CW01647584

Ares' Thirst

Quentin Black

Copyright © 2019 Quentin Black

All rights reserved.

ISBN: 19996006-1-4

ISBN-13: 978-1-9996006-1-7

CONTENTS

DEDICATION

To Mum—Thanks for your help

RYDER FAMILY TREE

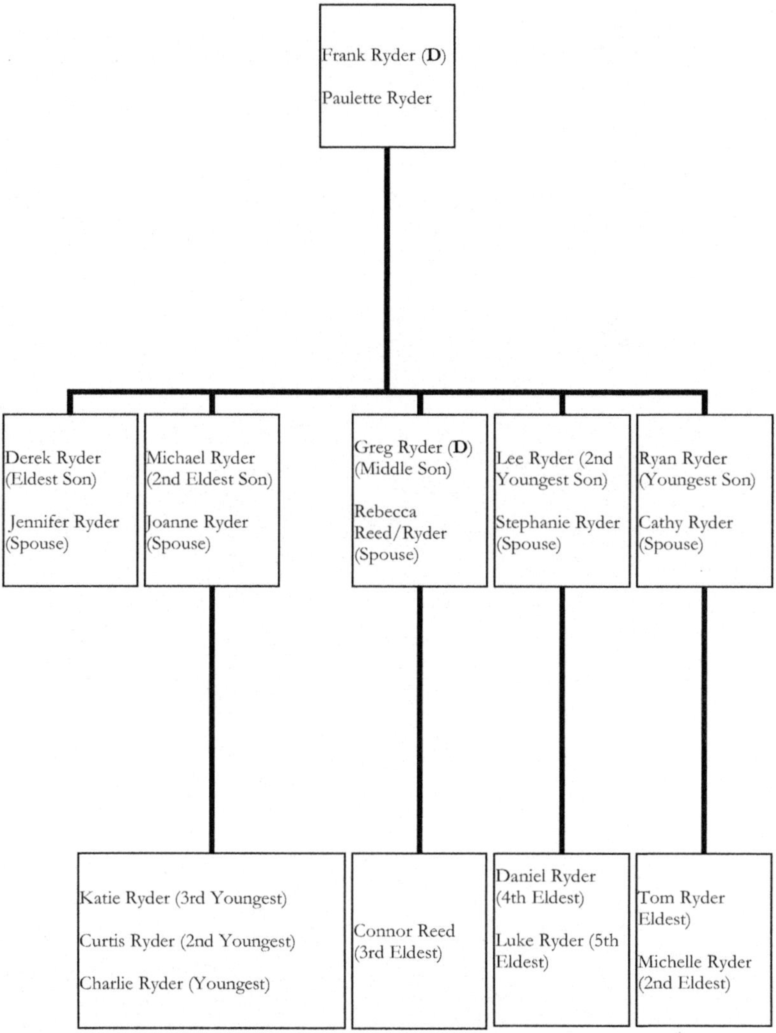

PROLOGUE

"Knowing your own darkness is the best method for dealing with the darkness of other people."

Carl Jung

ACKNOWLEDGMENTS

Thanks to Aquaflow Plumbing and Heating, in Carnoustie for the investment of time, effort and finance.

To Holly Mew, Dean Robertson, Jay Gardiner, Lee Barret and Sam Laird for your encouragement and support.

To the Evolution of Combat MMA promotions.

Andy Screen for the cover design.

Chris Searle for his polishing critiques.

Special Thanks to fellow Royal Marine, Jake Olafsen, author of *Wearing the Green Beret*

AUTHOR'S NOTE

Any specific terms and phrases have been highlighted in italics and can be found in the glossary.

1

As Grace Templeton walked the hospital corridor of chipped plaster and damp patches, she felt a sense of purpose within herself she had not felt for a long time. She had finally qualified as a paediatric surgeon—five years for her medical degree, two years of a post-graduate foundation course, and three years of specialist training in paediatrics.

No sooner had she qualified than she had taken on aid work in Ukraine with the UK-based charity 'Britikrane Aid'. The country, already in poverty, lay suffering from internal conflict, not helped by the Russian military excursion. The subsequent displacement of people had resulted in around three million people in need of aid, over half a million of which were children.

Grace had been thorough in her research prior to arrival in Ukraine and knew it to be one of the poorest countries in Europe— indeed one of the articles she had read stated at its current growth rate it would take fifty years to catch up with present-day Poland. And yet she had been pleasantly surprised upon her arrival in Kiev, seeing people drinking, dining and shopping.

The Ukrainian liaison officer for Britikrane Aid had been pleasant and attentive to her questions and requests. Within a week she had been sent to her post, and saw how stark economic disparity within a country could be.

The town of Mariupol had borne much of the brunt of the conflict between the Donetsk People's Republic (DPR) separatists and government forces. The hospital's conditions had shocked her—the dearth of proper medical equipment and supplies would have shamed 1920s Britain—water dripped, and the lighting from the shades, with blue stencilled birds, flickered on the basement hospital beds. Still, she never once thought of turning back and made the best of what was available.

She dealt with a plethora of medical ailments, from resetting bones, stitching wounds and dressing burns, to removing shrapnel from a seven-year-old girl's stomach due to an artillery blast. Despite all this, her satisfaction in her work soared knowing she was making a difference. Notwithstanding the comfort of western life, she had not missed much about her native Durham or her adopted home of Leeds, apart from a man—a fly by night she hardly saw.

She had known Connor Reed for a while, without really knowing him. She met him when he had been in the Royal Marines on a secondment to the hospital she had worked at for hands-on medical training. He was funny, confident, and had a fascinating combination of rough masculinity combined with a sharp and evolved intellect.

And on one night he had protected her and a petrified staff nurse from three aggressive thugs, reeking of alcohol by savaging all of them with his bare hands.

However she did not know what he did now—he was always cagey about it, and she did not press him. He would call or message when he was back in Leeds, or vice-versa, and they would go on a date and fuck. And despite the violence he had displayed that night there was never any 'hard man' posturing of any kind.

Then he would be gone—no messages, no calls, and he had no discernible social media. She had thought maybe he had a girlfriend or even a wife, and had confronted him about it; Grace would never allow herself to be 'the other woman', and hated hearing moral justifications for seeing a taken man.

However, he laughed, telling her, "I have too much respect for women to make one my girlfriend." And despite the randomness of their meetings and long periods of non-contact, she really enjoyed their 'relationship' for what it was—small adventures, stimulating conversation and banter, great sex, and a warmth in spending time with a decent man. She had, despite herself, occasionally envisioned them in a more conventional relationship.

She found the mystery of him both intriguing and disconcerting.

Then a YouTube video of Connor and two other men overcoming an attack by seven men in a Manchester nightclub surfaced. In the aftermath, which had included a court case, it had come out Connor was the son of former criminal underworld 'Godfather' Greg Ryder—Reed was his mother's name. The other two victors in the video had been his cousin Tom Ryder and a Louis Allen, a gang leader from south-London. At first, Grace had found the notion of Connor being this ruthless gangster hard to correlate with the man she knew.

But it made sense—the coming and going, the lack of social media, and the violent streak. Maybe it had been a good thing not getting attached to him.

She had finished for the day and met her assigned bodyguard and driver Dimitry to take her back to the hotel. She had felt self-conscious among her co-workers for having a driver. They were lovely to her, but there was an undercurrent of her being an outsider; she could leave whenever she wanted. She wore no makeup and tied her red hair up without any attempt at style; still, her attractiveness had made all the men thus far take a second look. The tall and compact Dimitry had kept his eyes and words to himself. Grace had been told jobs like this had been a godsend to some Ukrainian soldiers; better money, shorter hours and more comfortable work. Losing it for being inappropriate was not an option.

"Hi Dimitry," she said.

"Hello, Miss Templeton," he answered in thickly accented English as he held the door open for her.

They began the fifty-mile journey to the port city of Berdiansk. Grace settled into the boxy Nissan's seat, using the handle to wind down the window a half inch, glad it was the end of the day. Fifteen minutes in, she was enjoying the meditative experience of watching the world go by while listening to low-volume Ukrainian music with indecipherable lyrics.

The brakes slammed, shunting Grace forward onto the collarbone-digging seatbelt. The front window of her car shattered with blood. Grace's brain quickly registered the shooting of Dimitry.

The cold air of her door being wrenched open hit her, and a pair of rough hands gripped her, freeing her from her shock. She attacked with a primal vigour despite the gun being aimed at her. The butt of the pistol snatched her consciousness away.

2

A simmering sense of frustration lay beneath Adam Lloyd's skin as he lay on his bunk, staring at the ceiling in Frankland prison, stewing on the crumbling of his criminal empire.

Twice now he had attempted to deal with Louis Allen, the Southwark Union Gang's top boy. Allen led an amalgamation of several black southeast London gangs to create a monopoly in Lloyd's old manor. The SUG had begun operating 'OT'—out of towning— in small rural and coastal towns. A few of Lloyd's drug dealers had been beaten and thrown out of several of them.

He exhorted his younger brother to deal with the gang leader a couple of months back. Terry—or Tris as he had been known for years—had contracted three of his goons to handle the formidable Allen. It had resulted in their ambush, where an associate of Allen's shot the kneecaps of two and broke the fingers of the other. After that, Lloyd decided to use his own people, sending seven of his guys to ambush Allen in a Manchester nightclub. What he had not contended with was Allen socialising with a pair of the Ryder clan, part of the notorious Yorkshire crime family. The massacre of his team of seven at the fists of the three had been caught on more than one phone and plastered across YouTube. As Louis Allen, Tom Ryder and Connor Ryder—or Connor Reed as the news reported his name being—had all walked free from crown court on the grounds of self-defence, their standing in the UK underworld had rocketed as Lloyd's plummeted.

In the interlude between his first and second attack on Allen, his brother had been shot dead. The rumours were his brother had dealings with Tom Ryder.

He now had a more immediate concern— 'or an opportunity to seize', he said to himself.

Michael Ryder, the uncle of Connor and Tom, had been moved to Frankland.

Lloyd, now forty-six years old, had done a spell in prison back in his early twenties. Back then, prison clout had been directly related to which gang or organisation that person belonged to and his position within it. A ruthlessness in physical altercations had helped too. Now influence belonged to whoever controlled the prison drug supply— junkies would do anything for a hit. The quality of the drugs was secondary to the amount that could be obtained. Lloyd's supply chain recently slowed with his brother's absence, and his operations were squeezed, but these fiends did not know yet.

There was a knock at the door. One of the guards—the ginger one—stood imposingly in front of two young, shifty inmates. One kept grasping his fingers like he was trying to crack the knuckles as a collective.

"Take a walk," said Lloyd to the guard as he swung off his bed to stand. The pair shuffled in, surrounded by a kind of anticipatory nervousness.

When the guard had disappeared, Lloyd said, "Alright, you sure of the geezer? You got the target?"

Both nodded animatedly. Lloyd noted how fidgety they were—*fuckin' junkies.* He continued, "Got your tools?"

The taller of the two reached into his overalls and pulled out a weighted sock. The other produced a toothbrush with the handle sharpened to a point

"What's in that?" Lloyd asked.

"It's a rock I got from the fish tank, init."

Lloyd nodded. "Make sure this 'appens as soon as you get a chance."

The taller one replied, "We're gonna."

The stone sent a daze cracking into Lloyd's skull. His collapse into hollow limpness against his bed was met with the plastic spear plunging into his throat.

His assailants shot back from the blood spray.

Time slowed, with his brain whisking him away from reality to a pool table in his mind. A black ball with the white lettering of 'Lloyd' was over the pocket, shielded by a yellow 'stripe' ball. A green 'dot' ball with the black lettering of 'Ryder' knocked the yellow into the black and potted it.

Adam Lloyd's life drained away as he sat in the dream of death.

3

The players around the pool tables turned their heads towards Viliame's booming voice. "Here's my brother, the YouTube star."

The silver boxed overhead light shone on the black vested, hulking Fijian flinging a pair of strong arms, full of tribal and Parachute Regiment tattoos, around Connor Reed. The Yorkshireman returned the embrace but felt a little child-like in the seventeen-stone Viliame's bearhug.

"I've always been a star. You know that, Vili," he said upon release, while smoothing his white t-shirt. The players returned to their conversations, taking shots, sipping drinks and chalking cues.

"How you got away with that, I'll never know, man."

"Self-defence wasn't it."

Newcastle's 'The Hustler' was one of the city's better pool and snooker clubs. This setting contrasted to the one Connor had first encountered him in. Vili had been the heavyweight boxing entrant for the Parachute Regiment when they battled the Royal Marine team Connor had fought on. Although Connor had won his bout, The 'Reg' team had beaten the Marine team. Vili's annihilation of the corps' heavyweight had been particularly hard to watch. The lads attributed their loss to the para boxers being *tracksuit soldiers* and *"All they do on that team is boxing, we have to do a bit of soldiering!"*

Vili had been a member of 3 Para which, Connor was led to believe, had acquired the reputation of being the 'reprobate' battalion of the Parachute Regiment, and also its most successful at boxing. Vili had apparently embraced its hard-drinking, hard-fighting culture. When conventional operations in Afghanistan closed, the political climate changed and certain behaviours were now taken more seriously by the top brass, as Vili discovered after knocking out two bouncers on a night out in Colchester. One suffered a broken jaw, and a military court-martial sentenced Vili to fifteen months in the Military Correctional and Training Centre. It was there Connor became reacquainted with the Fijian.

Inside, Vili had sworn off alcohol—the source of most Fijian violence. And now, playing pool, Vili sipped on lemonade.

"I know it was self-defence. How you doing, bro?"

"I am good, Airborne. To tell you the truth, I am surprised you're still off the *grog*."

"Ah, I have other things— Jesus Christ and the Motorcycle Club. You should join, brother."

"The church, or the club that only allows former or currently serving *Bootnecks* and Paras in?"

"Both are good for the soul," said Vili.

"You flipping a coin?"

Vili won and broke. Connor refused to play snooker due to his incompetence at it, but agreed to a few games of pool. He prayed he did not get *'seven-balled.'*

"Brother, I am serious, you should join the club," said Vili after potting three balls. The fourth rattled out of the pocket.

"I haven't got a bike license yet, mate," replied Connor, potting two before failing an attempt at a snooker.

"Well, get one. Be part of a brotherhood again. Cut around looking cool as frik on a Dyna like me," said Vili. Connor smiled at his friend—who was capable of huge violence—using *'frik'* instead of 'fuck'.

"A Harley Davidson? I'm a patriot, you know. It'll have to be one of those Triumphs, if I do get a bike."

"Foley has a Thunderbird Storm which is pretty cool," said Vili.

"What's happened to him? He's been off the grid lately. He still in?"

Connor had also met the para headcase John Foley in Colchester. The Essex man had a wicked sense of humour but could not stop getting himself into trouble.

"Oh mate, haven't you heard? He's in the shit again. He'll get booted out."

Connor frowned. "Go on."

"Bro, he got pissed around town. Picked up a homeless girl and snuck her on camp."

Connor thought for a moment, "So? Surely that's *RPs* at the most? Unless it was against her will?"

"Nah it wasn't, but she stayed there for six frickin' months. Lads were feeding and *getting around her.* She was all up for it."

Connor's burst of laughter caused the heads of the other patrons to snap around like a shoal. After a few moments with his teeth pressing into the edge of his hand, Connor asked, "Wait a minute. What happened when inspections came around?"

"Just moved her between rooms, didn't they? Loads of lads going through her."

"She must be riddled. Loads must've bare-backed her," exclaimed Connor.

"Must've."

"How did Foley get caught out?"

"Well, I think the lads took her to the *NAAFI* for scoff or whatever, some *crow* officer noticed. The *CO* addressed the battalion, saying he'd restrict the entire camp unless whoever brought her onto camp owned up. Foley did. Think he'll get fucked for it."

"He'll land on his feet," said Connor, believing it.

"Listen, brother, if there's anything you need just let me know," said Vili looking him in the eyes.

Connor nodded. "And if you ever need my help, send me a text. Then I can ignore it before blocking your number."

Vili laughed.

Laying on his bunk, with a copy of *A People's History of the United States* open on his chest, Michael Ryder smiled as he heard the 'serious incident' siren go off, and prisoners herded to their cells. He let the smile die on his face—*Adam Lloyd might have overpowered the fiends.*

The guard—'Ginger Cliff'—came to lock him down and said, "It's done," before disappearing.

Michael Ryder was one of the elder members of the most powerful, white crime family in Yorkshire. The diversion in the river that had led to him and his four brothers switching from law-abiding—if rough around the edges—men, to controlling the organised crime of Leeds and beyond, had begun around the late eighties.

Their father Frank had been set upon by a group of thugs, after their abusing of some of the young women in the local pub. Attempting to intervene, he was eventually overpowered, before being horrifically kicked and beaten on the floor. Only the strength of his mental and physical constitution enabled him to survive. However, he spent a long time convalescing in hospital.

And so it happened that Michael's brother, Greg, despite being the middle in age and younger than Michael, led them all in a pursuit of vengeance: firstly against the immediate perpetrators, and then onto some of the more feared members of the Leeds underworld. When the smoke cleared, though their brother Derek—the eldest—had been shot in the shoulder, the brothers had left several enemies beaten and defeated, one scarred with second and third-degree burns. Also, the former 'Godfather' of Leeds had been left without a right hand and left foot, courtesy of a samurai sword.

A few months later, the police pulled over his brother Ryan with Greg as a passenger. The youngest Ryder confessed to his brother he had a gun in the car. The police must have been tipped off because they found it. Greg immediately said it was his, and quietened Ryan's protests—Ryan's missus had been pregnant.

When Greg came out of Armley after his two-year stretch, he took over the family business—organising it, establishing contacts and creating their code. The Ryder family made money, became feared by other underworld figures but, most importantly, respected by the civilian community. A decade of prosperity and respect followed until Greg's murder.

After a while, Michael had accepted 'the good old days' were gone and not coming back. Similar to any organisation, it peaks and then declines. Greed destroyed everything. Michael had read a lot more inside; during 'The Great Depression', America became 'great' when its peoples' entrepreneurial spirit and resolve were forged digging the country out of hard times. Hard times created hard and innovative men, hard and innovative men created good times, good times created self-entitled pussies, and self-entitled pussies created hard times.

The Ryder clan under his brother Derek had declined. However, his nephew Connor had carved a formidable reputation away from the family. He reminded Michael of his dad, Greg, in so many ways; charismatic, good-looking, awesome fighter and had a sense of honour. He was funnier than his dad though.

The charisma shadowed a dark disposition—a sadistic streak towards any bully. Some in the family suggested it had been down to his own father's murder, but Michael did not agree. Exacerbated maybe, but the truth was Michael had first seen it in his nephew when Connor was barely a teenager—years before his father's death. Michael had gone to *'the rec'* to pick up his nephews Tom, Luke and Connor. From the high ground of the upper football pitch, he looked down to the lower one at the circle of youths surrounding Connor and a much larger boy.

With the youth already bloodied and defeated, it was perturbing to see his nephew prolonging the beating by acting like Prince Naseem: winding up the right hand then smacking him with the left, standing in front of the flailing boy with his hands behind his back making him miss. The boy finally put his hands up in surrender. Connor still did not stop, and he knocked the lad flat onto his back. His nephew had then removed his belt and began the bestial whipping of his vanquished foe's face. Michael had shouted down to him to stop. Connor did not, and Michael had cut through the crowd. Cruel lacerations crisscrossed the youth's face.

As Michael restrained and dragged him away, his brother's only son's hysterical laughing disconcerted and angered him. When out of sight of the crowd he threw the blond youth to the floor. "What the fuck do you think our family are? When you've beaten a man, you don't just carry on to act the big man to a crowd of scrotters. Fuckin' disappointed in you."

"Leave him alone," screamed Luke. "That was Darren Pritchard. He's been at me for ages, picking on me, fouling me, smacking me… months. I told my cousin."

Michael could see the eleven-year-old Luke fighting back the tears.

Tom said, "It's true, uncle Mike. I let Connor 'av it as he and that Daz are the same age."

He looked at Connor who—seemingly unruffled by his man-handling of him—fixed him with a fierce gaze and said, "I fucking hate bullies.

4

Bruce McQuillan surfaced from the bottom of the pool and took a breath— the onlooking lifeguard's raised eyebrows and nod were subtle. McQuillan was a few strokes short of the two lengths underwater he was able to complete with ease in his youth. The fifty-year-old refused to accept the decline in physical performance ageing brought. He knew to accept it would lead to a lack of motivation in fighting it. He had completed his forty-five lengths.

The tall Scotsman got out, showered, changed and made his way to the sports centre's café. He ordered a cheese omelette, salad and a coffee. He resisted the urge to look at his phone, knowing it would suck him into triaging his tasks and working out how best to accomplish them. He had learned long ago the importance of taking a little bit of time for himself every day. He had seen the majority of his contemporaries fighting burnout with alcohol, pills, junk food, or recreational drugs.

He had led an unforgiving existence—*by Western standards*, he mused—from a childhood and youth spent in Glasgow, competing at judo to a national standard, through to soldiering at the highest levels and finally years conducting black operations. For over a decade and a half, Bruce had run his own unit— 'the Chameleon Project'— which had almost complete autonomy from MI5 and SIS. When he had been soldiering, life was a lot less complicated. There was the enemy, where you had to either: go and capture, disrupt, or kill them. Now he had to be constantly aware of all threats, even—especially—internal ones.

Bruce had finished his omelette and flicked open his phone. He began prioritising his tasks until he came across something particularly perturbing.

Connor fought to change his mindset as he climbed the cream painted stairs to the upper level— *Why are you nervous? You have been doing better every time you have sparred him. He is in his forties, and you are in your twenties. The old bastard should be nervous of you.*

Connor was about to commence a training session with mixed martial arts legend George Follet. He had trained with George for the last two years whenever he could. Due to Connor's continuous travelling commitments working for the Chameleon Project, there had been significant gaps of time in between their sessions. Because of this, George always sparred with him—hard. In the beginning, George had punished Connor with ease; staying a step ahead in the striking department, rag-dolling him in the clinches and dominating him on the ground. Connor maintained a training schedule even when on operations, by visiting the best MMA clubs of whatever city he was in. He had focused on his wrestling and grappling, and this had helped close the gap. This, coupled with George always giving him sound instruction—after the fact. Last time he had still been beaten but not before giving the former *Pride* and *Pancrase* standout a scare.

He opened the door of the fighting veteran's new dojo in Chorley, to be greeted by the sight of George, in white vale tudo shorts, holding his leg still in a high kick position. The flexibility on display gave credence to why the older man could easily reach him with head kicks, despite being three inches shorter.

The training hall George owned looked a cross between a traditional Japanese dojo, with its white matting and varnished wooden beams, and a western MMA gym with framed pictures of various star combat athletes, all signed with personal messages to George.

"How is the young apprentice?" asked George in his cockney drawl.

"I am fine thanks. Did you watch the fights last night?"

"I did. Very impressed."

Demetrious 'Mighty Mouse' Johnson had recently submitted an opponent with a never seen before suplex-to-armbar. George was one of the few retired fighters Connor knew that praised the subsequent generations of mixed martial artists over the era he fought in.

"Do you think he's the best ever?" asked Connor as he stripped to a pair of black vale tudo shorts and began his warm-up routine. He was always genuinely interested in George's stories and opinions. It stopped the awkward silences, too.

"I think he's the most complete fighter ever. Not sure about the greatest yet. Let's see if he takes a fight at the weight above and how he does."

Connor finished his warm-up routine and donned his MMA sparring gloves. George did not set the round timer as he believed it encouraged 'going into survival mode' and was to finish 'once they had a good fight'.

They began to size up one another. The standout boxer gave himself the mental reminder—*do not over-reach.* Connor, typically, would begin these sessions with feints and 'feeling out' jabs. Instead, he bolted out a combination of power punches forcing George to slip and block, before smashing into his *senpai* with a double leg takedown.

It worked.

However, Connor knew remaining on the ground with George Follet would be akin to a great white shark attacking the more formidable killer whale. He jumped to his feet.

As he watched George get back to his feet, he swallowed the urge to get high off his small victory. George feinted him then pounced—a one-two, which Connor blocked before he stepped back, avoiding Connor's counter right. George's overarching elbow smashed into Connor's cheek.

The former marine feinted the double leg, which George reacted to, before cracking George with a left hook to send him staggering.

He dived on the opportunity to take his mentor's back but failed to get his *'hooks in'* quickly enough. George span around and in the ensuing scramble caught Connor in *side-control*. The next ten minutes consisted of a struggle between George maintaining top positional control and Connor transitioning positions and threatening with sweeps and escapes from underneath.

Connor seized the chance to stand, only to find his foot trapped between George's feet. The martial arts veteran span around and tripped Connor into a seated position. George caught his foot under his armpit, with his legs trapping Connor's.

After Connor tapped to the kneebar submission, the sweat-stained George remained seated, drawing in oxygen. He looked at the younger man, and for the first time said, "Good."

5

Grace opened her eyes, blinking several times and shaking her hair from her vision. She gasped as recollections came flooding back. Bolting upright, her hands were snapped still by the handcuffs anchoring her to the matchbox bed.

Vulnerability washed over her as her eyes met with those of the man sat on the other side of the small room.

"Who are you? What's going on?" she said, feeling a swoop of vertigo.

The burly, moustached man did not answer, instead getting up, and banging on the door. With the sound of a bolt being slid back echoing throughout the room, he left.

Grace strained against the handcuffs, quickly realising it was useless. Looking around, the room was sparse but clean and tidy. The coarse blanket she lay on was tight over the bed's white sheets.

The door opened. She was drawn to his large nose first, then the shaven head, emphasized by the thick black beard. Then the dark suit—taller and broader than average.

He spoke with deep, Eastern European accented English, "If I unlock your handcuffs, will you be calm, Miss Templeton?"

"Who are you?"

He walked towards her with a key. She fought the urge to flinch as he loomed over her, before freeing her from her handcuffs. He sat in the seat vacated by the guard.

"My name is Vitali Agron. I represent the people of Ukraine."

Grace frowned. "What am I doing here?"

"Do you play chess, Miss Templeton?"

Grace took a moment to reply. "I know how to."

"So you understand the principle of sacrifice, yes?"

Grace's exasperation pierced her trepidation. "What is this? What am I doing here?"

Vitali stood and walked to her. His hand collided against her face, stretching the ligaments in her neck, and shooting her off the bed. She fell onto all fours.

"You will be a pawn for our cause. Do what I say, when we say it, or else there will be consequences."

The boot to her stomach slammed the pain in and her breath out. The sound of his departing footsteps clicked over her retching.

Derek Ryder liked the surreptitious stares of the other shoppers as he wandered around the Trafford Centre. However, he could not be certain if it was for his physique or his attractive wife Jenny, now in her early forties.

"Do you fancy helping me with these, Derek?" she said irritably, lifting the shopping bags hanging off both arms. Most contained presents for the family, though he could not remember who or for what occasion. He took some, feeling self-conscious to be carrying clothes for young women.

Three young lads blatantly eyed Jenny as they walked past, triggering Derek to bark, "Taking the piss?"

They quickened their pace at his flared posture.

"For goodness sake, Derek, they are probably still in sixth form," admonished Jenny.

"Then they'll have to learn not to stare at other men's wives, won't they?" he snapped, temper still raw.

He slung the bags into the boot and folded his aching joints into his Jaguar.

In his forties now, Derek began steroids ten years ago. He started off taking moderate steroid Deca orally— "Only smackheads jab up," he said at the time. The weights and his appetite shot up and he grew. He had been sensible at first, coming off them at the end of the six-week 'cycles'. These periods off were terrible, mentally and physically, but he disciplined himself to the task. Over the years, he moved onto the more potent drugs. The cycles got longer and the post-cycles got shorter as he began to suffer from body dysmorphia. It did not matter how many times people told him he looked big, or complimented him on a completed set, he knew he was so much better on the 'juice'—did not feel as small.

"I thought you were going to give it a rest. You've gotten worse this past year," Jenny announced.

He knew, because it had been almost a year since he had plunged into injecting Trenbolone. He had gotten huge and felt incredible but the side effects had been immense; temper, oily skin, hair loss but mostly the knowledge he probably could not perform sexually now if he were to come off—not for a long time anyway. T

And the huge and strong muscles had played havoc with his joints.

He bit his temper, "I'll wean myself off soon."

There were a few moments silence before she said, "I am glad you've patched up whatever needed to be with Connor. He's been spending more time in Leeds and it's nice to see."

Derek grunted; there had not been a falling out, it was just Connor had his own things going on in other places.

Six months ago, Derek would have welcomed his return. He had been nervous of his young nephew's activities away from Leeds, ever since he had left the Marines. Somehow, someway, he had managed to form a business relationship with Raymond Van Der Saar, probably the most influential white manufacturer of MDMA and ecstasy in *'the flat place'* and Europe as a whole, as well as being an importer of quality cocaine and weed. In addition, Connor had a friendship with Louis Allen, a southeast crime lord who led the powerful and notorious Southwark Union Gang, or SUG.

Connor had become closer to the family in recent months. Huge consignments of product out of Holland now came to the Ryder family for distribution. This had provided a cash injection, for which Derek was grateful.

"The family seem a little more, I dunno—lively when he's here," she said.

He had noticed it too—and did not like it. He had felt their subtle undermining of him in their body language. The cousins had said things like, "Connor thinks…" or "Connor said…" quite often. Even his brothers talked about him with a kind of reverence.

"As long as he never forgets who the boss of this family is," he said.

Bruce sat with Chen Zhao, nestled within an upper office of Interpol in Lyon, France. Zhao was now the president of the multinational agency.

An inoffensive bright cream paint covered the walls, and the white blinds were half shut. On the corner of the polished wood table, a pair of cups and a pot of tea separated the two men. A standing lamp-sized flag with the Interpol emblem stood on Zhao's side.

The organisation's remit was to support and promote co-operation between police forces all around the world, irrespective of the political relationship between nations.

Chen Zhao sat with his grey waistcoat over his light blue shirt. If Bruce had not known his age to be fifty-three, he would have guessed the oriental face to be well over a decade younger.

Bruce began, "I thought my request for information could have been issued by someone lower down the ladder?"

"Mrs Bainbridge speaks very highly of you, Mr McQuillan," said Zhao. "To be perfectly honest, your reputation precedes you and I wanted to meet you."

Zhao was referring to Kathryn Bainbridge, the now head of Scotland Yard.

Bruce answered, "That surprises me. We are from different worlds."

"Worlds that can and do coincide," said Zhao, pouring him tea. "Kathryn said you're wanting information relating to an incident in Ukraine, but did not tell me what specifically?"

Bruce sipped his tea, being pleasantly surprised, though not a tea drinker. Bainbridge had impressed upon him her trust in Zhao—he himself never trusted anyone he did not have to.

"A British national has been kidnapped. She's a surgeon who was working for 'Britikrane Aid'. This happened en route back from her place of work in Mariupol to the port town of Berdiansk. Her driver was shot dead and she's missing. It's been passed to me, I am guessing in the hope of resolving this before the media gets hold of it."

Zhao's fingers drummed on the table once, "You'll be aware our past involvement in that area has its controversies."

Bruce was aware. In the summer of 2014, despite the agency's remit not to undertake activities of a political or military nature, Interpol had apprehended the Ukrainian nationalist paramilitary leader Dmytro Yarosh at the request of the Russian authorities. Their subsequent reluctance to arrest former President Viktor Yanukovych in relation to the mass killings of protesters during Euromaidan had been widely criticised. Then came the revelations the Security Service of Ukraine liquidated a sabotage and reconnaissance group led by a former agent of the Ukrainian Bureau of Interpol.

"Are you saying Interpol have no contacts within the country?"

Zhao's face flashed a look of contriteness. "It's a complex situation. Traditionally, places like Cyprus, Latvia and Israel were the markets of choice for international money laundering. However, those places are losing their appeal as global pressure increases on them to clean up. This has coincided with the Ukrainian underworld co-operating more with their Russian counterparts—who are experts in this type of thing—and helps them as their economy is decreasing."

"So you're saying certain elements within the Ukrainian Government may welcome these ill-gotten finances running through their banks?"

"Yes, that is what I am saying. Ukraine has always been a thorn in our side—it's industrialised to the point of having large ports, banks and other services but doesn't have the means to regulate them tightly. It's hard to say if it has got better or worse since Yanukovych left office. There have been claims thirty-seven billion dollars disappeared during his reign. I am struggling for a foothold over there."

So that is the reason he is meeting me, thought Bruce.

"If you help me so I can establish that foothold, maybe I can see justice served, albeit in a different way."

"I am sure you are aware, given what you've just said, my helping of you could be construed as aiding the assassination of certain individuals."

Bruce had already considered this. "Then its fortunate it's me who you're helping, and not someone you cannot trust, or who wouldn't make a more than useful ally."

Zhao sipped his tea. "I am not sure if her kidnapping has a political agenda. Why would the Ukraine nationalists or Russian separatists kidnap a British aid worker? I think a criminal organisation has taken her."

"Why and who?"

"Why? Sex trafficking, perhaps. Maybe they wish to ransom her. Who knows. But if I had to guess, she'll be in Odessa."

"You think the Odessa Mafia has a hand in this?"

"Nothing of that sort would happen in that area without their say so, or at least their knowledge. At this moment in time, there is a war going on within it. Despite it being the bloodiest for nearly two decades, it has been kept out of the mainstream media. Again, because of the recent controversies, my contacts in the area aren't the best. I do not have a clear understanding of all the factors involved."

"I see, and you would like to?"

Zhao shrugged his shoulders and Bruce continued. "So there's been no infighting with the crime factions mirroring the civil unrest in Ukraine until recently?"

"Not really, the Odessa Mafia, indeed most of the Ukraine gangs, rely on the trafficking routes coming through Russia, particularly heroin arriving from the Caucasus, so they have to play nice. Indeed, the Russians have used Ukrainian criminals to do their dirty work during the uprising. There have been shootings, bombings, kidnapping and torture of these mafia members. These internal conflicts happen every generation or so. It's the rumours of the kidnaps of certain non-combatants that concern me the most."

"There's been more?"

"Reports of several Crimean Muslim children," said Zhao.

Bruce sipped his tea, "Why haven't I heard of this?"

"Russian media suppression is my guess."

Bruce nodded. "I am presuming you have a memory card or stick for me."

Bruce watched Zhao fail to keep the surprise at the accuracy of his prediction off his face. He then pulled a memory card out of his pocket. He held it up, but before handing it over he said, "Mr McQuillan, I hand you this more in forlorn hope than expectation. None of my officers have been able to operate in that area effectively. The gangsters that reside there are amongst the most ruthless, sophisticated and cunning in the world—like wolves, they'll sense someone who isn't one of them. You cannot send a group—groups are seen as threats and are eliminated. You need a single person who is ruthless, capable and intelligent."

Bruce took the memory card, "Don't worry about that part."

6

The black Audi A7 hummed through Connor's feet as he drove along the A58 towards an address in Alwoodley. The car had been a gift from Bruce a couple of years before, and Connor's Tom had it remapped because, "Those EGR valves are a nause to replace and your car will drive better anyway."

Tom had given him the address where he now headed and told him to be freshly showered and dress smart. When Connor had asked why, Tom had replied, "It's a business venture I want you to partner me on," but refused to elaborate. Connor had been staying in an Airbnb in Morley to the south of the city. He had taken the opportunity earlier that day to visit a superb gym there run by a former *Bellator* and UFC standout. Connor had been given a hard workout by some of the lads and enjoyed the friendly atmosphere of the place. Back at the house, he ate, showered, dressed in a light blue shirt, dark blue tie with a charcoal cardigan. His hands had hovered over the tie—was it paranoid or smart to remove it, as it could be used to choke him during a fight? He had relented and left it on.

He was now driving, engrossed in a podcast with a sixty-three-year-old strength and conditioning coach. The American had been said to be the United States' first bona fide Brazilian Jiujitsu black belt. Connor listened a little jealously as he described his minimalist, nomadic existence of travelling from country to country, conducting seminars without a fixed abode—*like a global Jack Reacher.*

It had been described to Connor how unfulfilling a life chasing money could be. When you make £100,000 per year, you move to a neighbourhood where people make £250,000. You buy a supercar, after a year of getting used to the performance and stares, you want a yacht. He had seen this in Derek over the years. His uncle liked the attention and notoriety—but he could be bitter. He complained about the trappings of some London gangsters, even the Manchester and Liverpool lot. Nothing was enough: not this car, or that restaurant, this house or that membership. He had also been hitting the steroids hard. Connor, because he only saw his uncle intermittently, saw with clarity the physical and behavioural change. When Connor was a teenager, any latent insecurity within his uncle had been masked by a raucous humour. Connor knew he'd had a bee in his bonnet about his criminal activities away from the family. Then he had seemed irked whenever Connor stayed in Leeds for any significant amount of time. His cousin, Tom, who helped keep things running smoothly in the years since Connor's father's death, had begun to confide in him about some of his side projects, although his main front would always be the car garages.

Though Tom still showed respect to his uncle, both in public and behind the scenes with money, Connor suspected he kept certain streams of revenue to himself. Like the one he was about to introduce him to.

Connor came up a long pathway leading to an archway gate with an intercom, a camera on the driver's side and another perched on top of the gate.

A beep sounded, followed by a female voice from the intercom, "What name is it please?"

"Connor Reed."

"Just one moment," and after a few seconds, "Apologies, but I am afraid you're not good-looking enough for admittance."

Connor smiled. "Tell my cousin to stop fucking around, or I'll one-bomb 'im."

Tom's voice came over the intercom, "You couldn't fight against the tide in a bath."

With that, the gates opened. As he drove up the pathway, the trees became sparser, opening up the scene of a modern style mansion. In the vast driveway sat an array of almost new Range Rovers, Jaguars, Audis, Mercedes Benzs and BMWs.

Connor parked and was met at the door by his cousin, who was a touch shorter and a little broader. He had black hair to Connor's dusty blond. Tom wore a green and white striped shirt with stonewash jeans. His short beard neither unkempt nor highly groomed.

"What is this place then?"

"It's my place."

"Fuck off. No way my play-it-safe, 'true Yorkshireman' of a cousin has forked out for something like this. Besides, what would you need a mansion for? It just screams *'Look into my tax return'*."

"It's not my house. It's a place of business. And one thing that's stronger than me being careful is providing for the family."

The last sentence gave Connor pause—he realised it was true. He asked, "What business?"

"You'll see, won't ya."

"How did you afford this? There can't have been that many gearboxes seizing up."

"Years and years of saving—compound interest."

Connor fought the urge to pry into his financial affairs.

"Does Derek know about this?"

"No. I want to keep it to myself for now."

"You sure? It's a mansion, it *'ain't a packet of facking peanuts'*," said Connor.

"I don't want 'im sticking his oar in just yet. He'll be happy with the kick up. This will be our thing."

"Let's see what all the fuss is about, then."

Walking in, the smell of perfume and aftershave hit Connor along with the attractiveness of the guests, particularly the women. RnB music played in the background. As Tom led him through, the male guests repeatedly stopped his cousin to praise him on the evening. Tom always introduced Connor, who noticed something strange—the men would greet him with reverence as the women blatantly eyed him up. One of the women had been particularly tactile with him.

As his cousin pulled him away, Connor asked him, "What sort of party is this?"

"Follow me."

They ascended the stairs, and Connor heard before he saw. The sounds of multiple people having sex echoed down the corridor.

"This a brothel," Connor chided.

"Nah. It's a private party."

They came to one of the open doors. An attractive blonde was being taken from behind by an in-shape forty-odd-year-old black-haired man. Her mouth filled by a man Connor recognised to be a Super League Rugby player. Upon inspecting other rooms in the corridor, there were similar acts of sexual debauchery. A scene confronted him of a gorgeous black woman standing up, being orally pleasured by two men, one from the front and one from behind, as she stroked their hair. She made eye contact with Connor and flashed him a wicked smile.

"Go on then. Tell me what the crack is," said Connor, as they stepped out onto a balcony overlooking a stream weaving through a wood.

"Private parties. A thousand pound per head plus a room for the night. There are thirty people here tonight. Been doing it for a few months."

"This legal?"

"How can't it be?" said Tom with a shrug, "They are guests at my house. A few thousand-nicker from each is a gift, isn't it?"

"Cash?"

"Obviously."

"Wait, a few thousand per night? How have you managed to convince these people to part with that."

"Convince 'catalogue Johns' to fuck 'worldies' with complete discretion? To have access to the best drugs and champagne you can get in the north of England? To sleep it off in a luxury mansion? Not that hard, when you know the right people. 'Ere, there's a room that opens onto the balcony specifically for taking drugs. Some people don't like to see it or smell the weed, Mormons like. The smoke flies out onto the night, meadow air."

"Eloquently put," Connor said looking around at the crystal chandelier lights. "You set this up yourself?"

"Yes, I don't have a partner."

Connor looked at Tom before giving him a wry smile, "I'll be honest, I know you're a shrewd businessman but I always pegged you as a careful one. I wouldn't have guessed you'd have taken a risk on something like this. I am impressed."

"What's that quote you once said? 'Necessity is the best motivator of all.' Risks need to be taken with the way things have been going."

Connor said, "The coppers are going to get a sniff of the drugs on sale here sooner or later, pardon the pun."

"That's the thing. The thousand covers the drugs. They are just left out. Who's to say I put 'em in there—anyone could have, any of the guests. I haven't said anything."

"You sure, Tom? Surely a determined task force and a switched-on prosecutor would still get you."

"Maybe, but it's about making things so difficult for 'em it's not worth them pursuing it. Like that fat, ginger kid at school, the one you could hammer but who would fight back an' maybe bust your nose—no one bothers bullying that kid."

Connor nodded his agreement and said, "How many months again?"

"Seven now. A million and a half so far. How do you think I afforded the first consignment from Van Der Saar. Because it wasn't Derek's money."

Van Der Saar was the Dutch drugs kingpin who now supplied the Ryder family.

"Fuckin' hell mate, a million and half net?"

"No. This place, the product, the background checks and that dig into it, but it's a tidy margin."

Connor looked at him, "You have surprised me."

"I want you to partner me in this."

"What do you need a partner for? It looks like you've got this handled all yourself. I doubt you need security— no one wants to fight when they are stoned, pilled up and just cum."

"You're the only one in the family I can trust with this. I need someone to bounce off, and if I am busy or get remanded, you can step in. Van Der Saar doesn't want his product cut, and in a place like this they don't have to be. The people here will pay for quality, it's a goldmine. Plus there are other considerations."

"Like what?"

"Listen mate, I am not stupid. I know however much you pay the coppers, and however quiet and out of the way we keep it, the gates could get busted down. Fuckin' arrest certain people, find they're high and that. Maybe some new chief constable looking to stamp his authority. And that's where insurance comes in. I need the guests vetted, which I have been doing, but it's a lot of graft."

"You mean, you need the addresses in case visits have to be made to stop 'em from grassing."

"Yeh. You can find the addresses after the fact."

Connor frowned, "I don't need to be your 'partner' to do that. You're my cousin, end of story."

Tom seemed to focus on a random spot on the wall for a moment before saying, "You know what you remind me of?

The whitest sheep in the family, painting himself black to remove yourself from us, and I can't understand why."

"Kind of like Michael Jackson in reverse. Which makes sense as its the children who molest me."

"You're fucking disturbed mate," said Tom, before his smile was replaced by a thoughtful look. "Listen, Connor. Derek is running this family into the ground. I am doing my best to keep the family afloat. I've paid thousands to various people he's pissed off in the last few years, and it still isn't enough."

"Then take over."

"I will if I have to. I am just saying if you want it, I'll follow you."

"I have my own thing going on. I'll support you. Just remember this is family. It's a sacred thing."

"I know it is. That's why he has to step down."

"Come on. It's been months since I've got high. And hopefully the black girl hasn't let anyone fuck her yet."

7

Xander Voitenko admired the view. The scene on high from Yalta's 'Mishor-Al-Petri' cable car was good for the soul. The time was sixteen minutes past three in the morning, and the moon light glinted off the dark sea. The green forestry had been turned black. It would have been a tranquil scene if not for his bound and gagged captive on the floor of the car.

Xander, with his suit, tie, well-groomed short beard and styled dark hair, gave the impression of a young businessman. Only the way he moved and the wolf-like sapphire eyes gave any indication of his physicality and the ruthlessness within him.

Xander looked to the man across from him and said in Ukrainian, "Artem, turn this piece of shit over so I can see his eyes."

The captive was roughly flipped over and Xander spoke Russian to the pleading man, "Vadim. As you can see, just at the top of the window is a hook, it is securely fastened to the frame on the roof by a length of strong, thick rope." Vadim craned his neck to see the hook on the outside of the car, and Xander continued, "We are around fifteen-hundred metres above sea level. Shortly, you will be suspended for the duration of your interview by your feet."

Panic shone from Vadim's eyes, and Xander produced a SKIF-knife. "I will ask a series of questions. For every refusal to answer or lie, I will draw the blade against the rope. I do not know how many strokes it will take before the rope snaps. And Vadim, if you scream for help, you will die. Understand?"

Xander did not wait for an answer, instead he gestured to Artem to proceed. The bitter night air whooshed in with the opening of the door. Xander made a final check of the rope and tape that bound the ankles. The pair hauled Vadim legs first outside, onto the hook.

Vadim hyperventilated against the masking tape, and Xander observed the strange scene of him struggling against the restraints that were preventing him from falling to his death. After a few moments, Vadim's brain must have engaged because he stopped.

Xander took out a tobacco tin and produced two cigarettes, offering Artem one. "Custom-made, black cherry."

They began to smoke. Xander savoured the concoction of nicotine, taste and cold air. The faint sound of the sea and the eerie panoramic added to his satisfaction. His attention turned to Vadim, who was crunching his neck and body in an attempt to relieve his head's blood pressure.

Xander reached down and tore away the tape, "You are Vadim Kumarin, a Russian criminal from Crimea now affiliated with the Odessa Mafia?"

"Who the fuck are you?"

"Artem, pull his trousers down—or up in this case."

"What the fuck is this. What are you doing?," Vadim exclaimed, as his penis and testicles were exposed to the cold air. "Who are you? What do—AARRRHHMMMPPPPPHHH!"

The tip of Xander's cigarette ground and scorched against the Russian's testes. The piercing scream had become muffled with Xander's clamping hand. The faint smell of burned flesh arose. Xander waited until the Russian quietened.

"I will forgive that scream, Vadim. Shall we begin again?"

Vadim did not answer. Xander said, "You know the rules," and cut a two-millimetre line across the taut rope.

"What? Yes, yes, I am Vadim Kumarin," wailed the suspended gangster.

"Good. What do you know about the kidnap of Tatar Muslim children in Crimea?"

"I know it's been happening. I do not know who. We wouldn't do it— it's bad for business."

"What are the rumours?"

"All sorts. Kidnaps for ransoms. Trafficking—"

"Stop. Why Muslims?"

"I don't know."

"Who would know?"

"I don't know."

Xander reached with the knife and scored the previous cut deeper. The rope screamed in its struggle to take the strain.

"No! Wait. Roman Ivankoe. He hates Muslims. His father was captured during the Russian-Afghan war. They tortured him. He says Muslims are 'rats in human guise'. He blames them for everything, even the revolution. It'll be him."

Xander knew of Roman Ivankoe, but not that he had that level of Islamophobia.

"Heard anything specific?"

"No. Unless it was for the sex trade then others in Odessa wouldn't look in favour on it. It has to be him."

"No one else?"

"No. I can't think of anyone. We're about money—that's it."

Xander nodded. "Okay. I am satisfied with your answer."

The condensation of Vadim's relieved breath was cut off by the masking tape Artem snapped around his mouth. The muffled protests came to naught as Xander's knife made a few sawing motions through the rope before it snapped. After several moments the fracturing of the forestry branches rose before a thud gave way to silence.

Xander looked at Artem, "They'll chalk it up to a gangland hit."

Connor drove, feeling a little like he had as a teenager creeping back into the house after being on the White

Lighting at the park with his friends, hoping his mum did not call out to him so as not having to put on the ridiculous show of not being inebriated. This time he was hungover, on a cocaine come down, and though his cock was still semi-hard from last night's Viagra, he felt drained after four orgasms. And this time it was his boss, not mum, he had to hide his condition from.

His attention wandered to the cylindrical shape of the lamppost heads of the road he was on, and how they resembled flying saucers—*fucking pack it in, you were meant to be a predator of evil, sharpen up.*

He was not too tough on himself; what was he going to do with two *essence* women, the best cocaine in the country and champagne—say 'no' and regret it on his death bed? Besides, this was an unscheduled meeting and he had only gotten the call around three hours ago. He had untangled himself from the two women—one a brunette stripper and the other was the black woman he had admired named Stephanie, a banker— and hit the M62 followed by the M6.

Ordinarily, meets with Bruce would be in a quiet pub out of the way—a different one every time. This time, it was to be at one of the safe houses in Shropshire.

The safehouses were used to questions detainees, and Connor knew two of the safehouses had incinerators to completely 'disappear' a body.

He remembered his surprise when he had first turned up at this particular safehouse in a small town named Wem in Shropshire. It had been in the early months of his career, and he had been expecting high walls, security cameras, electric fences and the like. Instead, it hid in plain sight. The owner of the farmhouse was the father of an SAS soldier who had died on operations—a friend of Bruce's—and had agreed to the building of another barn. In it a few rooms, all soundproofed, and the incinerator had been constructed to resemble a water storage unit.

Now, a few miles on a country road past the village of Tilstock, Bruce stood in the courtyard with a steaming mug when Connor pulled in. The Scotsman looked to the Yorkshireman like a meaner, modern version of Abraham Lincoln.

Connor got out, attempting to look alert. Bruce said, "Heavy night then?"

"Well, ahem—"

"There's coffee in the barn office," Bruce said, flicking the dregs of his mug on the ground. "It's like rocket fuel. Make us both one and we'll talk. The kettle hasn't long clicked off."

Connor walked to the barn, to find it derelict of the horses it was designed to hold. The stone floor slipped underneath the varnished wood and black painted iron stables. The wooden portacabin took up maybe an eighth of the total space.

Connor stepped inside—thin but clean black carpet, with the rest of the interior being made of grey marble and wood. The *wets boat*—hot drink station—lay in the corner next to the sink. A desk sat on the end where Bruce came in and sat with his back to the wall.

After Connor finished making the coffees, and sat in front of him, Bruce cracked open his laptop and spun it around on the surface so they both could see it.

"Tell me everything you know about the situation in Ukraine."

Connor sipped his beverage and thought for a moment. "The west of Ukraine wanted, or wants, a closer allegiance to the EU; the east and the southeast has more of an affiliation with Russia. Around the back end of 2013 into 2014 the Ukrainian president was blocking a promised referendum to join the EU, so the people kicked off in Kiev and he ran for asylum in Russia. The people in the southeast wanted to remain in Russia, so Putin blatantly but unofficially sent in troops to Crimea. Huge international outcry but fuck all happened really—well, sanctions happened, and then counter-sanctions. A civy plane got shot down, allegedly by the pro-Russian rebels with an anti-aircraft weapon allegedly supplied by the Russians. There's a continuing armed conflict going on in the east between government forces and separatists. What else?" he said, pausing to sip. "The port of Odessa is where loads of illegal imports and exports are shipped, like heroin from Afghan. And I saw the Ukrainian politicians having some handbags while Vitali Klitschko looked on, so they're a little wild out there. That's about it."

"You've got the gist," said Bruce. "The wave of civil unrest in late 2013 was because President Viktor Yanukovych suspended the signing of an association agreement with the EU. He appeared to be sidling up to the Eurasian Economic Union instead. Protests known as 'Euromaidan' became violent, and Yanukovych fled to Russia. In March 2014, a referendum happened in Crimea after pro-Russian separatists and Russian armed forces had taken over. They voted to become part of Russia. Most foreign governments refuse to acknowledge it. The war in the east is in the Donbas—refers to the Donetsk and Luhansk regions. Been going on since 2014 and ceasefires continually collapse."

Connor frowned, "That's what I just said?"

"You need to be sharper with the details."

"Isn't it MI6's remit?" Connor said, the coffee beginning to invigorate him.

"Well, something has come up. It's personal."

"I thought we didn't take things personal?"

"Sometimes the personal and business align themselves," said Bruce. "However, it's not personal to me—it will be to you."

Within a split-second Connor's brain—and stomach—figured it out. With his heart pounding, he braced himself for the answer to his next question.

"Is she dead?"

"I don't think so."

There were a few moments of quiet. His own reaction to the news surprised him.

"What's happened?"

"Her driver was shot dead, and she's disappeared. The initial guess is she's been taken to Odessa."

"Has this anything at all to do with me? I mean, has someone done that to her to get to me?"

"I think it's doubtful. It's a dangerous part of the world and her going has little to do with you from what I can glean."

Connor's blood ran cold as his reptilian brain activated. "What are our leads and contacts in the area?"

"Not many. Interpol had a couple of political embarrassments within the area. SIS is *sans* agents within the port—it isn't a place for outsiders. However, I think it best you go in cold."

"If SIS are struggling to insert people, why do you think I'll do any better?"

"SIS agents are made up from university graduates, military officers, or sometimes an outlier of a former special forces soldier. Odessa is a den of thieves with its mafia being one of the powerful criminal organisations in the world. The kind of place an audacious, young criminal would go to make contacts."

"You want me smuggling smack?" asked Connor with a hint of disdain.

"Calm down. The heroin will go to certain law enforcement agencies across Europe. I've made the potential arrangements. The 'busts' will make them look good. You'll get paid—not so much as its street value, but it's safe money and significantly the drugs get destroyed."

Connor sipped his tea. "Alright, you've sold me. But I don't have transportation to take heroin from the south of

Ukraine through Europe into the UK, so how am I going to convince these high-tech criminals I do?"

"You'll think outside the box," said Bruce.

"So you're saying I land in one of the most dangerous and volatile parts of the world, start asking questions, form links and a business arrangement with one of the most powerful mafias in the world, gain intelligence on Grace's whereabouts and rescue her?"

"He's got it now."

Grace lay on the bed staring at the ceiling. She had not long finished her first meal since arriving— two days and the Ukrainian beetroot soup—*borshch*—with bread had been delicious.

She had been taken to shower, with the wet vulnerability cascading over her as the guard kept a staring watch.

Now she lay, fed and clean—and scared. She resolved not to let it show, but flinched at the bolt sliding back. Vitali stepped through to her, pulling the chair close and they both sat.

"Miss Templeton, you are wondering what you are doing here?"

"Yes."

"You will help me with whatever I require—whatever the cause requires. From the me-ni-al, I think yes? To using your skills as a surgeon."

Grace felt a small wave of relief without knowing why, before realising, *if they are using me, they would not kill me.*

"What cause?"

"To loosen the Russian grip on our sovereignty."

"How?"

"Our civil war has weakened Ukrainian unity. My colleagues believe greater co-operation with Russia is the answer, but I know different. Russians have an in-he-rent arrogance— they look down on us, and we shall never be free with Russia strong."

"Why would I help a man who thinks it's acceptable to kill and kidnap others," Grace spat.

Vitali nodded perceptibly, almost to himself before shouting, "Vvedit'."

The bolt drew back. The guard shoved a girl no more than ten years of age into the room. She had dark hair, wore a green and white dress. Fear desecrated the innocence of her face.

"This is Alsu. I have plenty of these Tatar Muslim children in my possession. I will leave her in the room with you for a while, and might her presence will convince you to obey."

Vitali drew and levelled a revolver at Alsu's chest and fired.

8

Grace froze as her brain computed the scene. Finally, her primal scream burst forth and she rushed at Vitali. The back of his pistol-weighted fist whipped into her cheek, collapsing her across the floor. He left the room with the sneering words, "There are others" hanging in the air.

She fought to regain her equilibrium and scrambled over, but the inert anguish on the child's face convinced Grace hope was lost. She felt faint and staggered to the bed, her mind a jumble of thoughts and emotions, as a whispering horror swirled around her.

Connor liked Amsterdam for lots of reasons. The people were generally fun and easy-going. He walked, admiring the high buildings overlooking the canals as the cyclists spun by. He relished visiting the kickboxing gyms, knowing they were among the best in the world. He enjoyed chilling out in the coffeeshops—not coffee shops—that sold marijuana as well as beverages. Most of all, he adored indulging in the gorgeous women and appreciated the top-end drugs Raymond Van Der Saar almost insisted on providing him.

Connor now sat in the 'Meneer de Wits'—Mr White's—restaurant, buoyed by the cosy ambience and a coffee. He had got there early—*'five minutes before'* was the mantra of the British military regarding punctuality.

With his feet barely touching the ground since being given the mission, he had not time to analyse his feelings towards it. Now, he mentally shifted through the reasons why, in addition to his anger, he was feeling such fear. The anger part had been easy to assess—Grace had gone out there because of a need to care for those in dire straits, and had now lost her freedom to some sick and twisted person or group.

The fear was more difficult to look at. At first he concluded it was down to the fact if he failed, the world would be robbed of one of its angels. He realised his anxiety went deeper than that—and then it hit him; it was because she was the most moral, the purest, person in his life.

He loved his family, but they were criminals when all was said and done, and even the women could be seen as enablers. Bruce and Ciara were good people but they were killers just like he was. And on the sparse dates he had with Grace, he could forget not only was he a criminal and a killer, but that he loved torturing the evil and cruel.

Everything about her was about kindness and decency.

Upon feeling poisonous butterflies attempting to escape the cage of his diaphragm, he instinctively knew going down this rabbit hole would not help. He did not want his 'shadow' weakened when he, and Grace, needed it the most.

He resolved to cut off all thoughts and feelings of her until she was safe—any psychoanalysis could wait.

He searched for a mental distraction and felt a pang of happy nostalgia. Last time he had been here, he had been with Ciara, one of the Chameleon Project's female agents. Gorgeous, physical, smart and vicious, Connor had been attracted to her from the start despite his attempts to ignore it.

Despite her beauty and sexuality, she was a beast of a woman. Their survival of a Dutch-Moroccan Mafia ambush in large part had been due to Ciara's ferocious reaction to the attack. Immediately afterwards, they had sex in the hotel—*top four easy*—though he was almost emasculated by her domineering manner in bed. Over the short time they had spent together, he had even fantasised about a relationship; she was a fellow agent, smart and sexy as hell.

He knew she had experienced trauma throughout her youth. He surmised that was why she was like what she was like. That was why she had forged herself into a weapon.

Connor looked around the restaurant, being a little surprised at Van Der Saar's suggestion to meet here. For one, the proximity of the tables meant the other patrons were within eavesdropping radius.

Also, Connor would have thought Van Der Saar—a multi-millionaire—to be dining exclusively at places like Samhoud Places, Ciel Bleu and Bord'Eau.

The tall, craggy Dutchman entered the restaurant. He reminded Connor of a university professor in his dress and manner. Connor held out his hand, but as always Van Der Saar ignored it to embrace him.

"I think we're past your stiff British formalities are we not?"

"I guess so," said Connor, embracing him back.

They sat and Van Der Saar said, "If it's agreeable to yourself, I would like to discuss business after our meal?"

"Spent some time with Arabs have we?"

"Have you done business in the Middle East?"

Connor shook his head ruefully, already regretting the joke.

Van Der Saar continued. "It's very different over there. It's acceptable for them to keep foreigners waiting, or to even cancel the meeting upon your arrival. The meetings are not private until you've built a level of trust. Their enthusiastic acceptances mean only 'perhaps'. Their calendar revolves around their religious festivals. And always with a lot of small talk before anything of note is discussed. So no, I wouldn't inflict this Arab culture upon you."

Connor smiled. "Fair enough."

The waitress came and took their orders. They spent the next hour eating while Van Der Saar regaled him with stories of the New York nightclub scene back in the eighties, and how he watched—first in France, and then in Thailand—the first two of the four legendary matches between Dutch Muay Thai icon Raymond Dekkers and legendary Thai champion

Coban Lookchaomaesaitong. In conversation with Van Der Saar, Connor could forget he was talking to one of the most powerful criminals in Europe. He never felt that way talking to Bruce—he was always aware of what type of man he was speaking to then.

They had finished their meals.

"So, to business," said the Dutchman.

"Okay," said Connor, subtly indicating with his eyes his concern about the people around.

Van Der Saar smiled and clapped. "You can excuse us now."

With that, all five made for the door, and Connor understood. "They work for you, and they reserved the tables to ensure our privacy."

"Of course, I will always ensure our privacy and security."

Connor nodded. "Okay. I am going to scout for business in the south of the Ukraine."

Van Der Saar regarded him for a few moments. "Odessa?"

Connor nodded.

"You know Napoleon's and Hitler's decision to attack Russia led to their downfall?"

"You think I am over-reaching."

"I think it's a possibility, yes."

Connor had been debating how much to divulge. He decided to be as open as possible, but before he could Van Der Saar said, as a statement not a question, "There is something personal for you over there."

"It's a friend of mine."

Van Der Saar sipped his tea. "What do you need from me?"

Connor felt his gratefulness expand in his torso.

Jaime was back in the quiet suburb of Surrey, now waiting on Bruce McQuillan's arrival.

He had previously spent many months on his super yacht in the Mediterranean Sea. In the years leading to that he led a restrictive existence.

It had not been without good reason.

His passion and profession of computer hacking were bound to attract enemies. Although, being fresh out of college with Russia's feared state security service—the FSB—after you presented unique problems. He had reached out to Bruce McQuillan and had worked for him ever since.

A chime emitted from one of the computers, alerting him to Bruce's vehicle at the security gates. The hidden cameras relayed Bruce's image on a screen, and Jaime buzzed him in and made his way outside to meet him.

Looking upon his flowery garden, the smell of an English summer was mellowing to Jaime. Bruce, dressed in grey suit trousers and a white shirt, greeted him. "How yer doing, Jaime?"

"I am very well, thank you. And you?"

"Fantastic as always," he replied, clapping Jaime on the shoulder and motioning him to go in.

The kitchen layout consisted of an oval table top, with the window revealing a meadow view. The oven, hob, cooking table, fridge and shelves formed the perimeter.

"Missing the yacht?" asked Bruce.

"I miss some things of that life style I guess."

Using his skills in his work against some of the most powerful criminal organisations, most secure banks and governments had led Jaime into a constant state of hyper-alertness which had eventually begun to ruin his health. Over a year ago, deciding he was killing himself anyway, he cast off the shackles of this living and threw himself into the hedonistic lifestyle of a yacht owner. Being originally from Peru, the Mediterranean climate had suited him; indeed, with his jet-black hair and olive skin, it would be difficult to tell him apart from a native.

"So George Best was right in saying any money not spent on women and drink was a waste?"

"We both know that if I hadn't returned, I would be where he is now. It is a soulless existence and my work is my calling."

"This house is very nice Jaime. And the old you would not have had a window so large," said Bruce.

"We can look out but no one can look in. I think I have now achieved a balance of being security conscious without bad paranoia."

"Aye, you seem to be in a good place."

He meant it—he had a social life now, without it being careless. And his eyes remained fixed on his passion—his 'superpower'—his ability to hack the seemingly 'unhackable' systems of the world's most security-conscious entities. This was to be the first time Bruce had been to his home too. Before his yachting adventures, Jaime had always dictated the location and time of any meetings. He gave Bruce the general area, and when he was in it, the specific location. He'd hack into the local CCTV to make sure Bruce was not followed.

"Would you like coffee?"

"I would never turn down some of that Peruvian coffee."

Within a few minutes, both sat across from one another sipping their coffees.

"I am glad you're here. All the stringent countermeasures in the world don't alter the fact we're up against the most ruthless, powerful, and dangerous people on this planet. If you go out in the rain, you get wet."

Bruce himself had been kidnapped by the Russian Bratva over a year ago, and if it was not for the divergent that was Connor Reed, he would have died. Jaime's friend Ben Shaw had died a brutal death while assisting the Project, and the Peruvian carried a great deal of guilt over it.

Bruce spoke. "Do you remember when I got you to work up a background report on Connor not long after he came on board?"

"Of course."

"Remember he's been seeing the trainee surgeon—Grace Templeton."

Jaime thought for a moment. "I thought he was single—that it was casual?"

"All his dalliances have been casual as far as I can see. But she is the only one he consistently goes back to."

"Why is that?"

"I have my theory, but only he knows that—or maybe he doesn't."

"Okay. What is errr…Why we talking about this?"

"She has recently become fully qualified and took work with an organisation named 'Britikrane Aid', a scheme that sends aid workers of many sorts over to Ukraine. After a few weeks there, she has been kidnapped, her driver-slash-minder shot dead at the wheel."

"Where?"

"On the main highway from Mariupol, where she worked, and her safehouse was in the port of Berndiansk."

"And now Connor has found out and wants to find her? How are you going to stop him?"

Bruce sipped his coffee. "He found out because I told him. And we aren't going to stop him—we're going to help him."

"Help him?" said Jaime, frowning. "That is southern Ukraine— there is barely any presence of any western agencies there. I do not have any direct contacts there. And the criminals there are just as ruthless, if a little more subtle, than any in South and Central America. I sink—think—would be too much, maybe even for him."

"Aye, I know all about Ukraine."

"Can I ask, why do you want him to go? We protect the UK citizens from threat over here do we not?"

"When Brexit happens, the European arrest warrant will cease to exist. I need to begin to cultivate contacts now. And a lot of the shit that ends up on our streets comes in one way or another out of that port of Odessa. We need a footprint on the ground over there, and he might be the only one who could provide it."

"So this isn't about the girl for you?"

"It isn't 'just' about the girl for me."

"Mother Mary, Bruce. You're going to send him into a pit of vipers and hope he doesn't get bitten."

"Leaving a British civilian over there isnae an option, Jaime, and you already know that. Connor has the best computer tech in the world in his corner. And let's not forget who we're sending—this isn't a boy scout. Think of the situations he's already been in, how he appears thus far to be made of Teflon. And he understands criminality, perhaps even evil. And he has the motivation. If it's possible to bring them back, he'll find a way."

Jaime exhaled. "You're right as always."

For the next three hours, they planned as much as they could.

9

Connor landed in Ukraine International after a two hour and forty-five-minute flight from Amsterdam's KLM.

He walked through the calm atmosphere of the glass building. Three model-like air hostesses dressed in bold blue with yellow collars and gloves walked past him and smiled—*focus,* he told himself.

He noticed the stern-looking airport security staff, dressed in their stiff, military-like blue blazers, juxtaposed with the happy face of a sixty-something-year-old man floating around on a ride-on floor scrubber and drier. The airport seemed quieter than its western Europe counterparts, and instead of the token supercar displayed as a prize for some unknown competition, there was a new model Mazda.

He had spent an hour a day studying rudimentary Ukrainian ever since his meeting with Bruce. Through an app on his phone and a textbook, he had grasped several basic phrases.

Bruce had told him his contact in Kiev would be Danylo Kravets. In the wake of all the civil unrest, the corruption of the previous government had been widely acknowledged. In 2015, the Ukrainian president, Petro Poroshenko, brought forth several reforms, one of which had been a complete overhaul of the National Police. Kravets not only survived the culling but had been promoted to the head of a team that liaised with Interpol and other police agencies regarding Ukrainian criminals.

After getting through customs, Connor spotted his name on a piece of card, held by a man with dark hair and a nondescript suit. Sunglasses shielded the man's eyes despite his being indoors. Connor put it down to a countersurveillance tactic—one could not see where the eyes were looking—with the effect nullified in that it attracted attention. Already his antenna was up. He refrained from walking up and telling him to *'take those fucking things off'* and instead strode past him. He was irked— Bruce arranged a contact for him to meet him at the airport, and although Connor trusted him, he would not throw his lot in with a man dressed like an extra from *Goodfellas* holding a sign with his name emblazoned on it.

Connor left the placard-holding man behind and as he neared the airport exit a voice—in clear English—interrupted his thoughts. "I was told you were a smart one. Still, I needed to know for myself."

Connor stopped and took in the man—cropped dark hair, well-kept beard, better than average suit and grey eyes. Connor issued the premeditated challenge: "Vy dobre vyhlyadayete moyim druhom,"—*You look good my friend.*

The response received—"Ya pochuvayusya dobre," *I feel good*—was the correct one.

"So that was a test?"

"Of course. Now, if anyone is looking for a Connor Reed to greet them, they will think you didn't arrive. That, or else it has bought us time to remove ourselves from the airport," said the man.

Connor nodded. He followed the man through the throng into an underground carpark. He clicked his key fob, and a dark green Skoda Octavia bleeped. Connor remembered the passenger seat was on the other side and got in.

"Am I allowed to know your name?"

"My name is Danylo Kravets."

"You're Danylo? I thought a man of your stature would have had someone else pick me up."

"You are a special circumstance, and I had to make my eyes on you first."

"Where are we going?"

"I have for you an apartment in the Perchersk district. It is very nice—a final taste until your journey into the abyss."

Derek stood at the head of the table. He had called a family meeting. It had been a while since they last had one—years in fact. He realised he had let things slip, his grasp on the family was not as strong as it should have been. He remembered an episode of *The Sopranos* where the boss of the family—Tony—had noticed a subtle disrespect from the rest of the crime family creeping in, so he redressed the balance by beating up one of his underlings.

They met in the back of a pub named The Peregrine, on the outskirts of Leeds. His brother Ryan and nephew Luke arrived first. They shook his hand and he brushed off the small talk—he needed everyone to know he was serious.

His nephew Tom came next— he had never been one for small talk, although he seemed happy enough chatting to his dad and Luke. The young twins—Charlie and Curtis—arrived together, laughing and joking.

"Shut the fuck up and sit down," barked Derek. They all looked at him before shuffling into the chairs around the table. There were a few fleeting looks of derision, but it could wait.

"This meeting is so I can see what the fuck's going on, and 'ow we are going to fix this."

"What do you mean?" asked Luke.

"I am talking about the lack of money in our business," said Derek.

Tom spoke. "There's lots of reasons. Our relations with Bradford has gone down the swanny, so we don't have access to their Hawala banking anymore—we're having to pay money launderers. Law enforcement payoffs have shot up, especially as the grasses have multiplied—"

"You're blaming this deficit on us falling out with the Pakis and the coppers getting greedy?" said Derek.

"I am saying they are some of the reasons. Besides, there is money coming in now. Connor's shipments from Amsterdam are providing a healthy revenue."

Derek felt a flush of anger. "Those shipments could raise this family to the next level if he wasn't soft about us not cutting it."

"Uncle Derek, those shipments would stop soon after. The guy he gets it from is adamant they are not to be cut—"

"Spare me, he'll keep supplying as long as we keep paying. He's a businessman, and all businessmen care about 'tis money."

"Not this one apparently. Connor says he's cut off lucrative buyers before for doing that."

"Well the last time I checked, I was the boss of this family, not my nephew, not you, or any of you, unless anyone wants to make a grab."

There were a few moments of silence before Ryan sighed. "Derek, no one is making moves. But the import of the Dutch product is Connor's bag, and we have to abide by his—err—his conditions. Let's be honest, it's still plenty of money."

Derek saw the agreement in the body language of the rest and sensed he was losing his grip on the direction of the meeting.

"It's good it is, because the rest of your businesses have been failing for a long time now. And I want to know why."

"You want to know why?" exclaimed Ryan. "The why is, is we've stopped being respected. The why is, is we've made enemies we didn't need to make. We had a cooperative police force, or at least one that turned a blind eye because we were careful who we dealt drugs to. Now there's young mums and kids addicted to the shit you use the scrotes off the estates to deal. Throwing your toys out of your pram in negotiations with the Asians in Bradford, and the travellers—I mean, calling them 'Pakis' and 'Gyppos' like a schoolboy—has cut off a major source of revenue. These little deals with the Liverpool and Manchester lot you have made that we don't know about. And you have the balls to call a meeting and ask where the money is?"

Derek was taken back by the reply. Anger rushed into the void. "So you think I should have played nice with those PAKIS after the death of our beloved brother? Or should I say my beloved brother since it was for you he went to prison in the first place?"

Ryan raised his jaw and leaned back into his chair. "There's not a day goes by when I don't feel guilt for letting him take the rap for that. It was his choice and—"

"I am sure you argued hard," Derek said, and when satisfied his younger brother was back in his box he continued. "Anyone else want to give their two pence worth?"

After a few moments of silence, Charlie spoke softly. "Don't worry, Uncle Derek. Wherever Connor is now, he'll be sorting sommat, and we'll be back on our feet again."

"What the fuck did you say?"

Charlie looked up at his uncle with a perturbed expression. "Nuttin' what? I mean 'e sorted the Holland thing out din't he."

Derek began closing the gap between him and his nephew. "So he's the Messiah now is he?" His temper began to bubble.

"Nah, but he'll see us thro—"

Derek grabbed the youth by the throat and squeezed. Immediately Curtis jumped up but Derek punched him hard in the chest, tipping him back into the chair. He let the spluttering Charlie go with a shove. Derek turned around in time to see Tom had bolted around to his side of the table, presumably to stop him.

"What the fuck were you going to do," Derek spat.

"What are you doing? This is our family?"

"I don't give a fuck. Kindness gets mistaken for weakness. There's going to be some changes around here."

With that he walked out, shoulder-shunting Tom as he did so.

10

Connor looked around the flat, impressed. Despite the mish-mash of the colour schemes, and the lack of feng shui in the layout, it was spacious, the television large, the sofa was comfortable and the window had an expansive view of the adjacent buildings and surrounding greenery.

"I have coffee and your English tea in the cupboard. Also, our ryazhenka, so you can try," announced Danylo.

"What is ryazhenka?"

"Ah, it is wholesome milk that is baked. Cream is added. Very tasty and good for you."

"I'll try that."

When they were sat opposite one another with their beverages, Danylo asked, "So tell me, what do you know about our country?"

Connor sipped his drink and after deciding he liked it, began. "I know it is a country divided and going through a radical change at the moment."

"Tell me."

Connor summarised his knowledge on the Ukrainian conflict and some of its knock-on effects.

"I am impressed. What if I told you Ukraine is becoming the country most full with organised crime in the world?"

"I would ask you to elaborate."

"Of course. Please excuse, but there are several reasons. European policing agencies back over ten years ago, launched what you English speakers say 'a crackdown' on the Albanian Mafia and their drug route through the Balkans. So these Colombian kingpins and Afghan heroin suppliers began to use the Black Sea ports. Here in Ukraine, not only is there

Odessa, but there are Lllichivisk and Skadovsk, and now Sevastapol too."

"Alright. So that's one of the reasons."

"How much do you know about Vladimir Putin?"

"A lot. We could be here for a while."

"Describe him with a single word?"

Connor shrugged. "Strategist."

Danylo laughed. "Yes, Mr Reed. I was thinking 'tactician', which is the same, yes?"

"Yes."

"He is a strategist. He thinks long-term, and unlike his western counterparts, he has remained in power—whoever has the title of the president of Russia—since the year 2000."

"Yes, his interference in the US elections was particularly impressive. I suppose strategy and a combat mindset would be ingrained into a former KGB agent and judo black belt. What is the point, Mr Kravets?"

"Please, call me Danylo. And the point is I and many others believe Putin is making the further criminalising of Ukraine. The Ukrainian criminals who fought in the riots on the Russians' behalf and now denying them entry into the motherland. This means they will go into Europe and America—they will become the new Albanians. Indeed, Ukrainians have now been granted visa-free travel into most of Europe, we can see this already happening."

"Look, Danylo. Be under no illusion, my priority is to extract Miss Templeton. I understand this is your country, but I know how these things work— pieces of intelligence, delivered regularly, is better than getting myself killed to provide you with an avalanche of information from a single excursion. You don't win a war by getting killed in a battle."

Kravets took a mouthful of ryazhenka and said, "I agree, but I hope you understand this is a very different place than your United Kingdom. I do not know if your country could birth and breed a man needed to succeed down in the lair of the wolves."

"What makes you say that?"

"Because, you are aware of the Maslow hierarchy of needs, yes?"

"The need for food, water and shelter are at the bottom. Those need acquiring before concerning yourself with the next stage. So on and so forth until a person reaches the heights of self-actualisation."

"That is correct. I could make one about nations or societies. The people of your country no longer have to worry about survival. So soft, I have come to know a man in your country should cry if his football team is defeated. Brainwashed by television, the viewers cry when a cancer survivor sings well on your television singing contest shows. Your England and the Americans now say there are more than two sexes—excuse me—genders. And there are nearly two thousand mosques in your United Kingdom. What would you say to this?"

"How many mosques are in Ukraine?"

"Ah, a hundred and sixty, my friend."

Connor nodded. "I would say, only a few men cry at football. I will give you the television singing show one. I have never met anyone who identifies themselves as non-binary or whatever. And we don't have time to delve into the issue of Islam in my country." Connor finished his beverage. "I cannot deny that existence in your country is harsher and less—let's say—frivolous. But there's always an anomaly, an exception. And that's me."

For a moment, a ghost of a smile appeared on Kravets' face. "I hope so, Mr Reed."

John Merick sat picking at his rustic moustache in his office in London. He had moved into it a few months ago, and it dwarfed his previous office in size and amenities. When

Merick first set up 'Britikrane' ten years previous, it was from a small office tucked away behind a garage in Camden Town, with little more than a filing cabinet and a computer on top of a cheap white table. Now, his offices filled an entire floor of a building complex in the London borough of Southwark. His own office was behind glass, in which he had a view on his twenty-strong workforce—a double-edged sword at times but it kept everyone, including himself, accountable. Despite the softness of the leather chair, and the high-end air conditioning, Merick felt uncomfortable.

The kidnap of one of the charity's volunteers, a Grace Templeton, played on his mind as he shifted his bulk.

The chief investigator told Merick he was to expect a visit from a Bruce McQuillan, a man who worked in foreign affairs, and he was going to visit at two o'clock—five minutes from now.

Merick's phone rang from an unknown number and he answered. "Hello?"

"Mr Merick. Its Bruce McQuillan, I believe you're expecting me?"

"I certainly was, yes. Can't make it or delayed?"

"Neither. I am in the reception. Thought we should walk and talk."

"Ahem... Okay. I'll be out in a few moments."

Merick smoothed his tie and put on his coat. He passed his assistant, whose desk was situated between his office and the exit on the right.

"Marcy. I'll be out for an hour."

"Yes, Mr Merick."

Merick exited the office and floated his way out to the reception. He found a lean man with grey-flecked black hair sat perusing one of the glossy 'Britikrane' memorandum leaflets. He put it back on the table and stood to greet Merick—tall but broad at the shoulders, looking to Merick to be around his mid-forties.

"Mr Merick. Good to meet you," said the man with a light Scottish accent.

"Mr McQuillan. Please call me John."

"And call me Bruce. Let's take a walk," said Bruce, in a manner which made Merick accept the offer without questioning himself.

They stepped outside and began walking, having to part at intervals to make space for other pedestrians.

Merick was about to ask what the point of the walk was when Bruce spoke. "Dimitry Bondar, Miss Templeton's security— how was he selected exactly?"

Merick knew this was coming. "Usually with volunteers in Ukraine: the local police force guaranteed their protection. But Miss Templeton was the first one into that region—she insisted. The police in Kiev told us they couldn't guarantee her safety in that region, so they reached out to a local security agency down there."

"Meaning underworld types who do that sort of thing on the side."

Merick felt a flash of fear course through him. "There was a credible risk assessment done. Mariupol was not deemed to be a flashpoint for this sort of thing."

"How could it be? She was the first volunteer."

"I can only rely on what I am told. The relevant local authorities gave me their assurances—in writing—Miss Templeton would be safe. Despite a risk assessment being done, it states in her waiv er Mariupol is an unknown area to our organisation, therefore it was a higher risk. She read it and signed it," said Merick.

"Relax John, I wasn't pointing the finger. I am trying to gain a better understanding," said Bruce. "Who was your point of contact within the Ukrainian authorities?"

"His name was Viktor Kutz. He was a deputy within the Ukrainian Police's newly formed Interagency Liaison Unit—

I think he's since been promoted. It was he who assigned Miss Templeton her protection."

"What did he have to say about the kidnapping?"

"That's the thing. I haven't been able to reach him—phone or emails."

"Well, that's an interesting turn."

Grace had been locked in her room with the corpse for over twenty-four hours before last night's removal. If the intention had been to elicit her obedience, it had been successful as she now stood with Vitali hiding her fear and revulsion.

"You will look after these children's medical needs," he said.

They were peering through a window at a group of children. The realisation shocked her—a school assembly.

"What is this place?" she asked, as she felt a swirl of dark air in her rib cage looking at their anxious faces.

Vitali laughed. "An education. Come and follow me."

He led her around the halls, classrooms, the makeshift gymnasium and other facilities. She could see it was indeed a school—small, but a school nonetheless. And this left her reeling. She had expected a prison or barn complex. This was neither.

"Come, let us walk outside," said Vitali. "And Miss Templeton, do not attempt to run, as I will not chase you. I will kill one of the children, and leave the body in the room in which you'll sleep after you are brought back."

Grace looked at him in disdain—*he is evil.*

He led her outside. There were vast stretches of fields, with a river running to the right and a vehicle path to the left. This was all framed by woodland, with gentle hills to the side of them.

"What is this place?"

"This is a special place. We make use of these children."

"How?"

"That is not your concern," said Vitali. "Your concern is doing everything I say, so there's no more blood on your hands."

"You're a monster."

Vitali turned to Grace, his eyes drilling fear into her, "Yes, and do not ever forget that, or I will remind you."

Connor was impressed with the Golf R's handling on his way to Odessa on highway E95. Apart from the language on the road signs, and the four-headed lamp posts, the highway didn't seem dissimilar to a UK motorway. The flat scenery's vegetation reminded him of Sicily in the *Godfather* films.

Danylo had offered him an unmarked police vehicle and seemed put out when Connor had declined. Danylo had also suggested strategies for infiltrating the Odessa underworld.

Connor, though eager to glean any knowledge he could from the policeman, knew he would not be following his advice regarding how to go about his business. Bruce had always told him only to trust people if it was necessary, and to never let anyone know what you were doing unless you have to. He had likened it to being an orca—only surfacing when it had to.

The ringing from his phone filled the vehicle via his bluetooth connection.

"How's things, Airborne?" answered Connor, "I was playing pool with Vili not long back. He told me you were in bother again."

Connor tried not to laugh when recalling the story, but John Foley chortled for him anyway. "Maattteee, basically the CO told me to sign off and it'll be dropped. I don't think they want that story going to court-martial. I went on *Skynet* and did the *seven clicks to freedom* yesterday."

"How the fuck did you manage to keep a homeless chick on camp for six months without anyone finding out. At first,

I thought you grotty bastards never had OC inspections of the block."

"It's three para in'it, no one is going to grass. I was flapping waiting for my STI test results, but they came back negative. Must be because I always go for a hard piss and wipe the end of the old man on the curtain."

"You do know you're meant to do that after and not before?"

"Fuck— must be my dyslexia."

They laughed, before Connor asked, "What are you going to do employment-wise?"

"Private security, bruv."

"Where?"

"Between you and I, the Ukraine mate. Went out there last year on leave."

Connor had a brief mental flash of an orca surfacing. "Gen John, I am there now."

"What the fuck? Where are you? Kiev?"

"I was— on my way to Odessa."

The reply took a few moments to come through. "Why you going there, you mad northern bastard?"

"I can't disclose that."

"Connor. I went last year to meet members of our parent biker club, believe me there's some dangerous people down there."

"I know that—"

"It's not like back here. You take the roughest areas of London, Liverpool, Glasgow wherever the fuck, and they don't compare."

"I have had all the warnings. It isn't what you think; I have to do this. I can't tell you why, but I am going."

"At least let me make some calls to some of the people we're affiliated to, give you some advice an' that."

"I am fine for now, brother," said Connor.

"It's apparently kicking off big time in Crimea. Western media haven't reported on it yet, but there's untold going on."

"What over?"

"Rumours of some Muslim kids going missing. There'll be fucking murders when that gets out. It'll spread too, I reckon."

"I'll stay sharp," replied Connor. "One thing you could help me with, I know there's a war going on at the moment and I need to confirm who is who."

"Alright. Sling me an e-mail address and I'll make some calls. Stay frosty."

"Mother, why are you not eating?"

Ani Jovonich smiled across the table at her eight-year-old son Leon. "I am full, little bear," she said in their native Ukrainian, using her nickname for him. "I ate at work."

They sat in the en suite kitchen of their dilapidated apartment. Ani cherished this time of day with her son. Soon her mother would arrive and she would begin her night job.

The truth was she could not afford to feed herself and her son some days. The boy's father had walked out on them before his first birthday, and Ani now held down two jobs. In the day, working in a café as a waitress, trying to avoid the lecherous attention of her boss. At night, her mother watching Leon, she worked at a pay-per letter marriage service. She had listed herself on the internet as seeking a foreigner to marry. The company provided a comfortable cubicle with a computer and a phone. Last month, a fat, rich Frenchman—after weeks of communication and his sending money—came to visit her. She had made the right noises through the sex while metaphorically gritting her teeth. When he had asked for her to come and visit him in Paris, she had cancelled the communication upon receipt of the money he had sent for the airline tickets.

She felt dirty, not for conning him out of his money, he'd get over that, but for snatching the fantasy of her love from a lonely, old fool.

A knock rapped at the door. Her mother had come early again. Ani got up, a little annoyed at the intrusion into her alone time with her son. She opened the door to reveal a suited gentleman flanked by two police officers. Her heart went into her mouth—*was this the Frenchman's doing?*

As one of the officers showed his ID, her focus was drawn to the cobalt eyes of the man in the centre—they looked out of place amid the business suit and well-coiffured black hair. His dark beard was well trimmed.

"Miss Jovonich, may I come in?" he said in Ukrainian.

Ani nodded her illusionary consent—a woman in her position could not refuse the police entry.

He stepped in, but to her surprise the policemen left. She closed the door and walked over to her son, wanting to be close to him.

Leon looked at the man in curiosity before mumbling, "Hello."

"Hello Leon, what do you have there?" the man said, indicating the twenty-five kopiyok coin as he approached, which Leon usually used to buy himself a fizzy drink.

"My mother gave it to me for my chores this week," he said proudly.

The man held out his hand, and Ani felt a bolt of anger—*bastard.* She dare not voice her disgust.

However, the man did something with his hands and the coin disappeared. Leon looked on, awestruck.

"Leon, do you wash behind your ears?"

It took a few moments for her son to answer. "Yes."

The man reached behind his ear and produced two hryvnia coins which, combined, were eight times Leon's weekly allowance. "These are yours, but your mother decides when you get them, so behave for her," he said, passing Ani the coins. "This is your coin back. Go buy yourself something from the shop downstairs."

Leon briefly looked at his mother, who nodded. When he left, the man spoke.

"May I sit?"

"Yes. Would you like a drink?"

"No," said the man, planting himself on the chair. "My name is Xander Voitenko. I run a special investigations unit."

"What kind of special investigations unit?"

"One that tries to maintain or produce stability."

"Mr Voitenko, without being disrespectful, it's an open secret there is co-operation between the police, government and criminals here."

"I am not from here. Please call me Xander."

"What's your office or unit called, Xander?"

"I cannot disclose that. That was the reason the two police officers came."

"What can I do for you?"

"What if I told you there was a person, or people, out there kidnapping children?"

Ani shrugged. "I do not know?"

"Would you consider such people evil?"

Ani frowned. "Of course."

"I will not pretend to be a white knight, but if you help me, I will relocate you, your son and your mother to a lovely apartment in Kiev. Your mother assisted, your son given an education and you will be given clerical work with a comfortable salary—more than both of your current jobs together."

Ani's heart pumped harder—*how does he know about me?*

"And what must I do?"

11

Tom Ryder sat in the corner sofa and table unit in a pub with his father, Ryan, located near a roundabout dissecting Halifax, Huddersfield and the M62.

He watched a queue of patrons for the carvery and the harried-looking carver explaining to a rotund, unhappy looking couple that the gammon "will be a couple of minutes."

Ryan said, "These carveries attract fat people like women to a conclusion."

Tom smiled, he only just realised he missed time with his dad. They had not long collected a debt in Huddersfield worth £23,000 and decided to have a drink before returning to Leeds. Usually, Tom took one or more of his cousins on jobs like these but his father wanted to talk with him, so he decided to kill two birds with one stone. The collection went off without a hitch, due to Tom having the dealer's brother kidnapped. He released the sibling unharmed.

"I am not sure how this is exactly going to go, but it's not going to end well," said Ryan, his thumb caressing the edge of his pint.

Tom sipped his own. "Has Derek always been like this? I mean, back when you were all lads and that?"

Ryan tilted his head. "Ahem, —sort of. Think he always had a chip on his shoulder from being the eldest, but he was a fun guy growing up. He used to let me shoot crows off neighbours' roofs with his air rifle when he was younger."

"What happened to him then?"

Ryan took a gulp of his pint. "It was when our old man got beaten up. Firstly, it was Greg who retaliated by himself. He caught hold of Paul Farron, the leader of the group who filled Dad in, outside the gym where Farron used to bang out the weights. He was a big, huge cunt but our Greg mangled him. Ripped one of his ears off and broke his ankles. I remember Derek trying to 'av a go at him, saying he should have been the one to have taken care of Farron on account of him being the eldest. Thing is though, I think Farron would have handled Derek, definitely back then."

"Yeh?"

"Yeh. Derek could have a bit of a fight, could handle himself in a pub an' that, but Greg was an ABA champion, proper banger too. Honestly, having hands like him was like having a gun."

"Like Connor?"

Ryan squinted his eyes. "He has a good punch does Connor, but he's a bit more of a combination puncher, whereas his dad could 'one-bomb' almost anyone. Although Connor has a nasty streak in him. Anyway, what changed Derek was when all this was going on, he got shot in his collarbone by someone on a bike. While he was in the hospital, Greg rounded us all up and people got their limbs severed and another got burned. Then Greg's the man of the city and that burned Derek. He always had to prove himself. And he did do some stuff, hence why he's a big name. And why he was able to take over when Greg got killed."

"What actually happened to uncle Greg? I keep getting a different story on who shot him."

Ryan sighed, "No one knows for sure, son. Derek always blamed the Bradford Asians for some reason, and with him repeating that all the time saw a dive in our relations with them. See, in this game there's always gonna be arguments and scores to settle, but Greg was good at keeping the peace, and smoothing things out. That's why no one could understand it. No one could understand why he was in the middle of nowhere—well, Saddleworth—on his own."

"No one ever found out?"

"Nah. We didn't have any massive dramas or anything. We shook everyone but came up blank."

Tom nodded subtly. "You say Connor has a nasty streak, it came from this?"

Ryan shook his head. "It didn't help but no, he's had that from being a child anyway. I don't know if something happened to him, or if he's seen something he shouldn't 'av but I noticed, say when he was around six or seven, this weird devilment that would appear. It was—and is— usually towards the right people right enough. But you never was capable of that sort of ahem cruelty—I mean, take so much 'appiness and find it funny to torture fuckers. You know all this anyway, you're his cousin."

Tom did know.

His dad continued. "You know, I don't know what it is with that lad. Or you. Either one of you could take over this family. Especially with the support of the other."

"Well. Something is going to have to come to pass soon. Remember Derek has a lot of contacts—"

"Contacts? You mean people who make money from business with our family. They'll go where the money is. Besides, he has more enemies than 'friends'."

"Let's see how everything plays out first. He's our family, and Jenny is my aunt."

"Talk to your cousin when he gets back from God knows where."

12

"Why is your hand shaking, Mother?" asked Leon.

Ani Jovonich looked down at her son clutching her hand. They were walking down the Odessa street towards the barber shop she always took Leon.

"I am just a little cold, little bear," she said. This was the most nervous she had ever been. Xander had told her there were only two things she had to focus on: their future life in Kiev, and her mission. That and to calm her breathing.

She peered into the window and flinched upon seeing her target. Roman Ivankoe was sat in the barber's chair as she and Leon entered. He looked as if he was squeezed into the chair, his ruddy complexion contrasting with his straw-like hair.

The head of the gangster's hulking bodyguard snapped onto her for a moment before returning his attention to the outside. He sat on the edge of the wooden bench nearest the door.

Old Mr Skliar, the barber, greeted them warmly as always—Ani would clean his shop once a week in exchange for Leon's haircut. "Oh hello, Miss Ani, Mr Leon. Please take a seat."

"Of course, Mr Skliar." She smiled, mortified her voice came out strangulated with fear. No one seemed to notice.

Her forefinger on her left hand felt like it was on fire, for rested on it was a miniature microphone transmitter and receiver under a piece of brown stick-on fabric. Xander told her it was an exact match to the fabric of Ivankoe's cowboy hat, which he liked to wear to cover the sparseness of his hair at the back. It was hung up on the hook, with two empty ones either side— she was told it would probably be laid on the bench. She controlled her trembling—she would now have to turn her back to Ivankoe and the barber to do this. She gestured to Leon, and he removed and gave her his baseball cap.

She gripped the peak of it and, using it to disguise her actions, slid her finger underneath and attached the microphone to the rim of the crimelord's hat.

She turned and surreptitiously looked into the barber's mirror. Roman was looking at her but she could not read the expression.

I have either freed my family from poverty, or I have signed our death warrant.

Connor was surprised; he had not thought the city would look this nice—*what were you expecting? Mordor?*

He stood on the balcony of the fourth storey home he had rented online. The homeowners were away on holiday for a few weeks. He had a triple layered view; the residential area, some forestry and the sea. He had spent time each day from when he had first been given the assignment familiarising with the different areas using Google Earth. He devoured what he could on the city. He had also absorbed the information that Foley had e-mailed him regarding Odessa's most influential underworld figures.

Jaime had sent him an amped program that could plug into the TOR network so Connor could access the deep and dark web.

In his role with the Chameleon Project, Connor had become proficient at browsing through these hidden corners of the internet for information otherwise inaccessible. He had been surprised at some of the products and services that could be bought—via cryptocurrency—on it: PayPal stealing programs, WhatsApp spyware, fake credit cards pre-loaded with money, insider tips for stocks and hitman services. At first, he had been reluctant to use it, knowing it was a haven for paedophiles to gratify themselves. Upon telling Bruce McQuillan this, his boss asked, "Well, do you find children attractive?" When Connor answered, "No", Bruce said, 'Well I could walk over London Bridge as many times as I want. Doesn't mean I want or am going to jump off it."

He also used the subsurface network to confirm not only Foley's account of violence between Russian government officials and its security on dissident Tatars over missing Tatar children but to cross-reference his e-mailed intelligence.

Ever since he had been given this assignment, Connor's brain—both consciously and subconsciously—had been formulating a plan.

He decided to take a walk around.

The sun radiated a pleasant warmth, and the air had the smell of the sea in it. *Everything looks better when the sun is out*, thought Connor. He began to memorise anything pertinent: street names, shops and other establishments. He memorised as many of the faces he could behind his sunglasses, taking care not to be distracted by the Ukrainian women in their summer dresses—*do they have a monopoly on gorgeous women here?*

Subtlety in surveying the surroundings and people had been ingrained into him in his training, not only to avoid being caught by the target but by the potential person 'watching the watcher.'

His heart skipped a beat upon seeing a redhead across the street before realising it was not Grace.

He cursed the way his heart rate had bolted up. The truth was, if he were forced into spending the rest of his life with a woman, and had the choice of who it was, he would have chosen Grace—*if she would have me anyway.* Her decency had struck him several times.

He remembered an incident in a café in Horton-in-Ribblesdale after they had walked Pen-y-ghent, a 694 metre mountain in the Yorkshire Dales, together. They had finished an all-day breakfast and Grace had insisted on squaring the bill. She stood behind a woman paying for the food she and her three young children had finished. The woman's face went red upon opening her purse, before quietly declaring to the café owner she could have sworn she had the thirty pound in her purse. Connor had a clear view of the queue and what happened next. Grace bent down and pretended to pick up her own money.

"Excuse me, pet, this fell out of your pocket," she declared.

The woman looked at her quizzically before accepting with a profuse thank you. Connor had wondered if the woman knew what had happened. And he doubted Grace knew Connor had seen exactly what had happened—she never mentioned it either.

It felt surreal to him how chance had brought them together in the first place, and how it had now.

Now Connor knew he should take his time, get completely used to the environment—*the atmospherics*—before making his move. *'Slow is smooth, and smooth is fast'* as they used to say in the Corps.

But the longer he took, the longer Grace would be held. *Besides*, he thought, *I am a gangster looking for a drug deal. I do not want to be hanging around.*

He would make his move tonight.

Xander sat in his Skoda Octavia smoking his custom-made black cherry cigarette. The nicotine helped focus his mind during the tedium of surveillance. Only the hard, alert and cunning survived this game on the playing board of Odessa.

The hardness of character embedded within Xander evolved initially from spending his childhood and youth as a Muslim in Crimea.

As a child, his grandfather had regaled him with the plight of their people—the Crimean Tatars—as they walked in the hunt for sika stags.

"We have always been persecuted. The world holds the murdering of the Jews in such horror, but forget Stalin deported nearly a quarter of a million of us to Central Asia—on trumped up charges! A few of us might have been friendly towards the Germans—for good reason. The Russians then take our homes," he had said, spitting on the ground before continuing. "The Russian Government backtracked—1967, I remember the year—but it took twenty years for us to be allowed to return. And still we are looked down upon here. Bastards."

Xander remembered the conversation because he had never seen his grandfather spit or swear before.

And it was true—growing up, Xander saw everything from mild disdain through to the outright persecution and abuse of his people by ethnic Russians. Xander spent a large amount of time with his maternal grandparents in Kiev. He liked the Ukrainian capital: it was thriving and more accepting of multiculturalism. Slowly, he began to get more involved with the pro-west sentiment that seemed to permeate the city.

It was not long before Xander joined the military and was accepted into Ukraine's Alpha group. Just in time for the 2014 Ukrainian revolution.

After the proxy war had simmered into a strained peace, Xander felt an anger and a sadness over the fracturing of his country because of Russian influence. Still, he could live with it, knowing it was the will of the majority of Crimean people.

Xander had spent the last eight days trying to corroborate Vadim's claims of Roman Ivankoe's hatred for Muslims. Ordinarily, because Xander and his unit was going in 'blind', the process should have taken weeks. But the trade-off was the longer the surveillance lasted the greater the risk of being made.

Finally, Ivankoe's bodyguard appeared from the barber shop, fifty yards from where Xander was sat, with Ivankoe in tow.

"He's on the move," said Xander into his wrist.

He watched the straw-haired, thickset Russian walk towards his Mercedes parked down the street at the corner of the park.

Ivankoe's voice sounded in his earpiece.

"What the fuck is this?"

"I will get rid of him boss," replied his bodyguard.

Xander knew they were referring to the man prostrating himself on a prayer mat, chanting in Arabic near Ivankoe's car.

The bodyguard who ran up appeared to briefly converse with the bodyguard watching Ivankoe's black Mercedes. They turned on the man at prayer, remonstrating with him before finally taking a grip of his clothes and hauling him to his feet. As Ivankoe caught up with his bodyguards, Xander was able to pick up what was being said, as he watched the scene.

"I have every right to pray here. It's a public park," the man said in Ukrainian.

"Not when it is by my car, you filthy goat fucker," Ivankoe hissed in the same tongue.

Xander saw one of the bodyguards throw the man, scrambling, and the other throw his mat after him. The man snatched it up and walked away.

Ivankoe turned to the man who had been watching his car, "Do not ever allow one of those Islamic rats near my car again. If it weren't so busy around here, I would have killed him."

Xander smiled, he knew his agent would not suffer any physical harm in their engineering an altercation with Ivankoe and his goons—the gangland boss liked to keep a semblance of respectability in public. And now Xander did know something for sure—*he does hate Muslims.*

Connor already knew the majority of the people in Odessa spoke Russian. He also knew there was an undercurrent of distaste for foreigners due to their migrating to the city for the sex trade.

He needed someone who could navigate themselves around the city's nightlife and underworld, someone who could translate for him but not ask too many questions—but it was not as if he could buy a guide. And so he stood on his balcony, wearing a white Oxford button-down underneath a tartan-lined blue bomber jacket. The darkness of his jeans made them look like trousers above the brown brogues. He had shaved, and styled his hair. All this, so he would not be shown up by the escort he had ordered before even entering the country a week ago, who he was now waiting for.

Upon initial searching of the internet, Connor had found only tacky advertisements and trip advisor warnings not to indulge in the prostitutes. He needed a higher class of escort rather than a streetwalker or a brothel dweller, due to needing her assistance. The girls that worked the streets or brothels tended to have children and/or a drug addiction to support.

He had entered the Deep Web and found what he needed.

The doorbell chimed. Connor pressed the buzzer, and twenty seconds later opened the door at the knock.

Her large, brown eyes were the first thing he noticed. Her cascading black hair framed a pretty face. The olive skin contrasted well with her sleeveless white blouse.

"Hello, Anya?" Connor said, then before she could reply. "Although it would be a pretty big coincidence if you weren't."

She laughed. "Yes, it would."

He made way for her and caught a hint of her perfume. Still, as gorgeous as Connor thought she was, he knew this was a transaction for her. A woman could never be attracted to a man who paid for her affection. He remembered a time, where he and his best friend Liam Scott had managed to get into a strip club in Leeds, a few months shy of their eighteenth birthdays. A couple of dancers came up and chatted to them at length. After their respective lap dances, Connor remembered how crestfallen Liam and he had been when the dancers chatted away with another pair of stooges, never giving them a second look.

"Anya, your room is that one there," he said.

"My room?"

"Yes."

She looked at him quizzically.

"Would you like a coffee or tea for when you come back out? I am having one."

She shrugged. "Yes. Tea. Black. No sugar," she said, before going into her room.

Connor lamented how constantly saying 'please' and 'thank you' was more prevalent in Britain.

He prepared his coffee and her tea. Upon her return he noticed her perfume was a little stronger and lips a little glossier—*Good fucking girl.*

He handed her her tea and nodded towards the sofa. He sat beside her, and she nodded approvingly after a sip.

"This is good. You make it well."

"I am a Yorkshireman."

"What is this, a Yorkshireman?"

"A man from Yorkshire. A very sacred land in my country," he said pronouncing 'my country' in an attempted Slavic accent while the tips of his thumb, fore and middle finger on his right hand were pressed together in an Italian gesture.

She smiled. "I shall remember this."

"Alright. So this is what I need. I need you to be my tour guide. I am looking to meet certain people."

She smoothed her hair away from her face. "What kind of certain people?"

"The kind who control the drugs trade here."

She sipped her tea again. "Are you a policeman?"

"I am far and away from a policeman," he said, meaning it.

"This place is not like your sacred Yorkshire. The sun may warm the city, but it just makes its serpents move more."

"I think you have missed your calling as a poet."

"I am serious, Mr Reed."

"So am I," he said. "This will not be a transaction for sex. I will pay you double. And I will always make the tea."

She looked into his eyes, seemingly bemused. She sipped her tea again. "Okay. What would you like me to do?"

Parker stood to greet Bruce, which took longer than most on account of his height. The overhead light of the SIS chief's office glinted off the top of his head. Bruce, a tall and broad man himself, was dwarfed by Parker.

The bear-like palm was held out, and the Scotsman shook it.

Parker said, voice deep and edged with aristocracy, "How are you, Bruce?"

"I am well, as always."

They sat, and the big man smiled. "You always seem to be, regardless of the circumstances."

"We have a purpose in life, don't we? We're very lucky. What's bothering you?"

It unsettled him that despite his decades in this business, the Scotsman could read him so well.

"The situation has escalated over there," he announced.

"I am aware. A Tatar revolt and a Russian crackdown."

"There's more to it than that. I have had two disconcerting calls and an email. It's reaching a crisis point with regards to the Ukraine, Bruce—as in, the British national is no longer the priority."

Officially, Parker was Bruce's boss. Unofficially, they had an arrangement—Bruce was still afforded to run his own operations as long as he liaised with Parker—however loosely.

It had been Bruce who had—through his information systems technician—been informed of Grace Templeton's disappearance, and had brought it to Parker's attention before taking responsibility for her repatriation.

"Why don't you elaborate, and I will see where Grace Templeton resides in my priorities."

Parker disguised his displeasure with a nod. "Turkish authorities accosted Tarad al-Muhajer attempting to cross the Black Sea into Ukraine."

Parker looked for a trace of emotion but could not find one. Instead, McQuillan replied, "Where are they keeping him?"

"They released him."

There was a flicker that time. "They had one of ISIS's chief financial negotiators and released him?"

"Money equating to thirty-five million pounds from Saudi coffers into various Turkish officials accounts seems a strange coincidence. What would you make of that?"

Parker had his conclusion.

Bruce said, "The Saudis are none best pleased about Iran's attack on their facilities and are now willing to finance their ISIS pawn to attack Iran's Russian queen so to speak."

What had taken Parker hours had taken the Scotsman seemingly seconds. Members of the Saudi Royal family wanted to undermine Iran's backer, Russia.

Parker nodded. "Then you see why I am imploring you to divert any resources we have to finding these children?"

"Forgive me, Parker, but why is the onus on UK intelligence to find them?"

"Because the Americans seem to have this romantic notion that we have relic Cold War *Tinker Tailor Soldier Spy* assets in and around that part of the world."

"Then educate them to the contrary."

"It's not that black and white. If I tell them I haven't any, and your asset or assets are successful, we cannot use that success to strengthen a relationship we'll need post-Brexit."

"I see."

"Can you give me any updates?"

"You know I won't do that."

The chief frowned. "Thought we had come to a place of mutual trust?"

The Scotsman shook his head. "I do not divulge anything to anyone unless I have to, regardless of who it is. You've known me long enough."

"What am I meant to say to the prime minister?"

"I know you well enough to know you'd have no problem telling any PM to keep their nose out. This is about you."

Parker sighed ruefully. "Can you at least tell me it's progressing? However slow?"

Bruce pursed his lips. "It is."

"That place—all of it—is a God damned nightmare. Whatever is said publicly, Putin marching in annexing part of a country was an embarrassment to us but especially the US. He's a constant thorn with the capacity to turn into something much more flammable if this situation isn't contained."

"He needs it as a buffer zone between Russia and the West. As far as I was aware, the majority of Crimea wanted to be part of Russia anyway."

"That's not the point, Bruce. People in Devon have been wanting independence for years. It doesn't mean it's a good idea."

"My concern is the return of Miss Templeton, which I feel is connected to the bigger picture over there."

Parker looked at Bruce, and said something he had never said to the Scotsman before: "Is there anything I can do for you?"

He knew it took a lot for the dignified man to say.

"Keep the politicians at bay. You know my unit is the best chance we have of bringing the girl back in one piece, and preventing any needless suffering."

Parker nodded. "Godspeed."

Connor was lamenting on how he should have picked a less attractive girl considering the attention. It was early evening and they sat at a table near the window in the Xmapa Bar. The oak tables and bars gave the place a rustic feel. The ceiling, wall and artificial candle lights shone soft ambers. Anya's features were highlighted; her large brown eyes underneath eyebrows that were well-shaped but a little thicker than the fashion in the UK, he thought. Her high cheekbones gave way to lips so full that they were almost caricatures in their sensuality. Her jawline was a shade off being considered masculine.

He lifted his drink. "What's this you've got me?"

"That is a *medovukha,* made from honey. There are berries in it. Low alcohol. Good for you."

Her English was good but abbreviated beyond grammatical correctness.

"Yes, it's nice."

"So, why a quiet bar?"

"I wanted to pick your brains. I mean, I wanted to learn some information."

"Yes. I know what expression is," she said.

"I am not sure what I was expecting when I came here. A more hostile place maybe," he said glancing at the festive drinkers.

"This face of Odessa. The city needs tourism and will put on a show. But not long ago fifty people die in protestor clashes at Trade Unions House, and people here do not forget."

"So there are tensions?"

"Of course. This city makes to increase tensions—the port is a high prize."

"Of course it is. Ports have been an enterprise for criminals since they have been around," he said, thinking of how savvy a lot of the criminals from Liverpool were in comparison to other UK cities.

A veil of derision crossed Anya's face. "You thinking of criminals like the mafia, or hoodlums. You should also be thinking of governments and suchlike."

"Who controls it now?"

"The Odessa Mafia of course."

"Where can we find them?"

She laughed. "They are everywhere."

"Obviously, but they must have a favourite hangout."

Anya nodded her head. "There is such place."

13

The casino had a Vegas feel to it, Connor thought. The noise of the slot machines mixed with the hum of the patrons and clinking of glasses. Unlike Vegas, the intention of rinsing customers of their money was less overt.

The people were all smartly dressed without being too formal. He and Anya sat across from one another on red leather elevated buffets with a small round table between them. It felt to Connor like they were the centrepiece of the room.

He had a double take at the bar when he noticed it doubled as an aquarium. He nudged Anya. "As if that has not been smashed in yet."

She leaned in. "It is of reinforced glasses. Besides, people are well-behaved in here."

"How come?"

"Because the security here like to break bones as a warning."

A tall waitress arrived and spoke to him in Ukrainian, and Anya answered her in the same tongue.

"What would you like to drink?" Anya asked him.

"I'll have a medovukha if you have them, please."

Anya relayed their orders and the waitress sauntered away.

She spoke. "Why have we come here?"

Connor ignored the question. "Who owns this casino?"

"It is officially under a corporation called Kinan."

"Unofficially?"

"The Russians own it. It is looked after by a Roman Ivankoe."

The waitress arrived with their drinks.

Connor took a sip of his and asked, "If there's a war going on within criminal factions here, why hasn't this place been attacked yet?"

Anya smirked. "They all know who one another is. Certain faces would be immediately recognised and stopped at the door."

He had thought of the security measures at the door; no doormen at first, just a camera and a revolving steel gate which was presumably activated by the ticket clerk after checking the person or persons over on the camera.

Immediately inside stood two huge doormen, with the others dotted around the casino being a little smaller. Connor had automatically made a note of their positions in relation to the fire escapes. No security camera blind spots either.

He knew the dangers of adrenal fatigue and so said, "Alright Anya, I want you to leave and meet me back at the hotel."

When he offered no explanation she eventually shrugged and got off her seat. She turned as if to say something to him, but instead turned back and walked away.

He watched her leave and noticed the glances his way. People must have assumed they had argued. He took his time with the rest of his drink, giving her time to distance herself away from the casino. Thinking of his next course of action lead to him musing over the Norse mythology of there being a heaven where only warriors slain in battle go—Valhalla. He liked the idea of it—scrapping in the day, wounds healed by night before being served the finest food and drink by the gorgeous Valkyries.

Finishing his drink, he got off his stool.

He made his way towards two of the larger doormen who stood with a view of the bar and surrounding area. He stood a couple of feet away from the larger of the two but leaned in with his upper body. The doormen inclined his head but did not take his eyes off the bar. Connor spoke,

"Do you speak good English?"

The man nodded.

Connor pulled out what looked like a lighter. It was a *Kubotan* disguised like one.

"Go fetch me a cigar from the bar. I like to smoke as I gamble. Makes me feel like Bond."

The tight suit still did not even look at him. "Sir, there is no smo—" The sentence detuned into a cry as the outside of Connor's foot scythed into his knee.

The cry alerted Xander. His head, along with seemingly a hundred others, shot around to look. One of the casino's security had collapsed to the floor as a smaller man with sandy blond hair stood over him. As the second security guard began to turn towards the scene, the blond stepped in with a four-punch combination—left hook, right hand, left hook to the body, and a final right to the jaw. The security guard crumbled against the wall and slid down it after his feet were swept. Xander thought he could see something in the blond's right hand.

The casino's security team were descending on the scene like tuxedoed lions to a kill, but the blond was already sprinting. The fire exit crashed open under his boot and he disappeared into the night.

Connor ran as fast as he could. Though the security team behind would not chase him, they would send out his description, and probably not to the police.

He cut through the back streets and took random turns. After ten minutes of running, in which he estimated he had cleared well over a mile, he stopped in an archway down a back street.

He fired up his phone and the GPS located his position within seconds. Then he logged onto an Uber, with fake name account and requested an address around four hundred metres away from his hotel. He did not fancy Russian gangsters calling around in the middle of the night. His phone showed the driver was three minutes away. He knew he was taking a risk as the driver could have heard about the scene at the casino and been affiliated with the criminal underworld. Many Uber drivers jumped on and off again, unlike an established taxi firm where the drivers tended to stay for years. Therefore it minimalised the risk of them being linked with organised crime.

The car appeared and Connor said into the partially open window, "Ben Leonard?"

The driver nodded, letting him into the passenger seat. Connor was thankful the driver was not the talkative type and the noise of the radio was the only thing preventing silence. Connor kept a maps app on in case the driver diverged greatly from the correct route, but after twelve minutes the driver deposited him at a block of flats. He feigned using his phone until the car had driven away. Then he began a route back to the hotel, taking the side streets when he could.

He kept on hyper-alert entering the apartment block and made his way up the stairs. He knocked on the door but kept to the right side out of the *fatal funnel.*

"Yes?"

"It's me. I lost my key card," he lied. "Open the door."

It heartened him that she answered the door quickly. If there was a team waiting, there may have been a pause to mouth instructions to her.

She opened the door. "What happened?"

"Nothing. I couldn't see an opportunity."

"An opportunity for what?"

"To make my presence felt."

"Stupid to think this. They can make a trace of you."

"They won't have to."

Leonid Honchar painted on a smile as he watched the patrons of the park avoid his gaze. Yet he came here for the same reason as most on Sunday morning after church: to play chess.

The leaves on the trees rustled with the chirping of the birds, and the morning sun provided a comfortable warmth.

Sometimes Leonid would get lucky and a person who didn't know who he was would play him; that was rare, being one of Odessa's most infamous crime bosses. Tall, broad, dark-haired and thickset in a way that made him look more intimidating than the bodyguard with him. Not that he purposely cultivated that impression, indeed he wished to be able to tone it down for occasions like this.

This morning had been interesting. The Russians' smooth-running casino had suffered a disturbance two nights previous. News had travelled fast, carrying the blaming of him with it; not that he had contradicted this. What he did do was to use a contact within the casino to record on his phone the captured CCTV footage. The Ukrainian had been impressed—an accurate but vicious stamp to the knee had dispatched one of the security, and four rapid punches had taken care of the other. What surprised Leonid was the man with the dirty blond hair did not seem to be all that big, maybe 180 centimetres in height—stocky and athletic, but not a heavyweight.

Leonid did not fancy the man's chances; the Russians would be scouring the city, dying to make an example of him.

It seemed no one was going to meet his subliminal invite, so he sat resignedly to play his bodyguard.

"Excuse me, do you have an opponent?"

Leonid looked up to meet the eyes of a man with dirty blond hair. He was right—*maybe not even a light-heavyweight.* He took a few moments to calculate whether or not it was a good idea to allow such a 'target' to be seen with him.

"No. Would you like to be white or black?"

The scene fascinated Xander— the man from the casino now playing chess with one of the most powerful Odessa mafiosos. Leonid could be spotted from a distance; aside from his bear-like stature, his beard was bi-coloured—black moustache and sideboards, and grey down the cheeks and jaw. His shirt was open in a V revealing a tattooed chest. The black and grey hair pulled back into a neat ponytail.

The logical explanation was Leonid Honchar had hired this man to carry out the attack.

It had been a piece of luck Xander had managed to find this man. At the casino, his colleague Sebastian had recognised the woman who left just before the incident occurred. She worked as an escort for a multi-international agency named 'Tulips'. Xander hadn't asked Sebastian how he knew. Her work name was simply 'Anya' but her real name was Sofia Moroz. Xander had used his influence to leverage information out of the escort agency's office in Kiev.

The name—Connor Reed—and the apartment address was traced. The only other information so far was the man was British—a surprise to Xander,

The team had attempted to follow him from his apartment block but he slipped them easily. Xander feared he had made them.

However, Xander's team were also keeping track of Leonid Honchar, so when they reported the appearance of Reed, Xander had arrived on the scene as quickly as he could.

Now he was watching the two men playing chess.

He spoke into his wrist mike. "Who's winning?"

Sebastian replied, "Ahem. Leonid has two of his pawns and bishop. The Englishman has a bishop and a horse."

"A knight."

"Yes, a knight."

Interesting—thought Xander—*he is not letting him win.*

The suspense was gnawing away at Leonid. They had been playing for fifteen minutes now, and the man in front of him had not attempted conversation.

Finally, Leonid spoke. "Does conversation while playing distract your focus?"

"No," replied the man. "Your English is superb."

"I have spent a lot of time in the United States— and love the films too."

The man's blue eyes met his. "Would you like your man there to frisk me?"

"Why would I want him to do that?"

"You know why," said the man, moving a bishop a couple of spaces.

Leonid considered his answer. It had been a while since anyone had spoken to him with even a hint of insolence—*refreshing.*

"I think that is unnecessary," said the Ukrainian, moving his knight to protect a pawn. "Especially given your performance in the casino the other night. I am quite surprised you are still walking."

"It was required I am afraid."

"Why?"

"One was to get your attention as I don't have time to waste."

"Why would you need my attention?"

"For a business proposition," said the stranger, moving his queen out.

"Really? And why would I be interested in a proposition with you? You are unknown to me. And my organisation is in a busy time at the moment. Maybe not the best time for new ventures."

The man smiled. "You see, that's why it is the best time. I do not know exactly why this gangland war—for want of a better expression—has kicked off, but I imagine at least part of the reason is the Russians want Sevastopol to be the port for all things exotic. They are already attempting to undercut you and, because military supply convoys are exempt from police and customs checks, it's highly possible they could undermine and strangle your business here. In which case, a foreign partner with his own heavy goods transportation company might be of interest to you." With that, he moved his bishop to threaten the crime lord's queen.

Leonid nodded thoughtfully. "One that has made himself such a target might not. And Crimean ports are now targets for those within Russia who hate big, bad Putin."

The man shrugged. "You are at war anyway. I would have been a target anyway. And big, bad Putin will quell that uprising soon enough."

"You say the truth that I am at war. But conflict within our circles is not simply two opposing sides. There are a lot of layers. The right hand can do business with a man as the left hand is stabbing him. I am sure you have had experience of this." He took his opponent's bishop with his knight.

"Of course. The man who steals from you today, helps you make money tomorrow."

The accuracy of the man's assessment impressed Leonid. "Precisely. So I need to know what it's worth to me, and to see if we can lessen the damage somewhat."

"Two artic lorries every six weeks."

"Maybe we could, Mr…?"

"Mr Reed. But call me Connor."

"Okay, Connor. I invite you to my club tonight. Eight o'clock. It's called 'The Sky Light'."

"I will see you there then," said Connor, moving his queen and standing up.

"Are you not finishing this game?"

"I'll allow you to," said the Englishman nodding to the board before walking away. Leonid looked at the board—his opponent had moved his Queen leaving himself open to a checkmate.

14

Grace looked at the child with agony in her heart. She must have only been around seven years old, bravely trying to halt the flow of tears after Grace—trying to do the same—had reset her nose. There was no anaesthetic.

One of the guards looked on impassively. She needed no coercing for this, although she suspected the guard's presence was more to do with ensuring she didn't talk to the girl.

Grace felt the child's gaze tug at her heartstrings; her bruised eyes held a longing for any semblance of warmth in a human interaction. Grace gave her a soft smile and caught the look of disapproval of the guard. She hated what they were trying to turn her into.

She had never experienced the heart-wrenching atmosphere of seeing children en masse living in fear. The system for keeping obedience amongst the children was if one stepped out of line, her friend would receive a beating in front of the offender. That had been the case this time. No one told Grace what this little one's friend had supposedly done. The incident had occurred a few days ago with Grace having to wait for the swelling to subside before manipulating her nose.

Grace took the risk and held the child's face before planting a kiss on her forehead.

The girl was ripped away by the scruff of the neck from Grace, and thrown into the corner. A sharp backhanded smack halted Grace's rise out of her seat. As she lay on the floor with the swelling creeping underneath her eye, she smiled—*some things are worth it.*

"He is a wild bastard. He is going to get himself killed, Bruce," said Jaime, exasperatedly. They were in the kitchen of

Jaime's Surrey home, and he had not even poured the coffees before his outburst.

"Tell me what he has done now."

"Tell you? I can show you."

With that the Peruvian swivelled the laptop around to face the black ops chief and hit play. "This is in one of the Russian-owned casinos in Odessa. He has been there five minutes and already he's jumped on a lion's back. They will kill him for this."

Bruce was inclined to defend his actions but realised he could not. What he had done had gone against everything Bruce would have done. The former marine seemed to have inexplicably painted a bullseye on his back.

"Let's hope there's a method to the apparent madness," the Scotsman replied.

Connor had cut Anya loose after giving her the rest of her week's payment. He did not need her anymore and did not wish to endanger her life by association. He had not expected her look of disappointment when he had told her upon giving her the cash. And her coming on to him surprised him further. Despite the escort agency's stipulated strict adherence to STI testing, Connor ensured the condom had been firmly secure. She had been good rather than great; when he gripped her throat, he was surprised to see a flash of fright in her eyes and he quickly released it. It had occurred to him afterwards her regular clientele were probably fat, self-indulgent bankers, accountants and rich kids—*beta males without a decent bag-off in them*, he thought.

He was glad he had sex as he walked towards the neon lights of The Skylight. He savoured the crisp air as he thought about how it could have been his last carnal session. He had gambled that his offer of risk-free transportation would usurp whatever the Ukrainian could obtain from the Russians for his head. The odds were close.

Before he could join the back of the lengthy queue, a voice boomed, "Mr Reed."

The voice belonged to a huge bouncer at the door who sported the perfunctory bald head and neck tattoo, gesturing him to the front.

Just own it, Conor thought, as the queue's eyes followed him while humming with a mixture of Ukrainian and English.

The bouncer's hand engulfed his like a baseball catcher's mitt. "Mr Reed, follow."

As he followed the doorman, he felt like he was entering a dragon's cave. However, he could not help but again admire the women in their different outfits. As a collective, their jawlines seemed tighter, wore less makeup and generally seemed healthier than their British counterparts. The men in the club were all well dressed, mostly in chinos and collared shirts.

The club was a collection of soft lights, Euro music, mirrored walls and ceilings which gave it the optical illusion of being huge.

"Mr Reed, I must search. Can follow me?"

"Of course," replied Connor.

The doorman led him through a door to a small room with a table, with what Connor recognised as a handheld electronics detector on it. Connor's adrenaline eased; it seemed the man did just want to search him—fighting a man this size in such a tight area would not be a good day out.

"Mr Reed. Please remove shirt."

He did so and handed it over. The man felt around the collar and sleeves before laying it on the table. The man knelt to one side of Connor. Before he began the frisk, Connor said, "I have a Kubotan disguised as a lighter."

He knew the man was going to keep hold of his phone and check the lighter to ensure it was not an audio device. He did not want the big man to be suspicious by the weight of it.

The man paused for a moment. "This not help if they find you."

"You heard about that?"

"I think you may be crazy. You safe in here. Can I keep this and phone until I have word on the side of the ear of Mr Honchar?"

Connor already knew his asking was just out of politeness. "Of course."

The man frisked his legs after Connor had removed his wallet, keys, phone and Kubotan. The detector was run up and down his legs and around his crotch.

"Done," grunted the man.

They made their way out after he had put back on his shirt and the bouncer pocketed his phone and Kubotan. The throng parted for the doorman like the sea for Moses, and he led Connor up the stairs to a balcony floor.

Leonid Honchar perched on the edge of a huge booth. Connor thought his grey suit jacket with his red shirt bordered on '70s but the man still cut an impressive figure. His security stood by—tall, broad and Slavic. There was a pretty waitress stood by in a well-fitting but oddly masculine type of suit.

"Mr Reed, my friend. Glad you made it. Sit and drink."

Connor nodded and took the seat across from him. He knew it was customary in these parts to go through a preamble before business. He had not wanted to get drunk but he knew to refuse drinks would be considered rude.

"Do you have any Uzvar?" he asked, referring to a Ukrainian drink made of fruit and berries.

Leonid frowned. "Of course, but that is a no alcohol drink?"

"Stick some vodka in it."

The Ukrainian smiled, clicked his fingers at a pretty waitress who disappeared after a brief exchange in their native tongue.

"So tell me a little about yourself," Leonid asked.

"I am sure you have already done your due diligence Leonid."

"Of course. You are the only son of Gregory Ryder. I hear about this man years ago— he defeated the Triads trying to take over his turf."

Connor nodded. "Well, it wasn't 'the' Triads, per se. It was a triad and his gang who decided to try for a takeover of West Yorkshire without permission from his boss—his Dragonhead."

"Maybe but this triad had a hundred men at his disposal, and your father still defeated him."

"I am not sure it was hundred, but yes, he did."

"So, are you your father's son?"

"Time will tell."

"Tell me a little about your operation."

The waitress came and set the drinks down. Leonid had a glass of peppered Horilk, a kind of vodka which practically constituted the national drink. Connor observed the word Horilka was similar to the Ukrainian word of 'hority'—which meant 'to burn'. The waitress left the bottle on the table.

"It's small so far, three four-axle artics capable of holding thirty-six tonnes. I'd have to pad the edges and back out with legal commodities to pass a cursory glance by a customs officer. We're talking up to a potential fifty tonnes every six weeks or so of whatever you want, if you could pack it that tightly, which I doubt is possible. Still, very sizeable amount, and no financial risk to yourself as I'll pay up front. The mark up for cigarettes will go higher as it's more difficult to offload them than in the past. Vaping seems to be all the rage now."

Leonid rubbed his beard. "Heroin?"

"If you like."

"I hear it's not as popular in the UK, and hasn't been for years."

"You're right. Kids don't see being a smackhead as sexy, to be honest, blame *Trainspotting.* But there's still plenty of fiends about, and I was planning on doing drop-offs throughout Europe."

"I like *Trainspotting*. The film, not the act," said Leonid. "But I don't like this making a lot of customers in Europe. More people means more risk of leaks."

"Well, it's not you taking the risk now, is it?"

"Maybe no, maybe yes. Maybe they grab you and make you be an informant for me."

Connor shrugged. "Then make someone else the point of contact."

Leonid took a drink. "I like this. No 'I will never tell, never break', just reality advice."

"Practical," Connor said.

"Yes advice practical. Money can be discussed on a shipment by shipment basis but it will be agreeable to you. You have to understand there are new routes established through the Balkans as Iran and Turkey have achieved some success in halting the heroin from Afghanistan, but this route needs a lot of cash. There are other things beside heroin. Our crazy Islamic cousins are selling crude oil at an attractive price also."

Connor knew all about stolen oil being one of ISIS's sources of income. This was going to be a tricky one. It was unlikely Leonid would tell him who to sell drugs and counterfeit cigarettes to but he might for guns and oil. The vast majority of guns flowed the other way he knew, from Russia, China and Eastern Europe back to ISIS. However, there might be a possibility of Leonid asking him to supply guns to cells in Europe. He would refuse on the grounds of being a westerner and former military. The oil posed a moral dilemma. Refuse to transport such a valuable commodity and Leonid would probably deem their proposed venture as not worth the trouble. Agree to transport it, then the Chameleon Project would be responsible for directly funding terrorism. And then not even McQuillan's influence could save him.

Connor spoke. "I don't have a problem transporting oil, as long as I find my own buyer."

The Ukrainian raised his eyebrows. "You know people who trade in crude oil?"

"I might."

"Maybe that's acceptable. There are other products as well. Our clients—"

"I am not transporting arms for ISIS."

Leonid stared at him. "Why not?"

"I won't be responsible for putting arms into the hands of these backward extremists."

"But you would pay for their oil?"

"You'd find a buyer for that anyway. Besides, the more money they have, the longer they can carry on fighting Assad. The longer they carry on fighting him, the more of them die. The Russians won't let Assad lose. The Turks hate ISIS too. The Americans can't find a cohesive rebel group to back with commitment. But supplying guns or explosive components to cells across Europe is a no-no. Splattered kids at pop concerts aren't my thing. I'll take guns, but again they will be my own buyers."

The mafia boss looked on thoughtfully for a moment or two.

"How much do you know about Greek mythology?"

"I know the general chronology, and that Zeus tops the 'who's the hardest list' after leading the Olympians to marmalize the Titans in the twelve-year war. What else do you need to know?"

"When I am of beginning to know a man, I like to play a game in the mind of what the Gods would think of him. Ares would favour you, Connor."

"I don't agree. I am not an advocate of war—well, unnecessary war—as there's always innocents affected, but I am not averse to evil, or bad-beyond-rehabilitation men dying. I'd be more Hade's favourite. Do we have a deal on the guns?"

Leonid nodded seemingly to himself before extending his hand. Connor shook it firmly.

"Are you a boxing fan?" asked Leonid.

"Yes."

"Do you know of Vasyl Lomachenko?"

"Yes, he's a wizard."

Leonid frowned. "No. I mean a boxer named Lomachenko."

"I know. I meant he's a wizard at boxing."

"Yes of course. I apologise, my English needs practice with Britishers more." He smiled. "Do you box?"

"I used to, yes."

The Ukrainian gestured behind Connor with his fingers and the doorman appeared. He handed Connor his Kubotan and phone back.

"They were clean," he said simply to his boss before leaving.

Leonid said, "So boxer. We have another matter to take care of."

15

Connor was in the back of a chauffeur-driven car as it cut through the back streets of afternoon Odessa.

He had had to employ a range of methods to control his fear, ever since Leonid told him what was required to limit the damage of his actions at the casino. A bare-knuckle *vale tudo* match against the Russian he had laid out with punches before escaping. There was to be no referee or rounds either.

Although Leonid stated the match would be over when one was knocked out or tapped, Connor was not naïve—the larger Russian would want to make an example out of him, maybe break a few bones or take an eye.

Though Connor had already beaten him, he'd had the advantage of surprise—and the Kuboban—on that occasion.

One advantage Connor had was that upon being given the name Taavetti Jirov, he had found and studied footage of him on YouTube. 'The Tiger' looked a scary fucker; muscled, strong and aggressive.

Taav seemed to have good basics at every range without being advanced in any. He had a strong jab but was a little lazy pulling it back.

Connor could see the sambo background of the Russian. Because of his own judo background, Jirov's preferred method of takedowns consisting of throws and trips as opposed to a freestyle wrestling 'double leg' did not unduly worry Connor, but the leg locks, heel hooks and toe holds on the ground did. He had become more proficient in applying and defending them in the past year as the international No-Gi grappling competition scene had proved their effectiveness, and thus their popularity filtered into the BJJ and MMA gyms he frequented. Still, he could see the Russian was better versed in them.

He had hoped it would not come to that; he thought himself the better striker, and if he could avoid being taken down he would be fine—*hope for the best, and plan for the worst.*

The advantage he had, was there was not much the Russian could find on him even if he was so inclined. Connor's teenage boxing and Thai boxing matches were put up under his father's surname of Ryder, not Reed. There were not any of his judo matches in the Corps and only the combined services boxing highlights of which there were only a few seconds. The Russian also would not know of the training he had done with George and other MMA clubs for the past few years.

He felt his confidence grow and as the vehicle pulled up at the venue, he smiled—*I am going to torture this cunt.*

Xander stood amongst the baying crowd awaiting the entrance of the sacrificial lamb. Bets were being offered back and forth amongst the crowd although none, as he could hear, were with regards to who would win—no one fancied the foreigner's chances. "If he was good enough to beat Taav," Xander had heard one say, "we'd have heard of him."

It seemed a logical argument.

He had taken a risk being here. He had already been to the casino, and although he had been mindful of keeping his head tilted away from the cameras, if he kept frequenting Ivankoe's establishments, a keen-eyed member of his security staff might notice.

He saw the collective ripple of the turning of the crowd's heads. The Englishman was making his way to the elevated cage. There was no music, which added to the sense this was to be an execution.

Connor prepared himself to be pelted or at least spat on but neither happened, even the jeering was sporadic. The whole atmosphere was one of a sombre reverence.

He dressed in grey-and-white combat shorts. The large, cylindrical light made the elevated cage look as if it was about to be lifted by an alien spacecraft.

He took a final gulp of water, put his white gumshield in, slipped his flip-flops off to the side and entered the cage.

He began to breathe deeply, swilling saliva around his mouth. Tricks to take the edge off the fear response. An adrenaline dump was useful to the caveman running away from a sabretooth but needed to be controlled for fighting like this. Adrenaline made a person faster, stronger and sharper but too much was fatiguing and interfered with some of the fine motor skills needed for the correct timing of strikes.

He substituted every negative with a reminder of what he had to do—*do not over-reach, remember your leg lock drills and use your feints.*

He hated this part—the waiting. Fortunately, the Russian had not taken the opportunity to let him suffer, and came right out. Connor felt a spike of ephedrine because he knew as soon as the cage door locked, they were fighting.

The Tiger seemed in a hurry to get at him. He raised his hands to the bloodthirsty crowd and climbed in.

The cage was locked. Taav casually walked just short of the centre and he did the same. They were two metres apart.

Connor had a theory regarding cauliflower ears; those that were bulbous and stuck out were usually the result of impacts and the smooth ones—like the ones he looked at now—were a consequence of hours of mat time.

The Russian said with a grin, "I make this slow and painful."

"You reminded me of your mother when you said that."

The Tiger's eyes widened and he struck out with a half-step half-stamp. Connor slid to his right and slung a wide left hook through the guard and one to the stomach.

Taav pivoted so fast Connor did not immediately know what was happening until the spinning elbow crashed against his guard. He swayed with it and stepped out from the follow-up.

He *checked* the Russian's low kick and fired a jab to the solar plexus. Connor deflected the countering right hand off his shoulder and stepped away at an angle to avoid a flying knee.

They faced one another and Taav fired out a jab. Connor pulled his upper body back to avoid it, then rifled a right hand onto his jaw as Taav retracted his arm back, sending him stumbling though upright. Connor closed the gap, but the Russian ducked his left hook and wrapped his arms around him.

Connor felt himself hoisted into the air before being slammed. His lower back landed on the Russian's clasped hands, but the adrenaline turned off the pain that would pound him later. He began to push on his opponent's head to prevent him from securing mount. Taav released him and dived back for his leg.

Connor snatched it away while sitting and grabbing the wrists. He found his feet and flung the sambo practitioner's hands away, not wishing to engage in a vertical grapple with him.

The next couple of minutes consisted of the Russian stalking him as Connor skated around, darting in with punches and a few low kicks—*keep it to the basics*. Although he was getting the better of the exchanges, Taav was having success of his own, catching him with a couple of wide hooks as Connor pulled back, only for a flying knee to thud into his chest. The Yorkshireman's bare fists hurt; a couple of his hard punches had caught the Russians' forehead and others on his elbows.

He was vaguely aware of the storm of noise from the crowd.

Taav just kept coming, and Connor knew why—*fucker's trying to corral me against the cage so he can take me down.* One of Connor's strengths, he knew, was in his footwork. When he was a pre-teen boxer, his father made him do his shadow-boxing and even some of his sparring with runner's weights on his ankles. As a result, he could slip and slide around opponents easily. But his opponent was not only heavier, larger-framed and relentless—he was adept at cutting an opponent off.

Connor switched his focus to the body in an attempt to slow him down, jabbing to the solar plexus and hooking around the flanks. One particularly hard and well-placed hook to the liver had the Russian wincing. He went in to finish him only to find his nemesis had been play-acting before *underhooking* Connor's left arm and snatching his right wrist—*sneaky, fucking Russian.*

Connor overhooked and chopped his left hand onto his adversary's hip to block its was turning to throw him, as he tried torqueing his wrist out of the grip. Taav's strength meant Connor was Chinese burning himself but due to the Russian's physical size, strength and technical know-how, he guessed he would come off worse in a stand-up wrestling match. When he resisted the hip-throw the Russian switched to an *Ouchi Gari*—inside leg reap—that Connor barely escaped by snatching his leg away. Connor released his overhook and framed his left forearm against Taav's face and neck. When he felt the driving pressure of the head against it, he snapped it away and smashed his forehead into the Russian's face. He was immediately released as his opponent reeled back.

Connor kicked The Tiger between the legs like he was taking a Rugby field goal.

As the Russian crumpled to the floor, Connor punched the blade of his right forearm around the thick, corded neck from behind, wrapped one leg around Taav's torso while posting his other foot on the hip. With his prey secure he clasped his left bicep, knifed the back of his left palm behind the Russian's head and tightened the noose.

He saw the hand come up, seemingly to tap, before attempting to push Connor's elbow over his head—*good effort, you have to rage against the dying of the light.*

The Russian went limp and fleetingly Connor debated whether or not to kill him, before deciding against it—*You are the one who started it.*

He released his vanquished foe and walked to the door. After a moment, it opened.

He hid the damage he felt as he walked back to the changing room under a chorus of cheers.

16

With the entire bathroom filled with steam, John Merick numbly registered he had been in the shower too long. The effort of depriving himself of the beads of comforting warmth almost exhausted him.

He dried and dressed himself—smartly—on automatic before walking into his spacious bedroom.

He opened the medicine cabinet situated in his walk-in wardrobe. His heart plummeted upon hearing the rattle of the tablets in the container. He had overestimated how much he had been doubling up on his anti-depressants. Not that getting more would be an issue.

Today was Sunday, and he resolved to go to church. Maybe reviving his lapsed Catholicism would provide some sort of relief for the guilt and shame. Ever since the Scotsman had come to see him, he had felt a worm of fear too.

He would see the priest; a problem shared.

Ayesha Jehan never felt so scared and alienated in all her eight years on the earth. Her tears stained her pillow.

It had been less than three weeks since her father had revealed her birthday present. He had taken her to Simferpol and she watched with the other children the spells cast by the magician. It was as if she was in a dream, and she remained so after the show was over.

Out on the street, this wonderment was pierced with a burning arrow. She remembered vividly the shock of her father pushing her into another pedestrian—right before the car mounted the pavement and threw him into the air. He landed like a dropped fragile doll filled with red paint. He croaked her name, but quickly fell asleep. She stood trying to wake him as a small crowd gathered around her.

Somewhere in the melee a strange lady had held her hand for her and said, "We have to find a doctor, they will want to ask questions only a family member would know so they can treat him correctly."

She had a kind face.

The lady put her in the back of a car with a strange man driving and got in beside her. After a time, Ayesha began to get nervous. She tried asking about her father but the lady hushed her with a finger to her lips.

After a time the car went through a forest and stopped. She knew without knowing and screamed even before the man got out, opened the door, wrenched her out and threw her into the darkness of the boot.

She sobbed for what felt like hours while being bumped around. Finally, the car halted and the light attacked her eyes for a few seconds. They recovered to reveal a house the size of twenty surrounded by huge hills. The garden looked as big as her school's playing fields.

A man with a black beard like Hagrid but a bald head stood by the entrance.

With the driver watching her, the lady got out and spoke to the black beard. They had seemed to argue a little. The beard called out, and the driver gripped her and brought her over.

The beard looked down said, "I am Mr Agron. I am the headmaster here. You'll be staying a while as your father gets well."

She had been in a daze from then on. It seemed a strange school, and they learned strange things. And they were locked in their rooms for most of the day. All the other children were Muslim also.

She had made friends though. Kara was a bit younger than her and she had shared a biscuit with Ayesha.

One day, Ayesha had again asked about her father's well-being and where her mother was. One of the men had gripped

Kara by the arm and said to Ayesha, "This happen when ask of family," before smacking Kara with the back of the hand.

Ayesha had seen the shock on her friend's face before registering the bleeding. The room went silent except for a couple of the other children weeping. Another man dragged Kara out by her arm.

When Ayesha re-joined her classmates, she had an invisible forcefield around her pushing away the other children.

After a few days, Kara reappeared with two black eyes and her nose misshapen. And the forcefield kept her away too.

Connor had showered and changed surrounded by a sensation of vulnerability. Two of Leonid's guys stood by to look after him, but there would not be much they could do if Ivankoe had ordered his men to beat, kidnap or execute him in his lair. The whole point of the match was for Leonid to placate Ivankoe for Connor's transgression at the casino. Connor refrained from asking why this was necessary if the two factions were already engaged in a street war.

That aside, Ivankoe would not have expected his man to lose. Connor contemplated throwing the match to placate the Russian crime boss, but without a referee present and not trusting Taav not to break bones while he feigned unconsciousness, he had decided against it.

While pulling on his boots, there was a knock at the door. The two Ukrainians hands hovered by their waistband as Connor shouted, "Come in."

A tall, broad-shouldered man entered before Ivankoe.

There was a palpable tension in the room before Ivankoe roared, "That was facking good fight. Taav is good, very strong. You a very good fighter."

Connor nodded. "Thank you, Mr Ivank—"

"Roman. Please call me Roman."

"Roman. I want to apologise by the way I acted in your casino. I wasn't aware of who owned it."

"Let us not speak of this again. You made mistake but you here—you have big balls."

"And I want to apologise to Taav for attacking him, but I had to escape. And for kicking him in his big balls—like you said, he's very strong."

Ivankoe laughed. "He knew rules of fight. And, he will be better security now."

Connor shrugged. "Still."

"Of course. We go out tonight, anything you want. I will show you Odessa."

When Connor did not say anything, Ivankoe said, "Come now. With respect to these warriors, if I want you dead, you die."

Connor nodded at the confirmation of his own logic before saying, "Mr Hochar might not appreciate me going out with someone he's currently at odds with."

The sound of clapping came from the corridor and Leonid appeared smiling, "Connor, now I know we can do business."

"What was this? A test."

"Maybe." Leonid shrugged. "A stranger comes to me from nowhere—but now I know. I know police types, I know government types and I know none would be crazy-bastard enough to fight angry Russian in a cage and beat him with a kick to the balls."

He and Ivankoe began laughing, then Ivankoe's bodyguard and the Ukrainians did likewise.

So these two are best mates—thought Connor—*do not ask now.*

"So you don't mind me going out with him?"

"You cannot go out with this Russian. He pour so much vodka down your throat you will be singing Russian national song and dance like a Cossack."

Both Leonid and Ivankoe laughed. Leonid continued, "I make joke. It is free country, Mr Reed. You and I will have plenty of parties together. Tonight, let Mr Ivankoe hospitalise you."

Connor felt a jolt before realising Leonid meant something to do with 'hospitality'.

"Okay," said Connor before turning to Ivankoe. "You said anything I want?"

"Drink, girls—or boys if your thing— food, drugs—anything."

"Let's start with the food, shall we? I am famished."

Perturbed lines creased Xander's forehead observing through the powerful lens of his camera the sight of the man with the dirty blond hair dining with Ivankoe and his men including, Taavetti Jirov. *First Leonid and then Ivankoe? Who the fuck is he?* thought Xander.

The bar named 'Q1' was seemingly perched on the edge of the sea— a very famous spot. There seemed to be an influx of attractive women this evening, although Xander noted, they had not joined the group he was surveilling yet—Ivankoe would tell them when.

As Xander began taking pictures of the scene, he hoped his contact back in Kiev would be able to shed some light on the man.

17

A serenity passed over Merick as he said the words, "I accepted money I should not have."

He felt the sanctity of the confessional box keeping him safe.

"Go on, my son" prodded the voice on the other side of the latticed opening.

"Over two years ago, a man dressed like a banker named Paul Malone came to see me in my office with a proposal. He said he represented a multinational corporation named 'Ambow International' that wanted to fund our charity to penetrate the most hostile places in the world so we could provide aid to the most vulnerable—not just in Ukraine. That they would source and pay for all the security—manpower, their wages, their travel, accommodation and any risk assessments for our workers. He said all he wanted was that they chose the locations. Then he asked me to check the Britikrane account—right there and then on my phone. There had been a deposit of three-hundred and fifty thousand pounds made. He told me that was a token of their intent."

Merick took a few deep breaths.

"Carry on."

"A deal was hashed out on the spot. Most of the money went into the charity's account but not all. I justified to myself that I worked for years for others, and this money was a fraction of what bankers in the city who were only interested in themselves earned."

"The sins of another do not absolve you of yours."

Merick controlled the tremors in his voice. "I know that, father. But that's not all. I never met anyone from 'Ambow International' again in person. Everything was done digitally. After a while, their requests became demands. One day I put my foot down over something or other, and I got screenshots of the incriminating transactions regarding their money—things to do with tax. I told—typed—that they, whoever 'they' were, are just as guilty. Another email came through; 'Ambow' didn't even exist. I didn't fight my conscience—the charity's reach and influence had skyrocketed with the extra money."

There were a few moments of silence before the priest spoke. "Have you informed the authorities?"

Merick replied, "I decided to begin with God first."

"Good. Redemption can only be reached through Jesus Christ."

"Amen, father."

Connor awoke to fingertips gliding on his chest. They belonged to a dark-haired girl with cat-like eyes in bed beside him. He laid on his back with his head tilted towards her. It was bemusing to him how she had managed to get her other hand around him and onto his stomach before it clicked that they belonged to someone else. He turned to another gorgeous woman, with pale blonde hair—*My life is all downhill from here.*

The room colours were a blend of creams, white and light beiges and the sunrays sieved through the billowing curtains.

He felt drained and his head heavy, then he remembered snorting cocaine off the blonde's tits—*Fucking cliché.* It had been top drawer coke. His dad never touched drugs, saying, "Drugs aren't that dangerous—it's the natural human tendency of wanting more of a 'good' thing that makes them dangerous." Connor knew his dad was trying to discourage him from taking them but instead Connor had just resolved to use them sparingly. He liked the quote by Wilhelm Von Humboldt that the aim of existence is "a distillation of the widest possible experience of life into wisdom."

Still, he was paying for it now.

"Where are we?"

"You are in my home," yawned the blonde in excellent English. "I am Anita's flatmate."

"So you're Anita?" asked Connor, indicating the brunette.

The brunette looked playfully aghast and lightly punched him in the chest. "Oh my. You do not know my name after everything we have been through?"

Connor smiled, realising she was teasing. The recollections from last night came to him, and mercifully so did their names. "I make joke," he said in a parody Russian accent. "You're Maria and this is Alina."

"You have just saved yourself from murder," said Alina the blonde, gently gripping his throat.

He laughed, then smiled at the surrealism of the previous night. He remembered speaking to Taav at the bar, first apologising—which the Russian accepted—and then talking about MMA.

They seemed to have a similar taste in fighters, and the pair gravitated away from the rest of the group, including Ivankoe, who did not look too happy.

Taav seemed a popular guy in this part of Odessa, not having to queue at the night spot he had taken Connor to.

Connor had been wary any resentment over his victory might surface when the Russian was drunk. But the mafioso could not have been more welcoming—indeed, it did not seem like the alcohol had affected him at all. Connor had thought the notion of Russians being able to drink vodka like water and not get drunk was a myth, or at least exaggerated, but Taav seemed to be a testament to it.

Another reason they had come to this club was that Taav knew a girl, Anita—a dancer who doubled as a ring card girl, who was out for one of her friend's birthdays. The girls had been there for the fight and Connor inwardly revelled in the attention but outwardly remained cool, not only for the girl's benefit, but because he did not want to antagonise Taav.

It had been Maria's birthday, and it was Alina's idea he should stay the night with them. Because of the coke and sex, he had not had much sleep, and it was coming up to midday.

They heard some muffled cries from downstairs.

"Sounds like Taav is showing Anita he's a Tiger again," yawned Alina.

"Can either of you two cook?" asked Connor.

The girls looked at one another. "Of course, but it's my birthday." Maria smiled.

"It was your birthday last night, and I gave you your present." He winked. "Could you make me something, please. And coffee?"

Maria looked at him with a strange look on her face before getting out of bed, a little smile dancing on her lips, and left to go downstairs.

Connor turned to Alina, gripped her by the throat and kissed her hard. She responded enthusiastically. He slipped between the sheets and was about to enter her when a scream from downstairs bolted his heart rate up.

18

Connor slung the covers back and his pants, jeans and boots were on within seconds. Despite not having a gun he cleared out of the bedroom as per his *CQB* training.

He checked the bathroom before edging his way downstairs.

He found Maria sitting slumped against the doorframe of a bedroom, hugging her knees. She was not speaking, and instead seemed to be staring off into her mind's eye.

He made the final few steps before looking into the room himself.

Anita and Taav lay sprawled in the bed, decorated in their blood. The scene resembled a macabre contemporary art piece.

Something in his head screamed at him. He spun around, seeing the balaclava-clad figure creeping around the corner before the killer saw him.

Connor's left hand snatched the outside of the knife-holding right thumb and wretched it around. The edge of his hand whipped into the slaughterer's gullet, reeling him back clutching his throat with the knife clattering to the floor. A vicious jumping left to the temple knocked out the masked man.

He took off the balaclava—shallow skin and dark hair.

Connor took stock— calling the police was not an option—you did not talk to the police, not in his family and definitely not here, especially when you have met with two of the city's most infamous crime lords. Then who to call? He did not have Ivankoe's contact details and besides, Leonid was his new business partner and so his feigned loyalty lay with him.

First things first.

He turned and saw both girls staring at him. Maria seemed to have snapped out of her catatonic state. He addressed her sharply first to keep her from sliding back into it. "Maria. Look at me."

When she tilted her head from the killer to him, he said, "Do you have any rope or clingfilm?"

She shook her head.

"Take that off and give it to me," he said gesturing to her kimono-like nightie. "Alina, go fetch me a pair of scissors and anything that looks like tape from the kitchen now."

Alina seemed alert and dashed downstairs to the kitchen. Connor snapped his fingers in Maria's face and opened his palm. She took her nightie off and gave it to him.

"Go upstairs and put some clothes on."

As she numbly did so, he took out his phone before taking a picture. He hated having 'evidence' on him, but Jaime might be able to use his skills to identify the man.

Alina appeared with the scissors and a roll of black masking tape. He gave her the nightie after removing the belt.

"Cut strips from bottom to top around three inches—I mean seven centimetres thick. Okay."

She nodded and began, before being startled by the groaning of the killer.

Connor smiled and tapped her with the back of his hand. "Watch this."

The nonplussed man began to sit up, taking in his surroundings. Connor shouted, "Surprise motherfucker."

He kicked his head like he was taking a penalty shot and blood splashed against the wall.

He giggled. "Banter."

He shook his game face on upon seeing her bemused face. She handed him the strips and he hogtied the comatose man with them and the belt. He used the last two pieces to tie his fastened feet to the stair rail after removing his shoes. He wound the tape around the head covering the mouth and eyes, before doing the same to the wrists and ankles. He looked at Alina looking at him—*fuck me, she is sexy.*

"Go upstairs and check she's okay."

She nodded and climbed the steps.

He dialled his phone. Leonid picked up after the second ring. Bruce had told Connor stories of the capabilities of the CRAY supercomputer at the US's NSA and other systems within the GCHQ in the UK. Capabilities such as locking on to certain words if used within a phonetic proximity to one another and then recording that call; words like 'knife', 'stabbed', 'murder', 'kill', 'body', 'multiple', amongst a host of others, even if the phone was not directly bugged.

"Hello, Connor. Good night?"

"Yes, until this morning."

"Why until this morning."

"My friend who I danced with earlier let me stay at his girlfriend's house. They were both visited by a stranger who put them to sleep permanently with something sharp. I made him sleep temporarily. He's here tied up."

Leonid answered after a few moments. "Any others there?"

"Two girls. Flatmates with the sleeping girl," Connor answered. "Should I inform his boss?"

"No. I tell him. Tell girls, police are on the way. Tell them wait in one of rooms, and you leave. They tell your side of events for you, but if you are there Ivankoe will want you questioned. Understand?"

He did—they would torture him. Even he agreed it seemed a strange coincidence.

"Yes. What about the girls?"

"He knows the girls. He knows by their acting—behaviour—they innocent. You however are different matter. I call him now. Leave," said the Ukrainian before ending the call.

Connor looked over at the still-unconscious killer. He could not risk leaving him; if he managed to untie himself before Ivankoe's men got here he would likely kill the girls—the witnesses. He went over and rifled through the pockets, murmuring, "You *solid* fucking cunt," when he found a phone and a wallet.

He extended the killer's arms out by the secured wrists, located the elbows underneath the dark sweater, and stamped, fracturing them. If the killer awoke now, it would be excruciating to use his hands to free himself. Connor broke the fingers, laughing as he did so, as he recalled a joke about a patient pointing out to the doctor all the various places on his body that gave him pain when in fact it was just a broken finger—*Get a grip of yourself, tell the girls and fuck off.*

He bounded upstairs and knocked on the door. "It's me. I am coming in."

He opened the door and saw Alina holding Maria in a comforting embrace.

"The police are coming. Wait in here."

Alina stroked Maria's hair, soothingly, "We know who is coming, Connor. No need to lie. You go now."

Connor retrieved his top and made sure he had everything. He walked up to Alina, gripped her jaw and kissed her on the mouth, "Thanks for having me."

Then he left.

Xander observed Connor through a lens, leaving the apartment. He was on higher ground in his car, around 200 metres away, obscured by woodland. It was midday but the area was quiet with people either at work or university.

A lot of the residents of this area were students of the Unversity of Odessa, including the two girls who resided in the rental apartment—he had had a colleague check with the local city-district council, an Alina Kazan and Anita Malko. He had run checks through Kiev and discovered they were both from affluent backgrounds, and he mused their attraction to Taavetti Jirov and Connor Reed was borne out of the men possessing a testosterone level higher than the males they ordinarily associated. There had been a third woman whom he had not been able to identify.

With just Artem working with him, they had been unable to cover the back entrance of the house. Still, it had been cordoned off by a high wall and a garden.

As the Brit came closer, Xander saw blood on his face.

"Artem, follow the target. I'll stay with the house."

"Так, сер," he replied—Yes, sir.

Xander mulled over what to do. He sensed death from the house—*Why would the Englishman leave with flecks of blood on his face? Another fight with Taav?*

The Ukrainian agent mulled over his options. He could wait here for perhaps hours. He was a patient man, but anything could have happened in that apartment. If he had been on official police duties, he could have entered under probable cause. But he was not, which is why there was only him and Artem that morning. With his 'team' loaned from other districts outside of Odessa, limited funds meant he picked the times to use them sparingly. Had he told Artem he was considering entering the house alone, his fellow agent would have insisted on assisting him, and the Englishman needed surveilling.

He made his decision and got out of his vehicle. His fingers lightly brushed the bulge on his hip.

The treeline covered his approach until the final twenty metres, but he could not see any peering faces from the windows.

He reached the door, unholstered his pistol, keeping it hidden by his grey suit jacket. He slowly pressed on the handle and the door clicked opened. He stepped in, closed the door behind him while facing the stairwell. He brought his pistol up and began to clear the lower floor—nothing.

He crept up the stairs and saw a man trussed up in black tape on the floor. Xander recognised him through the bloody mask and taped eyes. It was Rinat Nureyev, an assassin and enforcer for a Crimean Tatar paramilitary group named *Povernuto*— The Returned—a reference to the mass Tatar deportation during World War Two and their coming back. Xander felt a wave of anger.

He continued sweeping, finding the bodies of Taav and the unknown girl lying in a blood pool of a bed. He attempted to compute why Rinat was there and why Connor Reed had not killed him. Xander turned his attention to the final floor when he heard the downstairs door open with Russian voices.

19

Derek Ryder lay back in his reclining leather settee staring at the premiership football on an eighty-six-inch LED smart TV. His thoughts yanked him back to the disrespect his family had shown him.

They would never realise how heavy lay the crown; he was the top dog, the lightning rod for the police and the bastard NCA. The half-time punditry began, and he listened to the discussion of Arsenal's drop in performances and the fans' displeasure at their long-standing manager, Arsene Wenger. *Disloyal cunts*—he thought—*after everything he has done for the club.*

He sipped his bottle of lager, realising what a mistake it was to encourage his nephew to return to Leeds. Not that he had moved back, per se—Derek was not aware of him buying or renting any property in or around the city—but his visits had been longer and more frequent. And he thought he could detect an undercurrent of dislike towards him; the mannerisms with him seemed a little—cold.

And he did not like how much of a name Connor—who used his mum's name of Reed rather than Ryder—had been making for himself in the UK and even European crime circles. And he and the leader of the Southwark Union Gang in London were friends.

He remembered when he had first realised just how much of a threat his nephew could potentially be—*that fucking boxing match.* His eldest nephew Tom had arranged a boxing show at one of the nightclubs and most of the family had attended and were placed at the VIP table. He remembered Connor walking in with a stunner of a short-haired blonde and his cousins and uncles treating him like a returning prince.

One of the main event boxers had pulled out at the last moment, and Connor had right then and there filled in for him. Not only that, he smashed and stopped the opponent in the fourth and final round. Derek remembered forcing a smile as the crowd chanted his name. And his wife Jenny had gushed all over her nephew.

Their marriage had been frayed. He had upped his steroids, alcohol and cocaine use, and his temper had gotten shorter.

She had been spending more time at friends recently, as she was tonight—*fuck her too.*

The second half was about to commence when the landline rang —*at this hour?*

He reached over and answered it. "Hello?"

"Hello Derek, how are you?"

"Who's this?"

"You know who this is."

Derek felt the blood cool in his veins.

"How did you get this number?"

The voice laughed in response, and Derek asked, "Why you calling me? Why now?"

"You think he knows. I mean, knows in his heart? I wonder what he's like around you? Although his father was taken in—never thought he would be. Then again, that man was all about family wasn't he?"

Derek tried to control his breathing, "What do you want?"

The line died.

The walk-in wardrobe surrounded Xander, looking through the slats, and keeping his pistol pointing forwards. He knew what he was going to see.

He recognised the leader of the three, one Yuri Alferov, a particularly vicious enforcer for Roman Ivankoe.

The agent was not under any illusions of what would happen if caught in here. The fact he was a law enforcement agent would mean nothing to them—in fact, it would exacerbate their desire to kill him.

All three had pistols in their hands. Alferov gestured to the other two and said in Russian, "Check upstairs. Be alert."

They both disappeared from view. Yuri began to move around the red painted corpses as if in thought, before coming closer to the closet.

Don't you do it—thought the Ukrainian bringing his pistol to the Russian's head height. Although he doubted there were more than the three, there was no way of knowing. Perhaps Alferov had left one or more as lookouts outside.

Alferov stood looking directly at the door. He walked over, putting his hand on the closet handle.

Xander's bullet smashed him in the face, instantly taking his life. The agent quickly burst from the closet and snatched a plant vase from the side. As he heard the upstairs bedroom door open, he launched it across the walkway over the stair railings. It smashed on the lower floor and he skipped back behind the door.

"He's on the lower floor, quick!" bellowed one of the men. Xander waited for them to bolt past—by the time they sensed his presence behind them, it was too late. He shot the pair several times, tumbling them down the steps like puppets with their strings cut.

He turned and bolted up the stairs and burst into the room revealing the one girl tightly embracing another cowering beside the bed.

"I am not going to hurt you. Quickly, tell me what has happened here," he said in Russian.

After a moment the blonde, who had been looking at him in defiance, said, "The man tied up in the stairwell stabbed Anita and Taav to death. An Englishman spent the night with us. He defeated him in a fight and tied him up."

Xander took stock for a moment. "Thank you."

He left the room.

"If it wasn't your lot. Who was it? A jilted lover of the girl?" asked Connor.

He rode in the back of the new black Mercedes with Leonid. There was a van of the same colour with the windows to match behind them as part of the Ukrainian's security detail. He had taken a risk and sent Leonid a picture of Anita and Taav's killer hours previously before meeting him.

Leonid smiled. "No. The man Rinat Nureyev is a mid-level enforcer for group named Povernuto. It is organisation dedicated to striking back for the hard treatment of Tatar Muslims in Crimea."

"I see," said Connor. "Can you tell me, or does that go against your *omerta*?"

The older man smiled. "I can talk about the Russians. But this will involve a history lesson."

Connor shrugged. "I like stories." He knew building a rapport with people was all about showing an interest in what they say.

"What you know of Tatar people history?"

"I know they all got deported under Stalin for possible collusion with the Nazis."

"Yes, a few maybe guilty of the crime but he exile all. It is word 'deportation' yes, sounds not so bad. Not so bad as word 'gassing' yes? But from this 'deportation' eight thousand people died, with thousands of others dying as time goes. It was not until thirty years ago they able to return."

Connor nodded. "And now?"

"And now tensions. Russia has Crimea. Before Putin came to power Russia was on knees. They humiliated. Yeltsin, could not even keep Chechnya under Russia control. The West laugh. They needed hope—hope their pride restored. Putin did this. One way was all the time remind the people Russia saved the world from fascism, and how world should be grateful for price the people paid."

The Englishman shrugged. "That might have some merit. Only the channel prevented Britain succumbing—that and Churchill's speeches on the wireless. The death toll for Russia was twenty-five million— the UK and USA had half a mil a piece."

"You are correct. However, rejoicing Stalin's Russia the saviour of the world, one cannot say bad about its leader. The anti-Stalin talk may be quiet now but people like the Tatars do not forget easily. And Povernuto did not like Russians controlling everything in Crimea. Up until two years ago they would have been crushed."

"Why two years ago?"

"Because Russian Bratva was beginning to become organised and have money to make all powerful. A Ravil Yelchin and Makar Gorokhov had reorganised organisation—changed Bratva rules that only former prisoners could join, and must have tattoos. Ex-Spetnaz and ex-KGB agents join. And they make much money in London. They die in gun fight in docks. Media say nothing. Many in organisation think the Moscow pahkan—the boss—ordered it. Bratva was plunged into civil war. It broke up into pieces with no real leadership. Povernuto like a wolf sensed weakness. Rumours they have relationship with ISIS—things could get bad."

The Chameleon Project agent's heart raised a notch. He had been largely responsible for the dismantling of Yelchin's and Gorokhov's infamous London Bratva. He had saved McQuillan's life who in turn saved his as Makar had been about to kill him. The entire saga had left McQuillan with a reconstructed knee, and a body count that included several Russian mafioso, Dutch mercenaries, an American hitman, and the former chief of MI5. That an Odessa crime lord was relaying him some of the details had a surrealism about it.

"Go on."

"Russians, although they deny, started kidnap Tatar Muslim children."

"I see," said Connor. "Taav was killed in retaliation."

"I think yes." Leonid grimaced. "I lived through dangerous times my friend. But this could set fire the world. Do you know why?"

"Because if this small group, this Povernuto, is seen as a sympathetic figure in the face of Russia and its criminals, the Islamic world, including Saudi Arabia, could come to its aid. And Putin could not tolerate that."

"You are smarter than I think first meeting you. This is correct. It is chess board with more than two players."

Connor nodded—*was Grace caught in this?*

20

Miles Parker sat in the Cabinet Office in Whitehall for his regular game of 'smoke and mirrors'. He had learned long ago most of these liaison meetings with representatives of the CIA were a waste of time. *Then again*, he thought, *so were the majority of meetings*. As the head of SIS he was obliged.

Sitting opposite was a Daniel Thornton, the deputy director of the CIA, several years younger than Parker at forty-two and a full half-foot shorter. This was their first meeting.

Ordinarily, given both his physical and metaphorical stature and completely shaven head, people tended to be a little intimidated of the British foreign intelligence chief. It did not seem that way with Thornton, though the undercurrent of American arrogance seemed mercifully absent.

Usually, it was Parker's direct counterpart within the CIA that met him with a couple of aides in tow, but not today.

"Thank you for seeing me, Mr Parker."

"You know as the deputy director of the CIA you can call me Miles."

"Of course, but we still need to go through the formality of me being formal and you correcting me."

Parker hid his approving smile.

"So, Daniel. We'll dispense with the rest of the formalities and you can tell me why you have come to see me."

Thornton gave him a look of respect. "Ukraine. It's getting a little dicey over there."

Parker shrugged. "Has for several years now."

"Our data and analysts indicate it could be the next flashpoint."

"We all said that a few years ago." Parker knew it was, and he knew Thornton knew he knew, but if he could force the younger man into relaying to him his findings it would be a small victory. Little wins compounded over time.

Thornton shifted a little. "It's not just a squabble over territory between the Ukrainians and the Russians. ISIS have taken an ass-whooping in Syria. Between Assad's forces, Russian air strikes, the rebels and our collective special forces, they are taking a shellacking. But let's say there's an area they could fight for and control, where they are only dealing with one of those enemies."

"If you're suggesting ISIS will try and conquer Russia, that is laughable."

"Not Russia. The port of Sevastopol, they want—"

"If there's one thing I know, it's that Putin would not allow Islamic fundamentalists running wild in his backyard."

"There are already organic Muslim elements in the region. With their assistance and a little Saudi money, they could prove a pain in the ass for Russia."

Parker kept the shock off his face as he got where this was going long before Thornton had finished speaking. "You want to assist them."

The CIA man took a moment to answer. "Assist them in their own destruction. It's like you said, Russia won't tolerate that. We both know Putin needs a buffer zone between Russian and the West. If international focus is more on these Crimean Muslims, it could open other avenues for us."

"Let's talk frankly. You're suggesting aiding ISIS and this off-shoot Crimean rag-tag Muslim revolutionary group—who are named 'Povernuto' by the way—through Saudi contacts and God knows what else, to inflame Russia into slaughtering a massive number of the Tatars. Or else, having your news channels make Putin appear he has. Alas, there is an international outcry which precipitates a global jihad. You'll stoke the fires of the old mujahedeen, and how they overcame the evil empire. And then add sanctions and so forth."

Thornton turned his palms over. "I would have expected your support in this endeavour. One enemy openly flaunts your laws by murdering its people on your soil. And the other has committed terrorist attacks against you."

"Daniel, do not use the phrase 'expect your support'; this isn't the Bush-Blair era. And you and I know what our meddling during that time has done."

"But we are coming up to a post-Brexit era," stated Thornton, before softening the statement with a smile and asking, "You don't agree with this strategy? Because we feel it's a bird in the hand."

"Who's we?"

"The director."

Parker nodded. "Why have you come to me? Surely it's not for my permission?"

Thornton scratched his chin. "We are limited to the number of assets we have in the region."

Parker knew that meant 'we don't have any'.

"What makes you think we do?"

"Because you're MI6."

"Flattery will get you everywhere," the spy chief said. "Leave this with me."

"Of course."

The two men stood and shook hands before Thornton left the room.

John Merick nursed the lager, which could not wash out the taste of anxiety. The barmaid seemed to be keeping her distance, despite the sparseness of other customers, perhaps sensing his mood. Only two other men were in tonight, a bar skeleton who Merick had seen regularly in the same corner table spot, and another man, mid-thirties, behind him whose attention was completely on his phone.

He immersed himself in his work during the day to distract himself. At night, without a family, the pub was his only refuge.

His confession had buoyed his mood for several hours before the dawning of what must be done deflated it. That, and the guilt that he had not told the man of the cloth the full story.

With his aid workers visiting these hostile zones, a series of strange events occurred. On three separate occasions, a member of security accompanying his volunteers had been shot while in the country and two had died as a result: three separate occasions, in three separate countries—Iraq, Syria and Nigeria. He understood after a time; 'Ambow International' was a front for a US government agency, and they had been using his charity to insert operatives in these places.

Whose attention would he even bring this to?

He slid off the stool and made for the toilet. He relieved himself and as he was finishing zipping himself away, the man who had been engrossed with his phone earlier entered.

He spoke. "Hey, how are ya?"

Merick felt a sense of unease—American.

"I am okay thanks, you?" he said cautiously. He felt more at ease when the American unzipped and began to urinate.

"Is it always this quiet on a Wednesday night?"

Merick shrugged, feeling strange having the conversation while the man was urinating.

"There used to be a quiz night. Not sure what happened to it. The 'Black Bull' up the road will be busier."

"Hey man, thanks. I'll check that out," said the man, finishing and washing his hands.

Out in the bar, the man walked past him and out the door.

Merick thought—*Now I am scared of Yanks in public toilets. Get a grip.*

He took a glug of his pint. *They need you too much to kill you now.*

Drowsiness swirled out of nowhere. He checked his watch—*it is past ten.*

He went to drain the last of his pint, but he could not seem to make his hand move forward. Then he could not move his head. His body refused to respond to his brain's command, and slid off his stool.

A coldness invaded his body as the barmaid appeared with her hands slipping under his armpits and trying to pull him up to no avail.

He died on the floor.

When Ayesha saw the copper-haired nurse smile at her, she felt like crying. It had been the first pleasant face in what had seemed like an age and she seemed to be the most beautiful lady she had ever seen.

Ayesha could not understand why the guards had not come in with her.

The lady said something in a foreign language. After a moment, she pointed to herself and said, "Grace."

Then she pointed at her. Ayesha understood and said, "Ayesha."

The nurse gestured to take her shoes off. When Ayesha hesitated, she smiled and the sound of the nurse's voice reassured her.

She stood Ayesha against a giant ruler and afterwards got on the weighing scales.

After, there were various tests. The nurse spoke to her in her strange but soothing voice throughout and Ayesha began to dread leaving her company.

When the tears broke the rim of her lower eyelid, she felt comforting arms slip around her and the nurse whispering comfort.

21

Connor and Leonid sat on loungers outside one of the Ukrainian's 'dachas'—a second home country house. This dacha overlooked an expansive garden, which ended as the view of the emerald sea began. The sun had just begun its descent and would plunge into the ocean soon.

The crime lord had insisted Connor join him for a whiskey and a cigar. Connor had informed him of his aversion to smoking, being a non-smoker for over four years, but when Leonid had explained the cigars were Cohiba Behike Cuban cigars and worth nearly $20,000 per box, he felt compelled to smoke one.

"I don't smoke one of these like a cigarette, do I?" said the Englishman.

"No—you are not all animal. I teach you to smoke like man. First, we cut end, and we do not use knife and no way we bite end off like some Hollywood pimp. We use this," said Leonid holding up a metallic oval with three holes in it the size of penny pieces. There was a blade in the centre.

"A cigar cutter? Or some other name?" asked Connor.

"Correct. A cigar cutter. Be quick and strong with cut," he said, and when Connor did so, he threw him a torch lighter and continued, "Use this. A cigarette lighter affects flavour. Light it underneath not on it. Make certain flame lights whole end equal. When end lit, draw smoke into mouth but do not inhale. Just suck smoke into mouth, enjoy taste and blow out. Understand?"

Connor nodded. "Puff, but don't inhale after I have lit it from the bottom and made sure its evenly lit."

"Correct. We will make a man of you yet. Cigar smoking is experience. Take your time, sip whiskey, breathe in sea air and enjoy view. This is not an endeavour for women, you understand?"

"Depends on the woman."

Leonid looked at him seriously. "When I say women, I mean the mentally weak. Not— what is western phrase?— gender."

Connor understood, before realising by inviting him to smoke he was showing him great respect.

He held the smoke for a moment, savouring the taste; he did not want to ruin the atmosphere by spluttering. The nicotine hit, and he took a sip of his whiskey. The warm air was pleasant on his skin.

The view of the sea combined with the birds' song had a hypnotic effect on him. He thought this was how meditation was meant to be. He had not quite grasped sitting on the floor cross-legged and paying attention to his breathing, but a cigar and whiskey made perfect sense.

Leonid's words broke the reprieve. "I have new information on scene you left yesterday."

"Alright."

"There was three more of Ivankoe's men found dead at scene."

Connor frowned. "I don't understand. You said 'found', or do you mean allegedly found after the police had killed them?"

"No, my friend—'found'. And more, Rinat Nureyev was nowhere."

"I securely fastened his arms and broke them for good measure. He wouldn't have been able to free himself, let alone kill three more Russians."

Leonid blew some smoke. "That is information I have from good source. Maybe he had back up who rescue him. Besides, what are you really doing here Connor?"

"What do you mean?" he said, feeling a worm of unease.

"What I mean is, is since I pick you up, and told you your life might in danger from the Russians, not once you ask me to get you away from city. Our business has already agreed. I ask myself 'Why does he stay?' Maybe you help me understand, no?"

"I do want to pursue our business relationship."

"I am sure. But that is not what I asked."

Connor drew in the smoke, blew and took a sip of whiskey. "A friend of mine was working in Crimea. She was kidnapped a few weeks back. I need to get her back."

Leonid smoked and said, "Then why did you come to Odessa?"

"Like I said. I have a dual purpose of being here. One was to make a business connection. And second, I heard any kidnap of attractive girls would normally result in them being sold to the sex trade."

"Do you have picture?"

Connor took out his phone and accessed a secret file, disguised as a calculator, before leaning over and showing Leonid a few pictures of her. He nodded in what looked to Connor like approval.

"Why she over here?"

"She's a surgeon. She was doing aid work in one of the hospitals."

The Ukrainian looked incredulous. "She is surgeon?"

Connor frowned. "Yeh. Surgeons can be gorgeous too. You never seen Grey's Anatomy?"

"What is this?"

"A television programme."

"Okay. I do not watch television. It is box for propaganda."

"In the UK we have something called flatscreens."

He saw Leonid frown, before his face softened as Connor smiled.

"I do not think your friend taken for sex trade."

"Why?"

"Because I would know."

A pool of relief formed within him that she might not be somewhere drugged and having sex forced upon her. A rock of disappointment was thrown in, with the ripples expanding in him—he was no further forward.

"You have any ideas?"

"The girls traded in criminal circles here begin as party girls. They are attracted to lifestyle. Our country is poor, the girls have taste of good life and want more. Drugs are a part of it." Leonid shrugged. "People think if have more of something that once made them happy, then more happiness they can have."

Connor said, "When in fact it desensitises you and you're on a hedonistic treadmill."

Leonid smiled. "'A hedonistic treadmill', I like this. Yes, it not take long for these girls to want more. More shopping, more holidays, more good times, more and stronger drugs. Then she at mercy of her dealer. Dealer becomes her pimp. Here they would not need to shoot driver, and kidnap a British surgeon to enter the sex trade."

Connor was surprised. "You already knew about her?"

"Yes. I did not know why you here—well, one of reasons—but I hear everything."

Fucking hope not—thought the operative. Connor refrained from saying anything. Leonid sipped his whiskey and both took a draw of their cigars.

The Ukrainian broke the quiet. "I like you. That is only reason you still live Englishman. I think your surgeon friend will be kidnapped for political reason. I cannot tell you everything. I will tell you this, the answer you seek is not here in Odessa. The place of your truth is more dangerous."

"Please do not say what I think you're going to say." Leonid laughed, and Connor continued, "How the fuck am I going to be able to move around Kremlin-controlled territory with impunity. If I bang out any Russian out there, I really will get killed."

"Bang out?"

"Yeh. Knock out," he said, making a punching motion. "The only reason I did it here was to gain an audience with yourself. There it will just get me dead."

The older man laughed. "Do you know you is—are—crazy, yes?"

"Depends on one's definition."

"Yes it does. But maybe only westerners can move around are journalists." With that, Leonid took a deep inhalation. As he blew the smoke out he looked over at Connor and asked, "Why do you smile?"

Parker sat at the window's edge overlooking the small lake. He observed the swan's elegant glide before taking in the fields and forestry surrounding the Sussex village of Lewes.

This small hikers' café had been chosen by Bruce McQuillan, who possessed the official title of 'MI5/SIS liaison officer'. The Scotsman performed superbly in the role but it was essentially a front masking his deeper role as head of the Chameleon Project.

Given McQuillan had an official role, they could have met at Vauxhall Cross, but he had asked Parker to meet here, simply stating they "should never set patterns."

The spy chief was glad—he had felt welded to his seat at times. And when he was not, his security was the most stringent of any civil servant which was why he was meeting McQuillan 'out of hours'.

The lean, keen-eyed McQuillan walked in and the two men shook hands. The Scotsman sat opposite Parker and the waitress bounded over.

"Anything I can get you, sir?"

"A black coffee, please," answered McQuillan.

"And you, sir?

"I am fine. Thank you."

She wandered off and McQuillan spoke. "Thought you'd appreciate the change of scene."

"I do, thank you."

"Why the unscheduled meeting?"

"Had a visit from one of our American cousins, one down from the top."

"To discuss their plans to bring their eighties South American tactics to Eastern Europe?" said McQuillan.

"How on Earth did you know?"

"I didn't. It was an educated guess."

Parker knew better than to probe him. "Can you take an educated guess on the specifics?"

McQuillan shrugged. "Riling up and maybe funding the few Ukrainian nationalists in the Crimea region against the Russians?"

"A shrewd approximation but off on its scale. They want to fund and 'rile up', as you say, a subversive group known as 'Povernuto' which is made up of Tatar Muslims. Seems they are unimpressed by what they see as the 'Russian invasion'."

"I see. So while certain sections of the US political structure want to prevent World War Three, another wants to inflame it by opening barely-healed wounds."

"What do you see specifically?"

McQuillan smiled. "I see the American media machine perched like a vulture when Putin's heavy-handed response ensues, probably with some veiled references to Stalin's treatment of the Tatars. He won't fuck around there. Donbas was a 'nice to have' for him, but his Black Sea fleet is in Sevastopol, so he'll ruthlessly stamp out any threat. Selected segments of the aftermath will be beamed everywhere and sanctions against Russia will become more politically viable."

Parker nodded. "Correct but incomplete. With ISIS nearing defeat in Syria, their gaze will focus somewhere else. Whispers will be made into the right ears, and the call for jihad against the oppressive Russian regime will sound."

"The Saudis are raging that the Iranians have funded the Yemeni Houthi rebels to attack their oil fields. Iran's backer of Russia will be seen as a perfect target. It's just money and denial for the Saudis."

"Thornton has made three trips to Riyadh in the past eight weeks."

"Russia, Iran, ISIS and Saudi Arabia— America's enemies are tied up for however long in a war against one another."

"Precisely."

"A fine plan if it didn't include the inevitable thousands of casualties, both combatants and non-combatants alike. It's not only ISIS that would come to the Crimean Tatars' aid, but there are Tatars all over the globe. Five million in Russia alone, even if you excluded the Crimean Tatars. Half a million in Uzbekistan. Thousands in other countries."

Parker had always been impressed by the Scotsman's retention.

"Quite. Our American cousins' involvement wouldn't be official, so they wouldn't even have to utter the words 'collateral damage'."

After the waitress came back with McQuillan's coffee, he asked Parker, "Are you getting soft in your old age?"

The Etonian took the barb well. "Just wiser."

"Why have you requested this meeting?"

"I told you last year of my reordered priorities."

A deep suspicion had marred Parker and McQuillan's professional relationship in the beginning. The evolution to a trusting rapport had been painfully slow. Last year had been a watershed moment for Parker. He—due to outside pressures—had not assisted McQuillan as much as he could have in his hunt for an American billionaire, Frank Schwimmer. The megalomaniac had devised an international scheme of lifting the homeless, before harvesting their organs for members of the global elite. Parker had been trying to protect his country from a man of comprehensive influence. It had been Bruce's actions and words that finally shifted his thinking that 'the country' and 'the people' were at times not mutually exclusive.

"You did," said Bruce. "What did you tell him when he made the proposal?"

"That I'd devote some thought to it."

Bruce nodded. "Think she knows?" referring to the CIA director.

"He said she did. He might be confident of my not bringing it to her, but it's a bold gamble if she didn't."

"Maybe not. If you ask her, she'll deny it anyway. If she isn't aware, she'll go back to him and he'll claim you made it up to feel her out about it. Claim it's your idea and you were pitching it."

"Surely the upstart wouldn't have such effrontery."

"I have done my research—he would."

Again, Parker did not ask. Instead asked, "What do you think we should do?"

"I'll make a few calls. Our cousins across the pond can't supply dissident Tatars with western weapons, or else Putin would have a field day splashing it over Russia Today. Remember there are around eight thousand media outlets in Russia across around a hundred languages and the Americans know that. Instead, they'll look to the Odessa Mafia to transport weapons to these rebels over there. If Kiev can focus their attention at the port it may avert disaster."

"Kiev might not want to incur Uncle Sam's wrath," suggested Parker.

"Their new allegiance is to Brussels, not Washington."

"That's if they even want to prevent it."

"Believe me. The last thing they want is their nuclear power of a neighbour and these crazy zealots fighting on their borders. They have enough on their hands trying to put in place a political infrastructure free—or relatively free—from corruption. Besides, they know how unforgiving the Russian backlash will be if they allowed an arms supply into Crimea to go unchecked."

Parker thought for a while how McQuillan should be his successor. The black ops chief had not shown any interest when Parker had pitched the idea to him.

"Any progress regarding the girl?"

"Not as yet," was all McQuillan would say.

"We need someone in there who can be our eyes and ears. I'll be honest, Bruce, I don't have anyone who I can rely on for solid information, even at street-level. It's sub-optimal that if this thing explodes, we will have no one on the ground batting for us."

Bruce left his meeting with Parker in thought. Though McQuillan had not said, he knew the SIS man had cut his teeth in this business through the back end of the Cold War. He'd always see the hammer and stickle when looking at Russia. Now Thornton had given Parker the impression this was a US-backed coup, maybe his interests would cross with his own.

He quelled the urge to ask his protégé for constant *sit-reps*. He thought of the coincidence of him sending Connor Reed to the region just as a touch paper was about to be lit. *The girl's kidnap must be linked to it, but how?* he thought.

As he got into his Jaguar, he was about to start the engine when he got the call. It was Reed.

"Hello, how's things?" he asked upon answering the call. Jaime had ensured end-to-end encryption, but they still kept the conversation as vague as they could. If Connor answered 'they are sweet', McQuillan would know he was under duress.

"Things are alright," said Connor. "I got directions to go further east. Towards the other port."

Bruce felt uneasy. If the man had to go there then he had to go—but there would be no diplomatic recourse to retrieve him. Also, he would not be sure he could use the same cover story twice. If he had already secured a trade agreement with Leonid, why would he be seeking one at Sevastopol—a place that was threatening to become a full-blown combat zone?

"Do you need anything from me?"

"Yes. I've been told only certain people from our neck of the woods can move with relative autonomy out there. One profession being a journalist."

"I see. And you'll be acting as the bodyguard."

"Yes," replied Reed. "Not that she fucking needs one."

22

Ciara Robson stood among the men with her back to the padded wall, looking over the mats at the instructor.

She had decided long ago wrestling was the physically hardest thing she had done that only lasted half an hour. She had been highly rated in Muay Thai, and although it hurt more and carried the threat of knockout, she found this more exhausting.

She was the only woman here who did it with any regularity. Plenty of girls took part in the Thai boxing class and even the Brazilian Jiujutsu sessions, but not many girls wanted to be thrown around, slammed and crushed by strong, sweaty, hairy men. In BJJ, the men could always *'play guard'*, but in wrestling the aim was the pin; that meant being thrown around, slammed and crushed, especially as she was too strong to be toyed with; in a choice between not wanting to be seen to be going hard on a girl or not wanting to lose to one, the men in the class chose the latter.

Still, for 'real' strength and conditioning Ciara found it had no equal, and her physicality was not something for social media posts—it was something that could save her life. And her ability to defend herself was something she cultivated to distance herself from the frightened young girl she had been under the same roof as an abusive man. She had heard a quote attributed to Bruce Lee— "A man with a good year or so of boxing and wrestling practise behind him, could beat a lifelong martial artist."

"Right," bellowed the instructor. "Until the end of the session we're doing winner stays on. Now all the under seventy-five kilo lads—and lady—to me left, and overs to my right."

The class divided themselves. Ciara stepped to the left, though not far off the upper limit. Indeed, the prominence of her musculature would have consigned her physique to be labelled masculine had it not been for the femininity of her face, breasts and posterior

"Three pairs to each side," called the instructor.

Ciara stepped out, with a dark-haired man who was shorter but broader. She remembered what the wrestling coach had once said, "For MMA I like doubles over singles so my hands aren't trapped, but if they're stronger than me then I prefer singles."

They assumed the wrestling position of arse out, elbows tucked in with palms open and head up. They shook hands—the wrestling equivalent of the 'slap hands and fist bump' of BJJ—and set about one another.

Her opponent reached to clasp the back of her neck. She grabbed the wrist with her two hands, pulling the arm across her body and drove her shoulder on top of his. She anticipated his fighting against the pressure, and took advantage of his bolting upright by snatching his right leg in both her arms.

"Finish it!" shouted the instructor.

She whipped her leg back while cannoning her shoulder atop his thigh. As he fell, she shot on top of him, her left arm around his neck and right scooping his far leg.

After three seconds, one of the lads on the side shouted, "Pin."

She stood, and he with her, shaking her hand despite the pained expression on his face.

She was in the most part bettered by the rest for the remainder of the sessions. Despite this, she enjoyed it as she always did.

"When we getting you into the cage, Ciara?" called out one of the lads, in reference to the general consensus that she would be 'a beast in MMA'.

"One day, maybe," she smiled.

She left for the changing rooms. After drying herself from the shower, she ran a comb through her short, silvery-blonde hair and looked at her phone.

She had an email notification.

Michael Ryder grinned upon seeing his kid brother Ryan. They were placed in a side room—two green cushioned seats and a coffee table— of Frankland. Previously, only Adam Lloyd had received that privilege on visits.

"Could you grab me a white coffee, please Bri?" he said to the guard.

"No problem, would you like a tea or a coffee mate?" the guard asked Ryan.

"The same, please."

As soon as the prison officer left, Ryan took out a scanner, stood on the table between them and waved it around the light.

"It's clean," he said, before handing his brother two doubled up polythene bags filled with wraps of heroin, equating to one and a half kilograms. Michael stuffed them into his grey jogging bottoms.

"Thanks for this."

"What are brothers for?"

"Where's Tom? You usually bring him."

"Just me today," said Ryan.

The door opened and the prison guard arrived with the coffees. He set them down and left without a word.

"Heard Adz Lloyd was murdered."

Michael nodded once.

"Won't be long until you're out," said Ryan.

"Nah, not long. It might be my release date by the time you get around to telling me what's on your mind, cocker."

A smile appeared on Ryan's face before disappearing again. "You might as well hear it from me Michael. Derek grabbed young Charlie around the throat at a family meeting a couple of weeks back."

Michael felt a seed of anger grow in his sternum. "Why the fuck did he do that?"

"He'd called a family meeting and it had gotten tense."

"Go on," said Michael.

"Derek was carrying on —asking why there had been no money, being more of a cunt than usual, with all his finger pointing. I snapped, telling him exactly what had happened to the family business. He had a go back, shit about Greg's arrest and 'im doing time fer us. But he must have still had a bee in his bonnet. Charlie was trying to calm things, saying Connor would sort it out. That just sent 'im over the edge and he grabbed young Charlie by the throat."

"What happened then?"

"Our Tom bolted around the table to stop him but he had already let go of 'im. Then he just skulked out of the door. Sent me a nasty text an' that."

The side of Michael's mouth twitched. "I'll be having words with him when I am out. You know what I think it is—Derek knows our Connor has done more for the family business with that Dutch connection than he has in years. That said, Derek is the point of contact for our connections in Manchester, the pool, and around 'ere in Geordieland."

"All them support 'im 'cos he's given them a way bigger cut than they were ever meant to have. Greg'd never have allowed it."

"We have to stop thinking about what Greg would do. Has Connor said anymore about coming back up here permanently?"

"Tom said he had spoken to 'im. He ums and ahs about it, but I don't think he's interested."

Michael squinted his eyes. "I can't understand—we'd all back him —what is he waiting for?"

"I don't know. I haven't heard from him for a few weeks. Couldn't tell you where he was, to be honest."

"One of the reasons the family is losing money is Derek believes more is better when it comes to foot soldiers. I've heard if off several lads in here. Pays for loads of little skagheads off the estates in Seacroft, some in Chapletown, rough areas in Wakey and Dewsbury just for little titbits. I couldn't understand it at first, then it came to me—he's doing it to get himself a little army in case there is a coup d'etat like. I think that's why he's keeping the Liverpool and Manchester lot sweet too."

"He'd get them involved if someone was to try an' take over?"

"I think so, but it might be inevitable. If Connor doesn't want to step up then one of us has to, or else we'll all be in here or dead."

In her North Finchley flat, with the light of her laptop screen illuminating her face, Ciara felt a nervous excitement upon reading the email. Her boss—her real boss—had just given her an assignment.

She wandered onto the balcony and looked over her view of London. The lights of the cars and street lamps began to appear as a darkened blue hue descended.

The silvery-blonde Ciara had two professions. One was as a freelance journalist, travelling from hotspot to hotspot, interviewing people, collating information and producing articles. The other was as an agent for the clandestine Chameleon Project.

Jaime, the mysterious tech guy whom she had never met, sent her a workup of the situation on an encrypted email. Her 'cover a story' for arrival in Ukraine had been detailed, as had the fact that she would be working with Connor Reed in the region to help locate a kidnapped British national.

She had worked with the Yorkshireman before in bringing down an organ-harvesting operation that preyed on the vulnerable and homeless. And he was not like any other man she knew.

One aspect of his character she bore witness to was a sadistic pleasure and even hilarity he found in hurting and humiliating people he considered 'evil' and 'too much of a risk to be allowed the time to potentially rehabilitate themselves'. Ciara had thwarted a gang attack on Connor, led by a thug who he had previously beaten. She had ordered the hoodlum to fight Connor one to one. After her fellow agent was victorious, he proceeded to sever the criminal's spinal column with a machete the victim had brought to the party. It had been the look on Connor's face as he did it she remembered the most.

On the same night, as they entered the safe house he had been inhabiting for a few weeks, they were accosted by an elderly lady who had waxed lyrical about how kind he had been to her, and how he had fixed her shower—and accepted his close-to-the-bone humour.

During their time together, Ciara had almost gotten killed twice, and despite that it had been one of the best times of her life. *His too*—she thought with a grin.

23

Connor sat in the same apartment Danylo had procured for him a few weeks earlier, feeling a frustration creep up within him. He quelled it—*I am still in the game, with cards to play*. The wrenching thought came into his mind that the longer he took, the more Grace would suffer, in whatever capacity. He expelled that too—it was not helpful.

He had heard a compelling career consisted of three elements: creativity, control, and impact. This profession had all those, he was the man on the ground and so McQuillan allowed him the latitude to attack whatever task his own way, and if he succeeded he would save lives. And he could provide credible intelligence to McQuillan, despite the *omerta* here.

Leonid had been cryptic regarding Crimea, and it was not as if he could press the Ukrainian. He told him his answers lay there and that was that. Connor had left the next day after Leonid had provided the security for him to return to the apartment and to collect his things.

Now, after a long drive, he was back here—waiting for Ciara to arrive. He was not sure how he felt. He had not had contact with her since they had worked together last year. On the one hand, there was not anyone apart from his *oppo,* Louis Allen, he would have to watch his back. Sharp and professional, but crucially she had a ferocious reaction to danger. When attacked by Moroccan gangsters in Holland she had slain two of them with a switchblade in a manner he could only describe as a berserk precision.

That had been the night they first had sex, he remembered, rubbing his throat.

His father had once said of a certain kind of woman—"Tigers are awesome and majestic animals, but you wouldn't have them in your house as a pet; they'd tear the fuck out of all your furniture."

Connor decided he was looking forward to seeing her. But then felt guilt for doing so. *It is OK*, he told himself, *you are single.*

The tap at the door sounded random but was not; he insisted Danylo use a prearranged knock, despite the police officer's assertion it was unnecessary.

Connor unlocked and twisted the door handle with an outstretched arm as taught in his agent training. Many in this profession had been shot through a still closed or barely open door.

He stepped back, welcoming in the Ukrainian and Ciara. She was just as stunning as he remembered. She wore a simple cream button shirt that revealed her defined forearms and did its best to hide her curves. Her jeans stopped at her strappy flat shoes.

The combination of her green eyes and short, layered silver-blonde hair drew like a magnet.

"Hello, stranger," she said, her hand on his shoulder, giving him a peck on the cheek.

"How are you?"

"I am not too bad, thank you. Not the best flight though."

"I guessed. Bathroom is over there. Go and put some makeup on."

He gave her a playful smile.

"There was a boy at school who used to kick me in the shins in the playground in front of an audience but then used to say sweet nothings to me as we walked back home. I forgive him now because he was ten-years-old."

"You know you look great."

"I know."

Connor turned to Danylo, who was watching the exchange with a bemused expression on his face. "To business *tak*?"

"Yes."

"Either of you want a drink?"

Danylo answered. "Yes. One of your English teas."

Connor nodded, still not entirely used to the lack of expectation in Europe regarding the words 'please' and 'thank you'.

"And you?" he asked Ciara.

"White coffee, no sugar, thanks."

"Alright. The kettle is over there. I'll have a black coffee."

She tutted with a flick of her fingers. "Off you go."

He made the drinks and Ciara dumped her luggage in the room.

They sat in an odd triangle around the coffee table.

Connor cleared his throat. "How do we get in? A request through the embassy would take weeks, I am guessing."

Danylo said, "Fortunately there are still back channels between ourselves and our Crimea, that can be greased with money. The problem is not really with accessing the region, it is your freedom to move there. They will want you to have an escort so you can only see what they want you to see. Understand?"

"But say if I am ill, surely they won't be firing people through to check on me. Ciara is the journalist; I am just the lowly assistant stroke bodyguard."

"Maybe, but be careful. The Kremlin knows Sevastopol is vulnerable to the West's infiltration. Putin fears the 'Mr Bonds' going there. They will want to know where you are at all times. Convince them you are not a threat, then you are safer."

Connor thought about what this would mean, then said, "You mean they despise western journalists over there, so when they are heavy-handed with me I have to pretend to be a beta male?"

The Ukrainian frowned. "What is a 'beta male'?"

Connor shrugged. "A pussy. A 'girlie-man' as Schwarzenegger calls them."

Danylo chuckled. "Yes. Oh—alpha male means a strong man, yes?"

Connor nodded. "But enough about Ciara. What is our actual route in?"

Ciara shook her head. "Your jokes are about as weak as this coffee."

Danylo answered, "I will drop you at border. They always change—rude, nice, rude, nice—no in middle. You arrive, they search you and belongings. Do not having anything they can use against you. Then will be nice— show you how wonderful motherland is. That is until you ask anything that could be against Russia, then you will be a 'propaganda journalist'. If you are too nice, they suspect you not a journalist. Too many not nice questions and they can make life difficult."

"What about leaving her on her own?"

"Her? Am I the cat's mother?" scolded Ciara.

"Cat's mother?" asked Danylo.

"It's a British, or at least English expression, I'm not sure," said Connor. "And I apologise. I mean, can I leave Ciara alone with them?"

"I would not trust. Foreign journalists treated with more respect to other western outsiders, but situation is dangerous. Miss Ciara, I would not wear makeup there."

Ciara said to the Ukrainian. "When do we leave?"

"I make calls tonight. There will still be bu-reauc-racy. I hope tomorrow we start journey."

As the liaison officer finished off his tea, Connor said, "Well Mr Kravets. We will await your call."

"Yes," he replied, then he shook hands with them both. Connor saw him out. He returned to Ciara standing with her hands on her hips, and her tits pushed out against the fabric of her shirt.

"You've finished your coffee, I see," she said.

"Yep, so I suggest—"

"I suggest—despite your infantile behaviour—you take yourself off to the bedroom, strip off and wait for me."

Connor blinked for a couple of seconds. No woman had bossed him around like this. He smiled and made his way to the bedroom.

Xander's eyebrows furrowed at the complication of the situation.

He sat in a non-descript Nissan over a hundred metres up the road, shifting his body position. He was not fond of sitting for any significant length. He had been in the boxy car for hours to trail the British man from Odessa.

He had failed. Reed had unexpectantly pulled over, and he was forced to drive past. Fortunately, Artem picked up the trail, as he was a couple of miles behind. As Reed converged on the suburbs of Kiev, he pulled into a cul-de-sac, and Artem had to park in it, get out and pretend to be a resident by walking confidently to the side of one of the houses out of view.

He had not been sure if he or Artem or both had been spotted, or if Reed was performing precautionary countersurveillance. Whatever the case, it was not a skillset typical of street criminals.

Luckily, though elements were attempting to turn off the baths of blatant corruption, most in government or law enforcement still showered in it. A female contact of his within the liaison unit had told him of a mysterious Englishman. She was not meant to know anything, except to book an apartment—"Kravets thinks that's beneath him." Kravets had let slip the gender and nationality because "he wanted me to make sure the cupboards were full with what the English liked."

Given the address, Xander had just observed Danylo Kravets—head of the Ukrainian Police's International Liaison Unit—walk in and now out of the same apartment

Connor Reed had walked into a few hours previously with what looked like groceries. Danylo had initially entered with a striking short-haired blonde. Was she a whore, some kind of payment for Reed?

Xander tried to work it out. Was Reed an informant? Why and how would Kravets look to the UK for a criminal for intelligence? Surely a Russian or Ukrainian would be a better and easier asset to recruit. Or maybe Reed had come to an arrangement with Kravets over a criminal enterprise. It did not make sense; the people who appointed him into that position did so because they wanted someone clean to present to the West, given the desire for EU membership.

Maybe he should ask Kravets himself. In an official capacity, the liaison chief would tell him no. It was a problem but still—*let us not make an elephant from a fly,* he thought.

24

Connor, laying back on the bed, blew lightly on the bite marks on his chest. Ciara was propped on her elbow looking at him.

"This is why you don't have a boyfriend," he said.

"Spare me. You know how I like it and were still in there like a shot."

He shrugged, hiding a smile. "A shag's a shag, isn't it."

"Yes, a shag is a shag. Especially when I can see the blood branches in a man's eyes as he cums."

"We're going to have to pack this in," he said, flinging the covers back and getting up. "We could have been slotted in bed just then."

"Could think of worst ways to go."

"I am not kidding, Ciara. It's other people's lives at stake now. We shouldn't be taking unnecessary risks."

"Alright, you baby. We'll keep our hands to ourselves then."

Connor felt a pang of disappointment. If she stopped initiating the sex, he could no tell himself she caught him in a moment of weakness. He began to dress, and Ciara got out of bed to do the same.

"Would you like another coffee, what with you being a lady of leisure now?" he asked her.

"Please, I work hard."

"You're an investigative journalist. You'll have more time off than Christopher Reeve's horse."

She pressed her lips tightly together and he left the room.

After a few minutes, they were sat by the coffee table.

"I take it this is your first time in Ukraine?" he asked her.

She gave a playful snort, "I was in Donetsk a few months after completing my degree."

Connor's forehead creased a little. "Gen, you went to Donbas fresh out of uni?"

"Gen?"

"I mean 'genuinely'."

"Yep. Our mutual boss had a hand in providing my security but it was, and still is a very volatile region."

"What were your observations?"

She took a breath. "In the Soviet era, the area was hugely important with its coal mines and iron smelting factories. I was shocked at how large the factory buildings were over there — like small cities. People came from all over, so it was never a 'Ukrainian' town, per se. The Soviet Union collapsed, and independent Ukraine didn't do much for the region. I think in the aftermath people's memories got distorted regarding the Soviet era—all the factual data indicates it was still very austere back then, with long hours and low wages, but the people I spoke to felt more of a sense of purpose. The heart-breaking thing is that masses of people there are affected by the agendas of a few. This old couple had worked their fingers to the bone and scrimped for the few possessions they had and bang, side of their small home smashed by a Ukrainian Army shelling—I remembered how broken they looked."

She paused momentarily, and Connor thought he saw a flash of melancholy. She continued, "They haven't got the means for precision bombing of targets like we and the US have. People like that old couple don't really care about the aims of Kiev or the DPR. They want to get on with their lives. Makes me angry."

Connor allowed her to vent, sensing this had been the first time she had properly spoken about it. This was also the first time he had seen the journalist in her.

"Who's at fault over there?"

She sighed. "You ready for a rant?"

"Alright."

"So, I said Kiev hasn't done much for that region since the Soviet collapse. Probably because its people are way over there, full of Russians and Russian speakers, ingesting Russian media. The Russians are not as subtle as us with their media manipulation; it openly terms the Ukrainian nationalist movement as Nazis and stirs up World War Two—or The Great Patriotic War as they call it—nostalgia. The thing is, there are Nazi sympathisers within the movement. Have you heard of Azov?"

"Yeah. Formerly led by Andriy Biletsky, an ultra-nationalist. His Azov were known as the 'little black men' to counter the Russians 'little green men' during the uprising."

"Exactly. The Ukrainian Government is doing more harm than good pretending the neo-Nazi movement doesn't exist, or downplaying it. People can see it's a cover up, especially when Putin's media is amplifying everything."

"I see," said Connor. "So if they said 'Look, there are some Nazi fucking dingbats in the ranks, but we're getting a handle on it' it wouldn't be quite as bad?"

"Eloquently put, yes."

"I take it the people there were under the impression the Kremlin would annex the region like Crimea?"

"A lot did. As I said, lots of people there were indifferent, but the media—and I know I am one of them—don't focus on them. They focus on the fighters and the players. Putin decided the risk was worth the reward for Crimea as part of his navy is there, and they need a port that doesn't freeze over every winter. There wasn't the incentive for Donbas."

Connor said, "And he got fucking smashed with sanctions. He can't have wanted another load hoisted on the country."

"No," she replied. "Especially since the oil and gas reserves are diminishing. They didn't diversify the country's economy when it was boom time. Those fucking politicians make out they are for the people and anti-West, meanwhile they buy property in Miami, Paris, Berlin and London."

"I know. I've seen *RocknRolla.* Great film."

"Why are you asking about Donbas when we're going to Crimea?"

"Leonid said something strange to me I didn't quite process at the time. He said something like, 'To find the girl you might have to visit more than one God-forsaken place here'. I wondered if he was including Donbas?"

Ciara blew her cheeks out. "We just going to follow the crumbs?"

"Yes," he replied, before asking, "Do you like cigars?"

Kravets lay in bed just after midnight debating with himself on whether he should go to the toilet. He knew he was delaying the inevitable but did not want to disentangle himself from the warm embrace of his plump wife and the comfort of the bed. It was a battle he had most nights and he always lost.

Finally, he began the slow slide out of his sleeping wife's arms and the warmth of the covers. The pyjamas he wore did their best to take the bite out of the cold. Despite his earnings, his frugality insisted the heating was switched off at ten before reigniting at six.

He tiptoed across the room, easing the door open and looking forward to relieving himself. He hurried to the toilet lest he wet himself, a phenomenon that puzzled him—*I can hold it for hours then almost piss myself a few seconds before the end.*

He sighed at the release. Tiredness slackened his jaw and he felt a full relaxation. He finished, shuddering as he shook off the last few remaining drops.

Fright bolted his heart as the metal pressed against his head.

"Scream and your brains will be splattered against the wall. I'd have to deal with your wife after that too. Understand?" said the voice in Ukrainian.

When Kravets took his time responding the tip of the assumed pistol jabbed him the back of his head.

"Yes, I understand," he replied in the same tongue.

"I will keep this pointed at you at all times. We will go down the stairs and talk. Move."

Kravets thought he recognised the voice, but he could not place it. A gloved hand gripping the collar of his pyjama top manoeuvred him down the stairs, across the corridor and into the kitchen.

"Sit," commanded the voice.

He saw who it was, and the fear threatened to envelop him, "Xander?"

"Yes."

"What is this?"

"Who is Connor Reed?"

25

Oksana, a former solicitor, sat with the other few court members, listening with both disdain and hope at the prosecution solicitor's closing remarks, the echo around the chamber resembling a school assembly hall. The defence's closing remarks were strong and this fool was merely embarrassing himself.

Disdain that the proceedings against Kirill and Stephan had even got this far. They were members of a human rights group named Krym Vmeste—*Crimea Together*—as was she. Months ago, they had merely stood on a bench in a busy Sevastopol park espousing the Tatar Muslim identity and solidarity to the small gathering, and for this had been arrested, charged and convicted for extremist propaganda in a process so blatantly corrupt it had defied belief. They had been in custody ever since.

Violent skirmishes had enflamed the city in protest to events such as this.

Hope, because the prosecution solicitor's bumbling effort had been torn to shreds by the defence. That, and the judge now looked bored by the old man's droning.

Now fifty-years-old, she had quit law to become a campaigner and journalist—both dangerous professions here in Crimea.

Her black shoulder-length hair had hints of grey she hadn't bothered to conceal; she could no justify hair dye as people starved. Her olive skin highlighted kind eyes and a crooked smile.

Oksana convinced herself that even if the judge had an anti-Tatar agenda, she would be unable to convict in the face of such a façade.

Finally, the prosecution finished with the concluding remark, "And it is to this end, why the actions of these two men threaten not only the social fabric of our way of life, but the security of our very nation. Thank you."

Oksana would have vomited if it was not so amusing.

The judge sighed, tapping her pen on her pad before announcing, "Both defendants will be sentenced to three months in separate corrective colonies. The locations of which will not be disclosed to the public."

Oksana felt her heart smash on the bottom of her stomach like a gavel. She remained speechless as the judge issued the sentences with less feeling than a motor mechanic quoting minor repair costs. Her face mirrored by those of her compatriots as the guards manoeuvred them up and out with prods of their rifles.

She sat motionless, before a burning resentment thawed her shock.

With corruption so brazen, who could help them now?

"How you doing?" came McQuillan's voice over the line.

"I'm okay," answered Connor. "Just waiting for our transport to the border now."

"Kravets come through?"

"Seems to have. Says he's squared an interpreter for us. He's going to be the driver too."

There was a long moment of silence. "Be careful around whoever this guy is. Kravets never mentioned him sourcing you an interpreter when I liaised with him yesterday. I had requested one from the very beginning."

"What you thinking?"

"He'll be a plant. Use him anyway. Kravets has a professional interest in you and the information you can glean down there. And a 'terp could be handy. There's been developments since we last spoke."

"Okay."

"Daesh's chief financial negotiator was intercepted by the Turkish authorities on his way to Sevastopol."

"Fucksake," Connor breathed. "They handing him over to the CIA?"

"No. They released him shortly after a healthy financial contribution from the Kingdom. This is all under the radar."

"What you're telling me, is I could now be heading into the flashpoint for the next major war?"

"Yes. I think the surgeon's disappearance is linked to whatever is going on there. Keep your eyes open and watch this 'interpreter'."

"I agree," he said as a silver Mercedes pulled up. "Speak of the devil. Is there's anything else?"

"No. Stay sharp."

The line went dead, just as the driver got out. As Connor appraised him, something his father had told him came to mind, "Dangerous men can always spot other dangerous men. It's the eyes. An ease of being able to hold your gaze without flinching or attempting intimidation."

Connor felt his dad had oversimplified, but he knew what he had meant. The driver's blue eyes took in everything with a relaxed alertness. He had combed, dark hair and a strong face—angular and grooved even with the rough beard. The well-fitted suit, without a tie, fit around a compact physique. Connor noticed his wrists, thick and vascular underneath the black wisps.

The man walked up to Connor without even acknowledging Ciara. They were of a similar height and build.

He spoke. "Mr Reed. Good to meet you."

So Kravets has told this guy the truth?

His face looked familiar. Connor shook his hand. Strong grip.

"Where I have seen you before?"

"Your exploits in Odessa have been impressive to witness."

"Who are you? Your English is excellent for a Ukrainian driver."

The stranger glanced at Ciara. "Should we go inside?"

Connor realised then, this man might not know Ciara was an agent, he might just know he was not her bodyguard or assistant—*Or he might be really sexist.* Besides, he wanted to keep the stranger not knowing.

"Alright."

Ciara said in what Connor knew to be a feigned exasperation, "Guess I'll just wait in the car shall I," before flouncing off.

The Englishman did not like having his back to the man, but he was the one leading. After the flight of stairs, they entered the apartment.

He turned around to face him. "Go on."

"My name is Xander Voitenko. I lead a special investigations unit here."

"You do not strike me as a policeman."

Xander frowned. "I will not strike you?"

"No. I mean you do not look like a policeman to me."

Xander smiled. "I was in an elite military unit, like yourself Mr Connor Reed."

"What do you want?"

"Several Muslim children, from the ages of seven to eleven years of age, have been disappearing from areas within the south and east of Ukraine. I want them back if I can."

Connor took in Xander's determined eyes. "Yeh, I would want that too."

26

Connor sat in the passenger seat not looking forward to the twelve-hour journey into Crimea. He had recalled doing a four-month training and advisory tour in Iraq as a marine after much of the hostilities had died down. They had made regular excursions from the port of Umm Qasr into Kuwait for supplies and drop-offs in thirty-tonne Mastiffs. The crew had comprised of a driver, *top cover* and the navigator all communicating with headsets and microphones. The banter was great for the first two and a half hours or so; games like 'twenty-one questions' and colourfully told stories provided entertainment. After that the conversation dried and the rest of the journey would be painfully boring.

Before he and Xander left the apartment, Connor had excused himself to the bathroom and fired Ciara a text: He knows I am an agent of some kind but I reckon he is unsure about you.

And she replied, I guessed.

Now he was grateful she was making the most conversation with the Ukrainian.

"Do you know Crimea well?" she asked Xander.

"Yes, I was born and spent my young days there."

"May I ask why you did not stay there?"

Xander looked in the mirror at Ciara. "I came to Kiev and found a city more including, is this the word?"

"Inclusive," Connor suggested.

"Yes, inclusive."

"Who taught you to speak English so well?"

"Myself. I watched English and American television shows in Kiev, and learned how your language is constructed. I am still not the best."

"Impressive," said Ciara, "I apologise for being so intrusive but do you now consider yourself to be Russian or Ukrainian?"

"I consider myself to be a Tatar."

Despite driving the Citroen Berlingo through the oppressive city traffic of Sevastopol to reach her home on the outskirts, Oksana Spetkor felt clearer headed than she had yesterday in the swirling aftermath leaving the courthouse.

That morning she had taken a walk to the top of Cape Fiolent, enjoying the greenery of the cliffs and the yellow strip of beach that separated the bright blue of the sea. Despite the austere conditions her people had had to endure, a walk on the cliffs remained mercifully free of charge.

As Oksana manoeuvred the car onto a quieter road, she remembered how she had wept last night, wondering if she would ever see the day when the Tatar population were free from Russian oppression.

As she approached her semi-detached house, she began to feel guilty; her respectable living allowed her to reside far away from the many for which she campaigned.

The horror punched her in the chest upon pulling in front of her house. She managed to halt the car but remained catatonic for a few moments. Gradually, her brain's messaging signals got through and she switched the ignition off. Opening the car door, the blood had drained from her now hollow legs and she struggled forward.

Her hopes of a hoax vanished—she had seen enough dead bodies, and the slash across the throat showed enough not to be faked.

The girl could be no more than twelve. A piece of paper was fixed on to her chest with a dagger. It read in Russian:

Для единой России—*For a United Russia.*

Connor was now driving.

Xander spoke of the borders they were now not far from, "There will be two checkpoints. A Ukrainian one, marked with blue and yellow markers, and a Russian one will have red and green border markers. There will be armed soldiers at both. Have helmets or cloth hats. Sometimes with body armour and sometimes not."

Connor knew by 'cloth hats' he meant berets. "How long do you envision it taking?"

"If a young soldier leading the checkpoint—longer it takes. They do not wish to make mistake yes. An older man is more ahem—"

"Jaded?"

"Yes. Worn out."

This is why robots will take over, thought Connor. He asked, "Will our pictures be taken?"

Xander shrugged. "It is a possibility, but they choose who. They cannot photograph all or even most."

He wanted to ask the Tatar if there was a possibility of him being recognised and detained at the border. However, he had to go along with the pretence Ciara was no more than a journalist. In the same way McQuillan valued him for his ability to roam various criminal underworlds without suspicion, Connor knew the old man would have held Ciara's ability to get herself into different hot zones as a journalist in equal or even higher esteem. He remembered McQuillan had once told him, "The first time you needlessly give away your true purpose, is the first time you encourage yourself to do it a second time. Never view a transgression in isolation." The more he considered the way his boss had recruited himself and Ciara, the more he admired it: 'saving' them from lengthy prison sentences after finding a use for them, thus imbuing a sense of loyalty to him. Even if it were a simple cold, hard calculation on the Scotsman's part, Connor would not have felt aggrieved—he loved what he was doing.

Though, as he saw the lights of the border, the nerves began their attempts to bite him.

27

"There seems to be more activity than normal," announced Xander as they waited in the queue of vehicles. He observed the Ukrainian soldiers speaking urgently into the wound-down windows of the cars in front. He spied one of the uniformed men at the stop gate with a single grey star on his rank slide. "And that is a major in Russian Army. It is not common for an officer to be at a checkpoint."

"Oh my God," whispered the journalist from the back.

"What is it?" asked Connor.

The blonde extended her phone out between the two men, and Xander's blood cooled.

Emblazoned in English was the title, 'Muslim girl found with throat slashed'.

"I don't recognise this news outlet," said Connor.

She replied, "It's an independent outlet on the dark web."

Shock iced Xander's diaphragm for a few moments. Eventually his fury expanded in his chest like a burning sphere. He snapped on to the journalist's voice.

"Bear with me, I'll use Google translator and decipher some bits. Alright, 'Eleven-year-old Hafsa Giray was found in a suburb of Sevastopol having died from a deep laceration to her throat. The child had gone missing from the Victory nature trail while on a school trip, four weeks ago.'"

"Is that it?" asked Connor.

"Christ," Ciara murmured.

"What is it?"

The phone appeared again. The picture showed the girl slumped, wearing a bib of red from her gruesome wound. A knife had pierced both a piece of paper and her chest, and had been left there. Xander read the Russian inscription.

For a United Russia.

Major Alexei Jirov, remembered his training officer's words regarding checkpoint security: "It isn't necessarily the man who's causing a scene who is guilty—he may have a nagging wife, badly behaved children, is rushing home after a long week and now he's having to contend with his day or night being disrupted. Fear or nervousness is what you should look for."

Jirov stood off and supervised the other men in their efforts in checking for fighting-age males, particularly any Muslims. He had not been told why, but the order came down from the Kremlin.

He could see a couple of possibles: two vehicles down in a silver Mercedes. The man driving looked in his early to mid-thirties, dark hair, a little colour in his skin. The blue eyes set in a sharp-featured face reminded Alexei of a snow husky—he noticed them even from this distance. The front passenger looked more Western European to Alexei with his dirty blond hair and strong face—maybe Dutch or British.

As the car pulled one closer, the Russian officer could see there was a woman in the back. Very pretty—*a volunteer to search her will be immediately forthcoming.* He watched one of his men ask a family of four the perfunctory questions.

His attention, and then his GSh-18 pistol snapped around in the direction of the silver Mercedes' door clicking open. The other four ranks with their AK-12s followed suit.

He shouted, "Остановитесь или я застрелю!"—*Stop, or I will shoot.*

As the girl from the back of the silver Mercedes got out, he could see she was more than just pretty. She called out to him, "Мне нужно поговорить с лидером"—*I need to speak with the leader.*

She was not a native speaker of Russian, that was clear by her dialect. He thought she might be Scandinavian. He beckoned her towards him before halting her five feet away from him.

"Откройте куртку и развернитесь,"— *Open your jacket and turn around.*

"I am sorry. I am English—British rather. My Russian isn't very good— I had to Google translate my opening," she said.

She is lucky—thought Alexei. Most of the soldiers spoke little or no English, not much more than one in eight. And maybe only one in a hundred who could speak it as fluently as he could. As an officer and a Muscovite, he knew how to speak it well. Maybe he could turn this into his advantage.

He repeated the order in English. She smiled at him, and pulled open the jacket. She twirled around— maybe flirtatiously or maybe he was imagining it

"Okay," he said finally. "Come to me."

She walked up close, and he was glad the illusion of her attractiveness failed to shatter.

"Hello, my name is Ciara Robson and these are my credentials. I am a journalist."

He checked them over. One of the papers included a faxed sheet with the Russian ambassador of Kiev's signature on it, stating Miss Robson to be let through.

"Why did you leave your vehicle to show me this?"

She bared her straight white teeth. "Well. I was wondering, well hoping, I could talk to you. About the atmosphere in Crimea? My bodyguard could wait outside and it looks like we do not need my translator."

Alexei felt only faintly tempted. The days of Stalin might be long gone, but to be quoted in a western article could result in career ruin—in the least.

"I am afraid I must decline your request."

"Please. Just a short interview. I won't even record it."

He laughed. "That would not be good for me."

"Why?"

"You in the West will always change the stories to suit your political agenda. I say something bad about Russia and you use a magnifying glass. I say nothing bad, then I am hiding the truth."

"My stories do not have an agenda."

He laughed. "If your stories are sold to the media they will have an agenda. Tell me, why are you in Crimea?"

"To gain an insight into what is happening here."

"No. You may think you are, or you may know you're not. I do not think your mainstream media would ever be seen to be saying good words of Russia. Your social media maybe, but not your BBC or papers."

As he said this, her silver Mercedes trundled to the checkpoint. He wanted to be rid of this woman now. She was either decidedly naïve or manipulative. To the men who were about to engage with the occupants, he shouted in Russian, "Leave them. This bitch is worse for talking than my wife."

The men laughed and stood off the car.

"What did you say to them?"

"I told them you believe your articles do not have an agenda. Now, Miss Robson, get in the car. As you can see, there are many other cars to pass."

He watched her walk off in a temper at his words. He thought of that western expression—'If it's too good to be true, it always is.'

As he watched the car drive through the checkpoint, he knew he should have allowed his men to check the two men, but the woman had all the relevant documents and the longer he spoke to her, the more time she had to prise a semblance of a quote from him. When the questions would get asked, then the other men would have to admit the major had been in conversation with her. *No*, he thought, *better to get her on her way.*

The soldier manning the phone appeared in the doorway of the cabin.

"Major. You have an urgent call from the embassy."

Alexei frowned. "Who?"

The soldier lowered his voice. "The ambassador."

He went in and lifted the phone to his ear. "Major Alexei Jirov, sir."

"Major. There is a woman, a journalist who I gave written permission to enter Crimea. Only now, the situation has changed and I would like to rescind this. Her name is—"

"She has not one minute ago left the checkpoint, sir. Her name is Ciara Robson?"

"Yes. Major, can you detain her?"

"Yes, Ambassador."

"How the fuck did you manage that?" asked Connor, as the checkpoint got smaller in his wing mirror.

"Played the dogmatic, crusading female journalist begging for an interview. No Russian officer wants his name to appear in a British paper with his quotes twisted to serve 'our' agenda. He just wanted to get rid of me in the end."

He smiled, then said to Xander, "I suppose they'll have other checkpoints within the region?"

The Tatar nodded. "Yes, but I know where they are. Well, the static ones I know."

"Alright," Connor said, "change of plan. Head towards the area where the little girl was found. A western journalist would want to know about it."

"I agree. However, the Russian way of silencing voices that go against doctrine is less hidden than in yours."

"Exactly," agreed Connor. "We need the hornets out of the nest before we can swat them."

Xander looked into the rearview mirror. "Looks like the hornets are coming out to sting."

They were all pushed back into their seats as Xander pressed on the accelerator. Connor looked back and saw the military five-door UAZ Patriot in pursuit with its siren wailing.

28

Ryan Ryder drove with Radio Two on low for background noise. He felt more optimistic than he had in a while, though he could not understand why as things were worse than ever. The realisation came—it was because the family was reaching an impasse; either Derek stepped down or there would be a takeover.

He still could not understand how things had reached this stage, and smiled remembering his father's reply when asked why blood was thicker than water: "Because, I am not having you lot fighting and carrying on at Christmases, weddings or funerals."

The red lights ground the traffic to a halt and he turned up the radio to erode his annoyance. He had a few stops to make today; the £11,000 he had under the spare tyre had to be distributed out—some in a safe at his paint and emulsions business, some to an investments firm for laundering and some to his employees.

The traffic began to move ahead and his hand drifted to the gearstick.

The glass beside him exploded, showering him and the interior. As he turned his head a hammer malleted his cheek, splitting it inwards. He raised a defending arm but the balaclavad figure only snatched the keys from the ignition. Despite the crater of agony consuming his face and doubling his vision, he saw the keys thrown to another masked figure at the back of the vehicle. Ryan realised through the pain fog they were after the money.

He rammed his shoulder against the blocked door but the figure had the advantage of standing purchase on the ground. Ryan managed to get a protecting arm up against another smashing blow of the hammer before clasping his head against any others.

They never came.

He looked to see the pair fleeing on a motorbike—the registration obscured in what looked like black soot.

As he opened the car door and stepped out, his legs threatened to give way. A pair of hands caught him. They belonged to a woman from the car behind who helped him back into his seat. He just about made out her husband calling the emergency services. The pain to his face shielded any other thought from entering his brain.

The rough terrain negated the Mercedes' speed advantage. Fields opened before funnelling their way into woodland. Xander had decided to hit the country road to avoid potential road blocks, which would have inevitably sprung up on the main highway. The Patriot, better suited to the conditions, was gaining fast.

"How good of a shot are you? With a pistol I mean?" he asked the Englishman.

"There's not many better," he replied flatly.

"You can shoot the tyres, yes?"

Connor nodded.

"There is a Fort 12 within a hidden back in the glove compartment. Here," said Xander handing him a glasses case he retrieved from the lower side shelf, "use the sharpened end of the glasses frames to unscrew the back."

Connor did within twenty seconds and removed the pistol.

Xander's hand touched Reed's arm. "Once you fire, even at the tyres, we will become the most hunted people in Crimea. You understand?"

"I am game if you are."

"What about our journalist friend here? This is not a game for civilians."

"Since we are about to step over the precipice together I think we can stop with the pretence," said Ciara. "I work for the same people he does."

Xander nodded. He suspected—no journalist would have shown that audacity at the checkpoint. *Did Kravets know?*

Connor wound down the window and unfastened his seatbelt, "The terrain looks smoother after that tree. Hold her steady after that."

The Mercedes hit a smoother run and Connor leaned out the window.

The echoes of two pistol rapports were whipped away by the dark. The British man slid back in his seat.

Xander looked into the rearview mirror. The Patriot weaved, slowed and halted.

Connor's voice translated Xander's thoughts differently. "Now the fun begins."

McQuillan entered his new apartment after climbing the four stories. He avoided lifts; inescapable traps should a professional team wish to kill him. Secondly, he believed life's comforts at times acted as inhibitors. It was the same reason the apartment—though it resembled a showroom in its cleanliness and modernity—was sparse of furniture—the ease of sofas, chairs and beds acting as unnecessary splints 'switching off' the muscles in the lower back and preventing healthy capillary refill. He had noticed an improvement in his back, which had received its fair share of batterings during arduous tabs through a career in the Paras and SAS in the eighties and early nineties. He never missed that aspect of his military service and could not understand why his retired contemporaries opted to voluntarily do it as part of their fitness regime.

He moved residence regularly, as both a security measure and a change of scene. He wondered how much happier man had been in his hunter-gatherer days; a few hours gathering, a few hours killing a mammoth, no financial problems, immersed in nature, a lack of disease and a lot of social interaction. A sabretooth may eat you but would that be worse than dying in a car accident?

Still, pointless to think back to a past that was not even his. He dispelled the negative thoughts from his mind. He had to do that a lot lately; ever since he had taken on his new role as MI5 and SIS liaison officer. His field days came to an end two years ago, though as the leader of the Chameleon Project he still handled the mission selection, funding and logistics. It had been a while coming but it had been a bullet to the knee cap and not his age that had 'retired' him.

The bureaucracy of the law enforcement, intelligence, and civil agencies he now witnessed up close made him grateful for all those years on the sharp end with a unit he had full control over. Now he had passed the reins to the younger agents and surprised himself with the feelings of concern that at times rose within him; not just that they were successful in their missions but of their safety. He had the vague feeling he was becoming one of those 'old, white men' sending others out to do 'the dirty work'.

His pager beeped, which meant Jaime. The pager had been his idea—because they were almost obsolete save for 'on call' doctors or special forces operators when in the 'black role', and sent messages with VHF, very high frequency radio signals typically broadcast in the range 138–466 MHz, they were not prioritised by any overarching countersurveillance net. The procedure between them was that Jaime would send him a thirteen-digit number with the fifth and sixth being random numbers, which meant he was not under duress. After removing said numbers, he would be left with the contact number which he would use a brand-new pay-as-you-go phone to call.

He went to his drawer, which had several mobiles still in their packaging. Within less than three minutes, he had activated one of the phones and called Jaime.

"What is it?" he asked.

"They passed the border."

Bruce frowned. "That's good. Why the cloak and dagger?"

"They were chased by the Crimean border guard. They escaped but not before firing upon the soldiers."

The Scotsman scrunched his eyes and quickly opened them. "Are you saying they smashed through the checkpoint after being chased?"

"The information is patchy. From what I can understand, they got through the checkpoint and were chased."

Bruce thought about the translator/spy Kravets had tacked onto Connor and Ciara.

"Was anyone of the guard injured?"

"No. The tyres were shot."

Bruce thought for a moment. "How well can you monitor the situation over there?"

"Strangely, the lower technology makes it more difficult for me to keep pace. And even my digital translators have difficulty with some of the dialects. But there's another thing."

"Go on."

"His uncle—the youngest uncle—has been assaulted not far from the prison in which one of the elder uncles is. Struck with a hammer while in traffic in daytime hours. They robbed money and got away on a motorbike."

Bruce sighed; he did not need his protégé distracted by his family embroiling themselves in gang warfare.

"All we can do is to assist our guys as much as we can. In the meantime, I need to visit our friend over there in the capital."

Jaime replied, "I'll arrange it."

"I can take us somewhere safe. We need to change this car and your appearance," said Xander indicating to Ciara.

Xander was handling the car down a country lane—they had filled the car with petrol just before crossing the border.

"Do you know someone close by?" she asked.

"Around twenty kilometres from here. A place named Dolynka not far from the Chatyrlyk river."

"Who do you know there?" she asked.

"I have friends."

"I am sure you do," said Connor. "And so did Charles Manson. So tell us where exactly we are going and who we are meeting."

Ciara saw Xander nod before saying, "I have a cousin who owns farmland and a farmhouse there. We will be safe until we make our move further south."

"So he is a Tatar too?" Ciara asked.

"He is a she. And yes, she is a Tatar."

Ciara asked, "Does Connor have to change his appearance too?"

"No. It is doubtful they would have an accurate description of him. People look at the weapon not the person in those situations."

"I think putting me in a Muslim dress would make me stand out more," said Connor.

She thought for a moment. "I am not wearing a burka, or shaving my head."

"A burka is not necessary. A Hijab—a headscarf—is good to cover your hair."

"We will have to split up," said Connor. "They'll be on the lookout for two men and a woman."

"You will not survive this place by yourself," the Tatar answered.

"We can't go as a three. End of story. And a Muslim woman with me, a white European—now we have decided on Ciara's conversion—will look suspicious."

"Yes, you are correct," he answered. "I may know a person to make it four. A guide."

"Why should we trust you?" said Ciara.

"What other choice do you have?"

29

Tom seethed, watching Derek orate from the top of the table. They were in a function room of a pub named 'The United Arms' in Morley. Tom knew the landlord owed Derek money. Only a wooden slider door separated anyone's ears outside from the rhetoric his coked-up uncle was spouting. He reminded Tom of clips he had seen of Hitler whipping up the crowds in a hateful fervour. The family leader's assumptions of the attackers—'that lot from Bradford'—was rankling him.

However, the insult that left Tom scalding with rage was that this—the first meeting since his dad's attack two days before—was not just attended by the family. Tony Angelis and Nathaniel Grimshaw—Derek's coke and weed runners for the Seacroft area of Leeds and Dewsbury respectively—were present. Tom knew, despite his uncle's denials, they sold smack for him too. They stood to one side posturing and nodded enthusiastically to his uncle's talk of war—*fucking shitbags without a square go in them,* Tom thought.

Brendan Chappel, a mid-level enforcer for the Kellings from Newcastle, stood at the other side—*shifty fucker.*

Tom's attention snapped onto his uncle's words, "And Tom gets first dibs when we find those rats in human guise who did this."

He bit his tongue. His cousins were looking at him furtively.

"That's that then," announced Derek. "Let's get out there and start cracking heads."

Cue the nodding and puffed out chests of Angelis and Grimshaw before swaggering out.

Chappel spoke in his reality TV Geordie voice, "We'll get 'em Des. My word, man, we'll find 'em."

Derek bowed his head sagely.

As Chappel rose, he and Derek embraced. Tom found the scene putrid. He never saw his uncle Greg act that way with strangers. He remembered once receiving a hair ruffle off his favourite uncle, which meant more to him—and still did—than any hugs from Derek. *Affection means fuck all off a slag.*

As Chappel left he felt Luke put a calming hand on his arm. Tom knew that it meant *'do not go too far yet'*. Tom had told the rest of the family not to inform Connor while he was away—wherever he was, this would just be a distraction to him.

"What was that?" he said, throwing the phrase like a rock at the family leader.

Derek frowned. "What are you talking about?"

"What I am talking about is that my dad is in the hospital and a 'family' meeting is called, and you bring in some sap of Newcastle and two heathens off the estates."

"They will be needed when the time comes."

"When the time comes for what?"

The flash of irritation on Derek's face was plain to see. "When we have to go to war with those paki fuckin' scumbags. We're goi—"

"Why do you keep saying that? We don't know who the fuck has done this or why. We have to find out first. Whoever has done this, knew my dad 'ad money in the motor. Knew he'd be visiting Michael. And probably knew he'd be alone. How would the Bradford lot know all that?"

"They have form, believe me."

Tom stood up. "It's my dad that's been attacked, so I will deal with it. And when I deal with it, it'll be worth a long time in the nick if I am caught, so I want to be certain."

There was tension-filled impasse before Derek said, "I'll give you a couple of weeks."

A coldness plumed in her as the silver Mercedes headed towards her home on a road laid over pancake flat terrain—*maybe they have found me?*

She refused to give them the satisfaction of chasing her and continued to take her dry clothes off the line; if it was the FSB, she would not get far anyway.

She could make out it was two men in the front seats—*a standard FSB arresting pair.* A few moments later she felt relief; the blue eyes were recognisable even at a distance.

After less than a minute the Mercedes arrived. Xander climbed out of the car, walked over and greeted her. "As-Salam-u-Alaikum."

She bowed her head. "Wa alaikum assalaam."

Two more people got out and she could tell by their features and manner they were not Ukrainian. The man had blond-brown hair, and was a similar height and build to Xander with eyes a less intense shade of blue.

She, to improve her stilted English, had practised reading a range of English books and articles. One had been on Viking mythology. She remembered reading about female Viking warriors named 'shield-maidens,' and in her mind's eye, the image of one was like the woman she was looking at now. Her hair—short for a woman—was a silvery-blonde, and her eyes shone emerald. The shoulders seemed broad for a woman, and her back straight.

"Irina," Xander said in English. "This is Ciara, and this is Connor."

That he did not tell her who they were spoke volumes.

"Nice to meet you," she said, being sure of the wording. "My home is your home."

"Thank you very much," said the woman, as the man nodded his agreement with a strange look on his face.

"Let's go inside," said Xander.

Bruce sat on a bench by a fountain overlooking the white and beige five-storey headquarters. The sun glinted off the ripples while warming his face. Just a few minutes before he had walked past the regal Saint Vladimir Monument, just as he had over two decades ago.

Ukraine had changed a great deal—in talking to people he detected more hope, but also more angst.

There had been something nagging at him ever since Connor had told him of the interpreter Kravets had sprung on him. The Ukrainian liaison chief had kept him abreast of all developments to the point of mentioning things Bruce did not think necessary. Now, he had lashed on an interpreter without notice. Bruce refrained from inquiring if there was anything untoward; Kravets would more than likely have concocted a story.

McQuillan had Jaime look back on a multitude of surveillance footage, intercept emails and call traffic to ascertain what time Kravets left his place of work at the police headquarters on Volodymyr Street 15. Bruce had decided a home visit would be too heavy-handed, and to announce his presence to the headquarters receptionist would allow Kravets time to compose himself.

Bruce got up and threw a handful of British pennies into the water as he spotted Kravets behind a throng of people presumably leaving work for the day.

The Ukrainian seemed deep in thought.

McQuillan called out, "Danylo." The policeman jolted to a halt and Bruce continued, "It's Bruce McQuillan."

He strode over with an outstretched hand to an open-mouthed Kravets. The Ukrainian's hand hovered into the Scotsman's before stammering, "I was not expecting this visit?"

"I wasn't expecting an interpreter to be attached to my agent and a British journalist without consulting me first."

His grip still firm on the policeman's hand.

Kravets opened his mouth to answer but produced no words for a few moments. Then he looked Bruce in the eye and said, "Please. I will tell you. Not here."

Bruce let go. "Fine. Let's take your car. Anywhere you want."

The Ukrainian took a breath and nodded.

Xander had invited Connor outside onto the back lawn to talk. The bright stars flecked the still night. The moon glint made the Chatyrlyk river visible even at a distance across the flat plain.

Earlier in the evening, he had a contact in the area exchange the Mercedes for a charcoal Lexus kept in a garage for events such as this. The Mercedes would be cut up and scrapped, with the number plates destroyed.

They had eaten a meal consisting of lamb roast and *Olivier*. The conversation had not quite shaken an undercurrent.

His hands were resting on the fence, looking out into the distance. When the Englishman mirrored this, Xander spoke. "We will rest tonight and leave in the morning. Irina will provide the woman with a few of her larger dresses to aid her disguise."

Connor nodded. "Except her name isn't Irina."

After a few moments, Xander asked, "How did you know?"

"I was fascinated with the legend of Roza Afandi—although I'll still call her Irina if you like—the daughter of the Chechnyan black widow Khava Afandi. I dismissed reports of a woman stabbing and garrotting Russian soldiers in the back streets of Kherson as a myth. I had seen pictures of said woman caught on CCTV in some of the areas where the soldiers died but decided they could be of any woman. That was until I saw Irina, a single woman apparently thriving in a place like this. And you, a law enforcement agent of some kind in Kiev, managing to rid yourself of that Mercedes and magic another in its place in less than a couple of hours. This is a safe house, isn't it?"

Xander rubbed his chin and nodded. The Englishman asked, "So, it begs the question, who are you?"

"So, who is he?" asked Bruce. Kravets knew he would have to tell him. They were walking in Maidan Nezalezhnosti, or 'Independence Square' in English. He had not wanted to bring the British man to his home but did not want to talk to him right outside of the police headquarters.

"Xander Voitenko heads a small investigative team. Politically sensitive things."

"Meaning he could be deniable depending on what and who he's investigating."

"Yes. Except…" Kravets stopped, conflicted to what he should impart to a foreign government figure. As if reading his mind, McQuillan said, "Whatever you tell me will not reach the ears of the higher-ups within my government or wider security services."

Kravets nodded; he had heard the rumours of this man's independent resources.

"Xander has been given a stay of leave for the foreseeable future."

"Why?"

"I do not know. I am not his boss."

"Don't feign ignorance. A man in your position would have at least heard rumours."

Kravets took a breath and said, "This is not your country Mr McQuillan. You cannot dictate to me."

There was no malice in the Britisher's voice when he said, "You know better than that, Danylo."

Kravets knew he was defeated. "Xander Voitenko may or may not be aiding a group named—"

"Povernuto?"

Kravets was surprised "How did you know?"
"A guess."

Connor looked at Xander and said, "There's no way Kiev has signed off on you aiding them. They might hate Putin—some of them—but that is different to having a global war between battle-hardened, Saudi-funded ISIS fundamentalists and Russian security forces."

Xander said nothing. Connor began Rubik's-cubing the information—a senior undercover agent of Ukrainian law enforcement, aiding what the Russians regarded as a terrorist group was dynamite. He and Ciara did need some native guidance; the region had the dangerous blend of volatility and unfamiliarity— going in 'cold', he and Ciara would lack a feel for local *atmospherics.*

And still, he did not know who had taken Grace or their motives. Who would benefit from snatching a British surgeon? Why was that girl killed and dumped outside the home of some anti-Russian journalist's house? Who would benefit from that?

The obvious conclusion would be an anti-Islamic, pro-Russian group attempting to bleed out the Tatars and other Muslims from the area. However, surely the Russians themselves would not want that? Putin has already had a win, annexing the region without a shot fired, and he would not want a media focus of dead children in Crimea.

Connor knew he would have to accept Xander's assistance—*what else am I going to do?*

He turned to Xander. "My concern is the return of the British national. But I will help you find these people who are murdering children. That said, if you're attempting to use Ciara and I for a political agenda, you and I will fall out. Be at odds with one another rather."

The Tatar met his gaze with his wolf-like eyes. He held out hand. "Does this still mean something with the men in your country."

"All you have to be concerned with, is it does with me," answered Connor as he grasped the hand.

30

Vitali Agron smiled, looking in the darkness beyond his window. The dead girl had been generating chatter on the web despite the attempt of a media shut out.

He kept in check the temptation to kill them all before littering the streets of Sevastopol with their corpses. But after that, they would know he would have no leverage left—better to remain patient and slowly ratchet the pressure.

Agron did not take any pleasure in killing children in and of itself. However, he had pride in being one of the few to do what was truly necessary.

The day he saw the Russian state on its knees, would be the day he could hold his head up in answering to God.

Oksana Spetkor sat amongst the rows of the other members of Krym Vmeste. The hall owned by one of their sponsors encased them, with the outside lookouts listening and scanning the dark for any sirens or headlights. The building lay on a valley floor with one side framed by forestry set back from it by around fifty metres. A river skirted the other side from a similar distance.

She had attended and hosted meetings such as this. There was always a contingent espousing how the Russians would only respect 'strength'—their euphemism for 'violence'. She had been a vocal dissenter to this sort of rhetoric. Mahatma Gandhi helped free India from the British Empire through peaceful demonstration while the Palestinians were still no further forward with their quest for sovereignty and to be treated with dignity.

Tonight, she had been quiet.

How could she speak up for non-violent means in the face of a murdered Tatar child? Did she even want to? She already knew she would never shake the tragic image of Hafsa Giray's throat-slashed corpse outside her home.

Oksana had ascertained some of the members of Krym Vmeste were also members of Povernuto. This group— 'The Returned'— had been waging a secret underground campaign against the Russian security services in the region. It had been threatening to explode for months now. Oksana knew if that were to happen, no Tatar would be safe.

The day she found Hafsa, she'd had the wherewithal to call the police under a false name with a payphone, claiming to be a member of the public; there was no telling what lengths the Russian authorities would have gone to in ensuring her silence. She had returned seven hours later in the evening, to find the body had disappeared and seemingly no evidence of it ever existing. Still, she ensured she had taken plenty of pictures and used her contacts to find the name. She was not naïve and knew she would be a target soon.

One of the men she suspected to be Povernuto was stood on a small podium waxing lyrical on how the Tatar people now seemed to have been demoted from the second-class citizen status to cockroaches the Russians deemed needing to be stamped out.

Just as the man seemed to be whipping the crowd into a fervour, a quietness descended with eyes turning to the door.

Three strangers.

The woman—despite the Hijab—was western. Tall and very striking. Both of the men stood an inch or two short of six feet and of a compact frame. The man at the front had dark hair, with a strange combination of having an olive hue to his skin with piercing blue eyes. It was him some of the men in the room were expectantly looking at—the men who she suspected as members of Povernuto.

Connor watched as Xander raised his hand and beckoned the man off the podium— the man did so without hesitation.

When Xander motioned to the chairs, Connor and Ciara took the seats at the back.

Xander made his way to the makeshift podium. Connor looked around; some had a face of confusion, and some had a look of reverence.

Recognition dawned when Connor saw the man with both arms in a cast— Rinat Nureyev, the killer of Taav. The assassin averted his eyes from Connor's.

As Xander began to address the audience in what Connor presumed to be Tatar, he knew then.

Xander was not just aiding Povernuto—he was the leader of it.

Oksana felt the man's strong, melodic orating in Crimean Tatar, gripping her.

"My brothers and sisters. My name is Xander Voitenko. I am the leader of the 'Povernuto'."

The murmurings of the crowd filled the room.

"I am also a law enforcement agent for the Ukrainian Government—a paradox perhaps, or perhaps not. Now, many of you here are now expecting my beating the drum for war, for violence, to fight back. That there's a dead child, one of our children, and that we need to act now."

Oksana could see the nodding of several people.

"But I won't ask you to do that. An armed uprising at this moment in time would be suicide for our people. With the judicial system this broken, and the media so controlled, we will be either incarcerated or dead before we could make any impact. Now is not the time for riots or violence. Curb your frustration, we will strike back but from a better position—a position of not only allies and funds but of knowledge. You can aid us in getting to that position by providing intelligence. Are there any questions for me?"

People looked to one another. Oksana raised her hand. When Xander acknowledged her she stood.

"My name is Oksana Spetkor. It was outside of my apartment the child was dumped like a dog. Before that, two members of our community were imprisoned for nothing more than speaking publicly about reclaiming a sense of community and pride amongst our people. An absolute sham of a hearing, so brazen in its corruption as to insult us. Forty-eight hours ago I would not have welcomed your presence here. But now, and in light of what you have said, I for one would be glad to help you."

Xander nodded almost imperceptibly. "Thank you. I was saddened to hear of Kirill and Stephan's plight. May I speak to you on the side, Mrs Spetkor?"

She was surprised and heartened this man knew their names.

"Of course."

31

On the outskirts of Kiev, Bruce walked beside the lake in Feofaniya park with brownish orange hues interspersing the greenery of the forest. In the distance, the Cathedral of St. Pantaleon looked regal even with red walls, green roofs and dark spires shaped like *Iced Gems.*

The call came through on his earpiece. He felt vaguely uncomfortable speaking through it, aware it looked like a person talking to himself.

"How are you?" he said.

"Same as usual," answered Jaime's digitalised voice; 'same as usual' meant he was not under any duress, whereas 'Same as always' meant he was.

"The highlights."

"Xander Voitenko, known to the myths around Crimea as 'Tatarskiy volk'—the Tatar Wolf. Born and raised in Crimea. Had family ties in Kiev on his mother's side. He relocated there with his grandparents at age sixteen. Left school and joined the Ukrainian military, and soon after joined was enlisted into the Alpha Group—a branch of the security services. And this is where it gets interesting."

"I am listening."

"From what I can gather Voitenko is alleged to have killed one of the snipers in his own team for shooting protesters during the 2014 Ukrainian revolution. He was held for a few weeks, but the organisation was purged and reorganised. Not only was he released, but he was promoted within the unit. The thread goes cold, but from what I can piece together, he becomes involved in clandestine operations during the war in Donbas."

"What happened then?"

"Upon his return, he was given his own small special investigations unit by the head of the SBU, the Security

Service of Ukraine. Eighteen months in, he goes 'dark'. I can't know for sure if it was with the blessing of SBU. There's no email trail, and I cannot trace a monetary link but, also, there hasn't been any directive to hunt him down."

"Either way," said Bruce, "he must have made an impression."

Grace had fought against the urge of accepting her situation—*in accepting it, I accept the fate of these kids*. She had begun to feel it in the last week. A pile of books lay in one of the classrooms—vetted of course—and she now lay on her bed with a copy of *The Cuckoo's Calling* on her chest. It had been written under J.K Rowling's pseudonym 'Robert Galbraith' and she thoroughly enjoyed it. She had fought to make the best of a bad situation by escaping and taking solace through the books she had been allowed to read out of the 'school's' library. They were a merciful comfort as her only verbal contact with humans was a few grunted orders by the guards and snatched conversations with the children she treated.

She was glad the guards had little contact with her. With a leader who had killed a child in front of her, she had feared her rape would have been acceptable to these reptiles. But it never came, despite the desire in their eyes when watching her showering. She could only thank God for whatever reason they were restraining themselves—so far.

Her interactions with the children had been gems to look forward to. Some of the guards, perhaps not realising the rules, had left the children alone with her. She had not seen one of the girls for the last few days and a strange mixture of dread and hope assaulted her—*had she been released or had the worst happened, like the girl that beast shot dead in my room?*

She began to wonder what the media outcry had been for her and all these children. Surely this Vitali and his thugs would be hunted by multiple agencies?

The theatre of her mind provided escape in the imaginings of being back home. Maybe she had stayed. Maybe she had got that rough diamond to pack in his wayward ways and they became a couple. Maybe they would have had—*no, you will not feel sorry for yourself, Grace. You are here, and you are the only adult here these children do not have to fear.*

The door flew open and her heart was briefly in her mouth, before she painted on a mask of defiance.

"I have a task for you," said Vitali. One word crept into her mind—*demon.*

She spoke after a few moments. "What is it?"

He took a seat and stared at her. "You need to take off one of children's arms."

She stared at him. "Why? Peripheral arterial disease?"

"No," he answered laconically.

When the horror sank in she said, "You fucking beast."

He smiled. "I do what's necessary for the greater good."

She felt revulsion in the pit of her stomach. Her mind whirred and she fought to organise her thoughts. Finally, she said, "I do not have the equipment necessary to perform the procedure."

"There are sharp butcher knives in kitchen. What more do you need?"

She attempted to control her breathing and said, "Even you could take a limb off. Taking it off without a child dying takes more than a butcher's knife. There isn't even local anaesthetic, never mind general. And there's a range of equipment needed that—"

"You make a list. I will get you what you need. Because if you do not—I will perform it myself. This is your purpose—to ensure children do not need to die needlessly."

Her disdain momentarily overrode her fear. "You'll kill them all anyway you evil, evil monster."

"It is easy for you to consider me a monster."

"Because you are."

"You have that opinion because you do not know what I know. Or seen what I have seen. In your world so free from the torments of humanity."

"I didn't have a choice in where I was born. But I chose to come here and help the less fortunate."

"I know of this. And this is why you are not violated sexually night after night, despite my men's wishes."

She could not believe it; Agron was not trying to convince himself he was a good man—he truly thought he was.

"Is this, your aim, going to be worth dead and dismembered children? You couldn't just fight these Russians man to man?" she said, half pleading, half with disgust.

He laughed. "There is a hundred and fifty million Russians to draw from. Even if I killed ten a day it would not be enough. However, there is short of two billion Muslims in the world."

She frowned. "What do you mean?"

"What I mean is what better way than to weaken the world of its greatest parasites than to have them fight one another?"

Grace could not speak. She was just numb in the face of insanity.

"Mrs Spetkor, how is your English?" Xander asked in Crimean Tatar.

They were in the back room of the hall. Three worn-out sofas were pushed close together, with Xander and Oksana facing one another, and Connor and Ciara sat together on one to the side. There was a small counter in the corner with a black kettle on it, and a broom cupboard on the opposite side. The carpet frayed in patches and the curtains hung loosely.

"It is good, thank you," Oksana answered in English. "Are we speaking this because it is the language of our two friends here?"

Xander nodded, and Connor leaned forward and reached out with his hand. Xander had told him the Islam practised in Crimea was a little more moderate than in Pakistan and Afghanistan, and thus he risked a handshake. She took it after a moment and he said, "My name is Fred. And this is Rosemary."

Ciara did not flinch, just also offered her hand. "Nice to meet you."

The Tatar woman smiled. "Me also, Rosemary. Nice to meet you, Fred. How can I help you?"

Xander spoke. "There must be rumours of who are taking these children."

"Of course, they are rumours. Everything from the Russian police to Stalin's ghost. But no one knows."

Ciara asked, "Has there been anyone who has said anything specific? Regarding a person or a location?"

Oksana looked to be in thought for a moment. "There was one person. He spoke of place in a 'forest of dead trees'. That there was school to be made for kidnapped Muslim girls. But he was a drunk. This was weeks and weeks ago, when only two girls had gone missing. He—"

Connor interrupted. "Where is he now? What's his name?"

"His name is Gavril Ivanov. He is held in a detention centre in Sevastopol. He will be soon transported to a Russian mental institution in the Urals."

"In the Urals?" exclaimed Connor. "I'd have thought St Petersburgh or Moscow would be more appropriate."

Oksana replied, "It is an institution for studying patients, not treating them."

Connor wondered if her bias against Russia would affect everything she had to say about the country. Surely she would not have been to this institution.

Xander asked, "On what charges?"

"Inciting social unrest. The hearing was closed to the public."

"I am surprised they did not kill him. Accusing members of the Russian system of kidnapping Muslim girls would demand something more permanent."

"It was not the Russians he said who were responsible," she said, looking at Xander. "He said it was a former Ukrainian Army officer."

Connor frowned and asked, "What motive would a Ukrainian Army officer have to snatch Tatar children? And how would he fund a 'school'?"

Oksana displayed her palms. "That is another reason why no one take him seriously."

There were a few moments of silence before Xander asked, "Did he say anything about this officer. Give a name or describe him?"

"I cannot remember."

Connor said, "Oksana, we need any information you can glean regarding this Gavril Ivanov, specifically any details on his transportation to Russia."

Ciara turned to him, "What are you thinking?"

"I am thinking Mr Ivanov made this claim in the beginning. Now a girl was found dead showing no signs of malnutrition, even though she was taken months ago. Some sort of holding pen in the hills under the guise of a school doesn't seem outrageous to me. As to this former officer's motives, I can only guess it is destabilising the Russians in the region."

Connor noted that although Oksana looked at him, Xander did not. He was about to speak before Ciara said, "Even if that was true, he'd still need people—need friends.

Well, employees at least. And employees cost money. It's Ukrainian politicians that were swimming in the money of corruption, not the army officers."

Xander cleared his throat. "Maybe the Russians have sponsored this man to carry out these acts. If he is revealed then he's a Ukrainian, not Russian."

Connor said, "Let's go fetch this Ivanov."

Oksana stared at him, "Are you crazy?"

"It depends on your definition."

Tom sat beside his father's hospital bed as he lay sleeping. A bandage was padded on the side he had his surgery done, covering his head.

The surgeon had explained to him exactly the type of procedure his dad had undergone: an open reduction, internal fixation and titanium plate fitting. The doctor had mentioned something about damage to the temporomandibular joint—'the TMJ' after Tom repeated it a couple of times—at the start of the jaw, to prevent malocclusion, which was something to do with teeth alignment.

Tom knew the hypocrisy of being outraged over his dad being attacked and robbed; it was the risk you had to accept in their way of life.

However, it was bad for business, and bothering Tom the most was that he was not sure who could have known his old man had that cash in the car. Tom had not told anyone. Maybe it had been the dealer they had taken the money off? He doubted it though—these guys either tailed his dad for a few days or had prior knowledge, and he did not think the Huddersfield wideboy would have that in his locker.

Still, it was a starting point.

32

"We can ambush them and take Ivanov to ask him hard questions," said Xander.

He and Connor stood by the moon-glinted lake not far from the Hall. The leaves of the surrounding forestry spoke to one another.

Ciara was still inside with Oksana.

Connor looked at him. "The most efficient way maybe, but we can't do that."

Xander frowned. "Why?"

"Why? Because it's killing people who to our knowledge haven't done anything wrong."

The Tatar laughed. "The guards? They protect oppression. They deserve to die."

"Listen, who knows why people pick their professions. And you have that opinion because you're a Tatar Muslim. Maybe young 'Sergei' or whoever has decided to join the Russian Army for a sense of security, or because he's from a broken home and wants comradeship? A person's notion of good and bad is based upon what he's fed throughout his life."

"So you are to say no one is good and no one is evil, just—"

"We're going down a rabbit hole. I don't want to be killing people for simply transporting a prisoner."

Xander looked at him. "What is alternative?"

"I will come up with a plan. If there's no other way then I wouldn't be averse to killing them for the greater good, but only if there's no other way."

Their attention was distracted by headlights in the distance.

"Do your pals inside have weapons?" Connor asked when they watched the lights getting closer.

"Maybe, but they will not use them."

"Why?"

"My people not to use weapons until I say. The Russians want them to use weapons so they have a reason to exterminate everyone. I do not know how they find us."

Major Alexei Jirov had been told to take at least the journalist alive. Moscow did not want a story of a dead western reporter—a woman at that— beamed worldwide. The ambassador did not extend that directive to include the two men who still might be with her. It had been one of those men who had fired at his vehicle.

He rode in the second armoured vehicle of a convoy of four, each with four armed soldiers. His superior officer had implied Povernuto members were present, and to be 'arrested'.

Alexei knew the likelihood of them coming willingly was slim and so a firefight would ensue if they were armed. He wondered the value of shooting Tatar Muslims given the rumours a Tatar child had been found murdered— a gifted propaganda coup for the Povernuto?

Alexei knew better than to voice disagreement.

He had a list of possible Povernuto members to take into questioning. Intelligence reports indicated very little in the way of structure and leadership.

He had instructed his men on the importance of speed and violence of action upon entry—the shock created could mean the individuals might be taken without bloodshed. Seeing two men bolt back into the building dashed this hope. The two likely reasons were either to warn the occupants or to arm themselves.

Jirov's men were well versed in the plan: pull in front of the building and use the vehicles for cover. Half the team would assault through the side entrance. The other half would wait for anyone fleeing through the front door. He would give them the option to surrender through a megaphone and so their fate would be in their own hands.

The voice of the driver of the lead vehicle sounded out of the internal speaker in Russian. "We will be smashing through the locked gates in ten seconds."

Jirov could see the men in his vehicle gripping their weapons tighter. The lead vehicle tore through the wrought-iron gates like they were matchsticks—leaving enough room for the rest of the convoy before resembling charging rhinos halting.

The soldiers spilt out. As inelegant as it made Alexei feel, his training ensured he followed the driver out of his side to protect himself from any potential firing from the house. He took a firing position over the bonnet.

The unison roar of multiple machine guns assaulted his ears. He ducked behind the cover of the vehicle a split second before realising the rounds were not from the building—but from the forestry behind them. The command to his men to initiate an anti-ambush sequence never made it to is mouth as a succession of rounds sledgehammered into his torso and face.

Connor watched the four muzzle flashes reverberating out of the forestry. The Russians did not stand a chance; their initial confusion ensured their deaths.

He rounded on Xander, over the din of the shooting.

"You fucking weasel. You're not interested in being certain of the truth. You have a fixation with killing Russian soldiers. You've probably signed the death warrant of all the members of your revolutionary group, you short-sighted mong."

Xander looked at him with a frank expression on his face. "This is not my doing."

"If you say it's Allah's I am going to fucking punch you."

Xander said more forcefully. "I know nothing of this. I can prove it."

The shooting stopped.

"How?"

"I think there were four PK machine guns. Yes?"

"Agreed."

"You and I can intercept them."

Connor's brow creased. "With what? Fallen branches? How do I know you won't be leading me into the hands of your bloodthirsty mates anyway?"

Xander reached behind him and whipped out a Fort-17, pointing it at Connor,

"If I wanted to kill you, I could do it here." He spun it around and held it out. "You're better with a pistol anyway. Let's kill them and see if they have anything to identify themselves on their bodies."

The Englishman's antenna rose—*he might want me to kill them so it absolves him of blame.*

Connor took the pistol. "No. I have a better idea."

The euphoria pushed the adrenaline out of the young mercenary's veins, his heartbeat ricocheting off the ground as he lay in the prone position. Back when he had first been taught the basic principles of ambushing, his training sergeant referred to it as 'legalised murder'.

It certainly had been that—easy money. The PK machine gun had not been particularly challenging to handle either.

Now Joe Airedale lay there watching his arcs as he and his team conducted a revolving withdrawal. Standard protocol dictated when the next member of the group took a firing position behind and offset to the front man, he was to have 'eyes on' him before either calling out or radioing through, depending on the tactical situation, for the lead man to 'revolve' past.

However, due to the density of the forest, visibility between points were only a few metres thus the *SOP* had been modified so the front man waited sixty seconds on the off chance a transmission from the next man's personal role radio was not forthcoming.

The former soldier's mental timer told him more than sixty seconds had elapsed.

As he got up, he snapped on to a sound to his right and swung the heavy machine gun towards it. He caught a movement to his left in his peripheral vision. He barely registered it was a swift-moving figure before a smashing impact on his temple took his consciousness.

His kids were jumping on the bed so hard his body bounced. It took Airedale a moment to realise the bouncing was not caused by his children, but by the terrain his captors were running over.

"He's awake. Put him down," said the one who had his arms.

The ground thudded into his back. The dark-haired man who had held his ankles whipped around and thrust the point of a knife under his chin. He began talking to Airedale venomously in a language he could not understand.

"I don't speak Russian. Just English," he said, his temple throbbing.

"Christ, a fucking American," said the fairer-haired one, who sounded British and was levelling a pistol at him. "Take his boots off and remove the laces."

As the other man began to carry out the task, Airedale asked, "What do you want?"

"What we want is to know why an American is in Ukraine shooting up Russians. I'd love it if you just told us here and now, so we can send you off—without your boots obviously—back to your team. I know that sounds too good to be true, but I don't want the headache of dealing with the ramifications of cutting up a Yank. But I'll do it if I have to."

"Why? You want to arrest us? You working for the Russians?"

"Do I look or sound like I am a Russian-friendly copper? Now stop time-wasting before my friend takes your eye out."

He wanted to believe the Englishman. He could be back with his team in minutes, telling them he escaped. He remembered the US Army creed, drilled into him: *I serve the people of the United States, and live the Army Values. I am disciplined, physically and mentally tough, trained and proficient in my warrior tasks and drills. I stand ready to deploy, engage, and destroy the enemies of the United States of America in close combat.*

He remembered it before remembering it no longer applied to him. He worked for money now and had only been thrown together with this current team forty-eight hours prior—he had no loyalties to them or the company. But would these two let him go if he told them what they needed to know?

"I am contracted by a private security firm named SouthArch Services Group. I don't know the endgame for the ambush."

"Fuck off," said the Englishman. "Your employer asks you to rinse Russian soldiers in Crimea, and you don't ask why?"

"Two hundred and fifty thousand dollars tends to stop you asking questions. This job wasn't handled by SouthArch Services; they just passed my details on to a third party and vouched for them."

"You ever find out who this third party was?"

"No."

"Half now, half when the mission is complete?"

"No. Payment after the job. SouthArch have always paid on time and told me it would be the same with these guys."

"Prompt paying after jobs in Afghanistan and Iraq for five figures. You'd have never seen the money for this job, you nugget. The reason you don't know is that whoever is behind this doesn't want any link between them and you, which was wise given your current situation. SouthArch would claim you had gone rogue. I am pretty sure you would have suffered an accident on the way back to the US. Let me guess, no immediate family?"

Airedale felt a worm of unease and shook his head.

"Maybe us taking you was good thing for you," said the dark-haired man.

Airedale looked at him, "You're going to let me go?"

The Englishman answered, "Yeh, I said we would. You can take this machine gun with you, but we're keeping the *belts*."

Airedale was about to protest but held his tongue— he could not convincingly argue his case to be allowed to keep both the PK and the ammunition.

The Englishman continued, "We're going to tie your wrists and ankles to buy us some time. Wouldn't want you running back and returning with your lads to mow us down now, would we? You'll perform a Houdini out of them in no time. I'd think of a plausible story in the meantime."

33

Bruce McQuillan enjoyed the outside ambience of the Kiev coffee shop 'The Skyberry.' He indulged himself in a white coffee instead of his usual black. The people walked briskly but without rushing as Londoners did. The way they moved and the expressions they wore seemed to him to project a happy, stoic pragmatism.

He liked the place.

He had learned long ago how to guard against burnout and panic; be proactive, plan, have contingency plans, and if he had to be reactive, to think through the options and take action— and not allow worry to creep in. He also knew the importance of delegation.

He remembered a story about a submarine nearing the surface in order to receive or send an important message via VLF (Very Low Frequency) radio waves. The skipper had passed over the command of the operations room to the executive officer (XO) as he went for a nap. Awoken by the turbulence of a storm affecting the submarine at the shallow depth, he immediately made his way to the ops room. He found his XO and chief of the boat, calmly and efficiently communicating with one another and instructing the relevant crew members of the actions they were to take. He did not say a word—he had simply left to return to his cabin. Similar to what it was like having your mind in order.

McQuillan's phone vibrated as expected; Jaime Rangel's punctuality as reliable as ever. The computer tech had been working on gleaning what information he could on the company which the man Connor had interrogated gave up.

Bruce read the email.

This is a summary of the company:

Registered in Venezuela, but with offices in Texas, Ukraine and the UK, SouthArch Services Group is a private military contractor that claims to provide "Highly confidential and effective security-related services designed to address the needs of governments, multinational corporations, non-governmental organisations, the corporate sector and prominent individuals." SouthArch's current CEO and president is a retired and decorated US Army lieutenant colonel and Gulf War veteran named Carl Nowak, who took up his post in 2008. The company's key services include security advisory and training, operational and intelligence support, and strategic communications. SouthArch also supports law enforcement agencies in the realm of terrorism, narcotics, organised crime, poaching, smuggling, maritime defence and the protection of natural resources. In 2015 SouthArch's revenue totalled $50.5 million.
N.B. Their systems are proving to be a challenge to breach. This is suspicious as I would have expected a high-level system but not to this degree. I make it a priority.

Bruce smiled; Jaime had waited until the very last line before making an error with his English grammar.

The black-operations chief mentally summarised Jaime's email—*US company. Based in Venezuela purely for tax purposes. Profitable and respected company. Clean-cut CEO.*

He had his suspicions who was behind the ambush but took the scientific approach of trying to prove himself wrong. He began to look at who had the means and motivation.

Povernuto had the ambition to kill Russians but he doubted they had the resources to reach out to SouthArch, not that the private security company would move against a superpower without the backing of an equal or more powerful entity. Nor did they possess the money, either short-term or in terms of future business, to be worth the risk to SouthArch.

That meant either a billion-dollar corporation or a nation. Bruce would instruct Jaime to look into exiled Russian billionaires with an axe to grind against Putin. The black operations chief could not see it though; the likes of Mikhail Khodorkovsky—the former Yukos oil company chief who had been sentenced to nine years imprisonment under Putin's government—were too high profile to try something this brazen, and Russia had demonstrated they were not averse to killing native 'miscreants' on foreign soil.

He thought of the various intelligence agencies potentially capable of initiating this.

He doubted anyone within the UK government or intelligence services would be audacious enough to action something like this. Discovery by the Russians would mean war, and no one desired that.

Israel and China's relations with Russia had been the warmest they had been for a long time. The conflict in Syria had been rocking the boat with Tel Aviv, and there were differences over Palestine, but economic relations had prospered in recent years with both the Jewish state and Beijing. Putin and Israel's Prime Minister Benjamin Netanyahu had a mutual respect, and Russia's trade agreements with China were flourishing.

It was these relationships, Bruce thought, that might make certain powers nervous.

Another email from Jaime pinged through,

Carl Nowak's cell phone has received messages from a 'Josh Taylor'. Always 'Hi, Josh here.' Always Nowak replies, 'What's your middle name?' And always a different middle name, and always from a different phone. I cannot trace any of them: Aaron, Able, Scott, Adam, Lee and Ffion. Then Nowak calls the number.

Bruce thought for a moment.

Where is Nowak now?

Ciara held a full splits position on the hotel room floor.

She had just completed a callisthenics workout consisting of pull-ups on the door frame, squats, press ups, bridging without the use of her hands, handstand presses and now a stretching routine. It had eased the boredom of the last twenty-four hours.

The previous day had been eventful.

The ambush of the Russian soldiers had caused everyone inside the hall to flee in panic. Connor had called her a few minutes after the firing had stopped and told her to bring their vehicle to the edge of the wooded area. She had complied, but when he nor Xander were there, she had begun to fear his capture. Just as she had chosen to get out of the vehicle and go look for him, he appeared with the Tatar.

When he said they managed to snatch one of the ambushers she had been shocked, before remembering something Bruce McQuillan had told her in his brief before she had ever met Connor—"He is the most audacious person I have known."

The revelation of an American contractor had stunned her.

Their primary objective had been to escape the area. Then lay low and wait for Jaime and Xander's contacts to gather intel to extract Gavril Ivanov. Laying low meant finding a place to stay where there were no cameras, and the staff were not the keenest eyed. They found such a place in the city of Simferopol, around two hours away from Sevastopol.

She had questioned the validity of choosing a city with known ties to the Crimean Tatars. The ambush had not made the media as yet, but now all the Russian security forces would be on high alert. She had worn a Niqab upon entering the hotel—her striking and unusual looks were a double-edged sword.

Connor had to take a room separate from hers as not to draw attention—an Islamic woman and a European non-Muslim would draw the eye. Instead, Xander had escorted her to her room but left as soon as she entered.

She ducked in for a cold shower. Ordinarily, when in a hotel, she would have taken a bath as per her training—the noise of the shower could mask an intruder's entry. As there was not a bath, she made it as quick as feasible before drying and dressing in the same manner.

She checked her phone and saw Connor had sent a WhatsApp.

'Guess what I have got?'

'Is this going to be an STI joke?'

'No. Unless there's something you want to tell me?'

'What have you got.'

'A chess set—all the pieces too. Rematch?'

'Well done. Now you're going to be remembered as the Englishman who asked reception for a board game'

'Behave. There's sort of a games room I noticed when doing my escape route checks. They won't miss it. Now are we playing or what?'

'OK. I'll leave the door open as not to show my western face in the hallway.'

Her lips curved upwards—she was glad she had showered.

Connor knocked on the door as he walked into the room. Ciara sat on one side of a small, rickety-looking table. Her hair still had a damp sheen from the shower she must have taken, and she wore a pair of denim shorts and a thin, white short-sleeved blouse revealing contoured arms and a couple of inches of her navel.

He set the board down and arranged the pieces.

"Your coffee is on the side there," she said.

"Thank you."

"No sexist comment?"

"You know I only say daft things like that to get a rise out of you—which to be fair never happens. I see you as every bit my equal and I'll pack it in with the 'jokes'."

"Well, maybe a little less," she smiled before gesturing to the board. "White or black?"

"You decide, being the lady."

She chose white and moved first. The time between moves was drawn without becoming tedious for him. There was no talking for the first twenty minutes, and they had taken several of the other's pieces, with he being a pawn and bishop up. Months ago, she had him on the run in the first game they had ever played due to his lack of concentration, and he had only just managed to salvage a stalemate.

"You know," she began, "you never talk about your mum."

He tightened imperceptibly before shrugging. "She's a Veterinarian. She emigrated to Australia and is living the dream. Is this background checking? Viewing me as a potential husband?"

"I have no desire to get married."

"They all say that apparently," he said. "But commitment is a biological imperative for women."

"You know how obnoxiously sexist that sounds?"

"Yes. Doesn't mean it's not true. Well, I mean it's true of my experience and research thus far."

"Do you think this woman we're rescuing—Grace—wants to marry you?"

"The boss told you then."

"Why wouldn't he?"

"Fair enough."

"Surreal isn't it? A woman you've been fucking is aiding you in rescuing another woman you've been sleeping with."

"I am kind of a big deal."

She smiled wolfishly. "It's a shame this line of work massively limits you in that area?"

"Sex?"

"No. Who you can settle down with. Can't spend your days hunting evil and powerful people and organisations, only to put someone you love in danger by settling down with them."

Connor had already considered this many times but he still felt a tinge of disappointment hearing it said aloud by someone else.

Ciara took one of his knights with her queen.

Gavril Ivanov sat on the hard bench of his cell, staring at the strange golden zig-zag prison bars. The voices of the guards and other prisoners echoed down the corridor of bare walls.

His fingers ran through his smooth grey-flecked brown hair, before rubbing his scratchy beard. He knew he would be getting transported in the next few days. There had been rumours amongst the detainees, and besides, it had made sense, the 'centre' as it was known was beginning to get full. If he had been a Tatar he would have been moved before now because of political pressure. Still, as he was merely an unruly drunk of a deserter from the Russian Army they left him, as a prison sentence would be inevitable and no one would be coming to protest over it.

He had almost felt relieved, as the waiting would be over. And he knew he deserved everything that might happen to him.

His desertion had not been voluntary—at first. He had been conscripted for the mandatory twelve-month draft when he had been eighteen years old. Many avoided the draft; some had educational deferrals, some had their affluent families pay bribes and he knew a few who had dropped blood into their piss test vial to escape via faux medical reasons.

However, he had wanted to join. He was from Tolyatti, known for the Lada and being one of Russia's poorest cities. The motor industry had been an option, but he yearned for adventure and travel so the army seemed a good fit.

Basic training had been condensed into twelve weeks for his troop—an experiment due to the draft period being shortened from eighteen months to twelve. It had been brutal both mentally and physically.

Ivanov had excelled and the instructors had laid off him a little after a string of strong performances. As the top recruit of his intake, he had been given the choice of which of the four Russian districts to serve in.

The administrative Stárshiy serzhánt had asked him, 'Where would you like to go, *Ryadovóy* Ivanoe?'

'Where is there likely to be action?' asked the new private.

One side of the senior sergeant's mouth curved, and his fingers danced over the keyboard. A moment later Gavril had been handed his papers—southern district: north Caucasus region, and south Caucasus near foreign states.

Grace sat amidst the eerie silence, looking across the meadowland and high hill. Vitali told her the guards would allow her ten minutes to smoke every few hours or so on an evening, and the time was so precious she endured the thorough frisking each time. The surgeon had not smoked in years, but she rationalised she would most likely die in this place, such were the things she had seen. She relished the cold flowery air mixing with the smoke.

Initially, she thought his allowance of her evening outdoor freedom had been an attempt to further curry her obedience. This belief vanished upon his reiteration any attempt of escape would result in the death of one of the children.

A few days ago, she had noticed the absence of one of the children and had felt a lurching fear in her stomach as there had seemed to be no reaction to it amongst the guards.

The number of guards had increased during the girl's disappearance, too. Not only that, but they had taken over the shifts of the other guards. She could not fathom why the manpower had enlarged but suspected the switching of sentries watching over her had been to prevent familiarity.

Still, she felt a momentary peace. The moonlight began to creep around the night clouds and bathe the valley floor. The nicotine hit helping amplify the feeling of tranquillity.

A guard's shout shattered it.

In her periphery, she picked out the movement of one of the children running, her nightdress fluttering behind her. More voices emerged into a chorus. Several guards burst around the corner, and one of them took chase.

Grace knew her capture would be inevitable, despite her hopes.

The man gained on her, and her apprehension seemed imminent.

The rifle shot cracked through the air, and horror pierced Grace as a piece of the little girl's head skimmed off in a pink spray. She collapsed face forward and did not move.

Grace screamed, with her legs running towards the girl of their own accord. She barely registered the sound of boots until a clip to her ankle sent her toppling.

The knee on the back of her neck pressed the side of her face into dew covered grass. Her eyes met Vitali's, as he perched on a balcony at the far end of this prison, scoped rifle in hand.

Ciara and Connor stared at one another across the table.

"Well played, Ciara," he said, not letting irk show.

"It's a pity you're taking it so well."

"Why?"

"Because you might have needed a release from the frustration, and then it could be me taking it," she said with a wink.

His cock hardened, and he felt a heady rush. He walked around the table and stood her up.

They kissed hard and deep. With his hands gripping her arse, he ground her onto him.

The rap on the door chopped through him—Xander's pre-arrangement knock. They smoothed their clothes and Ciara went to the door.

Xander quickly stepped in, and Connor saw him glance at the chess board.

"Who won?"

"I did," announced Ciara. "He's never beaten me yet."

Connor held the urge to defend himself.

"What's up?" he asked instead.

"Gavril Ivanov will be transported from Sevastopol to a small town called Kushva in the Urals two days from now," announced Xander. "He will be moved, along with three other prisoners, by an armoured vehicle. The journey is almost two thousand miles long and takes several days. There must be times where the guards change over—and vulnerable to ambush."

"You realise any shots fired on Russian soldiers, on Russian soil is a bad thing, Xander? Because with your choice of the word 'ambush' it sounds like you don't," said Ciara.

Xander blinked for a moment. "Yes, I understand this," he addressed Connor. "I know of basic route only."

"We might be able to assist in gleaning specifics as regards to the change overs and the personalities involved," said Connor. "Has there been any retaliation against Tatars for the ambush?"

Xander nodded. "Several arrests."

"Any of your guys?"

"No. They hide until I can prove their innocence."

"Do any of the arrested know where they are hiding?" asked Ciara.

"I am confident the answer is 'no'. Our security protocols are strict. But in this life, the only person's behaviour you can be sure of is your own."

"Be that as it may," said Connor, "we now have just two days to collate intelligence, make a plan, rehearse and then snatch Gavril before World War Three breaks out."

"And we need help," said Xander.

Connor caught on. "If she puts killing Russians in front of saving lives I will execute her."

34

Carl Nowak stared into the night from his hotel room: his view over the simmering Dnipro River highlighted by the hundred metres tall, gas flame-lit *Rodina Mat*—Mother Motherland, or The Motherland Monument. She held in her left hand a shield and a sword in the other.

Nowak felt a respect for the statue—many in now-independent Ukraine wanted to see the majestic symbol of Soviet power torn down or moved to Russia, but here she still stood.

He looked at his finished plate with a nip of guilt. The lobster fritta he had indulged in had been delicious but Nowak knew the expense of it had come from its rarity, not how it tasted. And these types of extravagances, once a rarity, were becoming a near-regular occurrence, and his still-solid physique had softened a little. This was not in keeping with the American warrior he had always been. He had memorised a quote by Genghis Khan:

I hate luxury. I exercise moderation … It will be easy to forget your vision and purpose once you have fine clothes, fast horses and beautiful women. You will be no better than a slave, and you will surely lose everything.

He imagined the old Mongol warlord would be shaking his head at the dark blue and turquoise silk kimono he wore. Nowak knew now, at a time where his empire was due to expand massively, was not the time to lose his sense of stoicism.

His throat felt tight, and his stomach a little nauseous.

He stood, and acknowledged that at fifty years of age, with his body still trim and his silver hair still full, he looked the part to others. But he had been slacking, and this feeling of sickness must have been a temptation to weakness. He fell to the floor and began his push-ups. He began to struggle before twenty—*fuck, I must have let myself slide.*

He felt relief at the interruption of the hotel phone.

"Hello, Mr Nowak. A Mr Joshua Taylor is here to see you?"

Nowak frowned and picked up his cell phone—no message. A sheen of sweat formed on his brow and shooting pains fired through his veins.

"Ask him what his middle name is."

"Excuse me, sir?"

"Ask him."

Nowak and his handlers had a system worked out where the second letter of the middle name always followed on alphabetically from the last.

After some muffled dialogue the receptionist's voice came back on the line. "He says he'll never forgive you for making him tell me but its 'Egar', sir, without a 'D' he said."

"He'll get over it," Nowak replied, faking amusement. "Send him up."

Replacing the receiver, Nowak picked up his wristwatch and flicked the communications switch before speaking into it.

"Angelo. A gentleman is coming up. Do not frisk him. Carry out perimeter checks and take Paul with you."

His handlers had insisted on the 'no frisk, no guards present' rule.

"Roger that," came the reply.

Nowak fought the urge to lie on the bed, and blinked his eyes rapidly. Minute men were rappelling down his ribs, stabbing them as they went.

A short knock at the door— he opened it to reveal a tall man with a chiselled face. A similar age to himself, the width of the man's shoulders and the narrowness of his waist reminded Nowak of a kite. He stepped back and allowed him in.

"We'll have to make this quick. I am not feeling too hot," said Nowak, downplaying the pain he was now going through.

"That'll be the poison you have ingested," answered the man.

Confusion jolted the American—the voice was British—Scottish. And he instantly knew what the man had told him was true.

"What was that?"

"The poison," the Scot replied, taking out of his pocket two transparent bottles with a clear liquid in each, one had a black cap and one had a white cap. "One of these is the antidote, and one is more of the poison. Now you can use your watch to summon your minders, but even if they managed to overpower me, an hour would not be long enough to break me. An hour is around the time you have left to live without the antidote."

The man sat on the seat Nowak had occupied to eat.

His panic seemed to revive him a little. "What the fuc—what do you want?"

"I want the answers to several questions. First one being, who's your backer?"

"My backer?"

"Don't play ignorant Mr Nowak, you don't have the time."

"Can I sit down?"

"I should think that's inevitable."

Nowak sat on the bed facing the man. He needed to think, but the pain began to cloud his brain. He had been on plenty of *SERE* evolutions in his time— both training and operational. This was different—his only potential rescuer was the interrogator. In those scenarios, the key was to prolong the time as painlessly as possible so any information eventually given would be redundant. Now the strategy was redundant.

Misdirection would be the key; he could not risk giving these people up. He was well versed in how to lie; give up something but not everything—mix lies with the truth. Watch the non-verbal cues.

"I never knew who it was. Only that a 'Josh Taylor' would contact me. The second letter of the middle name has to follow on alphabetically from the last one. It was always someone different. I have the bank records and have had some stills taken from far away."

Nowak searched the man's face for a reaction. All he got was a nonchalant stare. "I was about to say 'we can do this all day' but that would be a lie."

"What do you want?" replied Nowak, his voice straining hoarse.

"I know you know who it is, Mr Nowak. Now you have to ask yourself, does the potential consequence of giving them up to me outweigh the certainty of you losing your life before eleven o'clock tonight, because if it does, continue your misdirection tactics until you die on the floor."

An invisible hand began to choke him and he knew the game was over. He pushed the image of Genghis Khan out of his mind, and told everything.

Tom Ryder sat with his fingers lightly tapping his desk. The end of the working day had passed, and he sat inside the quiet of the garage's office, waiting for his cousin Luke to arrive.

It seemed one of his initial guesses, that Kirklees gangster Barry Sherman had been responsible for his dad's battering, had been correct. He dismissed the rumour—and one of his initial suspicions—that this was the case, as stemming from the idle bravado of a big-timer trying to claw back the reputation. But he put the feelers out anyway and discovered Sherman had not been back at home since the ambushing in the northeast.

He was proving a nuisance to track down. Sherman, who he believed to be flitting from mate's sofa to girl's bed to keep moving, was still in the town, he knew. His businesses were there and the rumour mill said he was pulling in money to abscond with. Tom knew if he was too open in tightening the noose Sherman would take whatever he had and be gone with the wind. The mechanic did not want his predatory anxiety pushing him into a mistake. Huddersfield formed a handy meeting and drop off point between the Ryder clan and various Manchester, and Liverpool gangs. Going in there causing a riot could compromise that, raising the ire of the local police and frightening Sherman into scarpering.

Tom had to find a way to surgically extract him before he left Yorkshire.

He leant back at the sound of the front door opening and watched Luke saunter into the garage. He would have been envious of the good looks had he not considered them boyish.

"What time do you call this?"

"Sorry," replied Luke, flopping into the chair opposite, "but I reckon I can make it up to you."

"Am all ears."

"Am shagging Jade, one of the strippers at the 'Dancing Bear'. Anyway, her sister is the manager there, a fucking worldie—she used to be one of those Instagram stars, ya know, 'if you like this picture then you want to check out my private content, swipe up'. Type in Cara Sinclair," said Luke nodding at the desk computer.

Tom did so, and images of a mixed-race girl, with shimmering dark hair, Rolo-like eyes, and perfect teeth filled the screen. Around a third of the pictures were of her displaying her jean-encased or barely-clad ass while staring alluringly at the camera.

"Alright, she's hot," said Tom. "What's the crack?"

"Well, made so much money from that Instagramming, she bought a share in that club—she's only twenty-six," exclaimed Luke. "Anyway, she's got a degree in business from Huddersfield Uni—quit being an Instagram star and that—but when she was at uni, she worked behind one of the bars in Huddersfield and this Baz Sherman we're after was pucker obsessed with her. Gave her free beak, and she just strung him along."

"She must've fucked him?"

"Nah—I don't think so—her Instagram was tame, more artistic like. She'd sell the coke on or give it away. I know loads of guys that have tried to crack into her but haven't managed it."

"Alright," said Tom, stroking the beginnings of a beard. "You said she'd bought a share in the club?"

"Yeh, a big percentage, and she runs it. But another bloke has the majority share. Jade said she reckons it's fucking Cara off, cos she picked up her share on the cheap as the club was on its arse and now it's banging. Bloke just feeds off her hard work, I reckon."

"Do you know her address?"

"I can get it."

Gavril realised he had gone nose deaf. He sat in the metallic box that formed the back of the security van along with three others. Their right wrists were secured by a chain just long enough to reach the open-topped bucket clipped to a steel fitting, there to relieve themselves.

The guards at the detention centre, either out of malice or absent-mindedness, had not allowed them to use the toilet before leaving. Six hours into the journey Gavril, knowing the others did not want to be the first to take a shit, did the honours, which prompted the others to take their turn.

Though no one had informed them, he knew their destination and the stops on the way—he had completed this journey before from the driver's seat.

Gavril recalled how the balloon of pride had expanded inside his chest upon being selected to return Crimea to Russia. Gavril remembered his anger at the parasites in Kiev screaming their claim to Khrushchev's gift to them when they were a part of the Soviet Union.

The pride became tinged with disappointment as there had been no severe fighting to secure the strategic positions. Still, he was happy to have played his role as part of the 'little green men', as the western press dubbed the Russian soldiers sans insignia. When asked by the locals where he had come from, Gavril simply pointed to the sky. His efforts in returning Crimea to Russian sovereignty received their rewards when he had been sent to the Donbas region to aid the people there in reclaiming their freedom.

People, who included his parents.

Nestor and Tanya had settled in Ukraine. A few years after the post-Soviet collapse, they had sent him away to live with his grandmother in Russia. Prospects in eastern Ukraine deteriorated with Kiev's neglect of the region and his parents wanted to give him a better chance. They had stayed through a sense of duty, and because of complications from his Ukrainian mother following her Russian husband to the former motherland.

Gavril set foot on the battle-torn soil as a soldier in August, and by the following September victory had been realised. It had been glorious: the heightened state of living, the camaraderie and a sense of purpose.

Then it began to change.

Tom Ryder sat in the strange dark living room, just out of the pool of light thrown by the Victorian-style street lamp outside. The décor surprised him, combining thoughtfulness and comfort in equal measure. The charcoal sofa and various complementary multicoloured cushions hugged him. The huge television stood at an angle to the modern gas fire replicating coal. Family pictures were mixed in with frames of iconic film posters.

At the sound of the car pulling up outside, Tom got up and positioned himself behind the door. He squeezed his eyes closed then opened them—the time constraint had compressed his planning to a bare minimum. Sliding the Czech CZ 75 pistol from the waistband of his jeans, he waited. He slowed his breathing and readied himself at the keys in the door, before the air sailed in.

The clicking of feet abruptly stopped, and the cold quiet surrounded him for a few moments. A shuffle got closer and the door budged against him. The moment the silhouette appeared his palm snatched over the mouth and the pistol's muzzle banged into the lower back.

"Don't make a sound, do everything I say and it'll all be golden. Nod if you understand."

Cara Sinclair did so.

35

Gavril's mind drifted to himself as a child, and the deep snow touched his soaked knees. He helped his grandma—a woman whose deeply lined face belied the relentlessness of her physical labour— in her sleet-layered garden. A flower of the deepest blue he had ever seen snatched his attention and transfixed him.

"Your grandfather brought that home with him. It's named a Larkspur flower, and it's a wonder it has survived," she said.

As he stepped forward, she flicked his ear hard. "Do not touch it. It will irritate your skin—poisonous—if you eat it, you can die."

A shunt in the road snapped Gavril back to the present. He sensed they were close as the van's average speed had slowed and changes of direction began to occur. It wasn't long before the truck slowed right down before finally stopping and the ignition died.

He had been briefly seconded for escort duty earlier in his career. The post had been less than three weeks and as such not officially recorded on his military record. However, he had made this exact journey and knew all the stopping points along the way.

The first changeover point would be a small holding centre in a forest west of Bataysk.

As the doors flung open, he scrunched his eyes in defence of both the bright daylight and the three masked guards barking. They punctuated their commands with flicks of their AKM-74s.

Unclipping Gavril's wrist bracelet, the guard said, "You, bring that shit bucket with you."

The rest were carefully filed out, and their wrists secured behind themselves. Gavril snatched a moment of enjoyment at breathing in the clean air and hearing the birds chirp. A muzzle prod to the back shifted him into movement towards the steel half tube entrance of the dank complex.

A guard stood at the entrance, armed with a vinyl skinned AK-47. Gavril was surprised the sentry wore a mask—Russian security forces were encouraged to wear one outside various government buildings in the cities to shield their identities from media glare and the attention of anti-Russian groups. Out here, there was not the need due to its seclusion and apparent secrecy.

The weapon system seemed out of place in this locale. The Russian military had received an injection of investment and revamping, but nothing was superfluous, and Gavril had presumed the better weaponry would be used in the ongoing conflict in Donbas, not an outhouse in the woods.

Gavril could barely make out the ringing of a phone inside the building.

As they got closer, the lead guard called out. "Where is Stefan? Drunk or sleeping again, no doubt?"

"Not today, there's been a security alert. Stefan will brief you inside," replied the sentry.

"Ah, I was about to ask why you wasn't smoking," replied the lead, chuckling at his own joke.

Gavril barely registered the exchange; he was too focused on the sentry's eyes—the same colour as the Larkspur flower.

Eyes he had seen before.

Tom perched on a handcrafted, back-supporting barstool with Cara sat across from him, bolt upright with her hands resting on her knees. The breakfast table top divided them.

The kitchen colour arrangement consisted of pearl and dusky turquoise, mixed with the wooden panelling and surfaces.

He had closed the blinds before she arrived.

"I am not here to hurt you or rob you," he said.

"What then? You a squatter? Sick stalker?"

Tom exhaled through his nose, spun the pistol in his palm so the grip faced her, slid it across the table towards her and sat back.

She stared at it for a few seconds before saying, "Like I'd know what to do with that anyway."

"Not exactly the hardest tool to master."

"Then what's to stop me from picking it up and calling the police, Mr…?"

"Ryder. Tom Ryder."

"You're Tom Ryder?" she said, her perfectly shaped eyebrows compressing. "You're barely taller than me?"

"I get that a lot."

She frowned. "So what do you want?"

"Baz Sherman. Do you have his number?"

"You broke into my home for a number? And how have you got in by the way? Have you broken the backdoor?"

"Not yet."

"What?"

"Nothing. I—"

"I heard what you said, very funny."

"I haven't broken any doors or windows."

"You'll have skills in stealthy little break-ins, I am sure."

He felt irked at her words. Though he could have broken in without damage, he had not had to; Luke had somehow found out the alarm code from the sister—and copied a key.

"Listen, I don't judge you sending strangers pictures of your flange, so don't judge me. I am sorry for frightening you, but it was necessary because I haven't got time to fuck around and I couldn't risk you slamming the door in my face and fucking me off."

Her delicate chin raised a little before she said, "I have never sent a stranger a picture of my pussy. Why do you think I work at a strip club—behind the bar."

"Look, I am not interested in what pictures you send to who. I am interested in Baz Sherman. He wasn't very nice to someone I am close to and now he's disappeared. It isn't his number I want. I want you to lure him out."

She tilted her head for a moment. "And why would I do that for you? He's a bit of a tit but he hasn't done anything to me—he might if I 'lure him out' for a pasting. You've given me this gun. I could call the police, or even shoot you—now you've told me how easy it is."

"Pulling a trigger is easy, killing someone isn't—at least the first time," he said looking into her silk-brown eyes. "And we both know you're not a grass. Just as we both know, the one thing you want the most is for your sack of a business partner to fuck off, and let you profit from your talent in running that club."

Her mouth parted a little. "What are you offering?"

"He's going to relinquish his claim to 'The Dancing Bear' to me. I am going to come in, take your thirty-five percent and be a silent partner. You'll have the remaining sixty-five percent. That's a thirty-percent upswing and you'll get your controlling share."

"Do you smoke?"

"Occasionally."

"Would you like one? Luxury cigarettes—there's only ten places in the world you can buy them. Or so the person who gave me them said."

Tom shrugged. "Alright. It doesn't smell like a house gets smoked in."

"I have had this pack for nine months now. Told myself I'd smoke one on a special occasion and this now is one. I'll put the extractor fan on. You drink whiskey?"

Tom pulled a face. "What? You do?"

"Why do you ask? Because I am a girl and mixed race?"

"Because you're a girl maybe. Not sure what you being mixed race has to do with it. Yeh, I'll have one. Neat."

While Cara busied herself with the glasses, Tom admired her from behind—*she knows I am looking too.*

She set his glass down in front of him. "Seventy-five to twenty-five."

"What the fuck? I've offered to increase your share by thirty percent without you having to put in any capital, and you're trying to squeeze me for more, you cheeky mare. I haven't even had a sip yet."

"I might not have to put any money in, but it'll be me putting all the work in—which I don't mind—but even with twenty-five percent I'll bet it'll be one of your better investments."

"The answer is no."

"At least let me have the option of buying you out."

He took a sip and took a draw. The nicotine lowered itself into his bloodstream.

"I'll always have a share in that club. You know why someone like me has bits and bats in a lot of places. But I'll give you the option of buying ten percent back. And that is as far as I'll ever go."

Her smile was wide, before quickly disappearing. "I don't fancy having to look over my shoulder for years."

"You do this for me, and Baz Sherman won't be hurting anyone, ever again."

A few moments passed before she said, "He might tell someone he's coming to meet me. Then they might put two and two together—one of his meaner friends."

Tom's fingers combed his beard. "We might have to convince people otherwise."

"How?"

"Can you take being roughed up a bit?"

"Yes."

"I won't mark you but—,"

"I am not made of glass. If you mean what you say about my controlling share, then be as convincing as you have to be."

"Fair enough."

She rested her cigarette on the lip of the ashtray and came around to his side of the table top. Her perfume mixed deliciously with the tobacco and whiskey.

"Then here's to our investment."

They clinked their glasses.

Connor began diaphragmatic breathing upon hearing the van grind to a halt. Even through his mask, the condensed air was visible in the bitter cold. He knew any form of fear could only be useful if it motivated him to take the right actions.

Or dissuaded him from taking the wrong ones.

They had gotten lucky so far. The guards had grown undisciplined and, expecting a prisoner drop off, were caught unawares as he, Xander, Ciara and Roza rapidly took over the compound. No shots had to be fired, and the four guards now lay in one of the cells with their mouths taped and wrists secure.

His concern did not just centre on surviving an ensuing gun battle—it focused on not getting into one in the first place. This holding centre lay on the east side of the Sea of Azov, over a hundred miles from Ukrainian territory.

The boss had made it clear what the potential consequences could be if he killed a member of the Russian security forces and was caught. They would take him and Ciara away, break them and the propaganda coup would be immense. The political ramifications would have a global effect. Particularly concerning to Connor, was the fact that Xander and Roza did not have the same agenda.

Especially her—he recognised the hate in her eyes when they locked onto the Russian guards.

The compound formed an L-shape with checking desk, changing room—which doubled as a recreation room, guard toilet and a search room on initial entry— and the holding cells around the corner.

Ciara watched over the prisoners and, as a result, was invisible to him. Roza matched him in both dress and back-to-the-wall position—he near the entrance, whereas she was further down next to the reception door.

They had a loose plan that each would cover one of the guards and take them down simultaneously without firing a shot, before taking control of them.

Connor remembered the adage from his days in the Marines—'No plan survives contact'. He had always taken it to mean that both an appropriate set of 'actions on' were needed, and that the individual and team had to have the ability to improvise. But it had always been impressed upon them to have a robust initial plan of action. And this plan seemed very vague.

Still, he dismissed the thought—it would not help him. Being aware and alert would.

He spun his head in the direction of the heart-piercing shrill of the reception phone. It was used by the QRF less than fifteen minutes away in Bataysk, to inform the guard commander of a shift change. Jaime had briefed him that the phone was always manned and answered. One ring out might not necessitate any action—whoever was meant to be manning it might have gone to the toilet—but a second would bring the QRF to the scene.

Because of the unrest in Donetsk, Syria and now the escalation in Crimea, Russia's more experienced soldiers had been stationed there. Jaime told him this rapid reaction was temporarily made up of a senior *mládshiy serzhánt*—junior sergeant or corporal—and a set of nine conscripts. He knew the Russian Army had pared down the conscription term to a single year, but Connor did not like four against ten, plus two armoured vehicles with mounted machine guns.

Of the four, only Xander could mimic a Russian soldier, so he stood outside, as Connor could not speak Russian with any degree of fluency and the sight of a woman might make the prisoner escorts suspicious.

The ringing became incessant, and Connor felt irritated on behalf of the phantom reception guard—*he is taking a fucking shit, call back in five.*

Finally, the phone died and Connor fought his sense of urgency, hearing the exchanges of Russian outside. They needed to take this escort team down before the phone went off again, convince whoever was on the other end all was well. That or there would be a large team of armed, amped up Russians on one side, and he, Ciara, and a pair of fierce Tatars who hated them on the other—*I should have been a fucking postman,* he thought before rebuking himself. *Pussy, check flashes and crack on.*

36

Barry Sherman lay in his mate's spare room bed, smiling broadly at his phone. Cara Sinclair DMing him out of the blue asking for sniff, and he had been dreaming of her ass for a long time. She must have heard about his bad lad exploits.

He knew girls loved a real gangster—the badder you were, the more pussy fell into your lap—but he always wondered if he would ever get his hands on her.

She always played it cool, and it made him want her more. He thought she might not be interested, and maybe back then she was not, but since the rumour went around that he had dealt with old Ryan Ryder she obviously changed her mind.

Not that he would have without the backing of his new boss. His sponsor told him to keep his nut down and move around for a few weeks as he dealt with Tom Ryder and his cousins. Sherman agreed, and he had been dossing between one slag's bed to another, sometimes hanging with one of his boys like now.

She had asked to meet him tomorrow night. She had messaged him an address—a posh end of Leeds. He wanted to suggest a different place but thought better of it. *Do not jinx it.*

The boss told him if he was to go anywhere out of the ordinary to take back up. But he did not want to take the lads, then make them wait outside, and he could just take a different car—no one would see him. His boss was not someone he wanted to risk upsetting though. He would have a think.

One thing he thought as he perused Cara Sinclair's Instagram page —*I will be balls deep inside that tomoz night.*

The door announced its opening with a clink. The outside air carried in the stench of excrement, and it took a moment for Connor to realise it came from the bucket of the man in front. And that the man in front was Gavril.

The lead guard looked furtive before another guard brushed past him bellowing in Russian.

Connor knew enough Russian to hold a pigeon conversation if he was the one leading it, but he could not follow what the Russian was saying as he strode past him towards Roza. Connor picked out the name 'Stefan'— *he wants to know where the guard commander is.*

Then the escort commander turned to Roza, and the belligerence in his raised voice did not need a translation.

Because Connor could not issue commands in Russian, it had been decided he would initiate the take down of the guards by his smashing the stock of his rifle into the back of the centre guard's head as he passed him. Except now, the escort commander seemed only seconds away from discovering the ruse, and the centre guard was still around six feet away. A word hurtled from the recall of his crammed Russian language study. Connor broke off the wall, walking towards the guard with his left palm outstretched.

He flicked his head up and snapped at the guard, "Klyuchi?"— *Keys?*

He knew his manner would divert the escort commander's attention off Roza. The guard's face of confusion turned into a mask of irritation. As he opened his mouth to speak, Connor, using the AK-47 as an extension of his fist, smashed its muzzle into the jaw. The guard collapsed like a Jenga stack. He fell in time for Connor to see Xander's rifle stock short-circuiting the last guard to the floor.

Connor span around to check on Roza's handling of the escort commander.

Only his superb reflexes allowed him to duck the bucket hurtling towards his face. Gavril's momentum doubled the impact of Connor's scything left hook. He toppled as the bucket exploded against the wall, scattering excrement over the other prisoners.

The echo of a gunshot smashed against his eardrum. Connor turned to see the headless escort commander tumble—*Now, we are fucked.*

Roza turned, barking at the prisoners, who lay face down with their hands still secured behind their backs. Ciara appeared at her side.

The phone began to shrill.

"That's the second time its rung," said Connor, with Xander already sprinting past him. As the Tatar burst into the reception and lifted the receiver, Gavril screamed out, "Vzlomshchiki!"

Connor's boot collided with his face, and he heard the receiver slam down. Xander rushed up. "They will send reinforcements. We need to leave."

Connor thought for a moment. "I'll create a diversion. This doolally fuck is our only lead and we don't know if he speaks English. I can tell you the vehicles they will be using are more powerful than ours. Use one vehicle and take Ciara with you. If she is caught there'll be a holy fuck of a diplomatic incident. If I am caught, the UK government can pass me off as a criminal."

"You aren't taking on a load of Russian soldiers on your own. You aren't Rambo, Connor," exclaimed Ciara.

"It's a diversion. This isn't up for discussion. Take him and fuck off."

"I stay with you," said Roza.

Connor's instinct was to protest, but he could not find a reason why.

"Fine. We'll position ourselves in the woods. Pass me the bag."

All four lifted a groggy Gavril by the wrists and ankles. They carried him around the corner of the compound, past the bound and gagged guards, and out of the exit.

"Take the Hilux. I am more familiar with the Duster," said Connor.

They stuffed Gavril into the back of the Hilux.

Xander looked at him. "We only need a few minutes."

"I know."

Ciara brushed past Connor on her way to climbing into the Hilux. "Don't be taking unnecessary risks and acting a hero," she said, punching him in the shoulder. "Because you have the potential to be decent in bed."

"Hey," Connor said, gripping her arm. "Take this, you'd be better with it anyway."

He slid out his commando dagger from beneath his sleeve, unclipped the sheath and gave both to her. She did not say anything, instead she snatched a grip of his jaw and kissed his lips hard before turning and getting in the Hilux.

It sped off just as the rumblings of other engines sounded in the distance.

He turned to Roza. "Use the treeline here on the left of this compound. I'll use the right. I need you to open fire to stop them in front of the compound. I'll take out their tyres. I'll throw smoke down and meet you back here and we drive off. Repeat what I have said back to me."

She spoke rapidly. "I on left—you on right. I shoot and stop them. You shoot tyres. Throw smoke and meet here."

"Yes, here you are," he said handing her a grenade. They sprinted off in separate directions.

The rumblings got closer and closer, and Connor hedged his bets whether or not Roza would be in position in time.

In the intelligence brief Jaime had sent to him, it had stated the BTR-90 armoured personnel carrier Russian QRFs used was too large for the track to the compound. Instead, this QRF used the formidable 4 x 4 GAZ Tiger. The top-mounted weapon this team used was a PKP Pecheneg 7.62 mm x 54mm general purpose machine gun, and if the weight of fire did not shred Roza, it might keep her pinned unless he could draw their fire. The Tigers were equipped with run flat tyres, but he also knew being punctured with a 7.76mm round would severely hamper their driving performance. On the winding track out, it might give them a chance of escape—*about as much chance of Oscar Pistorius catching athlete's foot.*

Connor did not ask Xander how he had managed to obtain the KSS suppressor for the AK, but he was glad of it now.

He prayed for luck—*do not drive around the back.*

Two Tigers burst into the clearing, passed the security van, and screeched to a halt in front of the compound. The two soldiers trained the machine guns on the compound door. The Tiger closer to him partially obscured the other. The backdoors flung open and the soldiers poured out. Connor spotted the mládshiy serzhánt by the way he gave commands and directed the others into various positions.

A grenade glided through the air towards them.

Although confident of being out of its fragmentation zone, Connor shielded himself behind the tree as it exploded. He counted two seconds and popped his head around just as Roza's muzzle report sounded off.

The weight of fire back in her direction drowned the air. He could see the mládshiy serzhánt laying on the ground, missing part of his head, like a horror version of a traffic warden making a halt sign.

Another with a red painted arm took cover behind one of the Tigers.

Connor took a kneeling firing position—firing in the prone would be more accurate, but if the soldiers picked up his position, he needed to be able to dive for cover.

He checked the safety was off, the change lever was set to single shot, and the sights set correctly. He aimed at one of the tyres—*come on Fortuna, be a good goddess and keep them looking the other way.*

He fired four shots in rapid succession, taking out three on the nearside Tiger, and a rear tyre on the other. The sound of the continuous firing hid the hiss of the tyres. Connor took advantage of the soldiers' initial confusion at the vehicles listing to one side by bolting twenty metres to his right. He took cover behind a hornbeam tree as a fusillade of fire kicked up the dirt and scythed down the tree branches around his previous firing position.

He could see five fallen bodies; if the initial grenade took out two—presuming the soldier with the bloody arm had bled out—then Roza had managed to gun down three others despite the horrendous weight of fire avalanching through the forestry.

Turmoil whirled in his mind; this angle completely exposed to him the other five soldiers hiding between the two Tigers; he could shoot them all now, and in doing so afford himself a stronger chance of escape. But they were just kids—teenagers doing the job they were supposed to, though not very well: their position and communication between themselves were both shocking. If this had been the regular Russian reaction force, they would have covered and manoeuvred through the wood before converging on his position.

Their weight of fire began to peter out—*finally. Lads, conserve your ammunition.* As he watched, he noticed something strange; the soldiers had not slowed their rates of fire to a deliberate rate—some had taken cover and stopped firing. Then another, and another.

They have fucking run out of rounds.

He felt relief; even if one of two of them still had rounds left, he could fling a smoke grenade in the opposite direction and use the foliage to creep back to the Duster. A risk, but he would not have the unnecessary deaths of young Russians on his conscience.

He stuck his hand into his day sack and felt for the smoke grenade. He began to lament on his lack of webbing when a masked Roza appeared from the farside treeline like a panther appearing from the dark mist.

Her approach was one of surreal nonchalance. With two of the conscripts focused on his previous position and the other three on the compound entrance and lower treeline, they did not see her sliding around the corner of one of the Tigers.

Connor fought the urge to alert the young men—he did not know for sure they were all out of rounds. She casually bowled—as if a ball to a child—a grenade into their midst.

He watched this time.

The frag ricocheting off the two Tigers shredded them like exploding tenpins. She calmly walked around to execute any moving bodies. She took her mask off and, like a mum calling her son in from playing with his friends, sang out to him. "Con-norrr, time to go now."

37

Barry could feel his anticipation rise as the maps app on his phone told him it was ten minutes to Cara's house. He felt the blood pool around his sinuses as the Viagra kicked in—he wanted to put in a performance that left her wanting more.

Not that he wanted her just as a bedmate; she was wifey material.

He'd borrowed a white Range Rover from one of the boys, and had shot up the M62 full of excitement. *No girl invites you to give her beak the next night, they want it there and then*—which is why he knew he would be in her pants tonight.

He slid off Scott Hall Road onto Kings Lane, admiring the nice houses and considering the worth of the jewellery in them.

Finally, the phone told him he had arrived. A gravel path divided the garden of the fully detached house. The neatly trimmed bushes stood like dwarf sentries leading to the door.

He looked down at his push-dagger, wondering whether he should take it. It was a chick's house in Bramhope—*not exactly dangerous.* Still, he and his boys had the motto: 'better to have and not need it, than need it and not have it'. His boss told him you could not be too careful, which is why he had sent Jordan and Phil the address and told them to come and wait a little way up the road. They were about fifteen minutes behind him. When he knew it was all kosher and he would be spending the night, he would send them a message letting them know it was okay for them to take off. Otherwise, he would go with them to a house party of a girl Jordan knew.

He walked up the path and chimed the doorbell.

The door opened and her perfume hit him with her appearance. He tried not to gawk. Her cascading black hair matched her choker and silk jacket. Her eyelashes looked perfectly curled, framing her gorgeous brown eyes.

"Where's my coke?" she demanded, holding out her palm.

The disappointment cut the words from him.

She laughed. "I'm just kidding. Come in."

Elation flooded him as he stepped in—*this is posh.* R&B played in the background. She floated into the kitchen, and called back,

"Do you want anything to drink?"

"Err, what do you have like?"

He heard the backdoor open and her gasp.

"What's wrong?" he called, she must have seen or dropped something.

She appeared in the doorway with fear plastered on her face.

"Whasup with you?"

He froze in his seat.

Tom Ryder appeared, pointing a pistol at him.

"You," Tom said, to Cara. "Is there anyone else in the house?"

She numbly shook her head.

"Where's your phone?" he continued.

"It's in my pocket."

"Alright, you do exactly what I say and you'll get through this. Understand?"

Barry could see his own fear reflected in her face—*how the fuck did he find me? She might have been bragging to her mates I was coming over.*

"I understand."

"Good," replied Ryder. "Take out your phone and show me the screen as you power it off."

She did so.

"Now face the window, interlace your fingers behind your head and lie down."

Barry's heart began to pound—*what is he going to do?*

Again, she complied.

Ryder faced him. "Right, you little cunt. Get off that sofa, interlace your fingers and kneel, facing away from me. I hope you give me an excuse to kill you."

Barry woodenly obeyed, adrenaline shaking him.

The heel of the pistol smashed the consciousness out of his temple.

Connor fought the urge to vent his anger as he drove. Arguing with Roza would not help him now.

He found watching her kill those soldiers eerie; the way Roza killed was as casual as watching other women apply their lipstick.

He kept his concentration, his eyes scanning the foreground for possible roadblocks and the rear view for any follow-ups. They were heading for a location just outside a small settlement named Ohorodnje. Roza directed him along a series of narrow tracks to avoid the main T0520 highway, which doubled the half-an-hour journey. Her knowledge of the area was evident.

"It isn't too far now. Down the end of this track."

After a hundred metres, the track opened to reveal three wooden huts, all joined by a floor raised a foot off the ground. The Hilux was parked to one side. Ciara appeared just as he switched the engine off. He got out and she walked briskly towards him, passing Roza.

"So?" she asked.

"I am fine by the way," he answered.

"What? Are you offended?"

He winced at the word. "Spare me. But all of the QRF soldiers are dead because of the Grim Reaper with tits."

"Tell me this is one of your jokes."

"It's not."

"Fuck."

"Not now."

"Connor, this isn't funny," she said with her eyes drilling him. "And I can't speak the language, but I think this Xander and Gavril know one another."

"What makes you say that?"

"The way Gavril looks at him—like he hates him."

"Maybe it's because he's our captive?"

"I'd be getting the same dirty looks if that was the case."

"Has he given up anything yet?"

"No. I insisted we wait for you and Roza before coercing him."

Tom prepared to set about rolling the unconscious Sherman in clingfilm. He knew from experience it would be an awkward job and placed the pistol on the coffee table. He had sent Cara upstairs; not yet knowing whether he was going to kill Sherman or not—he might have use for him if he left him alive, and Ryder did not want him to know Cara had been complicit.

When he had done, he'd grab the plastic sheeting and bolt cutters from outside. He bet himself Sherman would not make it until the second toe before singing. Tom had done the bolt cropper act several times and could never understand why the 'interviewee' would break at three toes—no one had ever gone over four. One for pride's sake maybe, but after the second he thought they might as well go all in.

Raindrops began tapping on the window, and Tom decided to bring the plastic sheet in early. The blood from any severed toes could be mopped with the towels Cara had brought down, but he did not want the claret mixing with the rainwater and dripping on the floor. Forensics were scarily good.

Tom flicked Sherman's eyelid to be sure of his unconsciousness—satisfied, he stood to make his way outside. The door was still ajar, as he had not wanted to alert Sherman by closing it when he had originally entered. He cursed himself—*your pistol, you fucking spastic.* He turned back, about to grab when a noise made him spin around.

A blur attacked him.

38

Connor watched Gavril's eyes. Even with himself, Roza and Ciara in the room, they remained on Xander, and Connor could not tell if it was fear or anger or contempt that filled them.

"He knows you, doesn't he?" said Connor.

Xander looked at him but before he could answer the captive's voice croaked, "Donbas."

Connor's eyes met Xander's, who nodded. "Let us speak outside—just you."

Connor followed him out, ignoring Ciara's eyes.

They walked to the edge of the treeline. Connor could hear the faint sound of rushing water from deep in the forest.

"Go on," said Connor.

"I worked undercover as a pro-Russian separatist. Putin had counter-sanctioned the west, and secret papers were intercepted showing Moscow planning on increasing gas prices to levels we could not meet—either my people lived back in dark ages or starved trying to meet the bill. Russia has used 'Holodomor' before. Merkel and NATO might talk tough in public, but their reliance on Russian gas stops them from making but gestures," he said dismissively. "My objective was to gather intelligence, specifically on where along these pipelines energy could be stolen. I would arrive at area and fight with the local militia, gather intelligence and move to another area. I began a reputation and came to attention of the Russian FSB, and I had to show my loyalty in a number of ways."

"They tested your 'attitude' to Ukrainians in a more definitive way."

"Correct. I did what I had to do."

Connor knew better than to discuss politics. "Tell me what you need to tell me."

"A Ukrainian special forces team were hitting the separatists hard. Their guerrilla warfare tactics spread fear for months and no one could track them down. I gained trust, but not quick enough to stop my country to be strangled. We could never kill enough Russian soldiers for Putin to give up the east. But sabotaging his pipelines is an effective strategy and was working. So, I used my contacts back in Kiev to tell me intelligence on the 'Ghosts of Blue and Yellow' and formed a team to capture them."

"And you were successful?"

"Not in capturing the team, no. Their commander sacrificed himself so the rest could escape. He pinned us down until he ran out of ammunition. We took him alive. The FSB took him. They also took me and wanted me to join them. The mission had been accomplished."

"What specifically did it accomplish?"

"The intelligence gathered helped the west be more strategic with their sanctions. Also, I able to find men willing to offload Russian oil and tap into their gas reserves to relieve some pressure on my country. As result, Russia has been forced to deal with China—and the Chinese squeezed them little bit. This had halted their aggressive actions."

"Where does Gavril come into this?"

"I try to come up with plan to free the Ukrainian officer—his knowledge would have provided the Russians valuable intelligence—but I couldn't see the opportunity without great risk of exposure. I did not think I would succeed in time. But he did not break and had been interrogated for nearly two weeks. Then I see chance."

"You used Gavril."

"Yes. I use him so Russians thought he had help the captive. I arm the Ukrainian, and sent them both away. I thought the Russian would simply be killed."

"Well, I don't think he's going to respond very well to you talking to him. I'll do it."

Xander shrugged. "If you wish."

"What was the name of the Ukrainian?"

"Agron. Vitali Agron."

Tom Ryder's reaction to shield his head with his fists facing palm in helped save his life. The blade caught the top of his left forearm, not the vulnerable underside. Wrapping his lacerated arm around his assailant's knife-wielding one, multiple elbow strikes smashed off his attacker's chin, severing his consciousness.

A swinging fist winged around the falling body, cracking off Ryder's temple. He fell sideways. The edge of the breakfast table hit his back like a spade into hardened clay. This second attacker ran at him in a fury. Tom stepped left, still dazed but avoiding the whipping cosh. He grabbed the wrist and stripped it back, using it as a lever to drive his opponent into the kitchen counter. When he hit it, Tom unleashed a series of pulverising punches that sagged the youth, before finishing him off with a knee to the face.

He stepped back and froze. Barry Sherman stood three feet to his left—pointing Ryder's own pistol at his head. Tom turned; this was the second time in his life he'd had a gun pointed at him. He felt a relief when Sherman said, "Follow me and I'll fucking kill ya."

The pussy is going to leave his mates and scarper.

Sherman turned, then turned back to face him again. "In fact, killing you would make me a legend, and I know my boss would love it too."

"And who is your boss?"

He smiled. "I'd tell ya, since there's nothing you can do about it now. But it'll be better you dying wondering—ya get me? All I'll say is that you should've looked closer to home."

Tom smiled back—when Sherman had turned to leave, he caught sight of the Sig Sauer P210's left side—the safety catch was still in its horizontal position.

He stepped towards Sherman whose frantic pulling of the internally blocked trigger splashed panic over his face. He swung the heel of the pistol at Tom's ducking head. His momentum sliding him on a splatter of blood from Tom's arm before sending him spiralling to the floor. The gun clattered away into the corner.

Tom grabbed a handful of Sherman's hair, to punch him into oblivion when his victim grasped the fallen knife. The blade angled towards him. Tom snatched the hand gripping it—all instinct now on the decimation of his would-be killer.

He forced the point with all his might into Sherman's throat.

His victim went rigid, and the gurgling sounded like the sound of a straw blowing into a milkshake. The warm blood ran Ryder's hand red as he rotated the knife—it reminded him of engine oil.

He removed the blade and let go of Sherman's hair, his face hitting the floor like a butcher flipping over a cut of beef.

He stood. Cara's deep breathing alerted him to her presence.

They did not speak for a long moment. He knew she must be in shock—but then she spoke,

"A hundred percent."

"Excuse me?"

Still breathing deeply, her voice remained strong. "You're going to buy me that club outright. You can have a share of the second but 'The Dancing Bear' will be all mine."

He stared at her for a moment, "I am not calling this in to the police—"

"I am not asking you to."

"I can't leave these two alive to be witnesses."

Surprise kicked him when she said, "Do we have a deal?"

"Yeh."

"Do you need a hand with anything?"

The question puzzled him before he shook his head. "I'll handle it."

"I'll be upstairs."

She left him counting his lucky stars. He had calls to make, but first he needed to deal with the other two men sprawled out on the floor.

He prised the knife from Sherman's fingers.

Daniel Thornton sat across from his boss in her office. The room was sparse of artefacts or pictures. The fan in the upper right-hand corner emitted a barely audible hum. To his right—her left—was a wall of tinted, and bulletproof, glass overlooking some of the forestry of Langley, Virginia.

She was still typing on her keyboard and Thornton's eyes were drawn to the CIA emblem wonderfully carved into the huge oak desk; the American eagle representing strength and alertness, the spokes of the compass indicating that the intelligence from around the world converged to this one point.

Thornton felt anxiety and annoyance billow within him. Anxious, because only an hour ago he had discovered that last night Carl Nowak, his point man in Ukraine, had been found dead after shooting himself in one of Kiev's most luxuriant hotels. Annoyance because this meeting was preventing him from taking action.

His boss, dressed in a light blue trouser suit with a light cream cashmere scarf, looked more like a high school headmistress than the leader of the world's most powerful intelligence agency, and that was one of her assets.

Finally, she finished typing, looked at him and said, "Daniel, you are to take one of the jets to Mallorca in an hour to meet a British liaison officer."

"What's the agenda?"

"Parker kept it vague, but said it was in our mutual interest."

Thornton's mind whirred. She was sending him—the deputy director—out on an unscheduled trip at the behest of her British counterpart and she did not even know why. It did not sound like her at all.

"Where am I meeting this liaison officer?"

"On a superyacht off Palma Bay. It belongs to Daniel O'Reilly, so you're on a trusted site."

"I've always found it strange that the company that supplies some of our most sensitive digital safekeeping is British. I wanted to ask you why the contract with the Asherson Group Incorporated was stopped?"

The director looked down her glasses at him. "Frank Schwimmer, our point of contact over there, died in a boating accident last year. Coincidentally, your predecessor retired and you were promoted. The contract with AIG and ourselves was mutually dissolved. O'Reilly's Verbatim Securities was our best bet going forward."

Thornton understood the subtext between the words—*Shut the fuck up and be grateful.*

Indeed, the deputy director of the CIA usually went to someone older, someone like his previous boss Michael Collymore, the director of the Counter-Terrorism Centre. However, Collymore had apparently refused the post and put Thornton forward instead. Thornton had headed CTC/SO (Special Operations) for several years and was involved in some of the most sensitive black operations conducted by the CIA in the past decade and a half. He suspected Collymore wanted him in that public office as a shit shield, and they could trust one another simply because of the goods they had on one another.

Thornton nodded. "Who is the man I am to meet?"

"His name is Bruce McQuillan."

39

Gavril had been left alone a while now, and he thought back to how different his life had been when he had first come to eastern Ukraine.

He remembered the sense of purpose he had felt upon arriving in Donbas, as part of the 'humanitarian convoy'. He was placed as a military advisor to the Donetsk People's Republic. The period of a few months from his arrival in Donbas had been the best of his life.

He and the other Russian military advisors had fought hard alongside their DPR and LPR (Luhansk People's Republic) brothers for their land taken by the Ukrainian Government forces.

One night, he had been sat on his military pack in front of a fire smoking a cigarette. His compatriots surrounded him, and a flask of vodka was passed from man to man as each took turns to regale the group with stories.

The news of the ceasefire—the Minsk protocol—had pierced the bubble of contentment he felt. While victory had exploded from his lungs, with a burst of rounds into the air from his rifle the same as everyone else, the smoke of anxiety plumed in his stomach—*What is my mission now?*

He need not have worried. Several violations of the ceasefire led to its collapse and Gavril had made a name for himself. So much so, he had been promoted in the field and had been one of the key commanders in the ferocious fighting for Debaltseve.

The door cranked open, and the sandy-haired Englishman stepped in.

"If your English isn't great, my friend will have to have a conversation with you," said the man.

"My English is better than yours."

"Why is that? I thought great English was rare even among the Russian officers."

"You do not need school to be able to learn."

The man nodded before dragging an empty barrel from the side and sitting on it.

"Do you smoke," he asked.

Gavril nodded.

His handcuffs were removed from his wrists, leaving his ankles secure. Three cigarettes and a lighter were pushed into his right palm, and the man resumed his seat on the barrel.

Gavril lit the cigarette and inhaled deeply. The nicotine filled his torso before swimming down his arms and under the skin of his face. He smiled.

"I doubt the kidnapped children will have smiled like that since their abductions."

"Perhaps not. Maybe you should ask your friend outside."

The man's eyebrows raised. "Go on."

"What do you mean?"

"I mean explain."

Gavril had no reason to withhold anything now. "In early days of the fighting, we had pushed Ukrainian forces back. I thought we had broken them. But we hear of stories. Stories of attacks—ambushes, sabotage and kidnaps—'The Ghosts of Blue and Yellow'."

Gavril took a drag as the man watched him impassively.

"The battle group try for months to capture the Ghosts until your friend led his team—they the 'Ghosts' of our side and they succeeded. Well, mostly success, he caught the leader who sacrifice himself so his men escape. His name is Vitali Agron."

"What happened then? Is that how you and Xander know one another?"

"Do you not smoke?"

The man shrugged. "It's been a while, and I don't want to be buzzed off nicotine."

"There is outpost under the command of the FSB, just over border in town named Kamensk-Shakhtinsky. This Ukrainian officer was taken there. I know, because I lead security team to get him there. The outpost's command think this man a security risk, so my team and I were ordered to stay."

Gavril's inhalation collected his thoughts. "Thirteen days they 'interrogated' him but he didn't break. Every man has breaking point, but Vitali escaped."

"I should imagine that to be quite a feat from an FSB facility and after two weeks of torture."

"I was on guard gate this night, so I know how."

"Don't keep me in suspense."

"You know your friend outside help him."

"He mentioned it."

"Tell you how?"

"Said he set you up. He needed the FSB to believe it was you who freed Agron so he could remain undercover."

"He did."

"I would have thought this Vitali would have simply killed you."

"He said I might be 'redeemable'."

"Go on, it's like pulling fucking teeth this."

"Pulling teeth?"

"I mean continue with your story."

"I can see he wanted to use me—make me a 'izmennik'. He is a mentally powerful man, and I begin to become convinced of his arguments. I began to not like my own country."

"Where did he take you?"

"A place near the Red Forest."

The four-mile square got its name due to the ginger colour of its dead pine trees following the Chernobyl disaster.

Connor frowned. "He's so mentally powerful he convinced you that you'd develop superpowers or something?"

"The facilities are what government workers live in before. But no one was there. He said we were not to stay long and he was right. In that time, a child come to join us. Agron said she a child of war—refugee—and he protected her. I never see her for days sometimes, she never speak."

"How old?"

Gavril shrugged. "Seven, eight, maybe ten. Few weeks later Vitali came up with plan. He said the Americans might look over us so he buy five coaches—I do not know how. We drive them out of Chernobyl. After miles down road, we stop and Agron order us to throw all smoke grenades we have—on top of the roofs more, to blind satellites. Vitali took his small army away on one coach. I hear the girl scream in Tatar."

Connor tilted his head back slightly. "Continue."

"Another man—did not give me name—and I, took coach to Kiev. He tell me of next phase. The next day, after dropping coach, we pick up van and went to bank in Kiev—XavierCredit Bank. He went in and come out with four huge—ahem—metal teeth bags—"

"Zipped bags?"

"Yes, zipped bags. Two of the bank's workers helped carry them to van. We drove into underground carpark and left the vehicle with the keys inside."

"Did you ask any questions?"

"Yes, that night. We in bar outside city and stay in small hotel. We have drinks and I ask questions. I ask how much money—same as four million American dollars-worth in the bags but part in Ukrainian hryvnia and Russian rubles. The plan was to set base in Zolotarivskyi forest in Luhansk Oblast, and hit the Tatar Muslims in Crimea. I could not understand logic but he said they would blame Russia. I told him it would not work—Russia could war with the Tatars quick—we won in Chechenia easy, the second time when we strong again. He laughed and say the whole Muslim world would come to Tatars' aid when dead children were found. That was plan."

"Did he confirm that?"

"Yes. I wake before him in morning and travel to Crimea—I wanted to visit my grandmother but was afraid Russian authorities have make spies of her neighbours. So I sneak back into Crimea, except I know FSB would think I help Vitali escape. I know what you are to think."

"How annoying these children must be?"

"What?"

"I am joking. What am I thinking?"

Gavril looked at him with bemusement before saying. "I am a traitor, that I helped facilitate what is happening now—these children, and—"

"Listen, I am not your priest," Connor interrupted. "But if there is a path to salvation, I can help you. If you help me."

"I will help you, but you keep your friend away from me."

"You have to hand it to Xander—that's his name by the way. Saw his opportunity, held you, I presume at gunpoint, circumvented the security apparatus, and sent Vitali on his way with you taking the blame for it. He's a bit like a Muslim James Bond—without the sense of humour maybe."

Gavril gave a sneering laugh. "Is that how you think he did it?"

Connor shrugged. "How else would he have done it?"

"He showed his phone—a video of my family being beaten. Then my Uncle Nicholas shot in face. When video clip ends, he tell me if I do not do as he say, my mother to be raped as my father watch, before both to be tortured until death. His eyes tell me it was truth. To my shame, I do anything to keep my parents safe."

Connor blew out, and said, "More of a Hans Gruber then—without the sense of humour maybe."

A strip of greenery separated the white of the Palma Bay buildings and the blue of the sea.

Daniel Thornton felt the breeze on his face.

He felt disconcerted that even in the short time he had been afforded, he could not find anything substantial on the Brit he was to meet.

His security stood a respectful distance back. As soon as Thornton saw McQuillan step on to the yacht, he knew what he was—a sharp and dangerous man, cloaked in the civility of a light grey suit and outwardly unthreatening body language.

Thornton stood and shook the man's hand—the grip did not belong to a civil servant.

They sat facing one another. Thornton gestured to the pots. "This one is tea, and that is coffee."

"This iced water looks the more appealing in this weather," said McQuillan.

"What accent is that?"

"Watered down Glaswegian."

"The military tends to do that, doesn't it?"

McQuillan smiled. "Your lack of knowledge of my background concerns you?"

"We are in the intelligence business. I'll happily answer any question with regards to mine."

"I don't need to ask questions regarding your background, Daniel, I need to ask questions regarding the present. Namely, was the kidnap and slaying of Tatar children the plan all along? Or was it an unforeseeable consequence?"

It was almost as if the vessel stopped swaying. The anger rose first. "Who the fuck do you think you are to come—"

McQuillan's voice cut across him. "I spoke to Nowak. Before he died, that is."

A cold liquid injected itself in his stomach, freezing some of the anger.

"You're lying."

"Check the spam on your personal email account."

Thornton's brain zoned out the background noise of the people chattering bayside. He blinked a couple of times before removing his phone from his pocket. Entering his email's spam folder, he found a message with a video clip attachment. It opened with a distressed Nowak, sitting on a hotel bed in what looked like a Japanese kimono. The questioning McQuillan had not even digitally distorted his voice.

(McQuillan) 'What was the objective?'

(Nowak) 'To drain Russian and Saudi resources and to increase international condemnation of them.'

'How?'

'False flag operations. Hit the Russians and fabricate a trail back to the Tatars. Vice-versa too. Please give me the antidote.'

'You'll get it when I am satisfied. How do I know this wasn't simply SouthArch acting alone out of its self-interest?'

'I have emails, photos and recordings to prove it.'

'I'll need to see them.'

'Yes of course.'

'Who is behind it?'

'The CIA.'

'Who specifically?'

'Daniel Thornton is the architect. We planned this together when he headed special operations at the CTC. It was his agent who helped free a Ukrainian POW from the FSB, recruited him to facilitate the plan and minimise our footprint in Crimea."

'What was the Ukrainian's name?'

'Agron. Vitali Agron. When Thornton became deputy director, he gave the handling to me. But rumours began to spread about Tatar children being kidnapped. I contacted Thornton and he said he had no knowledge of it, but that we had to play nice regardless as Agron could expose us. I offered to assassinate Agron, but Thornton vetoed it, saying that we should let the Ukrainian complete his mission first.'

The video ended and Thornton said, "Are you threatening me? What's to stop me calling my guys over and having you sleep with the Mediterranean fish."

"Because ninety minutes later, Nowak's video-recorded confession will hit every major news outlet in the world. Along with the evidence backing it up."

"I will destroy yo—"

"Shut ye fucking mouth. I am here to work out a solution. You were doing your job, and it was a good plan—I admire the daring. But you lack foresight, and now a psychopath is running riot over there. We have to stop him without it blowing back on you."

Thornton thought for a moment. "Why are you helping me."

"Because it's better the devil you know. Now tell me so I can help you help yourself. Your security can check me over with the wands again if you're nervous."

Thornton exhaled. "We provided Agron untraceable weapons, equipment and the objective of inflaming Tatar passions against the Russians. Meanwhile, we had people subtly turn middle-eastern Islamic heads in their direction—create sympathy which would turn into assistance. At the moment, Saudi money is being used to hamper the West's alternative energy research and development—it could be directed elsewhere. Have our dragons eat one another. I didn't envision how far this Agron would go."

"When did you know he was kidnapping children?"

"He never confirmed it except to give me the old omelette and eggs saying. I told him I would shut him down, and he laughed."

"Why not just shut him down?"

"I don't know where he is encamped. Originally we set him up—at his request—in the Red Forest."

"I am aware a few hundred villagers returned, but the government workers only stay in the exclusion zone for two weeks at a time. Looking after mercenaries financially is one thing. Paying them enough to increase their risk of cancer is quite another," said Bruce.

"It was his idea—he said he just needed the money and he'd take care of everything else. Frankly, I didn't disagree; it was easier to track his movement in an area with such a sparse population. Then after three weeks, he moved."

"Where?"

"I don't know."

"Don't lie to me."

"It's the truth. Five coaches arrived one day and made a convoy south with men getting into the lead vehicle. I could not contact Agron. They stopped fifty miles outside Kiev near a town named Ivankiv. Then they let off smoke grenades all around the vehicles, obscuring our satellite's vision. Because of the sensitive nature of the operation, I could only employ a small team so there could only be a single person covering the satellite surveillance at any one time. When the smoke cleared, there was no way of knowing who had gone into what coach, and only one could be tracked. The technician chose the wrong one that headed back to Chernobyl. So you see, I don't know where he is. If he'd have remained in Chernobyl after his atrocities, I could have leaned on the Ukrainian intelligence service to send a team to take him out. Maybe even Nowak's men, to attack it. A drone strike is out of the question. Then Agron gets in touch via email and says links between the two of us would be beamed out for the world to see if I happen to find him and try and stop him. I am fucked."

"Did you trace the email address?"

"To a park in Odessa. Probably one of his henchmen via a laptop, since destroyed."

"What about finances? What he's doing costs money."

Thornton sighed. "I couldn't fund him in increments. The more financial transactions there are, the more risk some Russian or Chinese cyber agent catches a pattern. Instead, I delivered all the funds I thought necessary across several accounts."

"Empty them. I know you have the technology and the influence to do so."

Thornton felt a hint of embarrassment. "That's the thing. I do not know how, but Agron managed to have all the funds from all the accounts transferred simultaneously to an account in Kiev the day of his escape from Chernoybl. The bank's name was XavierCredit Bank. Five minutes later, someone took out all the money in physical cash. I had the techs try and hack into the bank's camera recording—they had been switched off. That evening, the manager—a Denis Conrad—was killed in a hit and run."

The Scotsman stared at him. "How much?"

"Three point nine million dollars."

"Four million dollars to an unknown?"

"You and I know that's chump change in the grand scheme of things. If Russia and ISIS are undermined for the next decade or so, that goes a long way towards not just US safety and interests, but the rest of the West's too."

"I won't put you in a position of confirming or denying you had a hand in the drone attacks on the Saudi oil fields."

A flash of anger showed in Thornton's eyes before disappearing, and he said, "Thank you for that."

"But let's be honest Daniel, part of you still wants this Ukrainian psychopath to succeed."

"Hey, I have children myself."

"That's not what I asked."

"I am a patriot."

"A certain Austrian would have claimed the same thing."

Thornton stared at him. "That's a grotesque thing to say."

"How so? Manipulating two sides who might otherwise not have to engage in warfare, necessitating Lord knows how many lives."

"To ensure the survival of my nation, lives must be sacri…" he trailed off—that did sound like Hitler. "Look, what do you want me to say?"

"Nothing. I'll handle it from here, and I'll keep your name out of the fire."

"The soldiers around this Agron are Ukrainian nationalists hardened by war, supplied with the latest weapon systems, and I do not know if anyone else is funding him but his confidence is substantial for him to be able to shun our assistance. Mr McQuillan, what I am trying to say is that maybe the best course of action is to do nothing."

"That's all that's needed for evil to thrive."

"Things were less complicated in Kennedy's day."

"I think the quote is attributed, or misattributed, to Edmund Burke. But the sentiment is timeless. The only reason you believe that I would allow a major war needlessly break out in Europe, much less a psychopath who believes butchering children is a means to an end, is because you don't know me."

"What do you need from me?"

"I need you to remember this day. And remember who your friends are—if there are such things in our business."

40

Tom Ryder sat in the passenger's seat of the West Yorkshire Water van. The vehicle in front had the same logo. His cousin Luke drove the one he was in, and the twins drove the lead vehicle.

These 'work' vehicles were for times like this.

Tom had worn a cap and used the buses to reach Cara's the night he had killed Sherman and his two accomplices, so he had confidence he had not been tracked to the house. Tom had reached out to his contact in the West Yorkshire police, who told him the last place the police ANPR (Automatic Number Plate Recognition) cameras had tracked the Sherman crew cars had been on the M62.

Tom had Curtis and Charlie pick up and drive the cars around the next day. He had briefed them on DNA minimalisation, their routes and the points where they had to shield their faces by way of the sun visor from various cameras. The cars were eventually scrapped in a trusted yard in Doncaster. He gave his younger cousins this task to allow them to gain experience.

Tom knew various methods of how to dispose of bodies. He had done a couple of weighted burials into the sea until he heard a story of a captured shark being opened up to reveal a severed human arm in its stomach, and a murder investigation being triggered as a result. There were no sharks off the coasts of north England, but he realised as long as there was a body, there was a source of evidence.

The police rarely turned missing persons into murder investigations without a body, if for no other reason than the embarrassment it would cause if they reappeared.

"What's happening with their phones?" asked Luke, interrupting his thoughts.

"They're in the back of Desmond Hannaford's Beemer. If the police track them, they might even pin their disappearance on him," replied Tom, referring to a drug dealer from Pontefract who had been encroaching on Ryder territory.

"So Baz Sherman said it was someone close to home?"

"Yeh."

"I reckon it's Brendan Chappel. It was in his manor, and he's close to us."

"Why would the Kellings risk severing our relationship and starting a war over that type of money?"

Luke shrugged. "They are crims aren't they? Probably saw it as easy money, and they'd never get caught."

"It's not easy money. They would have needed a tip-off at least. I can't see how Baz Sherman would know we were due to visit Michael in Frankland and then have the gonads to tip-off the Kellings about the money. For all he knew, we could have already laundered it and they could also have told him to fuck off."

"I know, but that Brendan Chappel seems a shifty fucker, 'specially with all his mouthing off that day at the United Arms. Like he was guilty of sommat."

"We'll figure it out later. For now, we'll focus on not fucking this up. It's Curtis and Charlie's first time doing it this way."

"They'll be fine. Our Dan once said something like 'their sum is greater than their parts'."

He was referring to his only and older brother, who had gone to London to pursue a 'straight' life in business.

"The money that wheeler-dealer will make there will probably be a sum greater than all our money."

After ten more minutes they had pulled into a quiet country road near Digley reservoir. The four men, in their procured company uniforms, cordoned off a ten metre by five-metre area with logoed ticker tape and posts.

Tom opened the van's back. Amongst the assortment of hoses and various tools stood six 200 litre blue drums. In three were the bodies—each in several pieces—with some aluminium cans stacked in the bottom. The other three were filled with lye.

"Let's get to it," Tom said.

The pair of pothole diggers needed two men to lift and operate them. After an hour using them and a spade, a hole five feet wide and deep had been carved out—they lowered in the drums containing the bodies.

The sound of speeding cars burred in the distance.

"Hold it," said Tom freezing his cousins from hauling out the drums of lye. The sounds faded away, and Tom nodded for them to continue.

"Curtis, jump down and take off the lids of those lot," said Tom, indicating the drums in the hole.

"Fuck me, it's going to stink."

"They've only been dead a couple of days, soft lad," chided Luke.

Curtis slid in and began alternatively unscrewing the lids and balancing on the edges. Despite what Luke had said, an unpleasant smell emanated from the drums.

Curtis was about to haul himself out when Charlie screamed, "Fuck me, one's still alive!"

Curtis scrambled before falling to one side of the hole. His three cousins howled with laughter.

Curtis clambered out muttering, "Fucking pricks."

Once the giggling had petered out, Tom ordered, "Get the gogs and gloves on."

Once they had their protective gear on, the drums of lye were unscrewed. They steadily co-ordinated the pouring of the lye into the body-packed drums.

"And you thought they smelt bad before," said Tom.

The four turned their faces away from the stench.

"Fuck, it's a cop car," exclaimed Charlie, bringing everyone's attention on to the police car travelling towards them. "Fuck. We'll have to run, let's—"

"Calm the fuck down. I think they'd be more than one if they had been given a tip on us burying bodies. The sirens aren't even going."

"What we going to do, Tom?" asked Luke, as the car sped towards them.

As the blinding light attacked her, Grace scrunched her eyes shut and her body into a foetal position. There had been just enough ambient light to make out the shape of the toilet, and wash basin.

She did not know how long she had been kept like this for; there had been no sense of a timescale with which she had been fed. Every so often, the hatch to the tiny cell had been opened—sometimes, a cold meal would be provided and sometimes a half-eaten apple.

The door bolt slid open.

His bulk covered the entrance. Grace knew what she had seen in this God-forsaken place would haunt her forever—she came here to help and—*stop feeling sorry for yourself.* She looked at him, refusing to hide the contempt—the hate.

He spoke. "It not matter what an animal thinks of its owner, as long as it obeys."

"I ran to help a child you shot."

"You try to attack me."

"I suppose being attacked by a woman would enrage a man who gets his pleasures killing children," Grace screamed the last part of the sentence.

"I do not take pleasure. I do not take pleasure of the killing—"

"Those children never had a chance in life."

"Chance to do what?"

"To live."

"You had birth control when you first arrived here—no?"

"What's that got to do with anything?"

"How many chances of life have you stopped?"

She shook her head. "They could have gone on, had families of their own, achieved great things—"

"They could do bad things—maybe to their families, maybe to their communities, maybe to the world. You do not know. One thing is certain—the world is overcrowded."

She became aware her mouth was open. "You truly are evil."

"A woman label a man when logic fails."

"I don't care what you say. A world where children are killed for 'the greater good' is hell."

Vitali smiled. "I admire you, Miss Templeton. Maybe when all is done, you will one day see the light in this 'hell'."

"When this is done, the only thing I want to one day see is you receive justice for your horrific crimes."

"By God?"

"I meant here on earth—not in hell or one of your daft planets."

Bruce had the secure sat phone to his ear. Connor's voice came over with crystal clarity.

"Brace yourself, this is about as believable as my Nigerian lottery win."

McQuillan felt a tinge of annoyance at the comment; there was a time and place for flippant remarks and a sit-rep over a sat phone was not one of them.

"Go ahead."

"Gavril Ivanov fought in the thick of Donbas conflict. He said, despite smashing it, the separatists were being attacked regularly from all sorts of different locations by a group who they labelled 'The Ghosts of Yellow and Blue' or Ghosts for short. Roger so far?"

"Roger."

"This problem was eventually solved by Xander Voitenko, our supposed guide. Back then, he posed as a separatist to become embedded. He must have smashed plenty of his own countrymen, because Gavril said he had heard of him even before Xander's team managed to capture the leader of these 'Ghosts', a Ukrainian special forces officer named Vitali Agron who lay down suppressive fire so his team could escape. Roger so far?"

"Roger."

"There is or there was a command centre of some kind under the control of the FSB in a town just over the border named Kamensk-Shakhtinsky. Gavril had a team of seven guys under him and it was his section who were tasked with getting Vitali to the facility. When they did, they were asked to stay on to bolster security. Xander was at the facility too—his capture of Vitali had given him a golden pass."

McQuillan listened as Connor described the presence of a child—referred to as a refugee—to Vitali's group. He also detailed Vitali's escape and Gavril's descent into 'Stockholm Syndrome'.

As Connor confirmed how Vitali had escaped CIA surveillance, Bruce felt a respect for tradecraft—*an intelligent psychopath.*

"Why didn't the Russians in Crimea interrogate Gavril as soon as they found out who he was?" asked Bruce.

"Maybe an admin error. Or maybe they were moving him to a more secure facility. I am in between sessions with him but I'll ask. I had to touch base with you first because he's given me a rough area of where this Vitali character is holed up, amongst other things."

"Good work. Where?"

"You won't believe this: he says it was originally in the Red—"

"Forest."

"Yeh." There was a pause, then he said, "Mental isn't it? I thought it wouldn't be safe for hundreds of years, but Gavril reckons the compound was for government workers and is insulated from the radioactivity. Excursions outside are limited, and there's a changeover of the guards regularly. He must have had help within the Ukrainian security apparatus, surely. I can't understand where the money has come from for all this. He says he drove another guy—whose name he doesn't know—to a bank, where this guy came out with two of the bank's employees with four full duffel bags. Then they leave the money inside the unlocked van in an indoor parking facility—four million dollars."

"How does he know how much was in there if he was just the driver?"

"Because he and this guy got inebriated that night, and the bloke's tongue loosened. Something I skipped over telling you—where Vitali's men were playing musical coaches under the popped smoke, Gavril heard the child I was telling you about screaming in Tatar. When he and this guy were drinking, Gavril asked him what the crack was. This bloke confirmed this was how they were going to kick off World War Three—by kidnapping and topping these kids, and misdirecting the blame onto the Russians. Masses of Muslims will scream and rush to martyrdom against Putin's evil—that's what broke Gavril out of his Charles Manson spell and had him fucking off back to Crimea."

"The stirrings of it are happening now as we speak. Should hit the mainstream media soon enough," replied Bruce.

"Gavril says Vitali has moved to the Zolotarivskyi forest in Luhansk Oblast. Fucking nutcase."

"You know why he's done that, don't you?"

"If the Russians find him and assault whatever compound he's in, these Tatar kids will be killed as a result, having the effect he was after anyway. If any official units from the west try, then Russia will see it as an act of war."

McQuillan, because Connor could not see it, allowed himself an admiring smile at his protégé's deduction—*Getting better.*

"I would surmise that's correct."

"I'll need support from somewhere. Gavril says there are around twenty to thirty well-trained baddies. All of 'em armed with automatic weapons. Not to mention the headache Ciara and I would have getting up there in the first place. And I don't want to use Xander's group either—sort of defeats the purpose."

"This Russian might provide a way in. He's the best asset we have now."

"What do you want me to do?"

"Stay put for now. I might have some moves I can make. Can you stay alive for a day or two?"

41

"I'll handle this," said Tom. "Catch hold of this; you can manage it by yourself now."

Luke reached and grasped the drum on Tom's side.

The police car pulled up, and Tom, after removing his goggles, greeted them as the window wound down.

"Hi, officers."

The crowning policeman looked to be in his mid-forties. The young policewoman in the passenger seat smiled.

"You seen a black Golf around here?"

"No, but I heard a speeding vehicle over in that direction," Tom said, pointing.

"What's that smell?" said the policeman.

Tom's heartbeat raised. He had steeled himself a long time ago that he would never kill a law enforcement officer—if for no other reason that the heat it would bring down on the rest of the family would destroy them. But if this copper discovered the bodies, his cousins would not have a leg to stand on being tried as triple murder accomplices.

"It's the chemical mix for burning through and cleaning pipe work," answered Tom.

"What's causing the smell?" asked the policewoman.

"It's a sewage pipe," answered Tom.

The policeman frowned. "Around here? There's hardly anyone who lives here?"

Tom laughed. "That's the reason it runs right up here. We can open it up without stinking out someone's street."

His pride with his off the cuff lie was pierced by the Policeman's question, "Can I have a look?"

Fuck—thought Tom. He remembered his cousin Connor's words of 'you should have 'actions on' for every tangible situation.'

"Can do if you like. You'll both have to wear goggles as sometimes the acid spits and can blind."

The policeman seemed to hesitate, before dashing Tom's hopes as he shrugged and opened his car door, followed by the policewoman.

A plan raced through his head—kill the pair of them, throw them in the hole, drive their vehicle away and torch it—*no, I do not kill coppers.*

His cousins stood back, anticipating his command as they neared the hole.

"Curtis. Luke. Pass your goggles and gloves," said Tom.

As the pair reached out to receive their protective equipment, a black Golf burst over the hill two hundred metres away. Its engine screaming mockingly at the police as it sped past. The PCs scrambled for their car, got in and after a few jerking turns, gave chase.

"Fuckin' Nora that was close," exclaimed Charlie.

"Let's get this finished. Lob the rocks on first, then the sand, and last the soil."

They busied themselves with the task. After ten minutes, the disturbance to the ground would have only been noticeable if someone had been specifically looking.

As they drove off, Luke said, "Someone up there must be watching over us. Maybe uncle Greg, eh."

"Yeh, maybe," Tom replied. "But if our pictures get flashed around those coppers' station, and it clicks in one of 'em heads, I don't think any ghost will be able to help us."

Daniel Thornton picked up the phone—the phone he had not known was hidden inside his garage.

His Georgian-style home, complete with its well-maintained garden, disguised itself as a family home when Thornton had also considered it a fortress. The home itself had been fitted with a multitude of various security systems ranging from surveillance cameras, motion sensors and fingerprint scanners. In addition, most of his neighbours, if not employed by the CIA, worked in various capacities for the government, and as such kept a higher level of alertness than the average American suburb. He had always felt safe here in his residence, in Langley, Virginia.

He had received an email telling him of the phone's location. The fact the Scotsman—he had alluded to who it was in the email—had managed to discover one of Thornton's personal emails had been disconcerting enough. However, to be able to physically get a phone into his garage had been immensely disturbing.

Access to a hotel room or temporary accommodation in the UK or Europe was one thing, but here at his residence was another.

He powered the phone on, and within ten seconds, it rang.

"How the fuck did you do this?" demanded Thornton. "I am the deputy director of the CIA."

"I am aware. And I want you to continue to be," said McQuillan.

He has not even been bothered to disguise his voice.

"You think I'd let you—a Brit—blackmail me forever. I won't—"

"Save it. I'm a reasonable man. Yes, I won't hesitate to play my card if I have to, but I'd prefer for you to see this as mutually beneficial."

"You, or someone working for you, managed to plant a phone on my premises," Thornton seethed.

"How else was I meant to ensure the security of this phone call."

"How am I? Doesn't seem quite fair, does it partner?"

"I have everything I need if I wanted to expose you."

"You couldn't make that stick."

"You're right, in a court of law, you might be able to pull strings. In the court of public opinion, after it is blasted through every imaginable media outlet—now that might prove a little more difficult."

Thornton took a breath. "What do you want?"

"I have an approximate location for the thorn in our mutual sides."

"Where?"

"Zolotarivskyi forest in Luhansk Oblast."

"That doesn't make sense, unless…oh."

"That's right."

"I can't send any more Americans in there even if I wanted to. It was risk and effort enough to cultivate Nowak."

"I am not asking you to. But I haven't the manpower to recce—recon—the area. I need your analysts to work with the satellites. Look for thermals, any new builds with more than one route in and out."

"I can't give you a live feed, it would—"

"I don't need a live feed. I just need the precise location and up-to-date photographs. I'll handle it from there."

"Why did you go through all this trouble of planting a phone? Why couldn't you make this request officially?"

"Because I am trying to protect you."

"Because I am now your asset?" Thornton asked rhetorically.

"If you still see it like that. Destroy the phone. I have sent you an email address and password. Write a draft in there with the various attachments when you have the intel."

Ciara watched the two men without speaking. Roza was watching over Gavril inside the hut.

"Why would he lie?" asked Connor. He had told Xander of Gavril's confession that the FSB captive that Xander had helped escape was the man now raining terror on the Crimean Tatars. "The irony is that you released Agron when you were undercover as a Russian separatist—he'd never have known you were a Tatar."

"Gavril has reasons to tell lies when concerning me."

"I don't think he's lying. Be that as it may. You have to warn the Povernuto to stand down from retaliating because they might be getting involved in a war that martyrs them for the wrong cause."

"They have gone dark. No orders for attack have been given, except there is to be a meeting outside of Bakhchysarai a week from now. Then I can—"

"You told them to strike back, didn't you?" Connor said.

"I told them to protect themselves."

Ciara saw Connor's jaw tighten before relaxing. "They are going to get themselves killed while some demented Ukrainian prick pisses himself laughing."

"The Russian government and its military are not good organisations. Their soldiers deserve death. They would do it to us."

"Well, I know the Russian in there is going to try and kill you. So we're going to have to watch him. And the thing is we need him—and he knows we need him, he's the only one of us who has spent time with Agron," said Connor.

"We do not need him. He is danger to mission. We have what we need from him."

"We need a lot more from him. He'll know their weapon systems, rotations—"

"He could give misinformation."

"Then why the fuck did we risk all this to pick him up in the first instance?"

"Because I did not know who he was until I saw him," said Xander.

"He told me the story of how you had his parents captured to coerce him with a video of their 'treatment'. You could only have initiated that by first knowing his name."

"The video of which you speak was of Nestor and Tanya Kuznetsov. The son I threatened was Ivar Kuznetsov—the same Ivar Kuznetsov in there now. Gavril Ivanov—the real

Ivanov—was reported to be deserted presumed dead. I know because I reported it. I knew his real fate because I killed him."

"Why did you do that?" asked Ciara.

Xander shrugged without breaking eye contact with Connor. "Because he attached to my team of 'separatists' for the hunt of Vitali Agron's 'Ghosts'. During firefight, I saw opportunity and killed him. His body was never recovered. They never looked as I reported he ran off in different direction. This is why 'Gavril Ivanov' was left for weeks in Crimean security facility before transported with medium security? If Ivar Kuznetsov arrested, he would have been inside FSB basement and asked hard questions."

"Be that as it may, Ivar whoeverthefuckheis, is a valuable source of intel. We need him."

"You are wrong my friend. He turned on own country. When he arrive back in Crimea, he did not march to nearest military establishment, declare his true identity and lead Russian force to the location—no. And you wish to believe things he say. And you say yourself, he kill me at first opportunity and lead us to our deaths. That cannot happen."

Ciara watched Connor's eyes widen, and as he turned and sprinted for the hut, she understood.

42

Connor burst into the room, confronted by the captive lying in a pool of blood. So deeply sliced at the throat, it looked like an extra-terrestrial mouth opened to reveal a spinal cord thick with blood.

The sight of Roza wiping her blade off the cheek of the still wrist-bound Russian shot a fury into Connor. The back of his hand whipped through the air, cracking off her face, the force skidding her to her knees.

A strong forearm knifed around his throat. He caught the thumb, stripping the choking arm down off his tucked jaw.

The strength of the Tatar surprised him. His mind registered Ciara rushing towards Roza—*well triaged, woman.*

Connor attempted a headbutt but could not generate much force, held as he was. He drove Xander into the wall. His forearm blocked the knee strike, and the pair broke away from one another.

He fought the urge to look at what sounded like a vicious fight between the two women.

"There is a knife between them. We should split them up," said Xander.

"We should remove the knife. Always liked watching chicks fight."

"Chicks?"

"Girls. You're right, let's separate them."

He took a step back, and smiled at the scene. Ciara sat mounted on top of the smaller Roza, gripping her by the throat and detonating horrible looking punches to the face—he liked a girl who did not just pull hair in a fight. Connor rushed forward as Ciara leaned forward to grasp the knife in the pool of blood.

He hooked his arms under her, denying her the blade, but before he could control the arm grasping the throat, Ciara switched it to Roza's dark hair. She landed a couple more punches before he wrenched her arm over her head. When Xander prised her fingers off, Roza rose and punched Ciara in the face.

A surge of berserk energy rattled through Connor, as he fought to control Ciara, wrapping his legs around her in a body-triangle and pulling her back onto him. Her bloodthirsty scream shot into his ears.

"Get her the fuck out of here, Xander," he bellowed, but he could see the Povernuto leader having an almost equally desperate struggle to control his compatriot.

He felt tempted to let go of Ciara, but he knew if he did she would kill Roza.

"Stop!" he shouted, tightening his arms. "Ciara, fucking stop!"

His voice must have pierced her adrenal deafness as her struggling began to ebb, with Roza mirroring her.

"I am going to let go now. Please don't do anything."

"Okay."

He slowly loosened his hold and stood with her. He kept poised in case.

"That murderous bitch went for the knife after you slapped her," said Ciara, calm now.

The bruised Roza said nothing.

Connor spoke. "What's done is done now. But that's the last time you ever make a decision that important without telling me—us—first. Or you might become a liability."

"What is that?" said Roza, a little blood from her mouth.

"It means we'll kill you. Are you deaf as well as stupid?" answered Ciara, throwing the remark like a dagger.

"Fuck you."

"Let's cool down," said Connor. "Our goals at this moment are still aligned, and we are still better as a team than not. I think the best thing to do now is for you two to kiss, open-mouthed, for at least twenty seconds."

They all turned to look at him.

"Fuck crazy Englishman," said Roza softly.

"Broke the tension," he replied.

Ayesha lay clutching her thin blanket. She stared at the ceiling with numbness freezing her soul.

In the first few weeks in this place, she had longed for sleep as an escape from reality. Now she dreaded it. The nightmares would shake her awake, sometimes with her tears sliding off her face.

Her friend, Zoya, had boldly befriended her when no other would. Kara had stopped even looking at her.

One day, the guards told Zoya she could move into Ayesha's bedroom, and both were ecstatic.

They would make up and tell one another stories, as they peered out of the firmly shut window of their room.

Their favourite had been of how they would be rescued by knights on horses.

A week ago, one of the other girls disappeared, and there were whisperings. The next night, Zoya had announced, "There can be no knights to save us if they do not know where we are."

Ayesha had solemnly agreed.

"It is up to us, Ayesha. One of us must go for help."

Ayesha had pleaded with her against it, but Zoya insisted.

The silent time that passed after Zoya had tiptoed out of the room broke with the clonking stampede of boots and raised voices. Ayesha thought she heard a firework in the distance.

Ayesha had stayed awake all night wondering if Zoya had made it. She had almost hoped she had not—that she had been caught and would be her friend here again.

The next morning revealed the horrifying truth. The children were gathered in the assembly hall. Two of the guards brought in a lumpy, rolled carpet and unfurled it.

Zoya's corpse tumbled out, part of the top of her head missing. The children formed a crying and howling ring around her.

Not Ayesha—she could not feel anything.

Connor, Ciara, Roza and Xander stood in a circle outside the hut.

"The longer we stay here, the more dangerous it is. Besides, we don't have any supplies or amenities," said Connor.

"Any sort of haven is at least a hundred and fifty miles through war-torn east Ukraine," said Ciara.

"The only way we have a hope of pulling this off is if we trust one another, and agree what our main objective is."

"I agree," said Xander, "but you have no experience of this part of the world. We have to protect ourselves."

Ciara spoke. "You're right, and we'll defer to your expertise. But hate can cloud your judgement and killing every Russian soldier we come across probably isn't the best way to go."

"A mouth cannot tell tales of what the eyes have seen if the owner is dead."

"'Dead men tell no tales', is a better way of saying that," said Connor. "But bodies create excitement, and we already have enough of that."

Xander spoke. "We not kill unless necessary— my only promise to you. Do not be naïve, sometimes better their certain death than maybe ours."

"That's something that has been bothering me," said Ciara. "Chernobyl is firmly in Ukrainian territory. Less than two hours away from Kiev."

Hearing Ciara say this had the effect of removing a splinter in Connor's mind. He chastised himself for not seeing it earlier.

"What do you mean?" said Xander.

"What she means, is while we've been on a wild goose chase down Crimea and this hell hole, someone in your government has been complicit in aiding Vitali in his scheme. If indeed it is his scheme."

"Impossible."

"Now who's being naïve? Kiev has motive. No one, not them, not the US or NATO, wants to get directly embroiled in World War Three—but a group of nutty 'I hate Russia for air striking us in Syria,' ISIS terrorists would love to get stuck in if they could get a foothold. And your Povernuto could provide that."

"We not ISIS," announced Roza, her broken English thick with accent and contempt.

"Throw enough dead Tatar girls around, you'd ally with anyone who was an enemy of your enemy," said Connor.

Ciara said, "The point is you can't trust Kiev. Not until we know more. Which means we have to trust one another. Is this a Povernuto safehouse?"

Xander looked grave. "*SBU* safehouse."

Ciara began, "Who did—"

"There's no time. We have to get out of here now," said Connor. "Did you give them the vehicles we are driving?"

"No."

"Let's go. You take the lead," said Connor.

"Roza goes with you. Neither you or Ciara speak Russian."

They bomb burst into the vehicles; Xander and Ciara in the Hilux, with Connor and Roza following in the Duster. Their AKs were obscured underneath jackets on the backseats.

They pulled out onto the long, straight rural road with the trees forming a sun shield.

Connor saw them. A convoy of three cars, each filled with fighting aged males.

43

Connor spoke softly, "You see them?"

Roza nodded. He hoped all three vehicles would turn into the clearing.

"Don't do anything until I tell you, okay?" he said. Xander had told him Roza would understand almost anything he said but her speaking English tended to be monosyllabic.

She looked at him. "Okay."

Two of the vehicles peeled into the clearing. The third—a red and black JAC J5—dashed his hopes as it continued straight for them.

He dialled Ciara's number, and she answered on the second ring with, "Yeh, we can see. What were you thinking?"

"Roza and I will mask up. We'll try and get the drop on them so no shots are fired. I'll take their keys."

"Okay. We can assist."

"Negative. Roza and I will deal with it. They'll have already identified our vehicle— you're too far ahead for them to ID yours."

"Okay. Out."

The phone clicked off. "We'll try and stop them without killing them, understand?"

She nodded and he said, "Put your mask on."

Connor fought to quell the thoughts in his head.

The JAC gained on them rapidly.

"I am going to bang on the brakes. They might hit us. You ready?"

"Ready."

Connor slammed the brakes on. They both shielded their faces from the dashboard. Their burst from the Duster came a microsecond before the screeching JAC shunted it.

Roza screamed Russian commands while holding up her stop sign hand but it was to no avail.

All five seats of the JAC supported a fighting-age male. And Connor had seen many times the look when a man was about to attack—the look the man in the back left seat gave him. The others would follow his lead. In that moment he thought of Grace.

The windows disintegrated as the blood, bone splinters and brain matter exploded out. The sounds of the rifle reports, shattering glass and screams blended into a symphony of death.

When sure the threat was neutralised, he said, "Shoot the tyres."

The JAC gave a sagging hiss as they bolted back into the car. Connor gunned the engine and sped away.

He could see the two other vehicles closing in fast, before having to stop due to the shot up JAC blocking the way. Its flat tyres would prevent them from simply unlatching the handbrake and manoeuvring it to one side.

He dialled Ciara's number.

"Speak."

"We had to kill them. Managed to block the other two vehicles but this area is going to come alive in figures few. We're best splitting up now as its only my vehicle they have put out for ID. Roza will direct me."

A momentary silence echoed down the receiver.

"Don't trust her, Connor."

"You needn't be worried," he said. "I'll wear a condom."

He ignored Roza's stare.

"Anything else?" said the receiver.

"No."

The call terminated, and he steered the Duster around the corner.

"Was necessary," murmured Roza.

"I know," he answered quietly.

Bruce stared out on his view on London from his balcony flat. He missed Glasgow at times. Despite living in London almost as long, it would never be his 'bit'. His birthplace had a blend of visceral warmth London had lost a long time ago.

That said, the English capital had its many qualities, one of which being the way it looked on a night from this view. The moon peeked from the clouds like a giant's pupil-less eye. Thousands of orange sparks lay on the black landscape, turning blue as they neared the river Thames.

Sometimes he would stare out onto the scene like a form of meditation—his unconscious mind morphing ideas and dilemmas like a lava lamp before solidifying an answer.

His instinct had been to stay in Europe, but with his role as an interdepartmental liaison officer came mandated meetings and appointments. Parker could only cover for him so much when it came to missing them before certain people noticed.

Connor Reed had informed him via encrypted message of his suspicion that someone in the Ukrainian Government had been aiding this terrorist.

Another thought whirred in his mind—*has Thornton facilitated all this?*

It was not a question he could ask him over the phone, besides, if true, he would be working through an emissary in the Ukrainian Government. Bruce could not trust Danylo Kravets until he knew who Xander reported to. The flight over to Kiev would take three hours. Bruce would fly with a false passport and book a hotel in a false name.

Connor drove as fast as he dared without drawing attention. It was dark, which helped disturb the colour recognition of the Duster, but the roads were lighter on traffic.

"We need to ditch this car," he said. "We can't risk stealing one."

He adjusted the car's heating, chasing a perfectly comfortable temperature.

"Have friends— Pavlohrad."

Connor had snatched a map study as they had driven, and knew the city she was referring to was around a five-hour drive north-west.

"Povernuto?" asked Connor.

"No. Friends," she said, emphasizing the word.

"The members of Povernuto aren't your friends."

"'Friend' is…changeable word for others."

"Want to call your friends in Pavlohrad, let them know we are coming?"

She shook her head. "They not think I life—live."

It heartened Connor that her English was usable. He smiled. "I didn't think you ever existed until I saw you—and saw what you are capable of."

"Myth always bigger than real. And, no one hide from Allah's eyes."

"Surely he looks away when I am straining from a particularly big shit?"

As he looked at her, he thought he saw the corner of her mouth twitch.

He continued, "Why can't you call to tell them you're alive?"

"They think Russian trap."

"Whoever they are, they aren't going to be happy when the four of us land there."

"Just me and you."

"Explain."

"Well, Xander is Kiev."

It took Connor a moment to process what she had said.

"He's the leader of the Povernuto?"

"I no have see him in big—long—time. I do not trust one man."

"I can see why you are single."

"You trust people?"

"I trust my judgement of people."

"Why?"

"I come from a background where you have to trust people to achieve certain things. All the while, assessing their motives."

"Ah, criminal?"

Surprise at her guess jolted him. "Yes."

"You West saying—black sheep?"

He laughed. "Not for being a criminal—they're all criminals. I was the black sheep for joining the military. That and I don't carry my dad's name."

"Why not?"

"He didn't want my path in life made harder. I have my mother's name."

"You trust family?" Roza asked.

He thought for a moment. "Most of them."

44

Tom sat with his cousins Luke, Curtis and Charlie in a backroom of the Shibden Hall Mill Inn. The seventeenth-century establishment lay in a quiet valley of Halifax, and he liked its rustic charm. A fire and soft lighting warmed them inside the bare stone walls.

They were consuming various superb starters to their Sunday lunches. They spoke quietly, pausing or changing the conversation whenever someone cut through the room en route to the bathroom.

"Listen, like I said before. No one is to know what's happened to those three. Not until I say, and maybe not ever. You know the drill. You remember Mark Murray?"

"Your mate wasn't he, back in wild days eh," said Luke.

Tom smiled. "Yeh. Best mate. He stashed three bricks of coke for me in an old dog kennel. He'd have easy got fifty kay for them. I forgot about them because of things kicking off at the time. Came back to him nearly a year later and it was all still there to the ounce. Guess what he's in the nick for now?"

There was a collective shrug.

"Fucking robbing his grandad's plumbing van. Poor old fucker was a couple of years off retiring. He comes out not knowing who it was. Mark 'as a bally on, and because he's off his fucking face on drugs, he attacks his own grandad. Neighbours had already called the police five minutes before as the dozy fucker had stolen the wrong spare key and was fucking around trying to get into the van with it. What I am saying is just because you can trust a man today, doesn't mean you can trust him tomorrow."

"I thought you said it was only family that could be trusted?" said Curtis.

"I know." Tom smiled. "But it's protecting the family. No point burdening with something a copper or barrister might put to them—if they don't know, they don't have to lie."

They nodded their agreement.

"What's the plan?" asked Luke.

"No way did Barry Sherman do this on his tod—he's had at least authorisation from someone higher on the food chain. He said as much—'someone closer to home,' he said."

"I am just going to put it out there," said Luke. "You don't think it was a certain uncle of ours?"

Tom held back a smile. He had suspected ever since his uncle's 'Tony Soprano' speech in the aftermath of his dad's attack. Still, accusing his uncle without proof was not something he was prepared to do. For one, it could never be taken back, and if he was wrong, even if Derek outwardly forgave him, it would set a course that would break up the family.

If right, a move against his uncle was not to be taken lightly. Tom knew the reason the family hadn't yet been eaten by the new breed of youth gang culture was its outward appearance of unity. The reason the larger and more organised firms of Liverpool, Manchester and Newcastle had not was because Derek had agreed to distribute for them around West Yorkshire—forcibly removing Derek as head of the family would incur the wrath of certain gangland figureheads.

He needed proof—to himself. Part of him wished it was not true. And he needed it to get his family—all of them—on board. There was his Aunt Jenny to think about aswell.

He thought of Connor too. Briefly wondered what he would make of it and what he would suggest.

Tom looked at Luke. "We can't discount it, but no one here is to repeat that to anyone who's not present here, cos if it isn't true, it'll cause a storm in this family. This is what we're going to do. Barry Sherman's closest friends are now in the ground with him. But he has others. Wideboys like Sherman can't resist gobbing off—the old 'don't tell anyone I've said this but…' routine. He'll have bragged to someone. A pal, or a bird. You lot are going to keep diving into Huddersfield and knocking on doors—if you catch my drift—until we find someone who's going to spill."

"You said youse. Where are you going?" asked Charlie.

"I am going to make a trip to Newcastle."

Ciara tapped out an encrypted email draft to the address Bruce had sent through, using a miniature laptop Jaime had issued. Despite the advanced technology, McQuillan insisted sensitive communiques be written out in a draft but never sent. She had also been taught a method of messaging without having to resort to codes. Encoded messages attracted attention and were there to be broken.

She had transcribed the events concisely before shutting it off and putting it away in her backpack.

"You must know this place like the back of your hand now?"

"I have a good knowledge, yes."

"Roza hasn't told Connor where she's taking him to, so he hasn't told me."

He was silent for a moment. "She does not trust me."

"Why?"

"We have been apart a long time. She thinks my loyalty is to the Ukrainian Government rather than my people—rather than Povernuto."

"I don't understand. You're the leader of it. And she trusts you enough to let you come into her home with two strangers."

"It is complicated. I saved her from FSB capture, produce another identity for Roza and had her relocated. She was still not convinced. I used my skills and knowledge to arm and structure the Povernuto. I think she has suspicions I am a double agent."

She began to feel a stir within her stomach. She remembered how the Russians had attempted to ambush the Povernuto meeting.

"You know," she began, "if this monster is working in collusion with elements inside the Ukrainian Government, then when we cross the border out of Russophile 'Novorossiya' southeast into the nationalist north, we'll be out of the frying pan into the fire."

Connor and Roza sat parked on the edge of an embankment looking down on a residential street. The lack of street lighting had wrapped the houses in black.

It was three in the morning—the time where most people were in their deepest stage of sleep.

They had arrived a few hours earlier and agreed to take it in shifts to watch as the other slept. He had felt apprehensive of sleeping while this assassin he did not really know remained awake. He guessed the emotion she felt killing strangers might have been similar to what a geisha felt pouring tea. He had seen Bruce killing a formidable Russian Bratva chief enforcer with a professional ruthlessness, and Ciara kill Moroccan gangsters with a paradoxical furious meticulousness. For himself, it was either a steeling of resolve to do what was needed or an intense pleasure from torturing evil men before extinguishing their lives. The elation he felt when hearing their screams or sobs at times expanded into a release of laughter. Six months ago, despite its tactical imprudence, he had made two handcuffed men—one immoral, and one evil—take part in several leopard crawl races—after breaking their ankles. "The loser will die in this barn tonight. It pays to be a winner" he cajoled them while stifling his giggles. At the end of every race, the loser had a forfeit: at first a belt whipping, then an ear sliced off, then the other. Finally, he killed the loser. The best part had been the elation in the winner's face—the evil one—before Connor had told him "I didn't say the winner would live, did I?" He shot him in the heart so he could laugh more at the dying man's mask of incredulity.

This part of his psyche shocked anyone who came to know him. He guessed it was because it did not bleed into his everyday personality. It had been different with Ciara—it had been the very first thing she witnessed before getting to know him. She had tried to pry a couple of times now. The truth was that he knew exactly when the seed was planted. The recollection of what he had witnessed at seven years old was still vivid to this day right down to the American soap playing in the background as his mother was—

Roza's elbow pulled him gently out of his non-REM slumber.

He checked the time and nodded. "I'll crack into the green Skoda, then I'll follow you in it."

"Why you follow me?"

"Because we can't just leave this car here. It's likely been IDed and gives whoever is looking for us breadcrumbs to follow. We'll ditch it en route, and hope two and two aren't put together."

"I drive this?"

He knew she was wary of having to drive the IDed vehicle.

"I don't mind driving this car. Just thought it was more work me breaking into this just to then swap. But I understand your suspicions."

She looked at him. "Yes. You steal, and I drive it."

He got out of the car, hands in pockets and head down. The AK was too large to conceal on his person, so his *Kubotan* was his only weapon.

He kept his head still but eyes moving. He checked for any signs anywhere of awake humans while avoiding loitering. A Geely and a Hyundai were parked behind the seventeen-year-old Skoda. To Connor's mind the thatched, tepee-roofed houses looked like homes for Snow White's dwarfs. A bush—dense and large enough to hide two men—obscured the house immediately in front of the Skoda. He did not like not being able to see all the windows but needs must. He resisted the temptation the check the bush for imaginary men at three o'clock in the morning.

He felt his bumper key, designed to defeat the vast majority of vehicle locks and start their ignitions. Connor owned one from back in his early teens, which Tom had given to him. His had only been able to work on older models. Jaime had issued him a with a highly advanced one, and this was his first time using it.

The door opened without issue and he got in.

He softly cursed, angling his head down in response to the beams of an oncoming car.

It began to slow down.

He had been taught to act as his assumed character would in a given situation. In this scenario, he was a man working 'earlies' and pissed off he had to do so. He pulled on a mask of questioning as the vehicle stopped next to him. With his pigeon Ukrainian—Russian corrupted with Polish, he was told—as soon as he spoke he would have to go into some form of action.

Two burly men sat in the vehicle. Due to the steering wheels being on the left side, he and the driver were a couple of feet away from one another.

Connor's adrenaline spiked when he saw in the reflection of the window a man with a pistol in hand.

45

Connor's sharp, primal brain compressed the assessing of his options into less than two seconds. He could not take any aggressive action against the bearer of the pistol, the distance being too great and the obstacles too numerous.

If the man wanted to kill him here and now, he would have done it. This might be a kind of neighbourhood watch—Ukrainian style. They must have noticed him and Roza parked, and decided to ambush them—*Maybe this part of the world is self-policed?*

Deciding the man couldn't have noticed he had been noticed, Connor got out of the car. The two men began to bark in their native tongue.

Connor put a slur on his speech. "Whas sup. You hav' a keyysss for is?"

He began a drawling laugh to himself, as he swayed. He caught the reflection of the man with the pistol skirting around to his right.

Connor stumbled in that direction, sliding along his Skoda. He slumped in position with the back of his right heel pressed firmly against the tyre. The man stepped around the front end and stood before him to get his attention.

Connor exploded forward and snatched the top slider back against the hammer with his left hand. The man's trigger finger seemed to have been mid-pull when the Yorkshireman's right fist smashed into his jaw taking the control of his legs with it.

He swirled to the floor, as Connor's two hands tore the pistol from his grasp. He spun around to see the two men out of the car, bolting out of the car—towards him.

Roza's voice sounded loud from the darkness, "Стоп!"

The two men snapped around to her direction. They stood still at the sight of her.

Brendan Chappel looked at his year-old green Golf Scirocco R illuminated under the indoor carpark overhead light. The novelty had not worn off yet as he shuffled into it. He smiled, remembering the surprise on the salesman's face as he paid cash—nearly twenty grand. Two years ago, he had been driving a beat-up Beemer, but the Kellings had picked him up and put work his way. A recent job had coined him enough to pay for the Scirocco—except it was through someone else.

He had just completed his Wednesday night round of picking up the protection cash from a few local businesses on behalf of the family. He had started shooting up with Trenbolone two years ago, and his physique and Instagram had exploded as a result. Ensuring his tan was on point, his eyebrows perfectly shaped, and his chest cleavage always on display, he began getting gigs in some of the lower rent clubs in the city as a rep. His chance came and he auditioned for a reality TV show only to be told his four-year-old drugs conviction precluded him from it.

A coating of grey had splashed all over his world. His drinking and his cocaine habit got out of hand. He got into fights—and had been surprised how much his strength had aided him.

He ended up owing money to the wrong people—associates of one of Newcastle's most notorious families. One day he got a visit, and Kevin Kellings was a scary man. The slab of fat he carried could not disguise the immense power of his nineteen-stone frame. The shaven-headed goatee accosted Brendan in the gym carpark, and his heart rate ran riot. The beady eyes never seemed to blink as Kellings proceeded to tell him "you'll work for me, and dee as yer telt or yer legs will be broken."

Despite the threat, the Kellings paid him well. And it was not just the money he liked—it was the respect—and the fear. He had just come out The Hustler, a popular pool and snooker hall on the outskirts, and he could feel the room quieten as he walked in. Everyone averted their gaze—except this big, dark skinned bloke. Brendan knew he was not black as in West Indies. He looked like whatever race The Rock was. He would not avert his eyes when Brendan looked over and the gangster had to look away. Still, only he knew so he let it slide.

He impatiently drove through the residential streets to reach the long country road where he could make the four-cylinder turbo engines scream.

Finally the turn off came up, with a car following. There was around a quarter of a mile of winding before he could hit the straight and burn off whoever was behind him.

A full beam illuminated the inside of his Scirocco.

"Fucking doylem, turn yer—"

The rest of his sentence whiplashed short as his Scirocco shunted the airbag into his face.

It took a few seconds for his anger to pierce through the shock. This switched back as the window fragments shattered all over him. He was plunged into a terrifying dream as he stared at the gun. The pattering of the rain became louder with the realisation that the man behind was Tom Ryder.

"Put your hazards on now."

Brendan shakily complied.

"Unlock the doors," said the Yorkshireman, and when Brendan hesitated, he screamed, "NOW."

The doors were unlatched. "Don't fucking move. Unless you can run faster than a bullet."

Brendan remained stock-still as Tom slid around to the other side and opened the door. He did not get in, just knelt to obscure himself to any passing cars.

"Listen, you little cunt. I already know it was you and whatever cronies you have who attacked and stole from my dad," said Tom.

Brendan began to protest but was cut off as Tom raised the pistol and said, "Shut the fuck up now, before your brains are splattered out of what used to be your window. Now, lucky for you, I have two jobs for you. The first is to tell me who ordered it."

It took a few mere seconds for Brendan to answer, "Kevin Kellings."

"And who told him to?"

"Eh?"

"Are you fucking deaf? Who. Told. Him. It's not like he guessed my dad had that money in his car."

"I…I…never asked, man. He just told me. Never thought like."

"Well you're going to find out you little bastard. Because—"

Car lights shone before sidling passed, snatching away any hope of rescue as it continued on. The gun was obscured by the interior of the car.

Tom continued. "Because the video of you sucking cock might get out."

Brendan's blood froze. "What video?"

Tom removed a phone from his pocket, thumb tapped it and turned the screen to face Brendan. He could not understand—he made the lad delete it after he WhatsApped it to him. Then it occurred to Brendan—*Fuck, it will have been still in his sent folder.*

He began to panic and Tom seemed to read his thoughts. "Relax, that lad's an escort I hired. There's been rumours but this is the first bit of evidence of you being a faggot, eh. You forgot the mantra of being a gay gangster—you fuck them, they don't fuck you. They suck you, you don't suck them. Now," he said, "this can be our little secret—as long as you do everything I tell you to do. Your first little mission is to find out exactly who told Kevin Kellings about the money. Pass me your phone."

"Wh…why?"

"Because I fucking told you to, that's why."

Brendan handed it over.

"What's the pass code?"

"2810."

Tom tapped his thumb on the screen. "That's my number. It's under 'Stock'."

"Stock?"

"Yeh. To remind you that you'll be the laughing stock of the northeast underworld if this video gets out. You're going to be my little bitch from now on. And not in the way you'd like. And Brendan, if anything happens at all to your co-star, the next thing you'll be swallowing is a blade, you understand?"

Brendan nodded.

The living room was larger than Connor expected. The top of the walls were draped with what looked to him to be paintings printed on tea towels. The carpet ran in red, turquoise and black stripes. Lines of multicoloured beads formed the curtains with blades of light piercing through them. A green sheeted bed gave the appearance of propping up the window.

He stared into the wood fire as Roza and the man he now knew as Vladyslav talked. He had been the second man in the vehicle, and from what Connor could gather, the owner of the house. The same house Connor had attempted to steal the car from.

Roza told him Vladyslav was a friend, and how Connor handled the quasi-ambush had been a test—one which he must have passed, as Vladyslav allowed them to spend the night. Connor had slept on the green bed after subduing his feeling of vulnerability—*I cannot not sleep.*

It was now mid-morning, and Roza came through. He had not been sure where she had slept and did not ask.

"We breakfast here. Vladyslav gives us car. He destroys old car."

Connor opened his mouth to speak but closed it again—she would not tell him anything he did not need to know, and he respected that. Instead, he asked, "How is the man I punched?"

She shrugged. "Maybe embarrass. I make breakfast."

"I am honoured, especially since I am an infidel who's not your husband."

She blinked. "You no energy, no use."

She busied herself in the small kitchen. Connor noted she seemed familiar with the layout. Within half an hour, a plate with eggs nestled in a type of warm bun appeared in front of him, with a pair of replica plates either side.

She shouted something in Ukrainian into the corridor. Vladyslav ambled in. Around Connor's height and build, his green eyes stood out against his Slavic features. His brown hair was buzzed short.

The English was broken and halting. "You sleep well?"

"Yes, thank you."

Vladyslav pulled up a chair to the left of Connor and tucked in to his breakfast. Roza did the same to his right. There was not any talking for a few minutes before Roza and Vladyslav exchanged a few sentences in Ukrainian. Connor caught that he called her Irina. He turned to Connor.

"Who is best United Kingdom football player you see?"

Connor shrugged. "Paul Gascoigne. His career was— "

He gestured and made a noise denoting a bright burst into a fizzling sound.

"Yes, yes," said Vladyslav animatedly. "Like drink, like party. Football too easy."

Connor smiled—*Knowledge of the Premier League, wider spread than a pornstar's legs.*

"I agree."

They finished their meals and Roza took the plates to the kitchen.

Connor said, "Vladyslav—Спасибі—for the letting me stay and the car."

"It's okay. You friend." He pointed to Roza, then to himself. "You my friend. Be a lot care."

Connor nodded. "I will look after her."

Vladyslav scrunched his eyebrows, then laughed. "She look after you."

46

Danylo Kravets walked warily through the falling dusk of Park Feofania. Ordinarily, he would have enjoyed a stroll through the beautiful greenery and flora, intersected by canal and water features. The early moon overlooked St. Panteleimon's Cathedral as it, in turn, looked over the park.

Bruce McQuillan had asked him to meet here. They had had a brief conversation over the phone where the UK intelligence officer had stressed the urgency that they were to meet. Danylo had agreed, but had a flood of questions run through his mind from the moment of the call ending to now: *How did he get my number? Why was not I informed of his arrival back into the country? Should I be nervous? Why are we meeting here? It is a public place—is he scared of me? What could he possibly want to talk about that made this 'cloak and dagger' necessary?*

Although McQuillan had not asked him not to, Danylo did not tell his superiors as yet he was to meet him—*no need to excite anyone before necessary.*

McQuillan had told him the exact location, describing the bench overlooking one of the pools. Danylo knew exactly where one of his favourite parts of the park was—quiet enough to be peaceful.

From a distance of around two hundred metres, Danylo spotted McQuillan sat on the bench where he said he would be. He relaxed a little—at least he was there.

A man in a beige coat and matching hat came towards him and stopped him, saying, "Please tell me there are public toilets around here."

Noting the mild distress in the man's face and voice, Danylo smiled. About to answer, he heard a couple of steps behind him.

The 500ma of current through his armpit combusted his consciousness into pieces.

Ciara bit down on her anxiety as she read the news reports on her phone. A spate of attacks on Russian security services in Crimea. Putin had not yet made a statement.

Xander now drove—they had taken it in shifts to drive. She stared out of the window and divorced her thinking from her hormonally exacerbated emotions. Ciara had been taught to take notice of her cycle when on operations and this time was the worse—when the progesterone and oestrogen ran low leaving her stressed and aggressive.

Then again, she thought, *the fact there is stirrings of a third world war would piss anyone off.*

With her journalistic instincts biting, she asked, "Tell me honestly, what would be the ideal scenario for you?"

He looked at her briefly. "What do you mean?"

"I mean for the Tatar people. Ukraine as a whole?"

"For Russia to stop persecuting my people—we have suffered too much. I am not talking about the horrors under Stalin, I am talking about now. The harassment, intimidation, homes being searched for no reasons, attacks, and disappearances. Russia took over Crimea and human rights have dived. It isn't just Vitali."

A part of Ciara's brain nagged at her. McQuillan had told her, a sharp brain sometimes stored information it could not clarify until other information came to the fore; instead the embers smouldered in the background. This mental thorn centred on his outrage towards the Russians, but not Vitali—the man responsible for the kidnap of several children, and the death of at least one.

"Have your men—the Povernuto—had any dealings with Hizb ut-Tahrir?" she asked.

Hizb ut-Tahrir was the international Islamist movement that sought to establish a worldwide caliphate based on Sharia, but publicly denounced violence as a means to achieve its goal. In 2003, Russia banned Hizb ut-Tahrir as a terrorist organisation, Ukraine and most of Europe recognising them as such.

Xander shrugged. "We need friends. Just because Russia condemn them terrorists does not mean they are."

Ciara nodded in seeming agreement—she knew better than to argue with someone whose opinions were so emotionally rooted.

"Well here's a more pertinent question. Who do you report to exactly back in Ukraine?"

Four cars passed them coming from the opposite direction before Xander answered. "This is where I need your help."

"Tell me."

"This man promoted to the Ukrainian's police interagency liaison. I give him disinformation since our escape from safehouse—said we following lead in Odessa. If I return now he know I am of suspicions. I tell him you make way back to Kiev for demand answers from people. You will ask him for interview. Somewhere we can control."

"You want to ambush him?"

"I want to know if he helps Vitali Agron. If yes, he must pay."

"Well, we have much to discuss."

Danylo cursed his shivering—it was not the cold. He had hoped he could control his physical reactions to intense emotions when the stakes were this high, but reality had never lied.

He sat on a backless stool with his hands bound. A masked man stood to his front, and one either side of his eye line. He knew there was at least one behind him, which left him with a coolness running up his spine and the back of his head.

With woodchips and sand covering the floor, Danylo had guessed it to be a small animal pen, but the large tinted window to his right did not belong in any farm he knew.

He had come around to the blackness of the hood. He could not tell exactly how long the journey had been, maybe three hours, maybe five. A lot of twists and turns.

He now could not remember if he had slept or not in the van. He had been taught counter-resistance techniques by Ukrainian intelligence, but that was a long time ago.

"Danylo," said the man in front of him in Ukrainian. "I hope you answer my questions truthfully the first time. Nothing would make me happier than for us to have the information we need, and for you to be released from our care without there being any evidence of you being harmed."

Danylo felt hope flutter around his stomach. The man continued. "Because if you don't appear tomorrow, or appear with marks, that is bad for us—people ask questions. Then I have to decide if it is better to kill you, Danylo. Nothing personal."

Danylo pondered the logic of this, and then couldn't wait to answer.

"Shall we begin?"

Danylo nodded.

"Xander reports to you. Who do you report to?"

Danylo shook his head. "That is purposeful disinformation. Officially he reports to me, but in reality I am told to assist him."

"So who tells you to assist him and who does he report to? I will not ask nicely again Mr Kravets."

"Viktor Kutz. The new head of the Ukrainian Interagency Liaison Unit."

47

Connor and Roza drove through the lashing rain in the ten-year-old silver Volkswagen Golf Vladyslav had given them. Connor had been thankful for a reliable car that handled well. They had not spoken in the hour since they had left their benefactor. Connor looked out of the window as Roza drove, taking the opportunity to move the pieces on the chessboard of his mind.

If Roza did not trust Xander, would he be wise to? If he didn't, who would help him take on Vitali's mercenaries? Did he even want to engineer a full-scale assault given the children there the madman saw as sacrificial pawns?

It irked him he did not know exactly where they were going. Bruce had told him to head northeast, and he would call him. Connor liked having a specific target to break into segments. For some reason, he thought of the 'It's Only Pain! 500 Metres To Go' sign, depicting a caricature of a running, sweating marine with his beret pulled over his eyes and oversized boots. Connor smiled, thinking of the relief all Royal Marine and All Arms commando recruits felt seeing it, especially coming to the end of the endurance course.

He just needed a plan—but he could not make one until Bruce had shown his hand. Connor did not even know why he trusted the Scotsman so much—he had seen plenty of supposedly strong characters allow themselves to become blunted and weak.

As if on cue, his tactical phone rang.

"How are you?"

"I am alright."

If Connor had said, 'I am fine' it would indicate he was under duress.

"Head for Luhansk. Our tech friend has sent you the best route to the drafts box of the e-mail I am about to send to your phone, along with the password. He's going to update you as and when the situation changes through a series of emails. Once in Luhansk, he will send you your specific location."

"Right, ok."

Bruce put the phone down. He stood watching Danylo Kravets behind the reflective glass.

Yuri Kozlov stood next to him, looking not that different than he had over a quarter of a century ago. Such was the former revolutionary's competence, character and reputation. It was only the Ukrainian standing next to him that reminded Bruce he was over half a foot taller than his old friend.

"You look a little strange without your moustache, Bruce. Although yours did look a little like—what was that singer's name? Radio Gaga. 'Can anybody find meeeeee, somebody to love'."

Bruce smiled at the dangerous man's eccentricity.

"Freddie Mercury."

"Yes, Queen," he laughed, smoothing the right side curl of his own moustache that only held hints of grey. Bruce smiled at the SAS counter culture facial hair back in those days.

"Some things change," he answered.

"And some things no. I am your friend, and I will sacrifice all of my men before one hair harmed on this boy's head."

"Connor isn't exactly a boy—he's more than capable. He has a girl with him too and I'd appreciate it if she was protected as well. She's a Tatar Muslim, Yuri."

"You think a lot of this Connor, I can tell. Forgive me but I do not think it wise for a woman to be playing adult games in that part of the world, especially Muslim women."

"You'll understand when you meet her," Bruce said before turning to Yuri. "Listen Yuri, I appreciate everything you've done for me here. I know that—"

"Nonsense Bruce. I owe you my life and my riches. Nothing I could ever do would be enough."

Bruce had met Yuri in Ukraine back in the mid-nineties, back when the Ukrainian was one of the leaders of the Partisanen der Nato.

"Kravets might guess I've orchestrated this, but he cannot know for sure. I have to somehow meet with this Viktor Kutz character."

"I know of Viktor Kutz. I will work out a plan to take him."

"No, I can't let you do that—kidnapping a man that high up will be the end of you."

"Listen," said Yuri, extending the word. "My men will pick him up posing as working for this Vitali—he will tell us what we need to know."

"It's not that simple. Viktor Kutz's security is superb. Whatever he has in his head is worth protecting. You're no good to me dead. What I need from you is for you to protect and assist my man there. The only thing that matters now is how we stop this lunatic before his plan engulfs thousands, perhaps millions, of lives. And Connor will have another agenda in addition to that."

"What is that?"

"He has a liking for torturing evil men. The more abhorrent they are, the more pleasure he takes from it. And this Vitali Agron will be a prize for him."

Brendan stood in the shadow of Kevin Kellings. In Brendan's kitchen, Kellings had him lay out the collection money in such a way he could count it with his eyes—which Brendan knew was because he did not want to have his fingerprints on it.

The intimidating Kellings made Brendan feel like a visitor in his own home. It was the eyes that scared Brendan the most, even when Kellings was being sound or joking around, the whites were just about visible top and bottom of the pupils.

Brendan grimaced when he thought of what his reaction would be if that video came out.

"What's that face for like?"

Brendan flinched. "Nothing. Thought I'd miscounted."

"Just lay it out, you daft cunt. I'll count it."

Brendan still could not tell how to take the tone.

Kellings said, "Who dished ya car window in? Can't let that pass, marra."

Brendan's heart beat faster. "Not sure. There was a brick in it."

"Where was it?"

"Outside the pool hall on my last collection," he blurted. "How did you know?"

"Redders told me, why did you think you got it back so fast?" said Kellings referring to John Redman, an auto mechanic Brendan did not know Kellings knew.

"Yeh. He said he'd have to send it off or sommat. Wasn't expecting it to be the next day."

"That's the respect of being part of us," said Kellings. "And that's why we're gonna find this little fucking rat and break his legs. The pool hall has security cameras around it so we'll know."

Brendan felt a film of sweat circle his brow. If Kellings found out he was lying to him it could well be his legs that got broken.

"Well, I meant outside that paki shop on the corner. I popped in for a coke. Didn't even hear the glass smash."

It took an eternity for Kellings to answer. "Yeh, he cracks up the volume on the telly. Bangs it down when I go in."

Brendan nodded, with relief. He took a risk. "I can't think of anyone who'd dare to be honest. There's no one big time I've pissed off recently anyway. Unless one of those Ryders think we have sommat to do with Ryan Ryder's slapping."

Kellings snorted. "You think they're big time? The leader of that family is a shady little bitch. And the rest of 'em can't even see it."

"Derek Ryder's flaky?"

"Let me tell you something. When I was a lad, even us up here knew about the Ryder family, some of the stuff they did were legendary. That Greg Ryder dies, and now all their revenue goes to us, Liverpool and Manchester cos that fat 'roidhead lets us fuck 'im for protection."

"Protection from who though? Unless I am asking too many questions?"

"If you ask too many questions I'll fucking tell you, yeh. But Derek Ryder needs protection from his own fuckin' family. Well, two members of his family. That Tom Ryder, who's the only reason that family is still any sort of a force still. And that Connor Ryder, or Reed, whatever. Coz if them pair find out certain things about that Derek, he'll need help getting rid of 'em."

"Like what things?"

"Now you are asking too many questions. Wrap that money up, it's all there."

48

A pleasant surprise swept through Viktor Kutz; a woman who looked just as attractive in person than in her pictures. More so even.

He watched her approach and enter through the revolving glass doors of the 'Spirit Spa'. She moved with the athletic grace of a Ukrainian but with the deference of her English birth. Her sculpted, attractive face and womanly curves counteracted the masculinity of her height and powerful physique. The short silvery-blonde hair caught the eye.

Viktor had been to the UK enough times to know a woman as head-turning as this was a rarity over there—less so here, but she still stood out.

Kutz knew himself to be a handsome man, though he had downplayed it a little in his professional life—jealousy could kill a career.

His curiosity overcame his caution in agreeing to meet her. Xander had not updated him for days now, and Kutz feared he had died or was being interrogated somewhere.

Xander had gone dark since entering Crimea with this journalist. To find out what had happened to him was the only reason he had agreed to meet a foreign journalist. Her suggestion he choose the place assuaged him—there were only a few ways to be sure the person you were speaking with was absent listening devices on their person.

He sat on the soft cream leather sofa offset to the reception.

He stood as she approached. "Miss Robson," he said in impeccable English, "it is comforting to know you are safe. Shall we?"

"Shall we what?"

"Talk in the spa? Unless you feel uncomfortable?"

When her eyes studied his, he detected something behind them that was unexpected from a woman—an intelligent lack of nerves.

"I understand why a man such as yourself would feel the need for such measures, especially when speaking to a journalist."

Kutz smiled. "It's the first sauna room on the right out of the female changing rooms, it is smaller and more exclusive. The bill has been taken care of but your details are needed in the reception."

Kutz could have signed her in himself, but he wanted to be the first in there.

Ciara could tell the 'manager' stood by the receptionists was part of Kutz's security. It was not anything he said or in his body language that gave him away, but the women's behaviour towards him. The subtle uneasiness of the two receptionists would have been missed by the vast majority, but Ciara's already keen female instinct for detecting emotional nuances had been heightened during her agent training.

She noticed something she almost missed—it was not both women who were exhibiting the vague nervousness but just the younger blonde one. The dark-haired one smiled sweetly, but her eyes were full of professional assessment and the forearms carved with faint grooves of muscle.

If two were on the reception, there would be more in the saunas—*The secrets locked in his head.*

Xander, perhaps sensing she would only help him if he was candid with her, had opened up. He suspected Viktor Kutz had attempted to have them assassinated back at the safehouse. If true, he could only surmise that was because he had used Xander to extract Ivar Kuznetsov—the fake Gavril Ivanov— before he could spill the information of Vitali Agron to the Russian authorities. Although she had been there when Oksana had told them of the Russian captive—maybe Kutz just saw an opportunity.

He said he thought Viktor Kutz was the reason Vitali Agron had been able to set up a compound in Chernobyl. How he had been able to recruit despite being suspected KIA. And how he had now been able to set himself up in Luhansk, akin to an arachnid purposely climbing into a Venus flytrap.

Xander warned her about the level of security around Kutz but said he had one very definitive weakness—seducing gorgeous, professional women. Considering his wish to meet at a Spa, she had assessed before she bought a costume in the first side street shop she had seen. She did not wish to be given a bathing suit.

She thanked the blonde receptionist when handed the keys to her locker.

That the changing rooms were empty—convincing one of Kiev's most profitable spa treatment centres to cancel current bookings and not to take new ones during the day—spoke of Viktor Kutz's high-security status and power.

She changed into her blue and yellow bikini—maybe he had a sense of patriotism. She tightened the knots out of habit—if she had to fight, she did not want to expose herself. She smiled at how ridiculous the thought was—*my tits flying out would be the least of my worries if I had to fight in there. And I am meant to be seducing him.* Still, she did not loosen it.

She stepped through the door into the cooler air, before entering the sauna. The structure was a two-tier wooden seating plan with Kutz sat on the lower tier. She sat directly opposite him, and his eyes drank her in. She had to admit he did not look too bad himself, her usual cliché type of tall, dark and handsome—*At least it was until that blonde, sick-humoured Yorkshireman came along.*

Ciara enjoyed sex and knew just how much sex she could have with a man before her dopamine and oxytocin receptors clouded her judgement—*No man can reduce me to gaga after only one fuck.*

She sat across from him and admired how well he had maintained himself. She knew his age to be forty-eight—around twenty years her senior.

He spoke first. "As I said, I am happy to see you're safe. And maybe you could provide reassurance as what has happened to Mr Voitenko?"

"Your 'guide' decided to leave me to make my way back a good few days ago now."

"Left you in Crimea. And you miraculously managed to make your way back?"

"I am a resourceful woman."

"There's resourceful, and there's a foreigner making it back unaided out of one of the more dangerous parts of the world. Especially as your rather distinctive look will have been noted at the border. The shots fired may have escaped the attention of the media, but not me."

"Thanks for your compliment," said Ciara with a smile, interested in how he would take her flippancy.

The flicker in the eyes was barely noticeable.

"Can you imagine what it takes to be responsible for the protection of the interests and citizens of your nation?"

"A lot of pressure."

"A lot of decisions you will have to live with."

"Maybe a man in your position feels it necessary to stamp all over another nation's citizens and interests in the protection of his own."

"People would be naïve to conclude otherwise."

"Really? It seems to me the best way for any nation, dynasty, empire to fall is to attack others—make others have a reason to want to destroy you. Every action has a reaction—isn't that the basis of physics?"

"A bully only respects strength. You must know that?"

"I do."

"So, Xander is alive."

The sauna felt hotter.

"Can't believe I got out by my own volition?"

Kutz's smile surprised her because it was its first appearance. "No, Miss Robson. It's because he told me."

"Really?"

"Yes. Now we have a problem to solve. You and Mr Reed are pawns playing on a Ukrainian and Russian chessboard; you don't belong here and must be removed. Now you may or may not be just a journalist—your credentials with the newspaper check out— but your friend is running around with knowledge and intentions that are dangerous to the safety of my country."

"Knowledge of a Ukrainian war hero intent on plunging the Russians and Islamic world into a global war that could cost millions of lives, and intentions to stop it you mean?"

"Judgement is easy for those who sit on the sidelines."

"Is that what you think I do?"

"Even those who sit on the sidelines writing about it."

Ciara smiled. "So. What do you think happens now?"

He smiled back. "It's not what I 'think', it's what I 'know' will happen. We are going to escort you to a facility where you will make contact with Mr Reed. We will tell you what to say. Once he is in our custody, you will be both be returned to the United Kingdom."

Ciara snorted. "You'd just let us go?"

"Why wouldn't I?"

"Because we'd talk of course."

"I do not think anyone would believe you or that criminal."

"Well, I think I am going to have to decline your generous offer."

"It wasn't an offer, Miss Robson."

"I think in any situation a person has choices. Might not be the choices you like, but they have choices. Don't you agree?"

As his eyes flickered, Ciara exploded from her seat, her heel smashing through his face like a brick through a window. His head whipped back cracking on the edge of the upper seating.

To her surprise, he slumped unconscious. She waited for the inevitable rush from his men. When it did not come, she realised it was because Kutz really did think she was just an unthreatening journalist—*Maybe Xander did not tell him everything?*

She considered her options. She could not march him out of the door as a human shield; too heavy unconscious, still a strong, well-trained man conscious. It was her taking advantage of his underestimation of her that led to his current state, not her superior fighting prowess.

If she ran out, she might not get very far. They would be expecting their boss to leave the sauna first, so if she casually walked out, they would quickly check, then accost her.

She made her decision, and walked out of the sauna, into the changing rooms. Ripping out her jeans and top, she ragged them over her damp skin. Removing the commando dagger, she flung her bag over her shoulders just as the door flew open.

Her dagger punched through the first man's throat. The arterial blood spray warmed her face as he fell. His size momentarily blocked the path of two other men converging on the entrance. She ran for the opposite door leading out onto the reception floor.

It burst open before she reached it.

Without slowing, she drove the blade through the eye socket of the brunette 'receptionist'. Her hand gripped the dead woman's face, pushing as hard as she pulled to free the blade. The twitching corpse fell off, causing Ciara to step wide over it, eating precious seconds.

A boot to her back sent her toppling forward. The 'manager' leapt forward, snatching her wrist, controlling the dagger hand. She spun onto her back, hooked her left calf around the back of his right knee cap in a De La Riva guard. Booting his left ankle with her right heel, he was sent sprawling to the side of her.

Before she could free her dagger-clasping hand from underneath him, the seizing hands of three burly men restrained her. One sat on her legs, another knelt on her right arm, preventing her from using the blade, the third on her left arm. Despite the barrel of his pistol pushing hard into her face, her guttural screaming sent her threat resounding off the walls. "You're all gonna fucking die."

The man looked at her in alarm before his cheekbone and eye exploded.

As he and Roza drove through eastern Ukraine, Connor lamented how this was only the second war-torn country he had been in. Back in Afghanistan, Connor had equated the place to medieval Britain with the temperature cranked up thirty or so extra degrees—depending on where you were there. He had hesitated to think of the Afghan people as primitive, but the lifestyle of those living in the villages seemed more straightforward.

The signs of war were less apparent than they were here. Now he surveyed the inordinate amount of devastated buildings littering the landscape. The graffiti on some of the buildings would have been akin to 1970's Belfast had it not been in Russian. He noticed the look in the people's eyes—a grim stoicism.

Jaime had given him a concise report pinged through a secure message on his tactical phone. It listed likely separatist checkpoints, but the tech wizard stressed due to the lack of

CCTV, computer systems and a coordinating radio communications hub, he was unable to give a real-time feed of separatist movements.

Connor had only met the awkward tech genius on a handful of occasions, with the last time being a year and a half back. Bruce had told him Jaime had lost his close friend Ben, a highly talented inventor and engineer. Ben had worked on occasion—through Jaime—for the Project and had been killed through enemy action. Connor was not sure who Bruce or Jaime had contracted to be the new 'Q', but he had to trust them.

He mentally ran through his 'Actions On'. If they ran into a Russian/separatist patrol, there would be no 'good' choice. They could fight their way out, but even if they managed to escape in the ensuing firefight, the entire region was filled with armed, battle-hardened separatists that would be hunting them. If they gave themselves up, they would find themselves in either a dank basement or a sterile one depending on if the separatists or the FSB won the battle to interrogate them.

Driving away would be the only option, and even if the Golf could outrun whatever vehicles gave chase, the bodywork would not stand up to bullets.

"Listen," he said to Roza. "I don't know the specifics of why you hate the Russian so much—I get the generic reason but not the specifics. But, if we hit a vehicle checkpoint, I am going to drive through or away from it, you understand? I know you'd go down in a hail of gunfire, but that won't help anyone. I don't think the Houri applies to Muslim women. Besides, could you imagine what seventy-two male virgins look like? Several football teams of those blue-haired, pasty-skinned, no muscle tone, black fingernailed, unkempt types who would be stroking your hair then bursting into tears after they orgasm. Just think of that before you squeeze the trigger."

"Your sense of humour is not normal."

"I know."

She looked at him. "I not lose all fun. My vengeance not put in front those children. But if Russian separatists or us, I kill."

"I agree."

"We good warrior partners."

"Were you and Xander?"

"Was necessary. Like you and Viking woman."

Connor smiled at the image. "That wasn't a necessity per se. If I had to take someone to war with me, it would be her."

49

For a moment, Ciara lay under the three heavy bodies leaking blood over her. She rolled and heaved herself free and stood.

"Bruce," she exclaimed. He had three armed and alert looking men spanned out behind and to the side of him. He held his own supressed pistol with straight arms at a forty-five-degree angle to the floor.

"Where's Viktor Ku—"

His words fell short as the door behind her banged open. Ciara span around into an adrenaline-sharp attack mode. Her *teep* got to Kutz's stomach before the punches reached her face, firing him back into the changing rooms. As she entered, his guard was raised and his chin down. She considered tying him up in a clinch and kneeing him into oblivion, before deciding against it—there was a difference in a Thai fight with a girl of her own size, and an anything goes street fight with a larger, stronger male.

The door clicked open behind her, but Ciara did not turn to look at Bruce.

Barely able to keep the hate out of her voice, she said, "It's him. He helped keep Vitali Agron a step ahead all this time. He could have stopped those children's murders. Instead, he did nothing—all in the name of the Ukrainian people."

There were a few moments silence before Bruce's Scottish brogue commanded, "Miss Robson, take Mr Kutz into our custody."

Still only dressed in swimmer's shorts, Kutz announced, "No woman is taking me anywhere. If this bitch comes any closer, I will hurt her."

"Miss Robson, it seems to me Mr Kutz will need to be calmed, lassie. Would you like to do the honours?"

Her face split into a smile despite the splash of adrenaline cooling her insides.

"None of you will make it out of my country alive." Kutz sneered.

Ciara had been a high-level Muay Thai competitor for many years, and possessed a physical strength uncommon even among ardent female gym enthusiasts. But she did not lie to herself, there was a reason why women did not fight men in combat sports.

She wondered why Bruce did not simply use his men to wrap Kutz up. Then she realised—*He knows I need this.*

She did not enjoy this the way Connor would—*He would have laughed all the way through taking Kutz apart.* So far, her primal ferociousness only kicked when her life—or the life of a loved one— was threatened. Or when she was pissed off. She wanted to be able to tap into it at will.

She moved towards Kutz as he raised his guard.

He made a rush for her, which she sidestepped, jabbing him hard in the temple. He whipped around like an enraged bull after the red cape. Ciara fought against her panic—plenty of superior technicians had been taken out by a hard-charging aggressor. Keeping him off-balance with the jab, she moved out on angles, barely avoiding his wild swings.

She remembered something Connor had told her—*On the street, if you keep making them miss and jabbing them up, eventually they will make a dive to catch hold of you.*

She resisted the temptation to axe her shin into his thigh; although she doubted his ability to defend leg kicks, she did not want to compromise her stability.

She felt herself manoeuvred near the lockers. He ducked, and Ciara—anticipating another wild swing, shielded her head defensively. The headbutt still caught her with force on her barely turned cheek.

The hard jab of a locker key halted her skid backwards. Kutz tore after his prey with his eyes gleaming. Using her heel, she launched herself off the lower row of lockers. Her grasping his shoulder as she spun aided his momentum face first into the hard wood. Her survival instinct exploded into beautiful violence, tearing her bewildered victim backwards over her outstretched leg onto the floor.

His arms did not make it in time to block the stamp spilling his consciousness over the hard-tiled floor.

It was only on Bruce's third bellow of "Stop" that she ceased stamping.

Connor pulled the Golf over by an empty residential corner, surveying the scene. The street, barely wide enough to fit a vehicle down, sloped a mere few degrees for a hundred metres before flatting and curving left into disappearance. This urban setting on the outskirts of Luhansk reminded him of a frontier town in a western, except instead of saloons with swinging doors, wooden houses and quaint stables, there was an assortment of brick buildings displaying the marks of gunfire and frag grenades, though signs of shelling were absent.

He had been taught, back in his pre-deployment training for Afghanistan, to observe atmospherics. The lack of human life in a place where it would ordinarily be expected was never a good sign. When the Taliban entered an area with the intention of ambushing coalition forces, the local populace would abscond to avoid the crossfire.

This place appeared deserted.

However, this was the way the contact wanted it, for Connor to park where they had parked and for him to walk down the street to the far end alone. The crisp night air stroked his face, and he walked with his palms facing in. He had thought through all his possible options beforehand, and this was the only one that made sense. Through the tac-phone, Bruce had been adamant he arrive to meet this contact unarmed, and the duress code had not been used. The moon peaked out from behind the clouds, like a girl peering over her fingers at the build-up music of a horror film. The only weapon he possessed was his Kubaton, disguised as a lighter, limited in its usefulness to anything over two unarmed men. *Stop being a fucking pussy, Musashi killed the second-best swordsman in Japan with a wooden oar.*

He enjoyed the walk as much as he could. The night air had a crispness that reminded him of his teenaged early morning runs as an aspiring boxer.

He thought he could see ghost-like silhouettes in the fragmented windows but did not stop to check if they were illusionary. Thoughts rose in his head—*If you die now, those children will perish, along with thousands of men and women manipulated into fighting.* He countered the fear the thought induced with '*do your best not to die*'.

He could now see the wall he had been told to stop outside. The graffiti emblazoned on it was one of Putin eating the yellow and blue striped Ukraine like it was a bag of crisps, with the Kremlin in the background. He could not work out if it was meant to depict Russian superiority or anti-Russian imperialism.

He stood in front of it, and after a moment, a voice of accented English cut through the night breeze. "Are you lost?"

He answered with the challenge response. "I am exactly where I need to be."

A man stepped out of the darkness to Connor's right. Nothing in his hands, short, slight, dark-haired—*magnificent moustache.*

"My name is Yuri Kozlov. In this part of the world, I am your father now."

"Knowing my mother, you might be anyway."

Yuri smiled. "He told me you have wit, even in grave circumstances."

"Humour in the face of adversity."

Yuri nodded. "I like that."

"I take it we shouldn't stand on ceremony like this?"

"No. I will drive you to the safehouse. A man will take your car and burn it."

"Alright."

"Do you smoke?" asked Yuri, taking out a packet and using a match to light up.

"No, thank you."

"You used to though."

"How did you know."

"Your eyes when I offered."

Connor smiled. "Well observed."

"Can I ask. Why are you here?"

Connor looked at him and shrugged. "It's my job."

"No. Bruce would never force someone to work for him, not really—I have known him many years. And you—I know a little. You do not need this line of work for the adventure and money, you can get that in other ways. So I ask again, why are you here?"

"The truth sounds a little cliché, but I want the world to be a little better because I am in it."

"If you were to die now, would that be true?"

Connor felt his nervous system jolt. He searched the older man's face for any inference of his imminent death but could not see any. The question itself caught him off guard—this was his first time thinking about it. He quickly weighed his major sins against his significant good deeds.

"I think it would be."

"What about your friend up in the car there?"

"How would I know?"

"You know who she is, yes?"

"I've heard the stories."

"Me too, my friend, but I once doubted she ever existed. Maybe the stories are myths—propaganda."

Connor smiled. "They are true. I have seen her in action. She is capable of everything you have heard."

"If that is true, I cannot take her in with us. I asked you earlier, why are you here. Now I ask you, why is she here?"

So this is why you wanted me to come alone.

"This psychopath is murdering Tatar children. I should imagine she would like that to stop."

"Maybe. There is a difference between wanting to save those children and killing those responsible. Once upon a time, so the story goes, she led an assault on Russian soldiers in Chechnya. It was five floored apartment and circle steps," said Yuri indicating with his finger spiralling steps. "As her and 'comrades'—maybe not those words—brothers in arms assaulted this building, her fellow soldiers occupied various rooms to search the enemy dead and she continued to the top floor. They had not planned on the Russian reinforcements arriving so quickly. Many of the Chechens were killed but many were captured. She survived, acting as a frightened cleaner woman of the apartment—very famous story."

The cigarette shone on Yuri's face like a beacon as he inhaled, before continuing. "The Russians threw all the Chechen prisoners of war into a single room. Then they made a mistake—they all, after seeing their friends dead or wounded in this apartment, took turns to beat the Chechen prisoners. Your friend kills the single Russian watching over her, this tiny woman, took three of his grenades and walked to the door of the room all the Russians soldiers, and the surviving members of her team were in. Everyone in that room died that day. Most were shredded by the grenades. The rest were executed by pistol to their heads, including the Chechens."

Connor instinctively knew it was the truth.

"She made a tactical decision under hard circumstances," he answered, though the words felt hollow.

Yuri took another drag of his cigarette. "Is that the decision you would have made?"

"I don't know the circumstances."

"Very diplomatic—very English of you."

Connor smiled. "I am not English; I am from Yorkshire."

"What you say?"

"Nothing," he said. "Be that as it may, if I go with you, she's coming with me. I haven't come this far with her just to ditch her on the advice of a stranger."

"A sense of loyalty is a strange thing, my friend. It can be the making of a man or his downfall."

50

Tom's smile mirrored his Aunt Jenny's upon her opening the door.

"Here now, Thomas, what brings this surprise?"

Tom thought Jennifer Ryder—now approaching fifty—to be the best-looking of all his aunts, with maybe the possible exception of Connor's mum, Rebecca. Her chestnut brown hair cascaded over the shoulders, and Tom thought the traces of crow feet at the corners of her brown eyes when she smiled made them all the more charming.

"A proper breakfast for once?"

The crow's feet appeared. "You came to the right place, chuck."

Tom had not been to his Uncle Derek's and Aunt Jenny's house for a long time.

"If I knew this was here, I'd have come here instead of the cinema," he said, gesturing to the huge television.

"He spends more time in front of that thing than he does in our bed—although he's making up for it now," she sighed, tilting her head to the ceiling.

Tom frowned. "He's still in bed? It's quarter to ten?"

"You're lucky to see him before eleven nowadays."

"How long has this been going on?"

"A while now, although he's had a cob on for these last few weeks."

They made the usual chit-chat, quickly skimming over the well-being of each member of the Ryder family. As she put his plate in front of him, she asked, "And how is your sister?

"Michelle's fine. She's the manager now of the animal rescue centre down East Ardsley."

"She's a good egg, as is your mum. How is Cathy coping after what happened to your dad?"

"She's not happy. She knows what he is, but I think he's led a bit of a charmed life in this business so she wasn't expecting it. Could have had a custodial sentence all those years back if it hadn't been for uncle Greg."

He saw a melancholic smile pass over her face before sipping her mug of tea.

"Speaking of Greg. How is my rogue of a nephew?"

"He's away at the moment on business."

"I see. Like that is it, hush-hush."

"The truth is it's hush from me too. It's weird, I told him he's like the whitest sheep in the family who paints himself black."

She smiled. "What did he say to that?"

"Said it was like being a 'reverse Michael Jackson' or something."

"He and his father were a bit different. Greg could have a joke, but he was a bit more reserved than Connor. But you can tell Connor is his father's son," she said. He caught that look again.

The stairs creaked under what Tom knew to be his uncle's weight. Before he had even appeared half way down the stairs, Tom mentally projected himself into the past, where he had looked upon his uncle with love and frustration—not as a potential enemy.

Surprise splashed on Derek's face. His eyes darted around before he said. "Ehyup, weren't expecting you today. How long have you been here for?"

"About three-quarters of an hour."

"Why didn't you wake me, Jen?" His tone was abrupt.

"What? For you to be even more grumpy than you are now?"

Derek ignored her. "What brings you here, lad?"

"Can't I visit my favourite auntie?"

A ghost of a sneer flashed on Derek's face. "Bet you say that to all your aunties."

"I don't."

"How's your old man?"

"He's getting better. But when I get to the bottom of whoever had him attacked, they'll be worse."

Why have not you fucking visited him yourself? — thought Tom.

Derek walked over to the tea pot, weighed it in his hand before pouring himself a cup.

"Remember," he said, "we have to talk with one another at all times. Can't have the left hand not knowing what the right is doing."

"I know. That's why I am here."

Jennifer spoke. "I am going to get ready. Don't go without saying bye," she said, kissing Tom on the cheek. She walked past Derek.

"On the rag again," he muttered. "What's going on?"

"Been trying to get a bead on this Barry Sherman. You have any luck?"

Derek shook his head. "No. Besides, I think I know who it was."

"Who?" asked Tom, surprised his uncle was going to scapegoat a specific person.

"Zain Aziz."

It took Tom a few moments to free himself from the paralysis of astonishment. He thought his uncle might attempt to pin it on a gangster upstart or a mid-level player. But Zain Aziz was Bradford's 'Godfather', and because of the cultural proportions of that city, his reach was not only global but deep in other areas. Tom assessed—*maybe he is painting him as the target to put the frighteners on me to make me stop going after it.*

"Greg once told me if there was one person in the world outside the family I could trust, it was this guy."

"Ye', an' looked what happened to 'im."

"What you trying to say? Zain Aziz ordered uncle Greg's murder?"

"Put it this way—if Greg and Zain were so close in the nick, why didn't he help us turn the north of England upside down looking for his killers? You ask anyone. He just stayed quiet."

Tom's brain buzzed— *Maybe that is what Sherman meant by 'check closer to home'. Maybe I have been wrong all along.*

"Why would he have done?"

"Who knows? Greg had a lot of business interests that side of the airport, things probably we don't even know about—but Zain never reached out to me to continue them."

That did seem strange to Tom. There was something he held back from telling Derek. He had visited his uncle's grave not long afterwards. And he had seen the powerful Zain Aziz standing over it, appearing to murmur something. Tom had respectfully taken a walk, and when he had returned, Zain had disappeared.

Derek interrupted his thoughts. "As soon as you or I have the proof, we'll act."

"That's a war that could destroy us."

"Not necessarily. There're people in Bradford who would love that throne. And they'd love to work with us too."

Tom looked at his uncle, disconcerted. He now felt less sure of what was going on than when he first arrived.

As Connor looked over the rolling fields, he found it surreal to compute that he now stood in one of the most dangerous places on earth. The frost on the grass twinkled on the grass, and his breath plumed out.

He heard the steps behind him.

"When was the last time you smoked, my friend?" said Yuri. "It's nice to contemplate such a view with the company of nicotine-filled smoke."

"I had a cigar not long back. You're right, but I don't need the reminder of phlegm in my throat for hours afterwards."

"Ah, so that's the reason—not your health?"

"Well, my health too. I mean, according to Bruce you're my age, but you look fucked."

Yuri looked at him for a moment before laughing uproariously. "I can still fuck better than you, boy." Connor smiled and Yuri continued. "Speaking of which, Bruce tells me there is a British woman being held by this madman—a woman you're close to?"

"Wow. He must like you to spout off about things like that."

Yuri chortled. "We go back a long way. A few years after I met your mother."

"Touché." Connor smirked. "What was he like back then?"

"He was more…ahem…soldier-like, he took orders and executed them. He believed in queen and country more. Apart from that, he was the same, he'd die for his friends or to protect good people, and he is ruthless with enemies. Back then, it was his country, now it's who he decides is an enemy."

Connor allowed himself his curiosity. "You know, he seems to have resources beyond what he should have or ways and means that I can't work out."

Yuri smiled. "It is a strategy, and making the right friends over a long time. Friends like me, and friends like you. He might like you and me as people, I do not know, but make no mistake, if he didn't have good use for us, we would not know him."

Connor knew this to be true.

"Can I ask you when he became more a protector of the people than the realm so to speak?"

"Are you ready for this story?"

"I am ready."

"I was for the longest time a member of the Partisanen der Nato—Partisans of Nato. We used to help run western agents behind the Iron Curtain, and they in turn stashed weapon caches in the event of Russian aggression. Then the Berlin Wall comes down, and Russia becomes the fucking wild west. A Russian dissident group stole several 'suitcase' nuclear weapons, and Bruce—despite pressures and completely unsanctioned by your government— recovered them all with my help."

"I don't understand, why wouldn't the UK government want to recover nukes?"

Yuri laughed like it was a private joke. "Because let us imagine a dirty bomb from Russia had been released in Ukraine. The West—particularly Great Britain and the United States—would get to choke the then feeble giant to death with sanctions, maybe just the sanctions, and in doing so would gain enormous appreciation in my country. Gratitude leads to friendliness and voila, the West has an ally right on Russia's doorstep."

"You're saying the UK government dragged its feet for that reason?"

"I do not know for sure, but although these Russians were led by a man who would go on to be one of the biggest crime lords in Russia and Europe, at that time they were small-time—you English would say 'chancers'. How were they able to steal a piece of a nuclear arsenal? Yes, Russia was in disarray but still. Maybe they had help?"

Less and less surprised Connor as time had gone on, but this sounded a little far-fetched. "You're saying my government aided some lunatic Russians in stealing some of their own country's nuclear weapons to explode them in false flag operations?"

"I'll probably never know. I think Bruce might, but he never tells people anything they do not need to know. I think that was the time he decided no government could be trusted—so he played a masterful game."

Connor thought for a moment. "You mentioned the leader of this group going on to become a crime lord. What was his name?"

"Well, you know that."

"I don't, or I wouldn't have asked. I don't do cryptic unless I have to."

"What I meant was that you know who he is—or was. His name was Ravil Yelchin."

Less than three years ago, Yelchin's Russian Bratva had begun the task of controlling the UK underworld with the aid of the then MI5 chief. Knowing Bruce to be their main obstacle and a reservoir of valuable intelligence, they had succeeded in kidnapping him for interrogation. It had been Connor—still not even an agent then—Jaime, an American hitman and some fantastic luck that had got him back and thwarted the scheme.

Yuri smiled at him. "I can tell you are surprised he didn't tell you. Do not take it personally, he's very 'need to know', it's a security thing."

Connor smarted a little—*Get over yourself.*

"What was the fallout regarding that? I mean, I take it certain people were very pissed off with him."

"They never knew. He made sure I received all the credit, and for that, the Ukrainian Government made me an energy consultant. I am now a millionaire of many times over, thanks to him."

Connor looked him up and down. "It's true what they say—can't buy a sense of style."

Yuri laughed again. "I am in disguise. But you have the same gift he has—the ability to make the right allies. And you will need allies for this life. Ones only known to yourself, for when the time comes. Which reminds me, Bruce asked me to get you one of these."

With that, Yuri handed him a Fairbairn Sykes commando dagger—a carbon copy of the one he gave Ciara.

Connor smiled as he took it, before staring across the landscape.

Bruce perched himself on the small table. Across from him was Kutz, shackled to a chair by one wrist. He was staring impassively, presumably at a fixed point on the wall.

Two of Yuri's men sat behind him.

By the look of passivity on the Ukrainian's face, Bruce had expected a strategy of complete unresponsiveness to questioning, so it was a surprise to see Kutz's wide grin,

"You will not break me in time. If I do not get back, protocols will be initiated. No amount of pain will break me in the time you have left."

Bruce nodded. "Sounds familiar, and you're a tough man, I know, Viktor. Physically—despite your performance against the woman—and mentally, as a testament to your eighteen-month stint on the child protection task force. I know that was a pivotal role in your career; ten years ago now. The heinous nature of the images, the perpetrators and most of all the victims, I can't imagine. You're a very mentally tough man, Viktor. And I believe you when you tell me you have certain provisions in place—it's the sign of a forward-thinking man, and no one gets to your position without being forward thinking."

The barest expression of bemusement appeared and died on Viktor's face in the same instant.

Bruce continued. "And the knowledge most of those monsters are now roaming free. You remember a time back in the nineties when these beasts would have been executed, before Ukraine became weak."

Kutz nodded. "It was a mistake to abolish the death penalty. These animals cannot be cured."

“As much as I believe in the rehabilitation model, I think I have to agree with you there. However, Bohdan Chmara—child rapist—now works as a bartender in Kiev. Eugene Svetin, another rapist, lives in Hora. Vasily—in fact, pass him the list,” ordered Bruce to the man on Kutz’s left.

The man duly handed Kutz a list with a clipboard back. On it, Bruce knew there to be several paedophiles recognisable to the former policeman. Along with the names were various details, including their addresses.

After a few moments, Kutz looked up. “Where did you get this?”

“I am resourceful.”

“What does all this mean? Get to the point.”

Bruce nodded and gestured to the man on the right, who took out a phone, thumbed it and passed it to Kutz.

The light of the screen lit Kutz’s horrified face.

“You must have your men pick up your daughter from school often because, as you can see, she got straight into the van. Then again, most seven-year-olds are trusting, especially when the stranger is a woman. Now she is on her way to the address of one of the ‘animals’ on this list. The lady whose car she is in, will feign a family emergency and ask if they could look after Dasha for a few hours, or maybe until tomorrow. I am not sure if she’s already been dropped off or is about to. I can clear my conscience knowing as soon as you finish telling me what I need to know, I can stop it, or have her ‘rescued’. I don’t know how long it would take for this monster to begin assaulting her— you never know, he might not at all—but suffice to say the longer you leave it, the more time his resolve will erode. So your daughter’s innocence is now in your hands.”

“You’re lying. No way would you do that.”

“It’s not me doing it—her fate is entirely in your hands. Not nice when it is your children, Viktor.”

“Fuck,” he screamed.

"Breathe, and try not to think of his invasive fingers."

"I am going to fucking kill you."

"Not before you either tell me what I need to know, or your daughter is raped and probably killed. The beauty of this is the longer you take in telling me, the greater the chance it is both."

"For the love of God, stop this and I'll tell you everything."

"No, Viktor. You tell me everything and I'll stop this. And Viktor," said Bruce, who waited for their eyes to meet before continuing, "I will ask you some questions I already know the answers to. For every untruth you tell me, I will increase the time she stays by thirty minutes, no negotiation."

"Please, what do you want to know?"

51

Connor stood outside the landing and gently knocked on the door.

"Yes," answered Roza.

"It's me. Are you decent?"

The door opened to reveal a dressed Roza. "Decent?"

"I mean are you dressed. Can I come in?"

She stepped back and allowed him in. There was a towel laid perfectly on the floor, and Connor realised it was a makeshift prayer mat. A candle flickered on the bedside cabinet from the kisses of air let in by the ajar bedside window. The matchbox bed lay like a coffin beneath it.

He spoke quietly. "They think they've found the location, but they are gleaning as much information as they can. Then a plan will be made."

"You know location but not trust me."

"Would you in my shoes—or sandals?"

Grace stood in the corridor outside her 'office' watching the hive of activity around her. The guards now wore body armour, and there were more of them.

After the shooting, Grace thought her movements would be more hindered. Vitali must have guessed—correctly—she would not risk putting the children in danger. She was trapped into submission by her conscience.

She longed to have a conversation with someone.

What had broken her heart was the demeanour of Ayesha. Grace had always made a point of giving her surreptitious winks, smiles and once even sticking her tongue out. She had always been rewarded with a smile or a wink back, and it had made her heart soar—like a flicker of light in the darkness.

Ever since Ayesha's roommate's shooting, she had kept her head down or averted. It had wrenched at Grace to see her spirit broken—she did not even seem afraid anymore, just defeated.

Grace almost envied the state of resignation—it meant hope did not tear at your soul. And yet, she did not know what she was hoping for; she had no military experience, but common sense told her to overcome this many armed guards would require overwhelming force and firepower—and that would mean the children caught amidst it.

She remembered Connor had once told her James Bond-types did not exist. She'd had ridiculous dreams it would be Connor who would come to save her. She would wake, berating herself for believing it. He was a former Royal Marine, and a gangster, but no more than that. Besides, it was doubtful he even knew she had been kidnapped, let alone where she was.

Sometimes at night, she would escape into the happy scenes of her past, and it surprised her how many featured him. She knew she was tormenting herself.

Yesterday, Vitali had shown her a laptop, typed in 'Kidnapped aid worker + nurse + Ukraine' into the Google search engine, and nothing— her disappearance had not even made the news. There was not the façade this was a school anymore. The children were still taught, but even with the language barrier Grace could tell it was propaganda. That almost provided her with hope—why would they teach the children if they wanted to kill them all?

But there was something about to happen, and she dreaded to know what.

Xander stood on the wooden flooring surrounding the hut, amid the wilderness outside the city of Antratsyt. The rare combination of the 'moon illusion' making the red 'hunter's moon' appear larger than it was, transfixed Xander as nervous energy warmed him.

He had arrived a few hours earlier to await the arrival of his Povernuto soldiers.

The last contact he had with Viktor had been an envelope held for him in a Kiev post office vault—Vitali's location, satellite pictures, and a full intelligence report.

Viktor had not attempted to contact him since he had sent Ciara, which disturbed him. As dangerous as the woman might be, he found it hard to believe she could have fought her way out. Still, whatever happened would not change the course of his people's destiny. A calling he had become aware of months before; to destroy the Russian state once and for all.

He had needed allies, and he saw the opportunity in Vitali Agron, the brave, charismatic and now unhinged special forces officer. In the months after Vitali's rescue escape, Xander and Kutz had stoked and redirected his patriotism, hate for the Russians and thirst for revenge.

Xander had founded the Povernuto a few years ago, and his legend had grown with his anti-Russian exploits. He had recruited the loyal Artem, and the 'investigation' into who was taking the children had been partly for his benefit—he would inform the rest of the Povernuto of Xander's effort, thus ensuring a smokescreen.

Xander felt nearly as much of an aversion to a camera phone being pointed at him, as he did firearms. His fighting on the Russian separatist side against the Ukrainian Government forces and nationalist militia might not be understood amongst his Tatar brethren, no matter what explanations of the greater good he gave.

Cultivating Roza as a friend had been a masterstroke. Her legend preceeded her and she hated Russians more than even he did—which had blinded her.

When the time came, it would be Xander leading Allah's offensive against Russia. Unlike the Mujahedeen, who defended their homeland, his Povernuto would invade the enemy's. He had always known to cripple Putin's Russia would not only involve asymmetric warfare but had to be fought on multiple levels—the daggers stabbing in from all directions like the assassination of Caesar. He would draw Saudi wealth and the experience of ISIS, all the while heaping international condemnation upon Russia.

Weeks ago, he had told the members of the Povernuto to cease communication with one another until this night, when a chosen few of his most reliable and best soldiers would meet him.

First, he had to stop this savage murdering of his people's children.

When the distant vehicle lights panned across his face, he knew the time had come.

Connor and Roza sat opposite Yuri, having finished eating.

"Killing Agron's force isn't the issue, not really," said Connor. "It's getting those children out alive."

"I agree," answered Yuri. "What is the plan?"

"Our mutual friend broke Kutz. This has been years in the making. It was Kutz's brainchild, with Vitali and to some extent the CIA being puppet."

"What's the end goal?"

"He was going to have Xander tell his Povernuto Vitali was turned by the FSB while in their captivity—that narrative is to be spun to the whole world. He'll take some of his hardcore Povernuto soldiers there to martyr themselves in the attempt of rescuing these children. Grace Templeton will be used to draw the ire of the UK and international community.

Then the Povernuto and Islamic allies will begin attacking Russian targets in Crimea. The international community will impose massive sanctions. Russia will have to become China's bitch to survive economically."

"And what are our actions?"

Connor smiled. "Kutz will get word to Agron that Ciara is there to facilitate the release of the British national for an extortionate fee. Once she's in, she could provide intelligence."

"Could, not will?" said Yuri.

"We haven't the time to fuck around. I agree it's not ideal, but the skirmishes have already begun between the Povernuto and Russian forces in Crimea. If we don't act now, we won't be able to rein it in."

"How will she communicate? And how do you know they will not frisk her?"

"They certainly will frisk her. But unless they make her strip naked, the device will remain concealed."

"Where are we all going to be?"

"I'll get the maps out, but your team will be located around a quarter of a mile away."

"My team? Where will you be?"

"In the forestry close by, with Roza."

Incredulity passed over Yuri's face before he began laughing. "You two are going to storm the compound by yourselves?"

"No. We have to secure the children's safety before you and your team storm the compound. Then it's a mission by Ukrainian forces. At least, that's how it'll read in the media over the following weeks and months."

"This is ridiculous. They'll overwhelm you with numbers alone."

"They won't. There'll be a small window when the compound is manned by a skeleton crew of eight. Vitali has no reason not to believe Kutz. He'll tell him of an impending attack by Russian forces from the south side of the forestry. Roza, Ciara and I, might be able to extract the children without unnecessary bloodshed."

"Let me be sure of the plan before you go into details. Ciara is going to be inserted into the compound on the word of Kutz. Then Kutz will call, alerting Agron to a Russian assault on the south. When he deploys his men, the three of you are going to extract these children, without alerting this skeleton crew left, and—"

"We will have suppressors and knives."

"Oh. That's truly wonderful," smiled Yuri. "Will there be silencers on their weapons?"

"The idea is to neutralise them before they draw their weapons."

"Yes. Will Batman be helping you?"

"No. I think he tends to stick to the Gotham area."

"You seem remarkably calm given what you're up against."

"Yuri, I fully grasp the stakes and the difficulty of the situation. And I don't do false bravado. But not trying isn't an option for me. I can't think of a better plan of attack to get those children out. Now I'll take on board any ideas you have, but what I won't do is let fear consume me."

Yuri's nod was subtle. "I can see why he likes you."

52

The seventeen flint-eyed Tatars stared at their leader within the cabin. Xander had expected them to reach him without incident but remained impressed nonetheless.

"My brothers, the time has come," addressing them in Tatar. "Thank you for making the journey despite the last moment change of location. It was necessary—I have finally located the children."

They stirred in unison.

"I had to decide which men to take with me. Too many and you may have been discovered on your way here. And given what these demons are capable of, I couldn't take the risk of them being alerted."

"When are we embarking on this, leader?" said Beyti Pusat, one of the more notorious members.

"I have a detailed plan. Before I reveal it, I will tell you we will be outnumbered by well-trained, heavily armed men. In order to rescue these souls we must be willing to sacrifice ours. Allah may smile upon us, and we might not lose a single man. But the odds are against it. If the burden of responsibility is unbearable for anyone of you, leave now. Nothing more will ever be said. Not all men are warriors. Indeed some men who aren't may even be more of service to the cause in other capacities. But I need to know now exactly how many I am taking with me."

Not one flinched.

It was in times like these Tom wished Connor was with him. In this part of Dewsbury, his complexion made him *stick out like a eunuch on a nudist beach,* as he would say. His cousin could understand and speak the language. Though not as overt as it had been a few years ago, Tom still felt an undercurrent of hostility as he pretended not to notice the stares. He had deliberately taken an old banger down, as he'd have to leave it on its own.

He was here to see Dev Bhaskar. Tom felt a wave of guilt he had not done this before—sought out answers to his uncle's death. Until recently, he had accepted the vague narrative his uncle was killed by two British-Asians who hopped on a flight back to Pakistan immediately afterwards. His uncle Derek claimed he got the information from a bent copper in the West Yorkshire police who claimed a lack of evidence for prosecution. Now Derek was making out Zain Aziz had ordered it.

Tom remembered his uncle Greg once admonishing him as a teenager for a racist remark he had made.

Greg told him, he was never touched or even threatened inside Armley. He said at the time he assumed it was due to the reputation of his defeating and mutilating the men responsible for his dad Frank's attack and Derek's shooting. It had only been months after his release he discovered it was because his cellmate Zain Aziz had put the word out protecting him.

Tom knew one of the factors that made Greg's reign smoother and more prosperous than Derek's had been his ability to form relationships with various characters, in the underworld and beyond. That Greg had a good grasp of the language endeared him to the British-Asian underworld he had chosen to deal with from time to time, and his boxing to the Gypsies. When Connor went into the Marines, Greg began spending more time with Tom, showing him certain aspects of 'the business'.

One of the aspects was Greg had at times used the Hawala system for moving money. An informal money transfer system built on performance and honour, Greg had used a few Hawaladars so they would compete for his business.

Most had been in Bradford, but Tom could not go to them for the information he was seeking, as it would be certain Aziz would find out.

So he would come here to meet with Dev Bhaskar, a hugely respected Hawaladar who ran his business out of a vaping shop. The store was in the heart of the Dewsbury Asian community, and Tom fought to keep the balance of appearing confident without being hostile. He walked into the shop with a chime.

A man to his right, in his early twenties stood straight like a meerkat. A man around fifty sat reading a newspaper, a little greyer, a bit chunkier than the last time Tom had seen him. Before Tom could explain who he was, Dev Bhaskar exclaimed, "Thomas Ryder, look at you. All grown up. Wait, how did you get here? Taxi?"

"No. Car."

Bhaskar barked at the younger man in Punjabi, who quickly brushed passed Tom exiting the shop.

"He's warning anyone off your car."

"I appreciate it. Brought an old banger down, but didn't fancy catching the bus home."

"You must've been a teenager when I last saw you, init? When this was a corner shop?"

"Maybe just, nineteen or so. I've come to give you back that Mars bar." He smiled.

Bhaskar laughed. "I don't think I have seen you since Greg died 'av I?"

"No, I don't think so."

"A tragedy."

"It's what I came here to discuss with you."

Tom saw Bhaskar's eyes narrow, so he added, "I don't suspect your hand in it."

"Of course you don't. Aside from respect for the man, he put a lot of money my way over the years. That stopped after his passing. Maybe you could tell me why?"

Tom did not anticipate the question and said, "It wasn't on my call."

"I know." Bhaskar smiled. "What did you want to ask me?"

"I am still hazy with what happened to my uncle. The killer or killers were never found and all I have to go on are rumours."

"Which rumour did you believe?"

Tom shrugged. "Two unknown Asians were hired to murder him by an unknown. They fucked off back to Pakistan with a lot of money for it. Lost in the haze over there."

Bhaskar smiled. "What motivation would anyone have to off your uncle Greg?"

"To take over our trade and other business interests?"

"And did anyone do that?"

"Well, not really. We began having to pay out more to other players over the years, but I don't suppose anyone aggressively tried to take anything from us."

"Right, why didn't this mysterious individual follow through? As you say, there was no war in the aftermath."

"You know how Zain Aziz and my uncle met?"

"In Armley. Aziz must have liked—no loved—your uncle, because I know there was some seriously pissed off people in our community when Aziz introduced him to our, let's say, monetary system."

"Could those people have done Greg in?"

"Nah, that calmed when the money came in. Besides, you don't run all the naughtiness out of Bradford without being smart and terrifying. It's a different kettle in'it, some of these lads have been trained over in Pakistan. What I am trying to say is, crossing Zain Aziz has always meant death."

"That's what I can't understand. If two Asians did off my uncle, then he'd know about it, or at least ripped Bradford up trying to find out."

Bhaskar reached over and touched Tom's forearm. "If this was a courtroom I couldn't ask you leading questions, but because it ain't, you have to ask yourself 'who benefitted from Greg's murder?' You'll find your answer, ya get me."

The words punched a hollowness of confirmation into Tom's diaphragm.

Ciara kept track of how much time had passed since she had been blindfolded. She allowed her fear to show—she was meant to be a civilian bringing in terms of release; it was not difficult, as an air of icy vulnerability swirled around her.

The journey to Horlivka had taken ten hours, with a stop-over halfway, in which she and her escort slept in the vehicle. Her escort hardly spoke.

She was aware of the real possibility she could be walking into a trap. Xander was still on the loose, and there was no way of knowing if he had had communication with Agron.

She had been handed over in Horlivka and put into the back seat of a Land Rover. The fact they had not secured her wrists had been a good omen—if they knew how dangerous she was they would have.

She estimated two and a half hours had since gone by, and with the way she was rocked about, guessed they were on a road less well-maintained, if on one at all.

She began her diaphragmatic breathing; she could not afford to have her adrenaline zapping her energy.

Finally, the Land Rover stopped, her door opened and the blindfold was removed.

"Miss Robson, do come," said the burly driver.

She exaggerated the surprise she felt. The sprawling 'school' looked more like a huge manor stretched sideways. In the dimming light, the forestry looked more like an encircling army of green.

A bald, bearded man stood illuminated by the lights of the entry. With his hands clasped behind his back, it had seemed like his body wanted to burst from the suit he wore. She thought he might have once been handsome before the cruelty settled on his face.

His eyes were appraising without being threatening.

As she reached him, his bear-like left hand appeared, and she shook it despite herself.

"Miss Robson, I think you a television journalist, not newspaper one with no picture to find."

His tone was not flirtatious—more inquiring — his English a little stilted but clear.

"I did not want the way I look to get in the way of what I have to…ahem…impart."

Vitali lifted his jaw. "Rare in English-speaking countries today."

"Perhaps."

"I surprised your government would send journalist—a woman journalist—to me."

"Certain people did not think you would react well to a man, or someone who was not a civilian, coming here."

"Is that what you are?"

"A man? Not for a while now."

Vitali smirked. "You like to interview me?"

"I hadn't planned on it. My brief was to offer you the UK government's terms for the release of Miss Templeton. Besides, I didn't think you would agree to an interview—western media is often seen as propaganda in these parts of the world."

Vitali smiled. "Now we have internet—our phones can video and tape interview."

"You want an interview and for it to be recorded?"

"I want my cause recognised."

"I am sorry, Mr Agron, but I was led to believe you are a kidnapper of children, and there are some other frankly heinous rumours. If this is true, I do not see how this could benefit your cause."

"That is offer to you."

"What about the British national you have in your possession?"

"We can discuss, of course."

A raindrop fell on her cheek. "Of course."

"Let's go inside."

53

Connor hated being caught out in the rain. In the Royal Marines, the term for 'to quit' was 'to wrap'—and cold British rain was thus known as 'wrap juice'. He had a flashback to being laid in an exercise ambush serial on a training area in the north of England named Otterburn. With the rain splattering down the back of his neck, Connor had seethed listening to the enthusiastic young officer on the radio net repeatedly fuck up bringing the enemy detail down on the correct track.

In this scenario, he realised the shower was a blessing. It helped to disguise any sounds that might reach the ears of any wandering sentries in the forestry. The caveat being you couldn't hear a potential enemy either.

Roza and Connor were both armed with the Russian made AS Val, which fired a suppressed 9x 39MM round, either single shot or automatic. Yuri had allowed them both to test fire the weapons. Connor had been impressed that the sound had been reduced almost solely to the clacks of the hammer.

They kept a twenty-metre spacing, her face layered in *cam cream,* as was his. In the military, he had applied it as sparingly as he dared, knowing it to be a nightmare to remove afterwards.

In the brief, he had expressed how important it was to try to avoid alerting or killing any of the guards, as an alarm would be raised when the dead failed to check in.

They rehearsed the best they could, including the appropriate hand signals.

Now, they covered and manoeuvred slowly through the forestry, ensuring neither were moving at the same time.

The adrenaline pooled low in his gut, at the optimal level—just enough to keep him alert, and not too high as to drain him. He anticipated cutting through the forest with the stealth required would take about an hour to the entry point.

He took up a crouch behind a tree, scanning and searching over the top of the sights. He felt the bottom of his webbing rest against his upturned heel. He had always preferred belt webbing to a chest rig, even with urban combat.

Though he had both training and operational experience in *FIWAF* with the Corps, McQuillan had sent him on an intensive month-long course with Finnish special forces. It did not take long for him to discover how, during the hundred-and-five-day winter war from 1939 to 1940, the Finns claimed—by some estimates—five Soviet lives for every one of theirs.

Roza moved wraith-like behind another tree fifteen metres forward and to the right of him. She adopted a similar crouch and Connor glided forward, sweeping his feet from the inside out to clear his path from anything that might audibly snap underfoot.

His eyes caught a movement, and he snapped his fist up to freeze Roza. He counted the silhouettes, turned to Roza, gave her the thumbs down, stuck up four fingers and chopped his hand to the twelve o'clock of his position—*enemy, four of them, that direction.*

Ciara walked in marvel. From the outside, with its stately home appearance, it looked so out of place nestled inside a huge forest in eastern Ukraine. She had expected a state of dilapidation inside. Instead, it had an almost aristocratic air throughout.

"Who's that," she asked, gesturing to a portrait of a woman with a sniper rifle. Ciara guessed her to be a World War Two heroine.

"She only Russian I allow on wall. Her name is Lyudmila Pavlichenko."

Hearing the name triggered Ciara's memory. "Red Army sniper with over three-hundred kills."

"Yes."

"Well, I am surprised. She fought for the Russians against Germany's Nationalist Socialist German Worker's Party. Are you not a nationalist?"

"You compare me to Nazi?"

"I am asking questions. That's what journalists do."

"Nazi Germany wanted conquer world. I want my country free."

"At any cost?"

"Some great things cost a lot."

"I agree. Money, hard work, sacrifice—not sure if anything is worth the lives of innocent children," she said, shackling the venom attempting to rise to her voice.

"You English make me smile. How many children die from Dresden bombing? More casualties than Hiroshima and Nagasaki together."

"Firstly, as a journalist, I must inform you the city authorities at the time and in a new study back in twenty-ten suggests the death toll to be more around the twenty-five thousand mark. As an adult woman, I find your 'yeah but what about them' riposte to be at least juvenile."

"I make point, no one escapes horrors of war."

"Collateral damage is one thing. Actively kidnapping children and executing them is another."

"I thought your job as a journalist was to ask questions."

"You're right," she said. "So tell me, what was your reason for taking part in the Orange Revolution back in 2004? A bold move for one in the military."

"Viktor Yanukovych won a rigged election. He is Putin's puppet with no honour. We the people got the result overturned. Yuschenko was elected democratically and they try and poison him," he answered before hovering his palm over his face. "Make disfigurement of him."

Ciara nodded. "But in 2010, Viktor Yanukovych became president, which heralded four years of obscene and blatant thievery from the national coffers. Why no protest from you then?"

"A rat can attack a snake better from inside the snake's belly."

It clicked into place. "That's when the CIA approached you."

He shook his head. "That is when Viktor Kutz approached me for them."

"Then what?"

"I become Yanukovych security chief for a short time. That is when I saw how much he stole from his own country."

Ciara had seen too. She had taken the tour around Yanukovych's private residency not long after he fled to Russia. She had gotten a look at the opulence in which the president had lived; a piano worth around 90,000 euros, the extensive car and motorbike collection including the old style 'gangster' cars, a Faberge egg, gold monogrammed golf clubs, a private cinema with 3D glasses on hand, and a lakeside hot tub. Also a private zoo, golf course and helicopter landing pad aside an aircraft hangar. All this and more.

As if reading her mind, he said, "You and the other tourists pose for pictures at his home. My people were starving where I came from and Yanukovych lived like this, and fled like dog when curtains come down."

The ember glowed in her mind again. "But Yanukovych isn't your target—the Russians are. Tell me, what happened to send you so cruel, so…evil?"

"What happened to me is not important."

"Alright," said Ciara. "So all this is all for the greater good?"

Agron gave a nod. "Empires not toppled by other empires; they are defeated by the people who pay price. If price is killing some Tatar Muslim children, I will pay it.

Sacrifice is what the Bible is all about. Except, it will be the Russians who feel the backlash."

Ciara squeezed her fist to hide the tremor. "With that clear admittance, I guess you were never going to let me or Miss Templeton go."

Vitali smiled. "The US government would never let story of British woman murdered by Ukrainian CIA mole surface. Better story is two British women killed by Russians."

Before she could speak, one of the guards—very young looking—rushed to him, speaking rapidly. Vitali turned to her. "Urgency requires of my attention. Fedir watch you now."

Connor considered his options. Retreat was not an option now—the pace they would have to use to remain unseen would be too slow and the patrol would catch them. The bush and tree he was positioned behind would only hide him until the patrol came to a line abreast—ditto with Roza and her position—so they could not wait for them to pass either. Engaging them at distance was not feasible—their superior firepower would pin them, until the patrol manoeuvred up and killed them. His heart began to pound—*Stop panicking and start thinking.*

He looked around, then down. A rock protruded from the ground. He prised it free—the size of a half a brick.

He understood these four might be part of a larger patrol. As he observed them, it heartened him to see them remain close to one another. To a lay observer, they appeared professional; moving quietly, their eyes scanning the area, and using hand signals instead of their voices.

However, Connor knew they should be spread further apart: one, to widen their search dragnet, and secondly, so they would not all 'catch it up' if a grenade was tossed into their midst.

Though he had them, a grenade was not an option—it would alert Vitali's entire security detail in the target building. If he and Roza could strike as this teams' heads were turned, they might have a chance—small one.

The dilemma was if they caught sight of the rock in any part of its flight, he would have given away his position, signing his own death warrant. As he weighed the rock in his hand, an image of Carlos Schwabe's painting 'Elysian Fields' displayed itself in his mind. Instead of the lady with a harp, it was Grace walking with him in the flower-rich field, except they were both children—*Fucking pack it in and concentrate.*

He could hear their footsteps now. Still hidden, he slung his rifle and launched the rock in the air at the highest angle he could while still clearing over their heads. After two seconds— his weapon back in the low port—he heard it thunk off a tree. Which meant they must have heard it too.

He stepped out, steeling himself in anticipation of being shredded by a hail of bullets. Their backs were to him, facing the direction of where the rock had landed. Within two seconds, the pair to the left were punched in the back of their heads by Connor's silenced rounds, dead before their faces hit the ground.

Except, they were not the left-hand pair, they were the middle pair. He realised it as a rifle barrel peered around the tree to his left with the owner's eyes not far behind. He knew he was going to be shot, either by the guy to his left or the guy to the far right—*Fuck it, at least I can take this one with me.*

Whipping his slung rifle behind his back, his right hand dived into his left sleeve, and drew out his new commando dagger. He banged the rifle stock against the tree, pinning it in place. Swinging around, he uppercut the blade into the enemy's throat. Blood sprayed out onto Connor's face like an oil hose with a thumb partially on the end. As the dying man's knees gave way, his index finger caught the trigger, depressing it. The sound of the shots echoed over the valley floor.

Connor spun around into a crouch, expecting the fourth member of the patrol to be drawing down on him. He saw his corpse laying beyond the middle two with a shattered skull.

Roza silently appeared. "We must bring Yuri forces now."

Connor nodded. He lifted his wrist mike, but before he established comms, a familiar crescendo from the firing of multiple weapons erupted from the other side of the forest from a third of a mile away.

54

For a moment, Ciara imagined fireworks before the sound of rhythmic gunfire shattered the notion. Her heart sank—*He must be compromised.* The guard—Fedir—was sitting too far away for her to have a hope of disarming him. He looked anywhere from seventeen to twenty years of old, the beige and brown combat uniform hanging from him. McQuillan had once told her, in some war-torn parts of the world, teenagers might have participated in more combat than the average western career infantryman.

During her training, 'female intuition' had been explained and techniques instilled to enhance it. A woman's ability to read social and individual cues were generally much higher than a man's. Part of this was an evolutionary trait left over from ancient times when a woman needed to be able to read the moods of the larger, stronger males from his expressions and mannerisms, as to soothe or avoid his tempers that could result in physical harm towards her. This ability also translated to mothering of children not yet able to verbalise their wants and needs. Women, usually subconsciously, will mirror the posture and expression a person and their memory bank would send an interpretation of it.

So she studied his face as the battle raged—concealed anxiety.

"Can you speak English?"

He frowned. "I can speak. I understand it very well, more than I speak."

"This is not good for you is it."

"Why?"

"Your fellow soldiers are in a battle. If they lose, it will just be you. If they win, you will have had nothing to do with the victory."

She caught him stiffen.

"They not lose. They know I am brave soldier."

"Not the same. Every time the story of their victory is recounted, it will stab at you—knowing they only trusted you to look after a woman, probably because they can trust you not to fuck me. Virgin."

He shot her a bristling look. "I not a virgin. I am warrior. I fuck you good or I might shoot you."

She stood, and he shouted as he brandished his AK at her, "Sit down, now!"

She faced away from him. "Be known for shooting a woman in the back—pussy. Or," she said, undoing the top buttons of her jeans and struggling them down to reveal the top of her full, taut ass, "you can fuck this before we both die."

She knew one of the main culprits of unbelievably stupid actions is the young male sex drive; that and the male ego. There were a few moments of silence before she heard the scrape of the chair legs. She anticipated a hand or forearm on the back of her neck to hold her in place. She was excited—but not sexually.

She turned to look at him and saw his AK on the table and his hands reaching for her—*You silly, silly boy.*

She spun, snatched his outstretched wrist and rifled a smashing horizontal elbow strike into his jaw. Another came from underneath within a split second. He fell back, with his consciousness being expelled under her stamp.

She took stock and lingered on his AK. If she had to make a guess, she would have surmised all the fighting men in the building would be engaged in the firefight outside. However, there might be more than this guy left behind. That said, her running around with an AK would mark her instantly as a target. She looked down at the soldier, seeing little more than an unconscious teenager—*No, making a teenage mistake is shaving and painting your eyebrows on, not guarding kidnapped children to be killed. You can do this, Ciara.*

She knelt, pinning his arms, put her palm over his mouth and pinched his nose between her thumb and index fingers.

Connor's radio exchange with Yuri had taken thirty seconds. He turned to Roza. "That isn't Yuri's team under contact—I mean involved in that firefight."

Unsure of the ranges of the weapons being used in the firefight, he had ensured a tree covered him.

She said, "It is Xander."

The neurons fired in his brain. "Let's cover and move as quick to the target. John McClane it and rinse anyone who might be inside—most will now be involved in that firefight. We'll call Yuri in to transport the hostages out. Home for tea and biscuits."

"John McClane? Tea and biscuits?"

Connor ignored the questions. "Do you understand what we are doing?"

Just as he began to check his webbing pouches were fastened, Ciara's voice crackled through his ear piece.

"One Alpha, this is One Charlie, message over."

"Send."

"One enemy down. Enemy remaining in the building unknown. Location, lower floor room, south-west side. What's your ETA?"

"Three minutes."

"Roger, out."

Xander knew some would have to be sacrificed for the ruse to work. Vitali, well versed in guerrilla tactics, would not fall for what westerners termed a 'shoot and scoot'.

However, because Xander knew enough of the Ukrainian military commander's background, he could anticipate his reactions. After springing the murderous ambush of the four-man wandering patrol, Xander ordered his men to advance to contact the QRF Vitali would have on a moments' notice to move.

A sideways rain of fire chopped through the trees from a heavy calibre machine gun posted on the roof of the house. Because of his team's quick advance to the edge of the wood, they had avoided it — the thick canopy shielding them from the view of the machine gunner.

Vitali's QRF appeared from the north through the forestry.

Now Xander was caught amid a ferocious exchange of fire. Ordinarily, he would have ordered his numerically superior force to divide themselves into two and fire and manoeuvre to QRF's position, to overwhelm them.

He had something else in mind.

"Hold your position!" he screamed over the din, in case any of his men had lost sight of the plan in the whirl of the chaos.

He had drilled his men in the importance of switching their firing positions, but he could see some were failing to do so. They were not being punished for it yet, due to their greater weight of firepower. But Xander knew when Vitali's main force arrived, he would begin to take casualties. It was just a case of where they would come from.

Mercifully, the heavy machine gun ceased firing, which Xander assumed was to prevent a friendly fire incident.

He needed them to come from directly behind the QRF or he, and his force, would be martyred.

55

Ciara knew she had to gather the hostages now—they would not have much time. She decided to pick up the AK, and after an inspection of the chamber, concealed it in the jacket she had now taken off.

She looked around the door and stepped out. There had been no architectural plans from which she could memorise the schematics. The main stairs reminded her of where Jack stood waiting for Rose in a tuxedo in the film *Titanic*. She heard wails of children emanate down them.

Then heard the shouts of men.

It took a few seconds to evaluate her options—although desperate to engage the men upstairs, initiating a firefight would put the children in the crossfire. The AK was not silenced, but Connor and Roza's weapons would be—*Hurry up*.

She heard heavy boots chopping down the stairs and ducked behind a pillar just as one of the soldiers landed at the bottom the other side of it. He was so close she could hear him breathe. All she could see was his barrel pointing at the entrance.

Connor's voice whispered through her earpiece. "Breaching the main door in thirty seconds, over."

She could not reply. And if she did not respond he would come through the door into a hail of bullets.

Thirty seconds.

Her hand crept to her belt, grasping the leather tab of her dagger sheath clip. Covering it with her palm for muffling, she drew it up slowly. The click was barely audible.

Twenty seconds.

She slid painstakingly around the pillar, dagger in her right hand. He appeared, using the pillar to support his standing position.

Ten seconds.

Her left hand whipped around his mouth in the same instant the tip of the blade fired into the base of his skull, piercing the medulla oblongata—his trigger finger did not twitch.

She collapsed him to the floor as noiselessly as she could. The door slid open, and Connor and Roza appeared.

Xander smiled. He could see the main force manoeuvring up from the rear of the QRF.

He had drilled this moment into his men—rehearsing over and over.

His Tatar scream went up, "Increase fire for ten seconds!"

Several of his men echoed this command, and their weight of fire increased.

"Fall back!"

The Tatars began to pull back, not as efficiently as he would have liked, but the mechanics of fire and manoeuvre were present.

After a few bounds, the inevitable happened. He saw Zaman—one of the eldest in the group—have the top of his head blasted off like a red paint-soaked frisbee.

Xander had imprinted on his men that no casualty was to be attended to until after the battle was won. He braced himself, keeping a bound behind the rest of his men—if this rule was not adhered to, it could spell disaster. If one man tried to rescue a casualty, he most likely would become a casualty himself. If more went to retrieve both casualties, a domino effect would be set in place.

No one went back for Zaman.

Xander's heart gripped his throat when he saw Vitali's forces holding the line but not pursuing. He realised why a second before the heavy machine gun fire cascaded amongst his Tatar's positions. The bullets chopped through several of them.

"Pull back to the right!" he screamed.

In a disorganised fashion, they did so. The more trees Xander could put between his men and the sideways gale of death, the more protection it would afford them.

He could hear a dark spirit laughing at him. Half of his men now lay torn up, hit from both sides.

The superior forces began to move forward like a murderous avalanche.

Xander orientated himself. "Straight back. Straight back. Straight back!"

The tree line broke. Thirty metres of open ground.

His voice was hoarse from the battle cries. The tidal wave of their pursuers threatening to overwhelm them.

The zipping vacuum of the rounds whipped by his head.

Xander had always known they could not win a pitched battle—he did not have the numbers nor did his fighters have the soldiering ability as a unit. More were chopped down until only half a dozen remained.

At the last gasp, Xander made a note of the enemy's distance and dived behind the huge, solid tree. He counted slowly to ten as his scrabbling hands found the denotator. He resisted the urge to peek around and check their distance. Their voices were clear as day now.

He squeezed.

The boom felt like Allah had punched the earth, shaking him to his bones. Ten M18 Claymore mines, set in interlocking arcs towards the enemy, had fired simultaneously.

The vegetation floated down to meet the rising screams.

He popped his head out for a second to scan the carnage. Bodies were strewn everywhere, most still, some moving. He kept dancing his head in and out from behind the tree until he felt it safe no one was going to take a pot shot from the opposite treeline.

He bellowed, "Tatars. Not one of them escapes God's judgement tonight. Beware—three of you watch the opposite side from cover here."

He could see the euphoria of victory crawling over his men. The look died on the men's faces as their chests ripped apart. Xander stood still—they had been flanked.

He recognised the voice speaking in Ukrainian, "The man who had once freed me. Now here to destroy me. Turn around and tell me, was that the plan all along?"

Xander turned to face the hulking Vitali, surrounded by nine of his soldiers.

"You did not have to kill them—the children."

"Children who have disappeared are exactly that—disappeared. No one takes notice. But lifeless bodies are harder to ignore. A necessary evil."

Xander took a deep breath. "Was Kutz aware of it?"

"He gave me a long leash—an imaginary one."

"Did he even protest?"

"Meekly."

"What now?"

"Now my friend, you will see the cost of your failure—my contingency plan. This place is no longer secure, and I cannot take these children with me. Alive, they are witnesses. Dead, they are instrumental in our plan—to cut Russia's legs off at the knees, so it never rises to interfere or oppress our peoples again."

"Were you always a madman?"

"You will see the truth, my friend—their deaths will contribute far more than their lives ever could."

"Nothing justifies the killing of children. Only a man of *Iblīs* would rationalise it."

Vitali touched his earpiece, and his face changed. The Ukrainian barked to his men. "The base has been infiltrated.

We need to move. Andrei and Slava, seize him and beware of him at all times."

Connor breached the doorway and while sweeping his arcs, saw the soldiers' skull slide off Ciara blade—*I am going to need TRiM'ed up to the ying-yang after this trip.*

He heard the male shouts in Ukrainian up the stairs, correlating with Ciara's hand signals of *enemy, upstairs, number unknown.*

He pulled out a silenced pistol and gave it to Ciara.

After a couple of his hand gestures, they formed at the bottom of the stairs; he on the left, Ciara on the right and Roza behind him—*A poster of equality and diversity.*

He heard the children's wails. In this scenario, he had to make a decision—shoot for the medulla or fire 'failure drills'. The effect of shooting the medulla—sat at the base of the skull—was it instantly cut off any nerve firing to the rest of the body—no trigger finger twitch upon death. However, being around an inch in width, with the adrenaline racing, and using a weapon he was barely familiarised with, he knew the best course of action would be the 'two rounds to the sternum and one to the head' drill— *three times the ammunition and time.*

He reached the top of the stairs, turned the corner to see a guard corralling five children in a line against the wall. The surprise hit the guard's eyes. They stayed like that as the mandible disintegrated, tipping him lifelessly onto the floor.

Connor smacked his finger to his lips, not looking at the children to keep his eyes forward down the long corridor. He could hear Roza whisper to the children. There were hopefully more somewhere.

He reached the corner and began to 'slice the pie'. He saw the flame hair.

56

Ayesha held her blanket tightly to her chest. When the firing began she had dived under her bed. Her door had been flung open several times, but the owners of the boots had not lowered themselves to check. The shouts of the guards stabbed through the cries of the other children.

She felt a strange sensation in her tummy—*This might be a knight coming to rescue them.*

The sound of the guns and the men shouting kept her where she hid.

Xander, hands secured behind his back, was kicked and rifle thumped into keeping pace.

The clouds seemed to draw over the moon at the speed a woman would cover her modesty, dimming the valley floor into a raining darkness.

Vitali stopped the men on the edge of the forestry, a hundred metres away from the manor house. "One of you watch over the Muslim, and the other over the base. I need to know if any reinforcements arrive, and if anyone that isn't us escapes from the house—including the children—shoot them. Make him watch."

Pinned by the heavy knee in his back, he felt powerless.

Whatever, or whoever, was concerning to Vitali inside his fortress would not stand up to Vitali's men. The murdering of the children had never been the plan, or else he would never have supplied the intelligence for their kidnap.

The Povernuto never had suspected; he was the leader, borne through his ruthless actions against the enemy, with an uncanny ability to strike suddenly, with devastating effect and get away. They appreciated he was a weapon—a Ukrainian Government assassin and one of them. He could never explain to them, that to garner the support of the wider Islamic world to their cause beyond words would require an insidious outrage that would require sacrifice beyond measure.

The plan had been to stir Tatar fury, and he would further entrench himself with them by striking Russian targets in search of 'the truth'.

It had worked; his legend grew, as did their trust in him. Eventually, his authority became undisputed.

Then Hafsa Giray appeared dead. He appealed to Kutz, who told him he did not even know how or where Vitali went to, but he would find out.

Xander gave up Ciara in exchange for the location. With his trust in Kutz shattered, he had gone dark.

He might never know what had become of Roza and Connor Reed—shame broke over him like a wave upon the memory of the handshake with the Englishman. And if Roza had ever discovered his hand in this, she would not have stopped until either he or she was dead.

He reminded himself he had not departed this life yet. He surmised Vitali would take his best to quell whatever disturbance resided in the house. These two guarding him might be battle hardened, but still the worst of the bunch.

Grace froze at the sight of Connor, her mind scrambling to make sense of it. She stood powerless to move, as her brain slowed his action of aiming the rifle at her head. The anger on his face, and his mouth enunciating words she could not hear.

The bullet vacuuming past her cheek snapped her from her catatonic state, and his screaming words became clear: "Get down you ginger fuck."

She collapsed to the floor, watching him take a step to the right and firing his rifle again. It did not bang as she expected but clacked—unlike the gun firing from behind her.

A dark-haired, olive skinned woman appeared at his shoulder with the same rifle, shouting in another foreign language.

Connor and the woman bounded past her, first him, and then her.

The children pattered by her, then the woman. Finally, Connor appeared at her side, opened his palm out to her with a smirk on his face. In a strange accent he said, "Come with me if you want to live."

Connor lifted his wrist mike to his mouth, "Yuri, package secured. I need immediate extraction."

He stood, poised at the top of the stairs. The children were split by the corner of the corridors cleared, and Roza had counted them twice.

The manor was far too big for three of them to ensure it was clear. They had the hostages and extracting them was the priority.

He was unsure of the professionalism of Yuri's voice procedure.

"I'll be there. Out."

He shouted for Roza and Ciara's benefit, "He should arrive within three minutes max."

He heard the clank of the main entrance open.

He screamed, "Everyone back."

He ducked behind the wall at the top of the stairs. The explosion vibrated him off the wall.

"Roza," he bellowed. "Take the children and run them off. I'll hold the door."

He flipped open one of his grenade pouches. The weight of the fire coming up the stairs was too heavy for him to return adequately. Pin removed, the fly-off lever leapt off, and he waited two seconds before launching it down the stairs.

Upon the 'B' of the 'Bang', he flicked around the corner in a crouch—the lower position saved his head from a burst of submachine fire from the opposite corner. His instincts understood—it was fired by a soldier with a great sense of anticipation under contact.

He ducked back and ripped away another grenade as Ciara's voice cannoned down the corridor. "Contact."

Then an enemy grenade appeared.

57

Ciara saw him a split second before he saw her. Her three rounds hit him twice in the chest, and once in the head. Firing three had allowed the second soldier to draw down on her.

He flew back as if on an invisible, elastic band as Roza gunned him down.

"Contact," Ciara screamed.

Another grenade exploded, much closer than the previous one.

The grenade bounced as Connor threw himself into the adjacent room—mercifully unlocked—facing down and away, legs squeezed, fingers in his ears and mouth open in a desperate attempt not to have his ears perforated.

When the denotation hit, Connor felt an invisible giant use him like a cross-fit battle rope. He did not feel any tearing to his skin. His rifle, despite being slung, had somehow slid off and now lay three feet away. His ribs ached, and his face felt numb on the left side. His eye blinked the blood free.

Get up. The thrower is going to be bounding up those stairs.

He forced himself to his knees and spun around. In the process of standing a mini tank of a man appeared at the door and Connor instinctively knew who it was—Vitali. Like a sprinter from the starting pistol, Connor smashed his head into the man's groin, attempting to get his arms elbow deep around the back of the man's knees, he managed past the wrists, such was the size of the legs. The speed, coupled with the force, propelled the man toppling backwards.

In the scramble, Connor clamped his hand on his opponent's left hip, threaded his middle finger inside the trigger guard and over the man's index finger. The noise pounded the ears, and after a few seconds the PP-2000's magazine was spent.

The man's fist felt like a swung bowling ball as it collided against his cheek. He listed sideways out of his opponent's guard, who scrambled up and bolted for the door.

Connor forced himself to his feet, his palm steadying himself as he performed a mental inventory of his injuries. Cut above his left eye, swollen cheekbone. Jaw still intact due to his being able to ride the blow. His ribs were caning. However, he did not think he had any breaks or catastrophic bleeds.

He had no weapon and was relieved Vitali had not bolted into the room where Connor's AS Val was. His senses reopened, and he could hear Roza's exhortations in Tatar and the children's screams.

"Ciara," he shouted.

"Yeh?"

"Coming out." He stepped out to see the children filling the corridor. Roza was talking urgently to the children, as was Grace. Ciara was at the far end covering the retreat.

Connor went and retrieved his weapon, pulling back the cocking lever to make sure the round was seated correctly. Yuri's voice spoke in his ear. "We are here."

Connor lifted his wrist mike to reply when he heard shots fired outside, then a crescendo of fire returned.

"We have the enemy suppressed. You must hurry."

Grace's voice sounded. "We have to go back. One of the girls is missing."

"Fuck. What's her name?"

"Ayesha," she replied. "I will come with you—she trusts me—"

"No. You'll be a hindrance and she doesn't have to trust me."

"If you go back down that corridor, there's a big assembly hall on the right. Walk across it to the opposite door.

Turn left, and her room is down the far end of the corridor, on the right."

He turned to Ciara and Roza, and said, "If I am not out in three minutes flat, just leave me, and I'll make my way back."

Ciara stared at him for a moment. "There'll be a vehicle waiting for you outside."

Roza stepped to him, and stared into his eyes. "They evil men. God hide girl, so you can make them to meet him."

"Insha' Allah," he replied.

He saw her smile for the first time, and he knew it would be imprinted onto his memory. She and Ciara began to herd the children and Grace out, who looked at him as she passed with tears in her eyes.

Xander hunched and writhed as the burning, empty round casings rained down on the back of his neck. The man with a knee in the small of his back fired on the vehicles outside the manor. The other lay prone behind cover, touched his ear and shouted, "That's Vitali. We are needed inside the house to bolster numbers now."

Bits of barks and chunks of earth were flying around them.

"We dragging him together?"

"There's no time."

"Am I shooting him? This fuckhead, I mean."

The other man paused for a few seconds. "He's not going anywhere. Use the cable ties on his ankles and let's go."

"You sure?"

"Trust me. Vitali wants him to suffer."

Xander did not struggle as his ankles were secured together—*This is why Vitali did not take these idiots.*

58

Connor, alone now, checked the fastenings on his webbing and that the top round was seated correctly in the chamber of his Val. Two grenades left, plenty of magazines. It was not fear he felt—it was excitement. He remembered a nineties wildlife documentary about a dominant male lion savaging hyenas on the savannah. The advantage he had, was whoever might be still inside would not be expecting someone like him prowling inside.

He heard the sound of footsteps pattering down the corridor. He stepped into a small room and waited for them to pass. Stepping out again, he shot the pair in the back of their heads. The way they fell, made him suppress a laugh—*Jurgen Klinsmann would be proud.*

He ghost walked quicker now he knew—even though his weapon was silenced— if the two he had just killed did not turn up as expected, Vitali and whoever he had with him would be alerted.

He kept peering into rooms before he passed to ensure he was not a victim of his own tactic. He found the hall, but the heavy curtains—inside the glass—obscured his field of vision.

He stacked on the door, before darting in and to the left with his weapon raised.

The sight of Vitali with Ayesha assaulted him. His physical stature amplified against the child he held up under the jaw with his right hand. A black office swivel chair held his frame, and Ayesha's terror-stricken face partially covered his. His left hand angled a Fort-17 pistol against her temple. Connor knew he could not shoot the Ukrainian without hitting her, or setting off his trigger finger twitch. He kept his weapon trained on Vitali the best he could.

Connor counted five other men surrounding him, with their backs on the wall. All with their weapons half-mast.

"I knew you come back for her, Mr Reed."

"If you're trying to do a Bane impression, you need more bass in your voice," Connor replied. He enunciated his words to push the tremor off his voice.

"I hear great stories of you. But to see is to believe."

"I think experiencing is believing. Like when you experienced being taken down, and disarmed by a smaller, unarmed man recovering from percussion shock."

"Yes. And I remember swatting you like child. Still, I listen that you are excellent fighter. Girl and I will like to watch you take on my men with bare hands—one by one of course."

Connor smiled with a confidence he didn't feel. "What happens when I kill them all?"

"You face me for girl's life."

"What is this? Tekken?"

"Tekken?"

"A computer game."

"You see. My men and I did not have luxury computer games or other mindless entertainment. Our childhoods were mercilessly short."

"It's a shame. If you had a console, maybe you wouldn't find your entertainment in scaring, hurting and killing children."

"A man from where you from never understand."

Connor ignored him. "I just want to say thank you."

Vitali smiled. "What for?"

"This opportunity to take pieces from your minions that they will never get back."

"I like to watch you try," he said before bouncing Ayesha on his knee. He said something to her in what sounded like Russian.

When she did not answer whatever she had been asked, Vitali squeezed her jaw and growled, "Как много??"

Connor saw something in her eyes, before hearing her voice confirm it—defiance.

"Все они."

Vitali laughed. "I asked her how many does she think you'll beat. She said, 'All of them'. The hope of a child, not yet crushed by the world."

Connor knew that if Vitali wanted him dead upon entering the hall, he could have engineered it. He lowered his pistol. "Too much dialogue is killing the scene. Shall we? Who's first?"

"You choose. My reinforcements here in twenty minutes."

Connor knew he was telling the truth.

"The gomoseksual'nyy in the corner," said the former Royal Marine while gesturing towards the corner, and deliberately sounding out the Russian word for 'homosexual'. The jibe had the desired effect.

It occurred to Ciara that Grace had not asked her why they hadn't driven the Land Rover off yet—*She is more concerned with the little girl, than her own life.*

She felt an unpleasant jolt—*Maybe more concerned with him.*

Ciara spoke. "He'll get the girl out."

It took a few moments for Grace to reply, and her thoughts came out like a tap. "This Vitali, I knew that type of man had to exist. I have seen bastards before, creatures with no morals. But they were bottom feeders—socio-economic victims some might say. This man, he's different, he's—"

"The dark triad of smart, disciplined and evil."

"That's exactly what he is. He uses his intelligence to steer his hate. The things he's capable of…"

"I hope Connor meets this Vitali."

"You hope he does?"

"Yes," Ciara answered. "Then you can comfort yourself in the knowledge this monster is dead."

"How long have you known Connor?"

"Long enough."

The silence hung between them before Grace said softly, "I hope he makes it out."

She loves him—Ciara thought.

"I don't know who or what watches over him, but he'll make it out, and he'll have the girl with him."

The soldier ran at him with fury. Connor feigned surprise and an amateurish protective guard. Judging the distance and speed, Connor sprang forward. The contact of his right fist through his assailant's jaw felt like punching the corner off a giant block of butter.

The soldier fell, as if slipping on marbles, unconscious even before his head sickeningly hit the floor.

Connor leaned down and tilted his victim's head back as if to keep the airway clear. Straightening himself, he stamped with all his might onto the throat. Even under his boots, he felt the Adam's apple and larynx break like a ping-pong ball.

He wanted her to watch.

After a few moments, his opponent gasped like he had burst to the surface of the water he had been about to drown in. Glowing blood frothed from the mouth.

Connor giggled, despite wanting to maintain an appearance of seriousness. As his victim writhed and gurgled, he could not help laughing.

"There's always sign language," he said.

"Impressive," said Vitali, face impassive. "Just five more to go."

"Yep. You choose this time."

"Boris."

A man behind Connor put down his rifle and took off his chest rig. A touch taller, and a little slighter in build than

Connor. His long brown hair swept back behind the ears, looked out of place on his otherwise military demeanour.

Connor instantly knew this would be harder. The man stopped just out of range and took up his fighting posture—Thai or kickboxer. The shoulders and feet were squarer than a traditional boxing stance, the hands higher. Despite recognising this, the first kick—a high left—still caught Connor by surprise. Not just the speed but the complete lack of a telegraph. Without putting his foot back on the ground, Boris immediately stabbed Connor's torso with a teep.

The strategy was clear—to punish Connor from the outside with kicks. He had to get the kickboxer to the floor, aware a poorly executed double or single leg takedown could result in a crushing knee to the face. And without a cage fence or even ring ropes into which to corral his opponent, he would have to time it to perfection. That meant making the kickboxer concentrate on something else.

He faked shooting in, and the kickboxer lowered his arms in preparation to stop Connor's hands clasping around his knees— too low. Connor's left hook, right hand, left hook to the body and final right hand all landed cleanly.

The kickboxer fell onto his back, but the eyes were still alert as he raised his legs—*Hardy fucker.*

The Yorkshireman stepped one way, before ramming his knee behind onto the soldier's hamstring. He snatched the tip of the boot into his armpit, hooking his forearm beneath the heel before clamping his legs like a vice around his victim. Falling back into a sitting position, Connor wrenched on the heel hook, to the kickboxer's screams. He felt an amplified satisfaction of twisting bubble wrap—first the collateral ligaments, then the cruciate ligaments and finally the meniscus.

He let go. The screams sliding into ashen whimpering.

Connor sniggered. "Four million dollars, and this what you got? You cheap fuck."

Vitali's lip twitched before shouting in Ukrainian. Connor understood as the three remainders began to unlatch their assault rig and lay their weapons down in unison.

There was no furniture he could use to channel them. Wrestling and grappling of any kind would be suicide. Kicking would be out; he could not afford to sacrifice any mobility or balance. He remembered a Gyspy once telling his father "Two can worry a bull."

Now a lack of cage wall or ring ropes would work to his advantage. They zoned in on him. He slid off on angles to prevent any of them getting behind him. This was not the first time he had been confronted by multiple attackers. Connor, while knowing he could at least hurt most men he hit, wished for his father's 'touch of death' in times like this. One truth he found when dealing with more than one—*One of them has to be man enough to go first.*

He could see that by witnessing their two colleagues so ruthlessly and effortlessly dispatched, not one of them wanted to sacrifice themselves to allow the other two carte blanche on him. Still, he could not keep skipping around forever.

He flung his arms out and made a sound mimicking Bruce Lee as he took on the entire dojo in *Fists of Fury*. He laughed loudly as the three flinched.

Anger splattered the left one's face, and he zealously attacked. Connor slipped the punch and fired a harder, quicker and straighter one onto the nose.

He stayed in too long with the finishing touches. Hands gripped at his wrists and clothing. He became entangled in the three of them. A clubbing fist caught his cheek as arms wrapped around his legs. He barely kept his balance, as he pushed on the head of one hugging his right leg off the floor. He left hooked one who stumbled back but as Connor turned to release his limb, he was tackled below the right knee.

All three dived on him like piranhas, stamping, punching and kneeing. He refused to turtle up, knowing if he did so he would find himself booted to death. His attempts to stand were met by toecaps kicking his hands and feet out. Claustrophobia loomed, like being trapped in a box with holes cut out and fists punching you through them. That he would keep searching for a way to win was a given. His dad had once explained the difference in the mentality between Mike Tyson and Evander Holyfield to him—"When Tyson was getting beat, and there looked like no way out, he would take his beating 'like a man'. Holyfield, no matter how perilous the situation, would always try and find a way to win. Look at the tenth round against Riddick Bowe. Diego Corrales was the same. Don't ever take a beating 'like a man'."

Instead of trying to get up wrestling style, he rolled and spun over onto his back. Avoiding a stamping boot, he kicked the ankle out and toppled one of them. He sprang to his feet despite catching a few blows on the way up. He threw punches in different directions and created a distance.

His torso felt it had been drummed in by a procession of cue balls in socks. His face was hot with his left eye compressing. He drew in oxygen with the double nasal inhalation George had taught him, a 'su-su' to help him recover.

Back to the start, as they circled him, except his state had considerably declined. He was aware of the time. Vitali's reinforcements would arrive, and the game would be over.

He felt Ayesha's eyes on him, and felt his three opponents wary of going first again. This infuriated him. *Fucking child-harming pussies.* He pooled the blood in his mouth, and spat crimson in the face of the nearest. "Gomoseksual'nyy."

The guard bolted at him like a hot poker pranged rhino, only to have nose explode under the impact of Connor's forehead. As he slid around his falling opponent, his heel slid out on the blood-splattered floor. He was bundled to the floor again.

He would keep fighting to the end, but knew that end was coming. He would not have the strength to adroitly defend himself against Vitali, even if his attackers somehow knocked themselves out.

He shot his hand out and grasped a leg, but did not have the strength to pull its owner to the floor or get up. Instead, he sank his teeth into the inner thigh as hard as he possibly could. He barely heard the howls and shrieks, as he ragged his head. Punches thudded on his head. He felt his consciousness slipping, and with a mighty effort, fired an uppercut into the balls of the man his teeth were clamped in. As the crumpled man fell, the gunshot bolted through the room.

The gunshot straightened both women in their seats. Ciara knew she could not justify leaving Grace in the vehicle alone to investigate. The single firing set her to steel her nerves—Connor's weapon was silenced.

She turned on the ignition. He had either failed, which meant the enemy might pour out of the door. Or, he'd succeeded, which meant he would be out soon.

She gripped her pistol and prayed.

On the small road, less than half a mile away, there was a convoy of estate cars meandering towards the manor.

The rain of blows had ceased, just as he had been teetering on the precipice of blackness. His senses returned to a voice he recognised speaking in a language he did not. His eyes focused.

Xander had a pistol pressed against Vitali's temple. Vitali's Fort-17 lay on the floor—Connor guessed it went off as Xander disarmed him. His three opponents had stood back from him.

Connor processed the situation; if Xander shot Vitali, he might not have time to shoot the guards before they retrieved their weapons. If he shot the guards now, he would not have control over the brute of a terrorist.

"He says he has reinforcements arriving. Anytime now if he's to be believed," said Connor.

"It is true," said Xander. "I did not know he killed children. Take the girl and go. I will buy you time. They will not shoot me because risk killing him. You go now."

"You won't get out of here alive," said Connor.

"Lucky me. I have seventy-two virgins when I arrive." He smiled.

"I think that's the first joke I have heard you crack. It was a good one."

Vitali smiled, seemingly unperturbed. "I will find you."

"I am praying you do," Connor answered. "Ayesha."

He beckoned her to him while putting on his webbing and picking up his rifle. Tears silently ran down her face as she walked gingerly towards him. He knelt as she drew near to him before opening his arms. She nodded seemingly with understanding he was going to carry her.

The crash of doors being booted down and the foreign commands echoed down the halls behind Vitali and Xander. Connor snatched Ayesha in his arms, ignoring the pain cascading through his body and ran with her.

He came to the stairs and launched out of the main door. His heart soared upon seeing the Land Rover. He bundled Ayesha into the front and jumped into the back. Ciara accelerated, as Connor reached around and fastened Ayesha's seatbelt.

59

Xander didn't foresee the reinforcements coming in from behind. He switched his position to the side of Vitali,

"I hope for the both of our sakes these men coming will listen to you, or both of us will be dead," he said in Ukrainian.

Six men burst into Vitali's command of, "Don't shoot."

They stood still with their weapons pointed at Xander.

"I believe this is a Mexican standoff," said Vitali.

"This is what's going to happen," announced Xander to the collective. "Your boss and I are going for a walk down the hall— "

"You're not taking him—" started one of the men before Vitali's raised fingers silenced him.

"Continue," said Vitali.

"You and I will move down the hall to the exit. I will allow your men to keep their weapons trained on us. I escape, and maybe we meet another day. Now, I know you want to get after the Englishman, so it's time to make your mind up."

Vitali took a moment to nod, and said to his men, "If he shoots me, go after him. If he doesn't, we'll go after the British. Now Xander, are we ready?"

He opened his mouth to answer when three things happened simultaneously. Vitali's head snapped to the left, his bladed right fingers batted the inside of Xander's pistol gripping wrist, and the back of the chair smashed into Xander's torso.

Xander knifed his left hand around the bull-like neck, wedged his shoes against the bottom legs of the chair and fell backwards with Vitali on top of him. Xander shot two of the three men to his right, before Vitali's vice-like grip clamped his right wrist. Xander could not free it, and his choking attempt came to nought as Vitali's men pinned and disarmed him.

The former Ukrainian officer stood over Xander. He shook his head. "You could have led a revolution to free our people. A revolution against evil. You're so weak."

Xander smiled. "Your weakness allowed yourself to become evil. No good revolution starts with killing children. So pull the trigger."

Connor's adherence to the samurai quote, 'After a battle, tighten your helmet straps' proved correct. Just before turning the corner at the end of the near mile road, he caught sight of vehicles careening from the back of the manor.

When he finished tapping the screen, he put his phone away.

"Grace. From here on in, I need you to do what I say when I say it. Cars with men who want to kill us will be on us in a couple of minutes. Their cars are faster than this Land Rover, and this road has no turn-offs for miles. Understand?"

Grace nodded.

"Alright, I need you to get as low as you can and press your fingers in your ears."

He craned his neck around the seat to get Ayesha's attention and gestured for her to do the same.

As they complied, Ciara said, "Here. Yuri gave me these as a present."

With that, she handed him an AK-47 short barrel and a heavy satchel, full of magazines.

"How many?"

"Six. Standard thirty-round mags."

The cars gained on them. He loaded and chambered the first round. He estimated the death convoy to be at four hundred metres. He selected single shot—for ammunition conservation and accuracy. He cursed his lack of ear defence. *Probably could not claim on my PAX insurance anyway.*

His first round shattered the rear screen glass, raining shards on Grace and himself. He pressed his chest into the back of the seat and his feet into the front seat to better stabilise his firing position.

He fired. Each shot pounded his eardrum, and the smell of propellant filled the interior as the hot bullet casings flew back in. The cars chasing began to swerve before firing back.

This was the first live situation where Ciara had to drive to evade other vehicles. Her training had been extensive, first with top rally instructors for over two weeks and then another week of security protection driver training. Finally, a week of urban high-speed driving in different cities in the UK; a week that involved 'getting a chase' from various police vehicles, and after a period, surrendering and quoting a number. The bemused police officer would contact dispatch only to be ordered to let her go.

All that training seemed frustratingly negligent now on this straight road. All she could do was hold the vehicle straight as Connor was firing, and banking to the left or right when he said so.

The rounds came back. One smashed through the front window, and the spider web fragmentations obscured her vision. She took out her pistol and shattered a hole through the screen before using the barrel to enlarge it. Bullets banged into the boot. The cars were less than a hundred metres away and closing. Connor sounded, "Keep banking at irregular intervals."

She did so. Her eyes darted to the still intact wing mirror, and she saw them—motorcycles.

She knew the game was up, and they were all going to die.

Looking down at the young girl, with her fingers in her ears and eyes shut tight against the world, sent a pool of despair whirling within her, threatening to spill from her eyes.

Then she felt anger—anger Connor had stopped firing—*He should be fighting until the end, like the man I thought he was.*

It occurred to her maybe he had run out of rounds or the rifle had malfunctioned. She looked in the interior mirror and surprise hit her.

"Why the fuck are you smiling?"

He replied, "My brothers are here."

"You're an only child" she shouted over the din.

"Some brothers don't share the same parents," he shouted back. "And unfortunately for me, the same capbadge."

60

John Foley had requested his mini Uzi be fitted with a heavy bolt cyclic rate reducer. He had told the armourer, "I want to look cool as fuck shooting someone off my Thunderbird Storm. Not looking like a cunt if the kickback brings me off it."

There were three soldiers taking shots at the Land Rover through the cars' sunroofs. Despite everything Connor had told him about these boys, Foley did not feel right about shooting them from behind—*It is more fun when you see their faces.*

He also remembered the text Connor had sent a few minutes ago: *Try and keep the big bastard alive. Bald, beard.*

Foley and Vili had asked friends of theirs in the Night Wolves Motorcycle Club for an 'out of club business' favour. As Foley sat half-cut off the vodka Alexei—whose English was excellent— had been plying him with, he felt sure the chapter leader would not believe the story he was telling him. Indeed, Foley himself had been sceptical when Connor had told him over the phone a week ago. He and Vili had made their way out to Ukraine and petitioned for help. They had been owed a favour anyway.

To Foley's surprise, not only did Alexei believe him, but offered his assistance immediately. More of a surprise was when he reiterated his desire to help the next sober morning. Maybe it had been the part about the CIA's involvement—Alexei had gone into a passionate anti-American rhetoric—Foley did not think it wise to ask why the Russian rode a Harley.

Now, he and Vili—on his Dyna—rode up front with Alexei and his two comrades behind. Foley gave a *Brecon chop*, and the bikes swarmed to the cars like wolves on a buffalo herd.

The soldier turned his head but not his weapon to face Foley. *Bad drills.*

Two of Folley's shots smashed the head to pieces, and the body slid back down the sunroof. The Essex man's scan took a second— *No one bald with a beard*—and the rest of his magazine tore up the vehicle's occupants.

The sound of the wind whipping passed, and the reverberations of gunfire blended in his ears. Vili and Alexei were firing into the lead car. Up ahead Foley could see the Land Rover slowing down.

Connor watched with a smile despite himself—they were not out of the woods yet.

"Slow down."

"Why?" asked Ciara.

"Because I want a word with that Kojak with a beard."

Connor jumped out and jogged up to the carnage. Vitali had been torn from his vehicle, and now lay pinned face down on the road by two bikers.

"Fuck me, you look like you've had a fight with three Tysons. And how many times is 'the Reg' going to have to pull 'Royal' out of the shit?" were Foley's first words to him.

"Thanks for this." Connor smiled giving him the handclasp and half hug. Vili, as usual, ignored it, and gave him a full bear hug and said, "Why does God always use frickin' crazy men like you?"

Connor smiled before turning to one of the bikers. "You must be Alexei, I owe you a debt."

The Russian smiled, "There is no debt if this man has done what you say he has."

When a grey Lada Vesta appeared on the horizon behind them, Alexei continued, "This is mine. To get girls safely to Kiev."

Connor felt almost overwhelming gratitude and held out his hand. "Thank you for this."

As Alexei shook it, he said, "My only wonder is whether there's a punishment fit for this man."

"Not in the time we have. But I have an idea," he said, and then to Foley and Vili, "Can you get Miss Templeton to Kiev for me as discussed?"

"Of course, bruv," answered Foley.

Connor headed over to the Land Rover. Within a minute, Ciara, Grace and Ayesha stood with the bikers. The girl's face of fear upon seeing the pinned Vitali turned Connor's heart into a weight of compassion.

He walked over to Vitali, took out a silenced pistol and shot him in the back of his knees. The Ukrainian sounded like a wounded bear, and the two bikers struggled to keep hold of him. Connor walked around and, being mindful of the bikers pinning hands, fired rounds into Vitali's hands.

Connor produced two handcuffs and said to Vili and Foley,

"Help me secure this animal's ankles to the Land Rover's tow bar."

It took the five of them to drag and subdue the struggling Vitali enough to snap the handcuffs to a circulation cutting tightness around his ankles.

"Put him face down," said Connor.

The other ends of the handcuffs snapped onto the towing hook.

Connor addressed the group. "Ciara, take Grace in the Vesta to the designated location to be sent back to the UK. You can trust these men to act as convoy protection. I'll take the Land Rover and will raise comms and meet with Roza to hand off Ayesha, so she can be handed off to whatever family she has left."

Ciara nodded.

Connor continued. "Vili. John. There are around fifteen miles left on this road. Stay behind me until then. I'll have to release whatever is left of him before I hit the main highway and draw attention to myself."

"Mate, you still have to get out of this area alive. And by this area, I am talking about two hundred miles before you can start breathing out."

"Your priority is Grace. I'll only slow you down. I'll be alright, just please make sure she and Ciara get back safe."

"Brother," said Vili, "I will sacrifice my life so not a frickin' hair on their heads is harmed, so help me God."

"'They'll be fine, Connor', would have sufficed." Connor smiled.

Grace spoke. "You're going to drive off with him like that?"

The tone of her voice quietened everyone else.

Connor looked at her. "Yes."

Her brow furrowed, "He needs to be handed over to the authorities. To stand trial for what he's done."

"Grace, there are no 'authorities' to hand him over to. The Russians would use him as propaganda and the Ukrainians would cover it up. This is the only justice that can be meted out to him now."

Her eyes widened looking at him, something uncomprehending in them. "If that's the case, surely a bullet would suffice."

"No it wouldn't."

"Connor," she said, her voice tremoring. "This isn't you. This is… sadistic."

"This is me, Grace, at least part of me. And I don't care what it is—it's also a fraction of what he deserves."

"Please don't do this. If you do, there's no future for us."

Connor felt a whirl of emotion rise in him. All he had to do was shoot Vitali and have done with it, and life offered the promise of a truly magnificent and moral woman to walk through it with. He was aware of everyone's eyes on him.

He detached his voice tone and demeanour from the weight in his heart. "The day I change my calling in life to placate someone—no matter how much I think of them—is the day I stop living."

As he saw Grace's face wither into a mask of anguish, he quickly turned for Ayesha and guided her into the Land Rover. He dares not look back at Grace.

The sound of the bike engines being revved and the Vesta's ignition being switched on filled the air. He looked at Vitali—the Ukrainian's fear would have been invisible to a civilian but not to Connor. He knelt and said, "Thanks for choosing this deserted area—there's no one here to stop me turning you into Skeletor, you sick fucking cunt."

Ciara climbed into the passenger's side of the Vesta after gently escorting Grace into the back. The Slavic driver did not speak. A pair of red and blue furry dice hung from the rear-view mirror.

She knew now was not the time to process how she felt about the scene she had just witnessed. Ciara tore her gaze away from the wing mirror framing Grace with her head hung low.

Instead, she focused on the Land Rover in front, as it vibrated in starting up.

Her breathing became deeper as the Land Rover began to move—slowly at first and the Vesta matched its speed. The motorcycles remained thirty yards behind.

Vitali began to twist and kick with his legs. Pushing off with his hands before falling back to his forearms. She saw the pained desperation on his face.

As the Land Rover sped up, she saw the sleeves ripping into red. He turned onto one shoulder, and the same thing happened. His screams sounded through the inch open windows over the engine noise.

His face touched the scorching ground. He kept pushing off with the blood-stained bones of his hands.

Finally, he went limp. Ciara could not understand why she was still watching the macabre crimson paintbrush stain the dark road.

Epilogue

Connor had read that, back in feudal Japan, a child of one family would be given up as a 'hostage' to another family to cement an alliance or allegiance. The infant could spend their entire childhood under the care and tuition of their host family. So when Zain Aziz had offered to give up his nine-year-old son to Tom, for the duration of Connor's meeting with him, though Tom initially refused, Connor had accepted—why trust someone when you did not have to? The temporary release of custody of his son had been an assurance of Connor's safety during the meeting.

Tom drove off with the boy and Connor stood outside the vaping shop with Bhaskar. There were gangs of young British-Asian men set on the points of the streets surrounding the shops—and no other pedestrians. Other than his lighter-like Kubotan, he had no weapon.

"Shall we?" Bhaskar asked. Connor nodded. One of the stipulations of the meeting was that Aziz arrive first. They stepped into the shop.

"I must apologise. I must search you."

Connor doubted Bhaskar would have searched Aziz. Pointless arguing, it was not as if he was going to back out now.

Bhaskar finished and nodded towards the door. Connor shook his head. "No. You're going through the door first."

"Okay."

Bhaskar opened it and Connor looked around him—just one person—Aziz. Not that Connor had ever met him before.

"I am satisfied. Thanks."

Bhaskar nodded and left.

Aziz stood up. He was not quite as big as the image built in Connor's head. He had been fed the descriptions such as 'huge fucker', 'like a tank', 'barrelly', and his favourite, 'an espresso iceberg'. Still, Zain Aziz had a presence, not just his weight and frame—around six one and touching sixteen-stone—but the straightness of his back and a physique rivetted with strength. Although half-Asian, and half-Jamaican, Connor would have mistaken him for being Arabic.

He spoke in Punjabi. "Maiṁ khuśa hāṁ ki tusīṁ mainū milaṇa ā'i'ā sī." *I am glad you came to see me.*

"I hope curiosity doesn't kill the cat," replied Connor.

The dark eyes smiled. "Very good. Would you prefer English?"

"Saves anything getting lost in translation."

"I agree." Aziz nodded. "You look like your mother. Maybe not right now—been in the wars?"

"I get that a lot," replied Connor. "As for the state of my face, I fell off my horse while playing polo."

Aziz smirked. "But you are your father's son. Anyone can see—it's the… manner. Shall we sit?"

Connor lifted the chair in front of him and brought it around to the corner edge and sat down. Aziz smiled. "He never liked sitting with his back to the door either."

"My dad used to say you and he were very close."

"We were closer than you think."

"I didn't think my dad's prison sentence was long enough to contemplate that sort of thing."

It took a moment for Aziz to laugh. "I heard you had a sense of humour."

"Can I ask, if you were so close, why didn't you hunt down his killer?"

"We were close. I was the best man at your mother and father's wedding."

Connor bristled. "Well that's a fucking lie, they were never married."

Aziz smiled, showed him his hand before reaching into his pocket. He pulled out a heavy envelope, opened it and passed Connor several print pictures.

They showed his dad dressed in a light grey, checkered suit with a dark tie, his mother in a simple, backless pearl dress, her dark-blonde hair setting it off beautifully. It struck him how happy they looked, even on the photos they were not posing for.

"So he did marry her."

"Of course he did. The agreement was she would keep her maiden name in public. He never wanted her tarnished, or you."

"Is that your wife?" asked Connor, pointing to an attractive Asian woman.

"Yes."

"Wouldn't that be frowned upon, you being witnesses and honouring the wedding of non-believers?"

"Well, your mother and father had converted to Islam by then. Why do you think your father taught you the language?"

A jolt fired through Connor. "What?"

Aziz's straight face cracked into a huge smile, before laughing uproariously. "I am joking, you should have seen your face."

Connor smiled despite himself before asking, "When did this happen?"

"While you were in Wetherby," answered Aziz, referring to Connor's time in the male juvenile prison.

"Probably so they wouldn't have to pay to take me."

Aziz smiled. "They married in secret. There was another reason why your father chose the Bahamas and that waaaassss," said Aziz stretching the word out as he pulled some documents from the envelope, "to set up an off-shore account there in your name—the banking laws aren't under the same rules as the Bank of England. Only you and I know about this; your dad didn't even tell your mum. These are the details."

As Connor's eyes scanned the document, Aziz continued, "You can only draw out a maximum six grand per month. I guess your old man didn't want you blowing it in a haze of drugs and girlies."

"There's over three-hundred grand in this."

"Yeh, he'd been putting into it for a while."

Connor felt the room warp as he took in the information. His parents were married, and his dad not only left him money but he had been putting into it for a long time.

"Do you know who killed him?" he asked softly.

"Yes."

Connor's heart thumped hard against his breast plate.

"They still alive?"

"That person is, yes."

"If you were so close to my dad, why are they still alive?"

"It is a son's right to avenge his father's murder," said Aziz.

"I could have avenged his death years ago."

"Would you have believed me without evidence?"

Before Connor could answer, Aziz tipped out the remaining items of the envelope: a small MP3 player and a USB stick.

"This," said Aziz holding the USB stick, "is a recording of your father's murderer talking with former police officer Stephen Mahon. The clip is on this MP3 player, in case you're desperate to listen to it straight away."

The name flickered in Connor's head. "The same copper who died four or five years back?"

"Pushing six, but yes, the same one."

"How did you get this?"

"You don't need to know."

"How do I know this is real?"

Aziz shrugged. "When you find out who it is, ask yourself why I would lie."

Connor stared at the MP3 player. "Thanks."

Aziz stood. "If, after listening to that recording, you're going to do what I think you're going to do, in the aftermath you're going to need my help. You're going to create a storm we're going to have to get through."

He clapped his hand on Connor's shoulder and made for the door. Before he reached it, Connor asked,

"Why are you prepared to help me like this?"

"Because your dad saved my life twice—once in Armley, and once on the outside. I couldn't do the same for him, but nothing will harm his only son if I can help it."

A king-like confidence surrounded Derek, as he looked over most of his family in crime. The 'Buxton Arms' had been closed for a few months now undergoing the refurbishments. Set back off the main road, they would not be disturbed. He stood at the head of a set of tables.

Nervousness etched the faces of his nephews. He knew it was not simply over the fracas last time. It was because Kevin Kellings loomed beside him—like an oversized pitbull, exuding threat just by standing there. His henchman in attendance, Brendan Chappel, had to force the hardman persona a little.

His brother Michael was coming out of the prison in a couple of months, with his brother Lee being released shortly after. Derek wanted them both to know that everyone else considered his authority total. And the best way would be to deal with Tom in front of everyone.

Chappel had called him in a panic, telling him of how Tom had threatened him with a gun, asking questions about who had stoved in his dad and stole the money. Tom had thought Kevin Kellings had been in the know. Derek formulated a plan; Chappel would deny all knowledge and

Derek would allow Kellings to beat Tom for laying hands on one of Kellings' minions without permission from either of them. Kellings would offer Tom a straightener—either he would back down in front of all his cousins, or he could take his beating. Either way, he would be put in his place.

And Kellings was angry—because he was ignorant of the deal made behind his back, and thought Brendan innocent.

With Tom beaten down, there would not be anyone to threaten his reign. Michael might be a strong character, but he had not the contacts Derek had in Newcastle, Manchester and Liverpool. His concern about Connor had simmered—they had not heard from him in weeks. And it did not seem like his nephew had any interest in staying in Leeds—probably enjoyed his 'international' lifestyle too much. He might have something to say, but as long as Tom was still alive and not disabled—too much—there would not be a whole lot he could do.

Charlie opened the door, and Derek's anger, up already, spiked as Tom walked in—Charlie was told to warn him ahead of time. The cold splash of adrenaline cooled his anger when Connor walked in. Derek saw the fresh stitches above the eye and bruising to his face.

The splash became a flood when Connor pulled a pistol out and levelled it at Kellings.

"This isn't about you, so don't make it be," he said.

Kellings stood still, and nodded almost imperceptibly.

Indignant rage poked through Derek's fear as he said, "What the fuck is going on?"

The gun barrel's rapid shift in his direction made him flinch. Connor said, "One more word out of your fucking face, and you'll fall like a Jenga tower, you sack of shit."

Seeing the hate, stilled Derek's tongue. Connor nodded to his cousins, and they swarmed Brendan Chappel, ragging him face down over the table before pinning him to it. They controlled his arms by the wrists. He struggled and cried out for Kellings' help. Tom grasped his hair and banged his face into the polished wood. He whipped out and held the curved blade tip of his Emerson Karambit to his eye.

"Struggle again and you'll lose it."

Brendan ceased movement, except a craning of his neck away from the blade.

Connor said to Charlie, "Go get them."

Charlie disappeared for a moment, to reappear with handheld garden shears. Then Derek knew it had been planned—*How the fuck could they have known he would be bringing Kellings and Chappel down?*

As if reading his thoughts, Chappel exclaimed to Tom, "What the fuck is this? We had an agreement."

"Yeh, we did," said Tom. "An agreement to keep certain things between ourselves. Not you'd get away with this 'scot-free'. My cousin told me about this ritual the Yazuka do to atone for when they fuck up. Forget the proper name now."

"Yubitsume," answered Connor.

"Yeh, what he said," said Tom. "The cutting off of your little finger."

"Please, please, please, man. I know I fucked up but—" started Chappel.

"Shut up, Brendan. A little finger is fuck all. We were discussing it—the hard part is doing it yourself. But you'd take all day. So, this is the crack— you have sixty seconds to cut your little finger off yourself with my knife, or we'll cut four off for you. If you attempt to attack anyone, you'll be shot dead. Understand?"

"Please," Brendan croaked.

"Last chance."

"Okay, I'll do it."

Derek could not bring himself to utter a protest under the intensity of Connor's gaze. He looked over at Kellings, to see curiosity furrowing his eyes.

The cousins slowly released the pale Brendan. Tom handed him his dagger. "Because the blade is curved, you'll have to lie your finger on the table. Best doing it quick." He threw him a towel. "Wrap this around your finger. Maybe your boss will take you to *Jimmys*. Alright, your sixty seconds start from now."

Brendan snatched up the knife in such a way Derek thought he was going to get it over and done with. But the knife hovered. The edge crept into the skin. The tear of blood matched the tear spilling over Chappel's eyelid.

He looked up pleadingly, only to be met by Tom's stony face. Finally, Tom said, "Time's up."

"Told you," said Connor.

"How did you know?" replied Tom.

"Because the weak can't make sacrifices in the present to improve the future."

Tom stepped forward and said, "What we going to do with you, Brendan?"

He opened his palm and Brendan said, "Please, please. I'll do it, just need a bit more time."

"We're not going to cut your fingers off, daft lad. They'll be DNA everywhere. We just wanted to see if you'd do it yourself or not."

Derek knew Brendan should not have been wearing the look of relief. And he should not have given the knife back. No sooner had he, the cousins seized him and pinned him again. Tom stepped around, removed a transparent plastic bag with drawstrings underneath and rammed it over his head.

Muffled screams cut through Derek, as Chappel's steroid and terror amped muscles were surprisingly ineffectual under the Ryder hands. The scene of Chappel banging his head off the table as if in a fit seemed darkly surreal. Finally, his thrashing body stilled into a corpse. At Tom's nod, they let go, and it slid off the table.

Connor spoke to Kellings while keeping his eyes on him. "We don't believe you had anything to do with my uncle Ryan being hospitalised. The late Brendan Chappel recorded a conversation between him and the uncle here present to curry favour with us." With that, Connor under-bowled a glasses case towards Kellings, who caught it. "The recording is in there. Feel free to listen to it on your journey back to the northeast. We'll get rid of the body."

Kellings shifted to move, before pausing and saying, "Hadda'way man. The first place the copass are gana look is me."

"They'll come around to ask you questions. Tell them you dropped him in the town centre. We'll handle it so you're above suspicion."

Kevin took a moment before walking out of 'The Buxton Arms'.

Luke looked on at the scene. It seemed strange his cousin Connor—though shy of six feet—appeared to be the biggest man in the room, even though Derek was. Luke did not know why, but he had imagined a version of this day coming for a while. After Derek had gripped up Charlie and chest-punched Curtis, he had even dreamed it—though it was in his grandma's house, not in this pub. Connor defeated him with a sword that was embedded in their dead grandfather's chair, which he removed after Derek could not.

"Tom," said Connor, "play the recording. The first voice is a corrupt copper named Stephen Mahon."

The recording off Tom's phone began to play.

Mahon—*They can't come back to* (garbled) *live to tell this tale.*

Derek—*The money I am giving them pair is plenty. Besides, where are they going* (garbled)—*can't stay in Bradford. Aziz would have them torn up.*

Mahon—*How you going to get him into the moors without him telling anyone? If even one person knows you have asked him there, they'll know you are behind it.*

Derek—*If I ask my brother to come alone and not tell anyone he won't—all that 'a man is only as good as his word', the pious cunt. It will be bang, bang. I will take over, and you will get paid more.*

Mahon—*Think anyone will suspect?*

Derek—*What? That I had my brother killed? Nah—I'll make sure people's eyes look over to Bradford.*

The recording was clicked off, and Luke stood stunned.

"That has been fucking doctored by Aziz," exclaimed Derek, panic streaking his voice.

"How did you know Aziz gave it to me?"

Derek spluttered, "Cos, cos he's had it against me hasn't he?"

"Luke, go check if that fat cunt is carrying anything," said Connor.

Luke moved, shaking the shock off. Then he guessed why his cousin wanted him searched. He kept alert—his uncle was a big, strong man, and there was no telling what he'd do when cornered.

As he got closer he could see his uncle's left hand tremoring. Luke frisked him as Connor had shown him how to.

"He's clean."

Connor tilted his head, and Luke made his way back.

He watched his cousin unload and strip the pistol, before throwing the separate parts to his cousins. He lifted his sleeves, his jean bottoms to show his ankles and his t-shirt. "I am unarmed. If you beat me," he said to Derek, "we'll pretend your murder of my dad didn't happen. You'll walk out, still head of the family. But you will not leave here without us fighting."

Over a decade ago, Luke had followed Connor into the Reaper Boxing Club—and he was one of the stars of the club. Luke had always remembered his cousin's advice on handling pre-fight nerves, "Think of what you're scared of happening and focus on the ways you can prevent it. That's all you can do."

He would watch Connor in awe when he boxed in matches; he sparred well enough, but it was in matches he shone. Connor got sent to Wetherby around eighteen months after Luke had joined. One day the coach told him, "You're going to be the best boxer in this club", but he'd always look up to Connor. Tom too, but not in the same way.

Luke could hear the tremor in Derek's hand had spread to his breathing. After time stretched out the moment, Derek stepped forward.

His reaction to Connor's feint was more of a flinch than a defensive block. Connor's first landed punch was a jab to the face. More followed, from different angles—jabs to the body, screw jabs, double jabs. Luke—seeing the openings for more powerful punches—knew then his cousin was going to make it last. Derek's punches were telegraphed and easily evaded. Each of Connor's jabs sounded like a piece of defrosted steak slapping onto a chopping board.

A left hook axed into Derek's liver, and Connor's footsweep sent him crashing. He rolled into a crouch, sucking for breath.

Connor sniggered. "You never could fight. All show and no go."

Luke saw a flash in Derek's eyes when he eventually rose. He threw wild punches, sometimes starting from his hip, following Connor with them, who—always in range—stepped around the flailing. He slipped and ducked all of them. When he did not throw back, Derek's already porous defence became non-existent.

A mighty right hand fired off Derek's jaw, snapping his head around with a cartoonish force. He fell like a log. He lay on his back, his eyes unblinking, only the heaving of his chest showing he was still alive.

"Get up, you fat cunt," said Connor.

"Please. It was… complicated."

"Jealous brother wanted control. A yellow school bus passenger could pull his tongue off the window and explain that one."

"There was—stuff with our Jennifer, and—he wasn't the Messiah everyone makes out."

"Did he rape her?"

"What?"

"Did. He. Rape. Her."

"No, but—"

"Then shut the fuck up," Connor said, and held out his hand. Tom stepped forward and placed Connor's commando dagger into his palm.

Derek scuttled backwards. Connors' toe cap found his mouth as he attempted to stand. Derek roiled back, spitting out blood-laced shards of teeth like broken mints.

The sobs came. Luke could not believe the transformation of the man before his eyes. The large, coarse, domineering patriarch of the family reduced, after barely a round of bare-knuckle, to a sobbing mess.

"Please don't kill me—I know it's rich to ask but please."

"You think I'd kill my grandparents son?"

"I…I…I had your dad murd—"

"Yeh, that's what yooou did. There are certain things you can't come back from, and murdering family is one of them. You could die in a traffic accident. Or get stabbed by some chav you've been bullying. No," said Connor, pointing the blade at him for emphasis. "You'll walk out of here and leave for good. Not just Leeds, but the north of England. If you so much as set foot in West Yorkshire again, or set up shop anywhere north of Birmingham or south of Newcastle, I'll take it as an act of war on my family, and you'll die— and if there is a Judgement Day, I'll tell God why."

After a moment, Derek nodded and then said, "Why do you have the knife?"

Connor smiled. "You didn't think you were going to get off that easy. Lads, pin him down, and hold his head steady."

Derek's surges came to nothing under their collective grip. Tom's knees pinched the head like a vice.

As Luke clamped his palm over the blood-smeared mouth, Connor said, "Take your hand away mate, no one is going to hear but us. And I want to remember the sound."

As Connor began carving into the forehead, the agonising roars bounced off the walls in a cruel symphony.

The End

Glossary

Atmospherics—A soldier is taught to observe the 'atmospherics' while on operations for signs of an impending attack, encompassed in the saying, 'Look for the abnormal, and absence of the normal,' e.g., *Why aren't the kids playing outside when they ordinarily would be?*

Bag-off—Royal Marine parlance for sex.

Bellator—Currently the second largest mixed martial arts promotion outside the UFC.

Belts—Machine gun ammunition usually comes in 'belts' where the rounds are linked together.

Bootneck(s)—A nickname for a British Royal Marine.

Brecon Chop—A four-finger point used for either indicating a direction or emphasizing a point.

Cam Cream—In British military parlance means camouflage cream, applied with the fingers to break up the features of the face and to take away the shine and colour of the skin.

Check flashes—Tactical recognition flash (TRF) is the official term for a coloured patch worn on the right arm of combat clothing by members of the British military. Serves to quickly identify the regiment or corps of the wearer, in the absence of a cap badge. Royal Marine Commandos, prior to or during times of stress, are reminded to 'check flashes' to remind themselves of who they are.

CO—Commanding Officer of a unit or battalion.

CRAY supercomputer—The National Security Agency uses these incredibly powerful computer systems.

Crow—British Army term for inexperienced soldiers.

CQB—Close Quarter Battle.

Essence—Royal Marine term for 'gorgeous'.

Fatal Funnel—A term pertaining to building-clearing operations. It refers to areas such as stairwells, hallways and doorways that are generally narrow, confining areas that offer little or no cover or concealment.

FIWAF—Fighting In Woods and Forests.

FSB—The Federal Security Service of the Russian Federation; the principal security agency of Russia and the main successor agency to the USSR's Committee of State Security (KGB).

GCHQ—The Government Communications Headquarters is an intelligence and security organisation responsible for providing signals intelligence (SIGINT) and information assurance to the government and armed forces of the United Kingdom.

Grog (Kava)—A drink made from the root of the kava plant, which grows well in the dark, rich soil of the eastern part of Fiji.

Hooks in—A term in grappling martial arts that generally refers to the use of careful positioning of a practitioner's feet and legs to control and manipulate the movement or position of their opponent.

Houri—A beautiful young woman, especially one of the virgin companions of the faithful in the Muslim Paradise.

Iblīs—Features in the Quran as an archangel cast from heaven. Has been compared to the Christian Devil in some circles.

Icers—Royal Marine parlance for cold.

Jimmys'—Nickname for St James's Hospital in Leeds.

Kubotan—Is a genericised trademark for a self-defence weapon developed by Sōke Takayuki Kubota in the late 1960s. It is typically no more than 5.5 inches (14 centimetres) long and about half an inch (1.25 centimetres) in diameter, slightly thicker or the same size as a marker pen. The material is usually of a hard high-impact plastic.

NAAFI—Navy, Army and Air Force Institutes; sells goods to servicemen.

NSA—The National Security Agency is a national-level intelligence agency of the United States Department of Defense.

Olivier—A Ukrainian salad made out of cooked and chopped potatoes, dill pickles, boiled chopped eggs, cooked and chopped chicken or ham, chopped onions, canned peas, mixed with mayonnaise.

Omerta—A code of silence about criminal activity and a refusal to give evidence to the police.

Oppo—Royal Marine term for a friend within the service. Derives from 'opposite number'.

Ouchi gari—Japanese Judo term that translates to 'major inner reap'. It's an inside leg sweep.

Ryadovóy—The first rank received upon entry into the Russian Ground Forces (and Airforce) upon completion of basic training. Equivalent to a Private in the British Army.

RPs—Restriction of privileges, used in the British Army as punishment. E.g. confined to barracks and made to parade in uniform.

Senpai—Japanese term broadly meaning 'teacher' or 'master'.

SERE—Survival, Evasion, Resistance and Escape.

Seven-balled—When you lose a game of pool without potting a single ball.

Seven-clicks-to-heaven—The requisite number of mouse clicks a British serviceman has to complete on the military computer system in the process of resigning from the military.

Side-control—A dominant ground grappling position where the top combatant is lying perpendicularly over the face-up bottom combatant in such a way that the legs are free and he or she exerts no control over the combatant on the bottom.

Sit-Reps— Situation Reports.

Skynet—A nickname the Paras give JPA, the UK military's administration computer system, after the fictional neural net-based conscious group mind and artificial general intelligence system featuring in the Terminator franchise.

Sopranos—An American crime drama television series.

Solid—A term used in UK military meaning to lack intelligence.

SOP—Standard Operating Procedure.

Top Cover—Combat aeroplanes flying at high altitude to protect a military force from air attack, especially from other planes flying at a lower altitude. The term is also, more commonly, used to describe a protective hierarchy which breeds a confidence in the ranks beneath it.

Tracksuit soldiers—Soldiers participating full time in regimental and/or service sport.

Tren-train—Trenbolone is considered the most potent anabolic steroid by many performance-enhancing athletes, with the most adverse side effects. To go on the 'tren-train' is to start a course of Trenbolone.

TRiM—Trauma Risk Management; a method of secondary PTSD prevention originally developed by the UK military.

(The) Rec—Recreation ground.

Teep—A front push-kick used in Muay Thai predominately as a defensive technique.

The Flat Place—Northern England criminal parlance for Amsterdam.

Pride (FC)—A former Japanese mixed martial arts promotion company, known for its theatrics and 'looser' ruleset than its UFC counterpart.

Pancrase—A mixed martial arts promotion company founded in Japan in 1993. Palm strikes were permitted to the head in lieu of closed fist strikes.

Play Guard—To purposely fight off your back.

QRF—Quick Reaction Force.

Underhooking—Having your arms positioned under your opponent's arms while wrestling and grappling.

Vale Tudo—A Portuguese term that translates to 'anything goes'; derived from the full contact unarmed combat events that were first made popular in Brazilian circuses in the 1920s.

Wets Boat—A station for making teas and coffees.

ABOUT THE AUTHOR

Quentin Black is a former Royal Marine corporal with a decade of service in the Corps. This includes an operational tour of Afghanistan and an advisory mission in Iraq.

Black has competed in numerous boxing and Brazilian jiu-jitsu Gi and No-Gi matches.

AUTHOR'S NOTE

Any Amazon and/or Goodreads reviews would be greatly appreciated.

If you would like a FREE E-book copy of LESSONS IN BLOOD, or to contact me directly, you can through my website https://quentinblackauthor.com/. If you have spotted a mistake, I would like you to let me know so I can improve reader experience.

Subscribers will be given the heads up on any new releases and periods of discount.

The following is the second chapter of Quentin Black's follow-up novel—*Northern Wars*

Connor stood with Tom in the car park overlooking the bleak reservoir. Dawn crept from behind the horizon, turning Saddleworth Moor from black to the darkest of blues. The cold air stroked his face in the eerie quiet.

Tom said, rubbing his hands together, "The whole point of meeting this early was so as not to attract attention. Where is he?"

They were waiting for a notorious Liverpudlian criminal enforcer.

Connor shrugged against his dark blue sweater. "He'll still be fucked off that we made him come out this far, this early. It's a play for dominance. If he's not here in five, we'll fuck off. Speaking of attracting attention, why did you rock up in that Scooby Doo Mystery Machine?"

He was referring to the rusted 1972 Volkswagen T2 Camper parked next to the pub.

"Taking it down to Sheffield after this to sell it."

"Surely it'd barely be worth your fuel money."

"That's going twenty-five grand, mate. It's a done deal."

"That heap of shit? Fuck off," Connor exclaimed.

"Who do you think knows more about automobiles, you or me?"

"You," Connor conceded to his mechanic elder cousin. "Why, though? Looks like something Fred Flintstone would drive—or run, or whatever he did."

"It's the split-screen, patina windows, and that it's a classic—don't ask. Anyway, I thought you'd have got a motorbike by now?"

Connor smiled; his cousin must have eyes and ears all over Leeds. "Who told you?"

"The gaffer at the test centre comes in for his car repairs. He said you took their crash course. Thought you'd be riding around like Arnie off *Terminator 2*."

"Well, I am built like him," he said. "To be honest, mate, I'd rather have the licence and rent them out on occasion. If I bought one outright, I'd have to fuck around maintaining and insuring it."

"You'll end up buying one. What bikes do you like the look of?"

"I like the look of some of the Triumphs—especially that Thunderbird Storm. British company too."

"Made in Thailand," said Tom, with his hands thrust into his black Puffa jacket. "And those Thunderbird Storms are fucking beasts. I am telling ya, you won't enjoy riding it as a beginner cos you'll keep thinking you're going to die every time you pick up speed."

"What are you suggesting then?"

"I know a guy in Wakey who sells Royal Enfield bikes. He's got some of those new Interceptor 650s in…gorgeous bikes and probably better for you seeing as the only bikes you've been on are the scramblers we used to ride as lads, and the one at the test centre."

"Chicks' bikes, aren't they?"

"Why do you say they are chicks' bikes?" Tom frowned. "Cos you've seen girls sat on 'em on Instagram? They're proper bikes from a manufacturer that has been chucking out bikes longer than anyone—1901."

"I'll think about it," replied Connor. He felt a pleasant nostalgia remembering how his Uncle Ryan—Tom's Dad—used to take them to a disused quarry between Halifax and Keighley called the Flappits as young teenagers.

A Range Rover appeared in the distance and meandered down to them, zipping Connor into a demeanour of professionalism.

The Range Rover parked, and out of the passenger side stepped a man, taller than average, with a tanned face full of grooves and angles on account of his leanness. He wore jeans, and an oatmeal crew-neck sweater under a Parka. His light brown hair was shaved high up the sides and swept to one side.

Connor could see the Range Rover was laden with men.

Marty McKinley stepped towards them with a, "Fuck me, la, it's freezing, we going inside or what?"

"There's no need," said Tom. "This won't take long."

Marty nodded. "Mr Ellis understands there's 'ad to be some time for things to settle now Derek is off the scene and youse 'av had a reshuffle. Your Uncles Michael and Lee are out of the clink now and we heard good things—that you've massively grown your businesses, so fair's fair now. Derek had our money dropped off in cash in Liverpool at—"

"That's not happening any more," said Connor, flatly.

He met McKinley's stare with his own as Tom said, "We might be open to a business arrangement."

McKinley broke a moment of silence with, "I might have to discuss it with my lads in the Rover, and they might have to discuss it with youse."

"Of course," said Connor. "That's why we picked this place. So any 'discussions' won't have any witnesses."

Connor saw a flicker in McKinley's eyes and knew he was fighting the urge to look around. Instead, he said, "Mr Ellis isn't going to be happy. Sure youse want to go down this road?"

"We're sure," Tom replied.

"Look, I know youse aren't plazzy gangsters but youse two—your family—are still way over your head. This ain't *Emmerdale Farm*—this is a man who has been running things in the North since Ian Rush was still a boss striker."

"We're aware of Harry Ellis's CV," interjected Connor. "Now, you can either take the message to him, or you can get the lads in the Range Rover out to help you with negotiations. We'd prefer you didn't as it'll take time and energy filling the holes in."

McKinley's eyebrows compressed. "Not sure why you're being so aggy, la."

"I think you know the reason—"

"Nah, I don't, why don't—"

"But let's not cry over spilt milk. You take the message to Mr Ellis that there's no more protection money or whatever you rinsed our cretin of an uncle for. If he wants to discuss future business proposals, then we'll be all ears, but as of now, we don't have any with you."

McKinley said, "All right. I'll tell him. He won't like it but knows business is business. One of those things."

With that, he backed away, got into the Range Rover and Connor remained poised until it drove off.

The sun crested the hills just as the vehicle disappeared behind them.

"About what we expected," said Tom. "What's that look for?"

"It wasn't what he said that bothered me. It was what he didn't say."

"Meaning?"

"He never asked about our ghrelin-resistant cunt of an uncle, Derek—not what happened, not where he is, nothing. Over five years of a steady revenue stream for them and there wasn't one question asked."

"Maybe he's not bothered what's happened to Derek as long as he gets the money. Maybe he thought there was no point in asking."

"Or he might know what's happened to Derek and where he is because he's sheltering him. And, in exchange, he'll be singing like a choirboy regarding our businesses. You were right to hide some of it from him."

"What you thinking?"

"I am thinking we're going to have to put everyone on standby now. There's no telling what Harry Ellis's reaction is going to be. The way McKinley was all 'nicey, nicey' at the end bothered me too."

"How come?"

"'*Humble words and increased preparations are signs the enemy is about to attack*', according to Sun Tzu. Didn't you say you heard they've had an uptick in arms?"

"So I've heard," said Tom. "What does it mean to be ghrelin-resistant?"

"Ghrelin is a hormone that tells your brain you are full."

"A bookworm's way of calling someone fat?"

"Yeh," answered Connor. "When does Luke get back from Thailand?"

"On Monday. That's if he hasn't been arrested or murdered or whatever the fuck he'll have got himself into."

"Why? Has he said something?"

"No, but it's just him, isn't it, always getting himself in mither. Stupid too, he could get to the top—whether it's in our game or boxing—he's going to ruin it all if he's not careful."

Connor shook his hands out. "I stopped getting frustrated with how others live their lives a while ago—how hard is it to change something about yourself you don't like? Let's hope he gets it together soon."

Other books by Quentin Black.

The Bootneck

Lessons In Blood.

Northern Wars

Printed in Great Britain
by Amazon

62369249R00244